DARK LITTLE WORLDS

DARK LITTLE WORLDS

ICARUS CODE BOOK THREE

RYSA WALKER

STARRY NIGHT BOOKS

For everyone keeping tiny candles of hope burning. Let's put them all together to ignite a bonfire of change in our own dark little world.

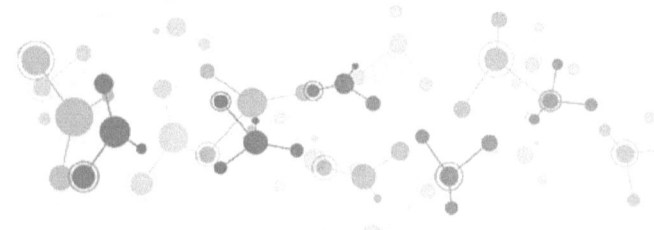

And the suns of the limitless universe sparkled and
    shone in the sky,
Flashing with fires as of God, but we knew that their
    light was a lie—
Bright as with deathless hope—but, however they
    sparkled and shone,
The dark little worlds running round them were worlds
    of woe like our own.

Alfred, Lord Tennyson, "Despair" (1881)

CONTENTS

PART I

PART II

CLAIRE

ANAK — TWO DAYS EARLIER

PART III

PART I

FROM THE JOURNAL OF EBERIN DAS

(Translation by John Beckett)
[Undated]

WE WILL FAIL. I now know this beyond all doubt. It is only a matter of time, and I fear that time is short.

I began this journal as a way to organize my thoughts. It was intended for no eyes other than my own. But this document will be the sole legacy   of our movement and perhaps we will not have failed entirely if it serves as a warning to someone, someday. My ego keeps urging me to edit, to clarify, to find the perfect word and most importantly, to make myself less of a villain before I hand these pages over to Navi for encoding. I've resisted that impulse, but as I look back through the entries, it's hard not to cringe at my moral blindness and naivete.

That's especially true of the entries at the beginning of my journal, where my hypocrisy is stunning. I was so smug in my moral superiority to the other Guardians because I lamented taking the life of my host. That was mostly because the unpleasant task fell upon my own shoulders, if I'm being completely honest, and there's surely no cause for being anything *but* completely honest at this point. And even as I gnashed my teeth over this immoral deed, I continued to dutifully play my part in the larger mission that doomed the entire planet.

What truly puzzles and shames me is that I didn't question everything *sooner*. I doubt that it would have made a difference in the end, but why did my qualms about our mission—about our entire culture—seem to begin only after I took on this particular host?

Bodae noticed it, too. He believes the procedure was flawed. I suppose it's possible, given that the transfer didn't take at all with my second potential host. The same thing could have happened again, just to a lesser extent. I'm sure this was part of the plea he made when he asked for leniency. When he begged me to turn myself in, to take yet another host, and throw myself on the mercy of the Triad.

Does some small part of my host's mind remain? Perhaps. Some oddity in my brain might not adapt well to the connection. There's no way to know for certain. Still, I prefer to believe that I arrived at these conclusions on my own. That it was a conscious choice, born of my own moral evolution.

If I am lucky, I will die with the people of this planet. If I am unlucky and my former comrades find me, I will die even sooner. However it goes, there can be no happy ending to my tale, and I'd like to believe that the unhappy ending is one that I chose of my own free will.

Either way, though, my Alliance name will die with me. It is my host's name that I used in our attempt at rebellion. It is *his* name that you found carved on my tomb if you are reading these words. That was a strategic choice, in part, as it will encourage my former brethren not to search too carefully for any messages I may leave behind, to accept the claim that my mind was no longer my own.

But it is also a tribute. If some hidden remnant of my host is what pushed me toward the light, then he has earned both that recognition and my deepest gratitude.

CLAIRE

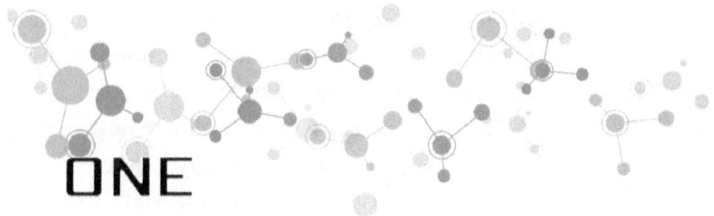

ONE

CLAIRE'S ARM flew up instinctively to shield her face from the massive flock of geese flying toward her. She knew they weren't real and would have felt ridiculous for overreacting if not for the fact that the two mining executives who remained at the table were doing the exact same thing.

The geese vanished into blackness and for several seconds, Claire sat frozen. The afterimage in her mind wasn't the birds taking off from the lake, silhouetted against the brilliant orange and scarlet sky. All she could see was the wreckage of Jonas Labs. The campus her father had designed, where her brother and Beck spent pretty much every waking hour, was one of six properties that Claire had just watched collapse, apparently in real time, as a woman's voice calmly informed them that they were not in danger, that they should not panic.

Most of the guests hadn't seemed to see or hear anything after the word *panic*. They were far too busy screaming and pushing toward the locked doors. Claire might have joined them, if not for the call from Beck a few moments before, telling her that she was safe. It had been hard to follow some of what he was saying, but he'd clearly said that the hotel at Beekman Place, the massive entertainment complex New Yorkers called *Kolya's Palace*, was not on *the list*. She hadn't fully understood what he meant by that until she saw the buildings on the screen.

Although, the fact that she recognized the voice in the video as Stasia Ljubic's would probably have been enough to keep her in her seat. That wasn't at all logical, but it was true. Stasia, formerly second-in-command to Anton Kolya, was now working with the Earth Watch Alliance, more commonly known as the Flock. Once content with harassment tactics, the Flock had shifted to full-fledged ecoterrorism under their new leader, Kolya's ex-wife Corbin Drexel. Evidence strongly suggested that the Flock was responsible for two bombings on Mars that had killed seven people, and very nearly killed Claire herself, but Drexel had yet to officially claim credit and according to Kolya, she outright denied having any part in the attacks.

The attacks hadn't been confined to Mars. During the past two weeks, Claire's house had been barraged by dozens of insectile nanodrones. The bugbots eventually found a weak spot in her security system and the home that she'd shared with her roommate Rowan and Ro's five-year-old daughter Jemma for the past few years was now a pile of rubble and ash. Four other people had died, and two additional buildings were destroyed, all in an effort to keep Claire from translating the document hidden in one of the biological samples she'd brought back from Mars.

So, yeah. Given all of that, the fact that the voice was Stasia's should have had her running for the exit faster than anyone. But something else was going on. The Flock's new leaders were clearly willing to risk some casualties, but they'd issued a warning to give the security teams at the properties they'd just destroyed a chance to evacuate the buildings. In the video, Stasia claimed that their goal for the bombings was to buy time, and while she didn't go into specifics, she really didn't have to. The Flock's positions had been essentially the same since they were founded—anti-science, anti-technology, anti-progress.

At least a quarter of the people currently in the ballroom were journalists, so the Flock's warning would be a top story for every major news outlet. But they could simply have destroyed the buildings and sent out the video via social media if publicity was their only goal. No, Claire was fairly certain that they had a more specific target for their message, two people they wanted to hit hard. In public. And unfortunately, those two people—Kai Jonas and Anton Kolya—had left the ballroom as soon as it became clear that something weird was happening to the hotel's communications system.

Claire scanned the crowd, but it was hard to see anything when the only light came from the flickering candles on the dinner tables and the few people who had thought to turn on their phone lights. Her eyes had been on the screen as Kolya led her mother offstage, but she had a vague memory of him guiding her to the left, away from the crowd. Maybe there was another door? She wouldn't put it past Kolya to have his own private emergency exit.

A small cheer rose up from the back of the ballroom. One of the doors was now open. That only seemed to make the panic worse, though, as everyone tried to shove through the same exit. A hotel-wide alarm was now playing over the speakers, instructing all guests to evacuate the building in a calm and orderly fashion. The two mining executives who had been at the table with her took this as their cue to leave.

Claire got to her feet, as well. She had no desire to join the throng at the doors, so she flicked on her phone light and headed toward the corridor on the side of the stage. If there was no exit, she could always turn around. It wasn't like she'd be getting out in the next couple of minutes anyway given how many people were trying to push through the one door that was currently open.

When she reached the end of the hallway, she found an exit marked *SECURITY ONLY*. She tried the handle, expecting the door to be locked, but it opened into a hot, empty stairwell.

After a dubious glance at the stairs, she leaned against the wall and slipped off her heels. On the plus side, she was going down, not up. Twenty flights wouldn't be fun either way, but she'd much rather do them barefoot than teetering on stilettos.

And she was alone, thank God, at least for now. She'd been in her office several years earlier when they received a bomb threat from a secessionist militia group, forcing everyone to evacuate. The *Atlantic Post* building was only nine floors high, but the slow, single file procession of the staff down the stairs had still been unnerving.

Well, *mostly* single file. There were always a few jerks in any office. Several people had elbowed their way through. Bryce Avery had been one of them, muttering an excuse about having kids—as though he were the only parent in the building—while he squeezed past his coworkers. He was probably doing the same thing to the other guests right now.

She felt a momentary pang of guilt for not going back to tell everyone that there was another way out, since that would siphon off some of the pressure from the main exits. But the security guards roaming around the place had to know about this door and, again, she really didn't think anyone in the building was in danger. She just hoped that the fifteen-minute warning Stasia said they'd given to the people in the buildings they destroyed had been enough to clear the premises. It was nearly nine p.m., so most of the Jonas Labs employees would have left hours ago, but several of the other buildings the Flock had targeted were in countries where it was still the middle of the workday. Even at Jonas Labs, dozens of employees and their families lived in one of the four buildings on the campus. Would fifteen minutes have been enough time for the security team to get everyone out of their apartments?

And had *Beck* gotten out?

One of the last things he'd told her before the call ended was that he was trying to save the biodome at the center of the complex. Was that because people were still inside? Or because he knew how much the place meant to her?

Claire began to pick up sounds from below as she passed the landing on the tenth floor. Two familiar voices echoed up the stairwell, along with the unmistakable clack of high heels against the concrete. *Of course.* There was no way Kai Jonas would be caught barefoot.

It was impossible to make out anything that either of them was saying, though, not just because of the periodic blasts from the emergency alarms but because Kai and Kolya were both talking at the same time. That almost certainly meant that they were on the phone with their respective security teams. Macek, Kolya's head of security, had left the ballroom a few minutes before the video began. Paul Caruso, who had taken over for Stasia, had rushed out a few minutes later, so they'd probably been responding to the warnings delivered to the security teams at the three Kolya International buildings that were on the Flock's list.

Now that she was fairly sure that Kai and Kolya both knew about the attacks, Claire slowed her pace. She had no desire to talk to either of them, especially Kai. No matter what sort of pressure her mother was under from stockholders, there was no way that Joe would have approved her decision to make any sort of public announcement about his stretch goals for Rejuvesce when the research was ongoing.

"Claire?" The voice came from several floors above and she recognized it instantly. Cursing softly, she stopped on the fifth floor landing and pressed herself into the shadows beneath the stairs. She had neither the time nor the patience for Bryce Avery right now.

TWO

FROM BELOW, there was a brief blast of traffic noise and then the clang of the door closing behind Kai and Kolya. About twenty seconds later, she watched from her hiding spot as Avery rounded the turn and continued down the stairs. Her phone began vibrating before he was even out of sight. A quick glance at the screen told her that the call was from Joe. She wanted to answer immediately, but she held off until she heard the door close behind Avery.

Her brother sighed in relief when she picked up. "Thank God, Claire. Are you okay?"

"Yeah. Mom's fine, too."

"So you know about the lab?"

"Yeah."

"They hit the Lomas Verdes plant and the one in Bangalore, as well."

"I know. I mean, I didn't know *which* facilities, but I knew there were two more. It was on the screen in the ballroom. Did they get everyone out in time?"

"Wilson thinks so, but it's too soon to tell. He's still waiting to hear back from the other locations. The lab and the floor below are completely wiped out."

The alarm inside the hotel sounded again but stopped abruptly halfway through. Had Beekman Place security canceled the evacuation so soon? Even though she personally didn't believe there was any danger, it seemed a bit premature.

"The death toll could have been higher, though, if not for Beck," Joe added. "He showed up about ten minutes before the warning came in from the Flock and convinced security to sound the alarm and contact the other two labs that he said were on the list."

"Is he okay?" she asked.

There was a long pause. "We're not sure. After he told Wilson to evacuate all of the buildings, he asked to see the security feeds. And he must have found something in the video because the guard who was in the room with him said he bolted out and took off for the biodome. Which was the last place he was seen. That section of the dome is completely down and … he's not answering my calls, Claire. He left me a weird message earlier, about half an hour before I got the call from Wilson. I was in the pool, so I didn't hear it ring. He asked if we were all okay here at the B & B. Kept apologizing about something. I called him back but had to leave a message. Told him we were fine, said to get back with me, but he never did. When did you last talk to him?"

"He called not long after Mom started speaking. Just before the Flock locked the doors and took over the communications system so they could air live footage of the six buildings they hit."

"*Six?* Wilson said there were only three."

"No, no. Three of them were Kolya's." She glanced down at her phone, which was vibrating again. "Hold on a sec, okay? I've got a message coming in from Wyatt. He's a few blocks over and might have heard the news. I need to let him know I'm safe."

Wyatt had indeed heard and said he was heading to the hotel. She sent a quick note to tell him that she was fine, and that she'd meet him at the Mexican restaurant where he was waiting. His response came back instantly.

> Already left the restaurant. Meet you halfway.

That didn't seem like a great idea to Claire since it would put him back inside the Beekman Place entertainment complex.

Macek's people had escorted Wyatt off the premises earlier when they caught him posing as a waiter and planting surveillance devices in the ballroom. They probably wouldn't be as friendly about it a second time, especially when they were on high alert at the moment. So she countered with a more precise location just outside the grounds.

51st Street entrance. Ten minutes.

Before she went back to her call with Joe, she noticed that Wyatt's message wasn't the only one that had come in. The other text was from the same number Beck had used earlier. The message itself was completely blank, but he'd attached two files. One text, one video. The text file was labeled *Journal*. The video file had no title at all, just a string of numbers.

She checked the timestamp on both files, hoping to find some bit of encouraging news to give Joe. No luck. Beck had sent them a little after eight-thirty, which was well before he called her and not long after she messaged him with a news-letter photo from forty years ago that clearly included his face. She'd added a snarky comment, asking whether she should call him Noah O'Brian, the name he had used nearly four decades earlier when he worked at a company that was bought out by Jonas Labs, or Anak, the name she was pretty sure he'd been using when he arrived on Earth back in the 1950s.

"Sorry," she said to Joe. "I realized I had another message from Beck, but it was sent before the explosions. I'll keep trying to get in touch with him."

"Okay. Listen, I need to get to the lab. Ro says that she and Jemma will be fine here with just the security team, but I wanted to let you know." He drew in a long, shaky breath. "Any chance that all of this happened *before* Mom started talking?"

"If the Flock had broken into their communications system

thirty seconds or so earlier, we'd have been in the clear. But ... no."

"So what did she say? She was hammering me earlier this week to let her mention at the annual meeting that we might be looking at a few decades more than the extra twenty-five years or so that we originally predicted. The meeting is still a few weeks away, but I said absolutely not. We need to wait until—"

"She asked the investors if they'd be more likely to invest in Kolya's next big thing—a project to terraform exoplanets—if they knew that their lifespans were potentially *unlimited*." Claire could practically hear her brother's blood boiling on the other end of the call, so she quickly added, "But like I said, she didn't have time to expand on it. The next thing anyone heard after that was Stasia Ljubic's voice coming through the speakers telling us to stay calm."

"What is going on, Claire? Not just with Mom. *Everything*. I mean, how was Beck able to warn Wilson that the Flock was about to attack?"

"I don't know." Her answer was automatic. And it was more or less true. She didn't *know* ... but she had a lot more information than Joe did. It was time she told him what she'd learned about Beck. But that wasn't happening over the phone. "I may have a few pieces of the puzzle, though. I'll meet you at JL in a few hours. I just need to grab my things from the apartment and then I'll head north."

"You really shouldn't be on the hyperloop with all this going on. Wilson said Mom flew down there on the Aerolyft. If you call her now, you might be able to catch a ride." It was clear from Joe's tone that he knew exactly how she'd feel about being trapped in an Aerolyft with their mother. "Or ... I could send it back down once she gets here."

"I'll just drive up. It will take a little longer by car, but I've got some reading to do anyway."

"Reading?" Joe gave a bitter laugh, and she knew he had to be wondering how the hell she'd be able to focus.

"Something Beck sent me. *Before* the explosions."

He sighed. "You're thinking all of this is connected to that manuscript, aren't you?"

"Probably. But … there's more going on. I'll explain when I see you, okay?"

Claire hurried down the last few flights of stairs and slipped her shoes onto her feet. Before she could open the door, however, a large hand closed around her upper arm and yanked her back into the stairwell.

THREE

CLAIRE JERKED her elbow back hard, sinking it directly into the stomach of the man behind her, and then brought the pointy heel of her shoe down on his foot. He let out a loud *oof*, followed by a yelp of pain, and she turned to find Bryce Avery hunched over with his arms crossed protectively over his abdomen.

"What the hell, Bryce? Are you insane? You don't sneak up on people like that. What do you want?"

"Just doing my..." He paused, trying to catch his breath. "Just doing my job. I saw you follow Kolya and your mother. Thought I'd follow, too, since that's obviously where the story was. You didn't stop when I called out to you. You didn't go outside after they did, and they were already gone when I opened the door. So ... I followed my journalistic instincts. That's how most of us get our information, you know. We don't have it handed to us on a silver platter. Who were you talking to? And what did your mother mean by—"

"I'm going now, Bryce. If you follow, I'll tell Bernard you're harassing me when I get back to the office. You may be our editor's golden boy, but I think he'll draw the line at that. And if you *touch* me again, I won't even bother with Bernard. I'll go straight to HR. Are we clear?"

Claire didn't wait for his answer, but just shoved the door open and spilled out into the alley between Hotel Mir and the casino. It was marginally cooler outside than it was in the stair-well, but the air was as thick and muggy as it had been several hours before when she entered the building.

Thankfully, Bryce was right on one count. Kolya and Kai

were long gone. Which was good news to begin with, but even more so after Bryce's last comment. At least he wouldn't be able to ask Kai any follow-up questions on what she'd meant by *potentially unlimited.*

As the door closed, she realized that one of the Beekman Place guards was watching her. His eyes narrowed, and she was pretty sure she was about to catch hell for using an exit that was clearly marked *Security Only.* But he just scowled at her for a second longer, then turned back toward the hotel where a group of employees was trying to herd the guests out of the street and into the small plaza on the other side. Judging from the guests' expressions—equal parts annoyance and relief—security must have decided to pitch it as a false alarm. Several other employees were reassuring a cluster of guests who had emerged from the casino next door. *Nothing to see here, folks. Why don't you all head back inside and lose some more money?*

Claire pushed her way through the crowd and continued toward the resort's 51st Street exit where she'd told Wyatt to meet her. He ignored the suggestion, though, intercepting her a full block inside the Palace grounds.

"Thought you said security told you to get out and stay out?" she said after a hug.

"They did. But you told me we're now sharing information with Macek, so I asked the guard at the gate to see if he could arrange a meeting. And he did. Not sure if Macek would have agreed on general principles, but I now have something to trade. Kes managed to recover part of the video from the house in Riverdale. No luck yet on the three days of recordings in the archives, but we've got everything from around seven p.m. yesterday until Kes sent the kill signal this afternoon."

Claire had spent a good five hours over the past two days skimming through video from the cameras that Wyatt asked Kes, his friend and technical assistant, to put in place after he received an anonymous tip that Drexel and other members of the Flock would be at an address in the Bronx this week. Macek would definitely be interested in that footage. He'd taken a small team out there earlier in the day—four people and five armed drones. Someone inside the house had turned those drones against him, killing one member of his team and injuring another. Macek himself had been hit in the shoulder, an injury that would have been much worse if he hadn't been wearing protective gear.

"The anonymous tip was from Wilson," she told Wyatt. "Macek got it as well, so they were already looking at the house in Riverdale. He and Wilson have been sharing information on the Flock for several months."

"Do you think he shared it with Beck, too? Maybe that's why he was at that house."

"No. I mean, Wilson *might* have told him, but…" She shook her head. "I've got a lot to catch you up on."

"Me, too." Wyatt nodded to a pocket park across the street, nestled between two buildings. "Let's find a bench. We don't have much time, though. I'm meeting Macek at Hotel Mir at ten thirty." He gave her a slow grin as his eyes traveled downward, taking in the blue dress. "Which is a damn shame. I'd much rather go back to the apartment and finish what we started this afternoon. I seem to recall that we have a roll of bubble wrap waiting. I should be back by midnight, though. Unless you want to go with me?"

She frowned. "I can't. I have to get to Boston. They managed to clear almost everyone out of the buildings, but Joe says…" She took a shaky breath. "Beck may be somewhere in the wreckage. They think he was in the biodome when the bombs went off."

"*Bombs*? What happened?"

"I … thought you already heard?" She sank down onto a bench, purposefully choosing one that faced out toward the street. The back wall of the little park had been designed as a waterfall, and she knew it would just make her think of the falls inside the biodome, which had almost certainly been destroyed. She really didn't need that distraction at the moment.

"All I heard was the NYPD alert saying the hotel was being evacuated," Wyatt said. "Then they sent out a follow-up maybe five minutes ago saying it was a false alarm."

"Well, it kind of *was*. For Beekman Place. Six other buildings weren't so lucky, though, and those of us in the ballroom had ringside seats. The Flock broke into their communications system and posted a video of the attacks. Stasia told us we were there to bear witness. That we weren't in any danger, and they were doing this to buy us some time."

"Time for what?"

"They weren't very clear about that."

Wyatt snorted. "Guess they have to justify their actions to themselves somehow. But why was Beck back at the lab?"

"I'm not sure. Maybe he was following whoever set off the bomb. Or it may just be that he thought Joe was going to be there and wanted to make sure that he was safe."

"But Joe is still in Maine, right?"

Claire nodded. "Yeah, although he's headed down to Boston now. He and Beck got into a bit of an argument the other day. It's a long story, but to sum up, it's like Joe has this infernal ticker in his head. Like every day he takes off is basically killing people. Beck wanted him to be around Jemma for a bit. To keep things in perspective."

"Whoa," Wyatt said. "Slow down. You're losing me. I'm guessing this is connected to the stretch goals you mentioned for Rejuvesce, but ... how many additional years are we talking here?"

Claire hesitated for a moment. She was really hoping Joe would be able to reason with Kai and maybe they could write her remarks off as a hypothetical question or hyperbole. It wouldn't be a permanent fix, but it might at least buy enough time for Joe to finalize his research. It seemed unlikely, though, given the number of reporters who were in the room tonight.

Even if they managed to roll things back, Kai had given voice to the possibility and Bryce Avery wouldn't be the only one determined to follow up.

"The words my mother used tonight were *potentially unlimited*," she said. "Everything went to hell before she could say more—which I guess is both good and bad—because there are some major qualifications to that statement. For one thing, it's entirely based on the computer models at this point. And a lot depends on how early the patient begins treatment. You and I would probably only be looking at three hundred years or so."

"*Only?*" He shook his head, clearly stunned.

"Maybe more. As Beck put it, cellular senescence starts around age twenty-five. If people start treatment before that, they think it might shut down the process entirely. Anyway, you can probably see why Joe is feeling pressured. On the one hand, he doesn't want to promise anything until he has solid results. On the other hand, he says that every day of unnecessary delay costs about a million people a few extra centuries of life. But on the *other* other hand, Beck has been trying to remind him that it's not just about death rates. There are also millions of children who won't be born because governments will have to start limiting reproduction. Beck was pushing me to invite Ro and Jemma to join us in Maine even before the fire, hoping to make Joe realize there's a balance. Joe is … humoring him, I guess? He decided to take a few extra days off and keep them company until I got back up there. I didn't mention it to Beck because Joe said he didn't want to listen to his gloating. And speaking of Beck, you need to see this."

She pulled up the message from Genni Chatterjee and handed him the phone.

"That picture was taken in 2049, when Beck was working under the name Noah O'Brian. He was originally with a company called VersaBio—which you may remember being mentioned in Tobias Shepherd's memoir. Jonas Labs bought them out and Noah quit not long after that, moved to Chicago, and died suddenly." She used air quotes on the last two words. "No clue what Beck did between then and the time he began working with Joe, but I'm pretty sure he's the one that Toby's Sentinel referred to as Anak."

Wyatt stared at the picture for a moment. "I guess I was thinking of Beck as younger than this based on the video taken outside the house in Riverdale. And your description, for that matter."

Claire just looked at him for a moment, surprised that he'd narrowed in on that small oddity compared to all of the others. "One of the things that Toby Shepherd overheard Professor Everett complaining about to the other head Sentinels—the Administrators or whatever he called them—was the unpleasantness of being altered. So, I'm guessing Beck has had to endure that *unpleasantness* at some point over the past four decades."

"Okay. So Beck is one of them. One of these Sentinels. And now he's working with Drexel and the Flock."

"He *is* one of them. But from what Wilson told Joe, and from what Beck said when he called me—"

"When did he call you?"

"Just before the explosions. I think he was trying to help them locate the bombs, but he said he was out of time. Joe has been trying to reach him, but..." She shook her head. "He *is* a Sentinel. But as for Drexel and the Flock? It sounds like he's working against them more than with them."

"Maybe," Wyatt said. "But why didn't he call Wilson and warn him well in advance? If he had that information, why wouldn't he give an explosives crew time to go in and defuse the bombs? Why arrive just before everything is about to blow up?"

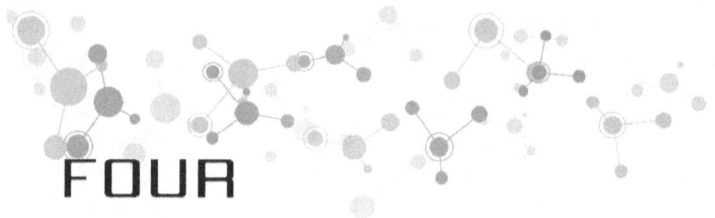

FOUR

AS MUCH AS Claire hated to admit it, Wyatt had a point. Even if Beck had flown from New York to the lab, it would have taken far longer than a simple phone call.

"I don't know," she said. "His apartment is less than a kilometer from Jonas Labs. Maybe he was there when he got the news? I mean, it's been more than twenty-four hours since he got into the car with Drexel. Who knows where he went after that? He sent me a couple of files that I'm going to look at on the drive up. Joe suggested that I call Kai and fly back with her, but … it was all I could do to keep from climbing onto that stage and punching her when she started talking about Joe's research. The two of us together in an Aerolyft would be a very bad idea."

"But she'll be heading back to the lab too, won't she?"

"Yeah. I'd obviously prefer not to deal with her at all right now, but I think Joe may need some backup."

"What I don't get is why she decided to make the announcement at the Ares Consortium conference," Wyatt said. "Especially knowing you were going to be there."

Claire shook her head. "Judging from her expression when she saw me at the table, I don't think she knew I was going to be at the dinner. Kolya seems convinced that we need to have some sort of heart-to-heart talk and resolve our differences, so this was probably his idea of a fun little surprise."

"But why would Kolya be willing to let your mother steal his thunder? Tonight's speech was supposed to be about the terraforming project. Something about stage seven, right?"

"Well, we did get a sneak peek at some of the lifeforms

they're planning to introduce in future stages, but it was more as a ... segue, I guess? ... into Kolya's new project. He's looking beyond Mars now, trying to get investors onboard for remotely terraforming exoplanets using the same basic processes they're using on Mars. The plan is to send tiny packets of recombinant biobots out to barren planets that we believe to be capable of supporting life. And that's where Rejuvesce comes in. One of the reasons Kolya gave me samples to bring home from Mars was because he was hoping I could convince Joe—and eventually, that Joe could convince Kai—that their research agendas are complementary."

"Sounds like Kolya decided to cut out the middleman and convince Kai himself."

"Yeah. And he's not wrong about the research agendas supporting each other. I mean, one of the inevitable objections to extending lives by centuries or more is that we're going to need to expand beyond Earth. Beyond Mars, even. Kolya's project would open up a lot of new frontiers for..." She trailed off and gave a bemused laugh. "I was going to say *for future generations*."

"Doesn't really fit anymore, does it?"

"Not if Joe's *in silico* results are accurate. But Kolya knew his audience well enough to understand that altruism isn't their primary motivation. It's hard to convince people driven by profit motive to invest in things to help the next generation and that tendency becomes even stronger when you move beyond projects that might help their children and start entering the realm of great-great grandkids. Kolya's hoping that the extra lifespan promised by Rejuvesce will convince people to invest in his new idea even if the payoff is in the very distant future. I'm thinking there's going to be a lot more interest in things like generation ships, too. If people have centuries to play around with, a hundred-year voyage isn't out of the question. And then there's the more typical investments in extractives and—" She stopped, thinking back to the conversation between the mining executives that she'd overheard during the cocktail hour.

"What's wrong?" Wyatt asked.

"Nothing, It's just, with everything else that happened, I almost forgot to tell you what I found out about Millex."

He chuckled and elbowed her. "You're such a slacker."

Claire's main reason for attending the conference had been to see if she could get information on the containment breach at Millex, a Martian tridymite mine, that had killed several dozen workers a few weeks prior. Wyatt's source had told him that one of the barracks on the outer edge of the Millex dome in Cerberus Fosse had been contaminated by the *Azospira oryzae* samples that Kolya's scientists released as part of the current stage of terraforming. The bacteria, which consumed perchlorates, had been modified to reproduce much more quickly and, as Davina Monroe had cautioned Claire during the demonstration, could rapidly form a biofilm on the lungs and mucous membranes when it was in its metabolically active phase.

That was one reason that the planet had been placed on a six-month lockdown during stage six, something that was highly unpopular with employers in the various mining colonies who'd balked at paying bonuses for the downtime. Bonuses were a huge sticking point in the labor negotiations, given that they were a major component of the mineworkers' compensation. And they couldn't just extend their contract in most cases, since workers were restricted to two-year contracts if they planned to return to Earth. Any longer than that, and they risked health complications due to the lower gravity on Mars.

Millex was KTI's main source of tridymite, the primary component in the hydrogel panels used to construct the domes, but they had contracts with several other companies as well. Wyatt's source at Millex, a union activist who had been funneling him information over the past year, had sent him a coded message indicating that the company had blown the barracks up when they discovered the deaths, telling everyone that the building had been constructed over a hidden sinkhole. What they hadn't realized was that several of the people inside the building had sent out messages the night before as they began to get sick. Some of those messages included pictures and videos. After seeing the neon green *Azospira* spread over the surface of Mars at the beginning of stage six, the recipients of those messages had no difficulty identifying the substance the miners were coughing up.

"Remember the woman I mentioned?" Claire began. "The chatty one I overheard at Daedalus?"

"Yeah. Were you able to place the camera at her table?"

"No. I still have it, if you want it back." She reached into her pocket to find the little card to which she'd attached the device.

He shook his head. "Keep it. Maybe there will be another chance."

"I actually didn't *need* it. Her name is Elizabeth Schwick. She's a source of Macek's, although he doesn't seem to fully trust her. Anyway, I listened in with the eavesdropping app on my phone while she was talking to two men, Valmer and Johnston. Valmer says that Dex Miller, the Millex owner, swears it wasn't a containment breach. He says it was sabotage."

Wyatt looked skeptical. "Not surprised he'd *say* that, but greed seems like a much more credible motive. Both versions of the story I've heard say that someone—either Miller or the company that the people in that barracks were subcontracted out to—was offering incentives for workers to start getting back out there before the lockdown ends."

"I know, but apparently Miller has surveillance video of someone wearing one of the biosuits—the older kind that they call puffsuits—putting a canister of something into the ventilation system. And..." She frowned, trying to remember how much she'd already told him. "Did I mention Westmoreland?"

"The guy who was killed in the plane crash on Mars, right?

Coming back from the labor negotiations at Daedalus City? You said Macek might have had something to do with it."

"Yeah. That was more of a gut feeling than anything I can pin down, though. I saw them get into a shoving match the day before, although the shoving was mostly on Macek's side. He could have squashed the guy like a bug, something that would have earned him a round of applause and free drinks from pretty much everyone I've heard mention Westmoreland's name. The general consensus seems to be that the guy was the scum of the earth—or Mars, I guess—and the son who took over his business interests in Lyot appears to be earning an equally bad reputation. Miller doesn't think Stasia or the Flock had anything to do with the bombing at Millex. He claims it was retribution by Westmoreland after Miller switched over to support Kolya on the issue of paying the worker bonuses. Then when Miller refused to break the lockdown and send workers out early to fulfill their contract, the younger Westmoreland had someone release the bacteria into the barracks."

"But ... why burn the building down if you've got proof of sabotage?"

"Macek says—" She stopped, remembering her agreement. "You cannot use his name or even say it was a KTI employee, okay? This has to be strictly on background."

Claire could tell Wyatt wasn't particularly happy about that condition, with good reason. He'd need to track down another source to confirm the information and that was much easier said than done when all of the witnesses were a few hundred million kilometers away and under a planetwide lockdown.

"Okay," she continued after he tipped her a grudging nod. "Macek claims Miller panicked on the sinkhole excuse. But he says it was a very good thing that they blew up the building. The heat from the resulting fire destroyed the *Azospira oryzae*. Otherwise, it could have spread and killed everyone in the dome. As for how the bacteria got into the barracks, Macek doesn't know. He thinks it could easily be that Miller decided to cheat and send a few teams out early. But he also wouldn't be at all surprised to learn Westmoreland had a hand in it. Said he wouldn't put anything past the guy given that he most likely learned his business ethics from his dad."

"Anything else?"

Claire shook her head. "Macek caught me snooping and sent a signal through my earphones that nearly deafened me. An *accident*, according to him, but he got a nice chuckle out of it." She reached into the pocket of her dress and pulled out the earbuds, one of which was now a flat, shattered disc. "Elizabeth didn't approve of my eavesdropping."

"Like I keep saying, you need to upgrade." He tapped the spot behind his ear where he'd had the implants placed a few years back and then laughed when she shuddered.

"I was actually leaning toward doing just that. Thought maybe I'd add an armphone like Alice Dobroski's while I was at it. But there's no way in hell now. I was able to get *these* out. I can't even imagine having that level of noise hit something embedded inside my ears."

"You just *tap* to shut it off. Tap twice and even the noise around you is muffled. How do you think I got through meetings with Avery when we had to collaborate?"

Claire groaned. "Avery. He was at the dinner. We had a bit of a ... confrontation as I was leaving the hotel. He might still be hanging around the place when you get there."

"I'll keep an eye out." Wyatt pulled something up on his phone and handed it to her. "Don't suppose you recognize any of these guys from tonight? Flip through. There are seven of them."

The first three—two men and one woman—didn't look familiar. When she reached the fourth image, she hesitated. She couldn't be certain. The man in the picture had longer hair and the beard was trimmed much more closely now, but he looked like the guard who had been staring at her as she left Hotel Mir.

"I *think* this guy is working with Beekman Place security.

Someone who looks a lot like him gave me the stink-eye as I left the building a few minutes ago."

She continued thumbing through the images. Numbers five and six rang no bells, but number seven set off full-fledged alarms.

"That's him. The guy who broke into the Data Sciences Institute with FBI Agent Wheeler." She shook her head, annoyed. "The *fake* agent, that is. Baby Bangs. The guy looks a bit younger here and he was a little more washed out in the headlights from the car, but I'm pretty sure that's him."

"Yeah, that's what I thought. The picture is from about five years ago. I had Kes enhance and run facial recognition on the two of them when they showed back up at the Riverdale house after the break-in, in part because the guy looked kind of familiar to me."

"Do you think he's connected to the Flock?"

"Ideologically? No way. He was a leader in the Lone Star militia. Not *the* leader, but one of the lieutenants. Can't see them finding common cause with a bunch of green activists."

Claire nodded. The states that seceded had one major commonality—opposition to what they viewed as federal over-reach, mostly on environmental regulations. Extractive industries like oil and gas had been especially hard hit. Two of the Martian colonies, including Lyot, had seen an influx of new colonists after the governments of Texas and Oklahoma rejoined the US, as owners and workers who weren't in favor of that decision sought a more permissive place to do business.

"On the other hand," Wyatt continued, "quite a few of them have been renting themselves out as mercenaries. If they're happy with the color of the Flock's money, they may not be too concerned about the color of their politics."

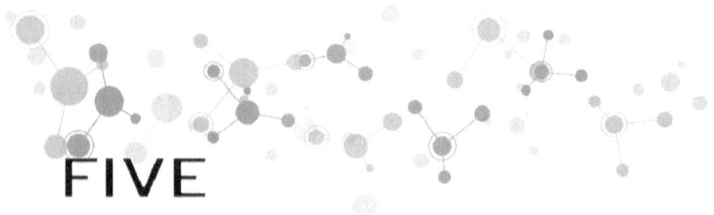

FIVE

CLAIRE TOSSED her bag into the back of the Aeris, gave the car her destination, and settled into the soft leather seat, cradling the travel mug of coffee she'd brewed while she tossed her things into her bag and changed into something less formal than the blue dress. It was a little after ten thirty, and she might regret the caffeine at such a late hour. But she needed to focus. Hopefully, the crappy sleep she'd had over the past two nights would balance out the jitters and she'd be able to crash when she needed to.

On the trip from Beekman Place to the apartment, she had reserved a two-bedroom suite at a hotel near Jonas Labs where she'd stayed on a few occasions while visiting. She sent the information to Joe, reasoning that he'd probably want to avoid staying in the house with Kai right now. Then she called Ro, who assured her that Joe was right. She and Jemma would be fine at the bed and breakfast. They had plenty of food, Jemma was thoroughly enjoying the pool, and she felt safe with the Jonas Labs guards that Wilson had sent up to watch the place. Claire wasn't entirely sure that she believed the last point, but there wasn't much she could do at the moment and there really wasn't anywhere else she could think of that would be safer for the two of them.

As the Aeris pulled out of the garage, she tried once more to reach Beck, but he still wasn't answering. She considered waiting a bit to open the video that he had sent her. Wyatt was in the middle of his meeting with Macek and he'd no doubt call as soon as it ended, which meant she'd have to stop the video and start again, and...

That was bullshit, though, and she knew it. She was delaying because she was afraid of what was in those files. Afraid of what Beck was about to tell her. She'd already figured out that the man was an alien—a freaking *alien*—and he'd been lying to her and to Joe the entire time he'd known them. That made her angry on a personal level. She'd trusted him. But she was even angrier for Joe. She had other people in her life—Ro, Jemma, Wyatt. Her brother had only two people aside from Claire, and he'd learned tonight that both of them had betrayed his trust.

After a deep breath and a long sip of her coffee, Claire opened her phone and sent the video file to the Aeris's viewscreen.

"Do you want a summary?" the AI asked. "Or shall I—"

"No. Play the complete file."

The timestamp indicated that it had been recorded late that afternoon, but Beck was still in the gray paisley shirt and black jeans he'd been wearing when they left Maine the day before. There was something white on the back of his neck. A bandage, maybe?

He was in a hotel room—a very *cheap* hotel room, judging from the generic décor and the tattered armchair. Given that he could definitely afford something better, he must have grabbed the first place he found with a vacancy. The bed behind him was rumpled, but judging from the exhaustion in his eyes, she doubted he'd gotten much sleep.

Although, on second thought, maybe he'd chosen the hotel because it was next to a liquor store. She'd never known him to have more than a couple of beers, but there was a flask on the end-table next to his chair. At least, she *thought* it was a flask. It was the right size, but made of what looked like glazed ceramic, dark red, with white symbols running vertically down the narrower edge.

For a moment, Beck simply stared at the camera, his mouth

set in a grim line. He looked completely miserable. And yes, more than a little drunk.

"I'm sending this to you, Claire, because you've already pieced some of it together and because I hope that you might be able to understand. And…" He shook his head. "I guess I'm too much of a coward to tell Joe, even indirectly."

Claire hit pause before he could say anything else and zoomed in on the flask. The symbols were stylized, but she had no trouble making them out as variants of the script she'd seen in the chamber at Icarus and in the children's book on the data drive Shepherd passed to her. The letters were more rounded, more like the variant Alice Dobroski had dubbed *New Martian*, although Claire was fairly certain they were going to have to change their assumptions about the script's planet of origin.

So, Beck was in a cheap hotel room drinking alien booze. Well, probably not alien to *him*, but still. Even if she hadn't already been worried about what he was going to tell her, that did not bode well.

She started the video again, wishing she could reach through the screen and tip a bit of whatever was in Beck's red flask into her coffee.

TRANSCRIPT OF VIDEO
BY JOHN BECKETT

(09/05/3084 18:43)

I'm sending this to you, Claire, because you've already pieced some of it together and because I hope that you might be able to understand. And … I guess I'm too much of a coward to tell Joe, even indirectly.

Because Joe will *not* understand. All he will see is betrayal. Which is completely fair in one sense and completely unfair in another. I don't know if you're watching this before or after you've read Eberin Das's journal—and yes, I'm now certain that it *is* a journal. I've learned several things in the past two days and…

Sorry. My mind is scattered. I planned to record this before the alcohol hit, but Sandjeel wasn't kidding when he said this batch of *evir* is extra strong. There's a fine line between being drunk enough that you're *willing* to slice a tracker out of the back of your neck and being *so* drunk that you're unable to safely handle an Exacto knife. I used my last few minutes of numb-but-still-sober to get rid of the thing and then passed out. I've got about fifteen minutes before I need to leave if I'm going to make it to Boston in time to take care of my end of the bargain. Hopefully, the effects of the alcohol will have worn off completely by the time I get there.

Still, *evir* plays a pivotal role in this story, so maybe it's fitting that it gets a little screen time. The word on this label was one of the first that I recognized from the journal. Aside from minor changes to the letters, it's written the same today as it was back then. Eberin and his compatriots drank *evir* when they met at Conclave. That would have been during the Second Alliance—no, I think Arbet said it was late First Alliance. Either way, you'd think by now, in the Sixth Alliance, millions of years later, we'd be on more solid moral ground, but ... we apparently haven't made much progress in that regard, since I'm facing the exact same dilemma as our friend Eberin. In one of the first entries I translated, he talked about the Alliance forcing him to choose between his blood-kin and his heart-kin. Between loyalty and justice. That's not an easy decision under the best of circumstances, but he knew the choice was futile. Nothing he did stood any chance of altering the inevitable. The only difference between my choice and his is that Eberin *knew* what he was signing up for when he left the Ufretan system. He changed his mind after a few decades working with the Martian people, but he understood the stakes from the beginning.

Maybe he's the reason they lie to us today. I don't know...

You know how in movies or books you have this character who says, "There's just so much. I'm not sure where to start." Then, the wise mentor steps in and tells them it's usually best to start at the beginning. Well, I'm going to ignore that sage advice, because like I said, I've got less than fifteen minutes. I'd hoped to do this on the flight to Boston, but I couldn't even get a shared transport, let alone a private one, and ... recording on the hyperloop obviously isn't an option.

Anyway, I'm going to start at the point where Eberin's journal began shifting from an interesting historical find to an unmitigated disaster. Joe was right when he said I've been a bit obsessed. I recognized the symbols as soon as I saw the video you recorded when they opened that chamber at Icarus Camp. I couldn't make out words, but the symbols were clearly some variant of the alphabet I learned as a child—which was about eleven hundred of your years ago, since I'm sure you're wondering. I'm one of the younger members of the Watch.

Anyway, I recognized the symbols, and it was a surprise, but not a major one. To the best of my knowledge, ours is the first Watch that the *Sixth* Alliance has sent into this star system, but I already knew that Ufretans visited Mars in the distant past because we learned about it at the Academy. I wouldn't be surprised now to learn that every Watch is provided with a similar cautionary tale. Mars was held out to us as an example of what can happen when we arrive too late to lend a guiding hand, when unbridled scientific advancement leads to chaos. We were taught that Mars was destroyed by its own inhabitants a few years *before* they reached the two milestones, which is the point at which the Watch is supposed to pack up and go home. That's when the diplomats take over to initiate formal first contact and, eventually, they offer the planet provisional membership in the Alliance.

Or so we were told.

When you brought that sample to the lab, I knew it was important. But to be honest, I was thinking more about the *historical significance* to the Alliance. Many of our records from the first two eras were destroyed during the First Great War and … well, I was thinking about what I might do next once I was back home. I had imagined returning to Parda with this important historical document. Translating it. Maybe even teaching at the Academy the next time they found a candidate world and recruited a new team of Watchers to guide its progress.

So, yeah. Joe was right when he said my focus was elsewhere. Even when we were working in the lab, my mind kept wandering back to the manuscript. And as I began compiling it, several words and phrases jumped out at me even before I got the translation software from the team at Berkeley. *Evir*, as I just noted. The words I've translated as *Conclave* and *Guardian*. I also recognized the word for *philosopher* because it was etched into the walls of a building at one of my schools—that's in the journal entry where Eberin says that he's trying to remember the name of some philosopher while he debates the morality of murdering his dinner partner.

And I should clarify that point. I don't know if the Martians were a closer match to our actual physiology or if they had a different method for transferring consciousness back then, but we don't murder our hosts. This body is a *clone*. With the exception of the Triad leader, who has to keep his original form, all members of the Watch are in cloned bodies. The worst thing that happened to the originals is that someone from one of our early scout ships collected their DNA. They weren't supposed to remember those encounters, but I believe a few of them did.

Where was I? Oh, yeah. Words I recognized. Probably the most important one was *ufret*. It's the root word for the name of our star system, the Alliance formed with several neighboring systems, and for the primary language used by members of our Alliance. Underneath all of that, however, it's the word for … family, I guess, although I think the phrase "found family" might be a better match. And it's as much an adjective as a noun. You can even use it as a verb, which makes it a bit hard to explain. One of the other Watchers once said it was like a merger of the Hawaiian words *aloha* and *ohana*.

In the journal, I translated the noun *ufret* as *heart-kin*, a feeling of shared sentiment and values. This is the core meaning of family in our culture, in part because we have limited ties to *ipret*, or blood-kin, who are from generations near our own. Siblings are almost unheard of, since most people in our culture are never granted a license to have even one child, let alone two. And because so few licenses are granted, parental rights are limited. Children *do* maintain ties to their birth families, but they're raised communally after the first few years.

This probably seems like a tangent to you, and maybe it is, but it's important. Maybe it's why I sort of … exploded everything at Conclave today. Not literally, but I definitely left an information bomb on my way out.

The thing is, I worked as a caregiver at one of the four regional child training centers on Parda—that's my homeworld. For most of the first decade of that assignment, I worked with the youngest students, many of whom were still processing the trauma of separation from their birth families. Most of the time, what they needed more than anything else was physical contact, a reminder that they were still among people who cared. That they were *ufret*.

That was one of my first postings, and by the time I joined the Watch, most of those memories had faded away. But they came roaring back in vivid detail when I saw you in the hallway at your dad's memorial.

I almost didn't go. I'm not sure if you remember, but I never actually met your dad. He was in the final stages and entered the hospital not long after I took the job. In the end, I decided to attend out of respect for Joe. But when they began sharing stories about your dad at the service, it seemed like a good time for me to make a discreet exit.

On my way out, I spotted you in that little side room, and the old instincts from my work at the Center just ... kicked in. I didn't think about whether I was overstepping personal boundaries or propriety. You were a child in pain. A child who felt abandoned, who needed *ufret*. I sat on the floor next to you, pulled you into my arms, and rocked you as you cried it out.

In my eyes, you will *always* be that child, Claire. And uh ... I don't want you to take this the wrong way, but maybe it will help you understand why I was relieved when your crush passed. A ten-year age gap would have been questionable even within your own culture back when you were eighteen, but on Parda—for that matter, on almost all of the worlds in the Sixth Alliance—you would be viewed as a youngling even today.

What I felt for you then—what I still feel—is ... well, maybe not parental, exactly, but close to that. It's just ... *ufret*. And that feeling was something I'd missed. I'd been on Earth for over a century at that point. Yes, I'd had good working relationships with colleagues, and even a few actual friendships but ... that was the first time I'd felt a real bond, a heart-kinship, with anyone here. I think it made me more open to connection, because I know that my bond with Joe is far, far stronger than any partnership that I had at VersaBio or my earlier postings on Earth. Stronger than any of the friendships I've made here. Hell, stronger than most of my friendships on Parda, although I don't see how my relationship with Joe is going to survive what I'm about to do and ... that hurts. It hurts a lot.

Is it crazy that my mind keeps circling back to that? Back to my guilt at lying to you and to Joe? I don't know. It seems odd to worry about destroying friendships when the planet itself is on the chopping block.

So ... let me get back on track here. I thought the Eberin Das manuscript was a great historical find. And yes, I thought it might be a warning, but not for Earth, given how close Joe's work has us to one of the milestones. The only thing that gnawed at me during those first months after you got back from Mars was how the Flock fits into all of this, especially after I learned that Drex had taken over. I'd obviously paid attention to the group when it was under Shepherd. Kind of hard to ignore them when they were releasing rats in the lobby of Jonas Labs and pelting people with blood balloons. But I hadn't thought a lot about Shepherd's ... what would you call it? His origin story for the group, I guess. The names were similar—the Watch, the Sentinels—but it's a fairly standard spiel, right? Humans are destroying the Earth, but some angelic group is coming to whisk the true believers away in their mothership.

The main reason, though, that it was easy for me to dismiss Shepherd was that the man got the key point *wrong*. He claimed that these Sentinels were *against* scientific progress, and that's the exact opposite of our stated mission. The whole reason we spent decades in training, in stasis, and well over a century here on Earth was to observe progress and report back. Maybe even give a gentle nudge in the right direction from time to time.

They left the question of whether to *nudge* up to individual preference, at least at first. But we've been here longer than anticipated. The first scouts thought the milestones would be reached by 2050. Not sure what they based that on, and maybe it *would* have happened by then if not for the political upheaval here in the US. But we're well past our target date and for the past few decades, one member of the Triad, Durav, has been urging those of us with active assignments to be a bit more *pro*active. I've never liked Durav, but I kind of agreed with him on that point. What could be wrong with giving the researchers a little push every now and then if Earth was going to get there eventually? Not that Joe was ever especially amenable to my redirection, but in principle, I leaned more toward Durav's position than Sandjeel and Arbet's.

So, that's where I was with all of this before you came back from New Haven with that nanodrive, which included not just a Ufretan version, but an English translation of *Tales from the Aveezi Forest*, a book that pretty much anyone who grew up on a world in the Sixth Alliance read as a child. At that point, I had to believe that at least *some* aspects of Shepherd's story were true. He *had* been in contact with a member of the Watch. And it had to have been more than a casual encounter if he'd spent enough time with them that he'd learned to read and write Ufretan.

After I read Shepherd's memoir, I also realized that the events in those first few chapters coincided with the only two deaths the Watch has incurred since our arrival. A member of the Triad, Djasa, was killed in 2046 when a secessionist militia attacked a cluster of research buildings near Duke University. She was replaced, as protocol required, by the seniormost member of the Watch, a man named Uden. I didn't know him well. He was in the other stasis group. All I knew was that he was based at an American university. And then about a year later, we were told that Uden was killed in an accidental fall at his home.

It seemed likely to me that Uden was Professor Everett from Shepherd's memoir. I needed to be sure, though. I'd had no luck in my attempts to locate Drex—she and Stasia were pretty much off the radar until they showed up in New York—so there was no way to ask her. I even tried contacting Arbet, the Watcher who took Uden's place on the Triad and the only one of the three that I know well. As a last resort I combed through the log of outgoing signals at Bellamy House—and grabbed Shepherd's contact info from your calls. Sorry about that.

I wanted to dig in a bit and see how much Shepherd knew but I decided to keep my question simple, based on your earlier observation that KTI censors all messages going in and out of areas they control. I just asked Shepherd if he could put me in touch with a mutual colleague, Professor Uden. There was a chance that Uden had never shared his real name with the boy, but judging from the memoir, Shepherd was a curious kid. It would have been a very natural thing for him to ask Uden's name when he was learning how to render his own name in Ufretan script. And sure enough, when he eventually got back to me, he confirmed that Uden and Everett were the same person.

Even then, it was hard for me to accept that Shepherd had gotten it right, you know? Everything I'd been taught my entire life argued against it. I went into the Conclave knowing on a rational level that it was all true, but desperate to find evidence to the contrary.

Only I didn't, and…

I'm nearly out of time. I might be able to record more later, but if not … read the journal, okay? What I sent you isn't the *entire* manuscript, just the parts I've managed to translate along with some notes. I started at the beginning, but when it became clear that I wouldn't finish before we left for New York, I jumped to the end and prioritized the last few entries.

I'm guessing it will raise more questions than it answers for you. As I suspect this video does. I will answer all of your questions. I promise. When you're done with your business in New York, find me. If you think back to our conversation on Monday, you know where I'll be. I'm hoping that place will still be safe, at least for a while. God knows I created an elaborate enough paper trail to hide it.

And now I'm wondering exactly *why* I did that. A moment ago, I'd have sworn that I never suspected anything was off about our mission, about the Triad and yet I have kept a secret hideaway for … what? Nearly eighty years. It's not the hardened fortress that would serve me best now that I *do* know the truth, but maybe there was some thread of suspicion at the back of my mind all along that one day, I'd need it.

Anyway, the code to the gate is the title. I'll tell you anything you want to know. About me, about the Alliance, about the Watch. About the bargain we tried to strike with the Triad. Their answer was no, but maybe this will show them we're serious. I think there's an equally good chance they'll just double down, but…

Be careful, okay? Bring Wyatt with you if you're worried about coming alone. Joe, too, if he's willing, although I don't think that will be likely after tonight. Just keep the gun with you. I doubt that Durav will continue honoring my right of *ufrete,* and apparently that was the main thing keeping you safe for the past few months.

The one thing I need to stress before I go is this—I didn't have a clue, Claire. None of us did. The Watch is supposed to be something similar to your Peace Corps. What I signed up for was … I guess you could call it an interplanetary development agency. Only now, I find out that Earth is maybe six months away, a year at the most, from the same fate as Mars, and I've been pushing it closer to the brink all this time.

There's a line in one of the entries near the end of Eberin's journal that haunts me. He knew they had no hope of success, and he was honest with the people who followed him about the fact that it was probably too late. Still, they didn't back down.

It's probably too late for us, too. Chances are, we'll fail the same way that Eberin Das did.

But like he said in his journal, when the fate of an entire planet is on the line, do the odds even matter? What choice do we have but to try?

FROM THE JOURNAL
OF EBERIN DAS

(Translation by John Beckett)

32.17.506

FOR ONCE, I arrived at the Conclave early enough to get a room with a balcony. It meant taking an extra day off, but it was worth it. It will be nice to sit out here with Bodae and catch up. I've missed our talks. We'll be spending most of the next four days in a closed room. I need a door that I can throw open to get some air once the meetings are over.

And the air is clear and fresh this high up on the slopes. Even during our first few years on Mars, I rarely needed nasal filters when we were here. At lower elevations, Martian law required them any time you stepped outside back then, even in smaller population centers like Reha. The remediation efforts have been very successful though, and they're needed only a few times a year now, during warmer weather.

The Triad chose this spot for our headquarters ostensibly because of its isolation. But I think they also liked the symbolism. The natives call this Emperor Mountain, a fitting name for the largest peak on the planet. And on the flight in today, anyone coming from the south—which is most of us—passed over the range of slightly smaller mountains that they call the Guardians, three stout gatekeepers. There are far more than three of us, but I'm sure the Triad considers the location a nice visual reminder. Emperor Mountain is the Alliance, and the Guardians are its noble protectors.

If our advance force had dug a bit deeper, however, or if the Triad had much interaction with the native population, they might have been less enthused about that allusion. Yes, the planet once had an Emperor, but in the stories that I've heard, the three Guardians represent the force that overthrew him when he forgot that his proper role was to serve and protect.

The people I've worked with and lived among since our arrival bear almost no resemblance to the warlike caricature we were taught to expect when we studied the culture at the Academy. They're not perfect. They still have squabbles between and even within their six regional governments, especially in times when resources are scarce. They haven't conquered corruption or personal greed. But what Alliance world has?

We are more alike than we are different. In many ways, the Martians come out better in a direct comparison. They've survived and even thrived in a far harsher environment than most worlds in the Alliance.

Surely, I can't be the only one who sees this?

Translator's Notes:

1. I've chosen to translate the name of the planet as *Mars* and the people as *Martians*. Given where the journal was found, I think this is a reasonable assumption, even though the phonetic rendering of the ancient Ufretan word is very different. Likewise, I've opted to translate most words related to the Alliance using the historical terms from what I'm fairly certain was either the First Alliance or Second Alliance rather than our current (Sixth Alliance) variants. Root words for the terms I've translated here as *Triad* (our panel of three leaders) and *Conclave* (the official meetings they

oversee) have remained the same over time. The root word for the larger group, however, has changed. I've translated the term used by Eberin as *Guardians*, but it seems to be used more in the sense of an advance force securing an area than as a protective force for the planet's inhabitants. Today, we call ourselves *Watchers*, and the root word is the same as our term for observation. Simply put, we are spies for the Sixth Alliance, and the Triad is our spymaster.

2. Emperor Mountain and the Three Guardians track closely with the Martian geological features of Tharsis Montes and Olympus Mons. Even if we ignore the fact that the manuscript and Eberin's crypt were found on Mars, this description is further proof that it's the same planet.

32.18.506

Bodae arrived just before the evening meal, which is thankfully a short and informal affair on the night before Conclave begins. He snagged an extra bottle of *evir,* and we split it on the balcony. We reminisced for a while, which was nice, and I was well-behaved, keeping the conversation firmly in the past and away from our jobs. I've long suspected that working on different milestones may be the reason we've kept our friendship intact for so long. Arguments over strategies and timing have come between several Guardians who were close at the Academy, but we've been able to avoid those. It's hard to argue too vociferously over work given that Bodae has no background in medical science, and I don't keep up with the intricacies of the Martian government's off-planet colonization projects.

Eventually, it was Bodae who shifted the conversation to work. "I'm sure you heard that Seeker Two returned safely?"

I nodded. After the loss of the first ship the previous year, every news source had gleefully hailed the safe return of the six-person crew several days earlier. "Hard to miss it," I said. "Congratulations. Did they find out what happened to the first mission?"

He winced. "More or less. They located the ship, which was largely intact. No survivors. There were remains inside one of the exosuits, though. And other bones nearby. Picked clean. Crushed in some places. And the crew got a glimpse of a creature they said looked perfectly capable of crushing them—even through the suits. We'd seen some pretty fearsome beasts through the cameras on the unmanned missions, but can you imagine actually being there with something like that approaching and you're barely able to shuffle because it feels like you're carrying around nearly twice your weight? *More* than twice your weight if you count the suit."

"That's not insurmountable, though, right? Won't the atmospheric adjustments wipe out most of the native creatures?"

"Yeah. Not much they can do about the gravity though. Would you want to spend most of your life inside one of those exosuits? They … haven't announced it yet, but they've already decided against sending another team."

He was quiet for a moment, letting the weight of that statement sink in. Earth is the sole viable option for colonization within this star system. If they were scrapping plans for colonies there, only two other options remained.

"So are they going with orbital habitats or exoplanets?" I asked.

"It's being debated in the committees right now. Opinion seems about equally split between the two. But most of the orbital habitat advocates see it as a stop-gap measure. There's a fairly solid consensus that they need to pick a couple of worlds outside this system and see what they can tweak remotely. So … it's pretty much over. I think the Triad will call it. If not now, definitely before the next Conclave. Which is bad timing, given that the transport just left this sector. On the plus side, though, my team will have nearly a full cycle of down time to travel. I haven't had a chance to see much outside of Wen Mievet. I'm looking forward to a nice long sabbatical. I'd like to spend some time hiking in this region, too. Maybe you can join me if you get some time off?"

"Oh, no. I'd be much too afraid."

He gave me a wary, questioning look. "Afraid of what?"

"Of the people we'd encounter. You know, the warmongering, imperialistic, morally inferior species they warned us about at the Academy? The brutish hordes who can't be allowed to spread to neighboring star systems? I haven't seen many of them in the cities, and this is one of the few remaining areas that's relatively unpopulated, so they must all be hiding in these parts, right? We'd probably fare better among the nasty beasts that you guys have spotted on Earth."

Bodae chuckled and topped off our glasses with the last of the *evir*, refusing to be baited into an argument. I didn't push it. We've covered this territory many times before, and I know that deep down, he agrees with me. He has friends in the native population, too. And he's not a monster.

But with the alcohol now exhausted and Conclave beginning early, he excused himself a few minutes later and headed back to his own room. It's well after midnight. I should sleep, too. I'm still here on the balcony, though, disturbed both by his rather cavalier dismissal of my concerns and my own cowardice. I should have pushed the issue. So what if it makes him uncomfortable? We're talking about genocide. If that *doesn't* make him uncomfortable, then maybe he's not the person I thought I knew.

The true irony is that the Alliance considers itself civilized and moral because we *wait* to destroy these worlds. We set an arbitrary line that they must not cross, but the line is invisible to them. Then we wait, we watch, and we weigh their achievements. And some of us aren't even content to wait. Reasoning that there's no point in delaying the inevitable, they nudge these unsuspecting people toward that line that they cannot see, toward the tripwire that will doom their world.

We think that we're somehow noble for refusing to swat them down until they reach the point where we might consider them equals. Not because they're suddenly dangerous to us. They're several sectors away from the Ufretan system and far, far below our level of technological power.

The painfully obvious truth is that the Martian people, even once they achieve the two milestones, will pose absolutely no threat to the Alliance for many centuries to come. We're just wiping them out because they might—in some distant day—*become* competition.

Translator's Notes:

1. An Alliance cycle is mapped to the Ufretan solar year. I have no idea how often retrieval ships returned to the sector back then. Now, it's about once every cycle, or roughly every three Earth years.
2. *Evir* is similar to vodka. The word also means *burn* in most Alliance languages. I suppose that makes it a linguistic cousin to the old Earth term "firewater."
3. I can't imagine any planet in the system that this could be aside from Earth. If I'm right about the journal being written in either the late First Alliance or early Second Alliance, then it would have been during Earth's late Jurassic period or possibly the early Cretaceous era, during which the crew could easily have encountered the sort of beasts that Bodae described. And it's much easier for the humans terraforming Mars today to adapt to *lower* gravity than it would have been for Martian explorers to adapt to the gravity on Earth.

32.19.506

I awoke today with a pounding head, a sour stomach, and a patchy memory. Bodae's look of fond disapproval over our morning meal confirmed what I already suspected. In addition to drinking too much last night, I'd also *talked* too much.

In all likelihood, I wasn't the only one from our group nursing a hangover. The Conclave isn't just a business event, after all, but a reunion. A time to celebrate our achievements, plan the upcoming cycle, and—most important of all—to remind ourselves exactly why we are here. The Triad does its best to ensure that we leave Conclave with a renewed appreciation of all that we have been sent here to protect, and they are perfectly willing to trigger a bit of homesickness in the process. All of the questions they asked before programming our stasis environment made it easy to ensure that they included small stores of each Guardian's favorite foods, drink, and music. These little touches of home are things that we can only experience at the Conclave, as scenes from our home worlds flash on the walls and as we watch messages from loved ones and record our own greetings into our *rezlat* to send back to them.

We're now thirty-seven cycles in, however, and they're getting a bit stingy with the *crestah*. That leads me to believe that the Ufretan supplies are nearly depleted. Still plenty of that foul *braber*, though. Not a surprise, I guess, when two of the three Triad are from the Durdjin system.

Drink, however, always flows freely at the Conclave. I've yet to visit an Alliance world without some variant of *evir*. It's basic enough that I even managed to create a passable version from local ingredients before I developed a taste for Martian brews. But I don't think the abundance of alcohol at these gatherings is simply due to the fact that there's a general consensus among the Guardians on their favorite spirit. The Triad *wants* us to overindulge. They probably learn more during the social hours than they do from our formal reports.

"Stop staring at me and just say whatever it is you're thinking," I grumbled to Bodae.

He continued eating for a moment before looking up. "I'm *thinking* you should save your wild hypotheticals for our private conversations. The others don't know you like I do. Eidjri is convinced that you're serious and she's not alone in that view. And by your fourth or fifth drink, you don't back down when someone challenges you. They could tell you that your ass was on fire, and you'd refuse to put it out just to be contrary. You've always been that way to some extent, but it's gotten worse recently. After you collapsed in the corner last night, I spent the rest of the evening doing damage control."

I didn't respond at first. How could he be right about so many things and still miss the key point? *Wild hypotheticals?* Maybe these subjects had been hypothetical—at least for us— back at the Academy. But how could anyone say that now?

He *was* right about one thing. I need to steer clear of Eidjri at these events. That's hard to do, though, when we're both on the team that monitors longevity research. Different labs, both hurtling toward the same goal. Hers is marginally ahead of mine at the moment, and I know why. The Triad leaves the question of whether we are to serve as monitors or as guides to our personal discretion. Eidjri gleefully assists her lab at every turn, pointing their scientists in the right direction if they seem to be veering off track. She's not the only one. The group was close to evenly split on this ethical quandary when we arrived on Mars, but as time has passed, more and more of them have drifted over to what they consider the pragmatic approach. We all know it's going to happen eventually and the sooner it does, the sooner we can get back to plentiful supplies of *crestah* and *braber.*

"Everyone already knows how I feel about interference," I said to Bodae, weighing my words carefully. "And Eidjri is one of the worst offenders."

"Except you called her a *murderer.* And a ghoul. I'm not

saying you don't have a point—it *is* almost ghoulish, the way she views our mission as a race. It's like she's sprinting toward the finish line. I find her attitude as abhorrent as you do. We have a job to do, and it's vital for the future of the Alliance, but you're right. It's better to let things take their natural course. All I'm saying is that you need to be a little more diplomatic in how and where you express those views." He gave me a warm smile. "The good news is that it sounds like we only have a few more Conclaves before this is all over."

I returned his smile automatically, but it felt strange on my face.

Good news for *us*, sure. We get to go home. But it was the worst kind of bad news for everyone else on the planet.

Translator's Notes:

1. Twenty-seven Alliance cycles are roughly fifty-five Mars years, which would be about a hundred and ten Earth years. Either the Martians advanced as quickly from normal aging to near immortality as Earth seems to be doing, or else the Guardians didn't bother to alter their host bodies to adjust for age, simply taking a new host instead. Maybe knowing from the outset that the planet was doomed resulted in less of a moral quandary over taking a life a few cycles early. Or maybe this was only an issue for Eberin as he mentions trouble with the transfer in the undated post I am interpreting as a preface.

2. Watchers still receive a *rezlat* at the beginning of each Conclave. I'm not sure if their device was exactly the same, but ours is a (supposedly) private recorder with a biometric sensor that allows us to exchange messages with friends and family in the Ufretan system. There's about a three-year time lag, but most

members of the Watch still very much look forward to this.

3. *Crestah* might be an early version of a confection we call *creshad*. A bit like pralines, but chewier and less sweet. *Braber* is a word I recognized immediately. You can find it on most Alliance planets. Similar to chocolate but with strong licorice undertones. As with your cilantro, people tend to either love it or hate it.

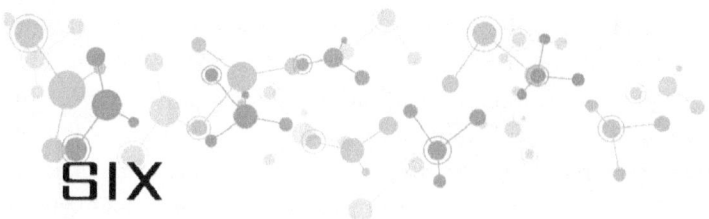

SIX

Wednesday, September 6 12:28 am

CLAIRE PLACED the tablet on the seat next to her and stared out at the lights on the highway trying to process what she'd just learned. She'd watched Beck's recording three times. The first two times, she just listened. The last time, she took notes. And she was absolutely certain that Beck had told the truth about at least one thing. She now had more questions than she'd had going in, both about the manuscript and the video.

Her first note was a single word: *Millions?* Because Beck had definitely implied that the journal was *millions* of years old. *You'd think by now, in the Sixth Alliance, millions of years later, we'd be on more solid moral ground.* She'd replayed that section several times and even used the captioning tool to confirm that she'd heard him correctly. Because assuming that the manuscript was indeed a history of the final days leading up to the planet's destruction, that couldn't be right.

Ben Pelzer, the geologist on the team she'd traveled with to Mars, hadn't been able to determine the age of the metal chamber. He had, however, been able to get a reading on several pieces of olivine they'd found around the edges. He'd estimated one of them at about four million years, others at closer to a hundred million. That wasn't surprising, given that the molten olivine could have shot up through the layers of rock at different times, molding itself around the edges and corners. Nothing seemed to adhere to the sides of the chamber, and Pelzer still couldn't identify the alloy, although he had told her that it contained some materials not previously found on Mars.

The chamber itself, however, would have to be much older than the olivine if Mars was inhabited at the time. Even the most generous estimates had liquid water evaporating from the surface more than two billion years ago. While a few scientists theorized that life was possible without water, the majority begged to differ. Leaving aside the very obvious H_2O symbol she'd seen in the lower chamber, Mars had retained subsurface water and the native bacterial life that had been found was water-based. Without water, the civilization that Eberin Das described would have died off *billions* of years ago, not millions.

So, yes, she had several questions on that point alone. But even if she'd been in the same room when Beck was speaking, she'd have been hesitant to ask him for clarification in the moment. The anger and pain on his face had been palpable, and he'd clearly been working toward something that was of far more consequence than exactly *when* Mars had ceased to be habitable.

The second question on her list concerned the nature of this *bargain* he was heading back to Boston to complete. Given the timing, the answer would seem to be that he had played some role in setting the bombs. But that didn't make sense given both his call to her during the Ares Consortium dinner and what Wilson had told Joe about his efforts in the minutes before the explosions.

And bargain with *whom*? Drexel?

Her third question involved the two milestones, but she'd scratched that out after reading the journal. The first milestone was biological immortality or something very close to it, since Beck said that Joe's work had Earth on the precipice of that achievement. Based on her interpretation of Eberin's journal, the second must be colonization outside the solar system. Beck said that he believed Earth to be years away from that, but his conversations with Stasia and Drex must have given him a heads up that Kolya was about to announce the plans for his scattershot method of terraforming exoplanets.

She had also jotted down the word *youngling*, in part because it wasn't commonly used. People generally say *child, kid, youth,* or even *youngster.* But it jumped out mostly because she remembered it from one of the stories she'd read in *Tales of the Aveezi Forest.* Maybe it had a more specific meaning in Ufretan culture. Personally, she was going to translate it as *young adult,* because the idea that she could be considered a child at nearly twenty-nine was disconcerting, to say the least.

The code to the gate is the title raised three more very obvious questions. *What title? What code? What gate?* And she didn't even know where to start with this right of *ufrete* and how it might have kept her from harm.

As for the journal, there were huge gaps in the narrative, but she had no idea how many of those gaps were sections that Beck hadn't finished translating and how many were times when Eberin Das simply hadn't written in his diary. Occasionally, there would be several months—assuming she was interpreting the date format correctly—where there were no entries at all and then he would fire off three or four in a matter of days.

More than ever, she wanted to dismiss the manuscript as a work of fiction or the product of delusion. Had it been originally written in English, she would have read it again, trying to pick up on subtle nuances that could help her decide whether the author was lying or even insane. In this case, however, she had little hope of being able to tell.

Even more worrisome, the translation was undoubtedly colored by Beck's own thoughts and experiences. How was she supposed to suss out the truth in a document with not just one but *two* potentially unreliable narrators?

ANAK — TWO DAYS EARLIER

things went badly, he'd be hiding out there in a few days and the harder it was for the Triad to track him down, the better. Disappointment because he loved the place, and if things went *very* badly, there was a chance that he'd never see it again.

Claire was asking him something else, but the only word he caught was *cat*.

"Sorry. What?"

"I asked if you usually bring your cat up when you visit."

"Sometimes," he said, before remembering that had been a different cat, the one he'd owned many years ago, just after he bought the place. Was that when he was still Noah O'Brian? It might even have been the assignment before that. "I usually have someone come in and feed him now on the rare occasions when I travel. Crichton is a bit of a homebody."

"Oh, yeah. We have one of those, too. Siggy *hates* going out of the house." Claire pointed to two pink lines on her upper arm. "I earned these battle scars trying to wrestle the demon into her crate to take her to the kennel before I headed to New York the other day. I very nearly left her grumpy little ass to the tender mercies of the auto-feeder." She shuddered, clearly thinking about the fire that had destroyed her house a few days earlier. "Very, very glad I didn't. I can't even imagine breaking that news to Jemma. Ro is going to have a hard enough time telling her that our house is gone. So ... how long has it been since you've gone to one of these reunions?"

Ah ha ... there it was. They were now back to the topic that she'd been trying to get him to talk about since he mentioned it inside the biodome at Jonas Labs a few days prior.

At first, Anak had been puzzled as to why she was so curious and a little worried that the crush she'd had on him during her college years had resurfaced. Claire's interest in him back then had been obvious enough that even Joe had noticed. In fact, Joe had actually encouraged him a bit at the very beginning, saying maybe his sister would come home on her breaks from Stanford more often if he asked her out. He'd quickly backtracked, though, joking that he didn't want to deal with the moping around when Claire inevitably dumped him.

Joe wasn't usually adept at reading social cues, so Anak suspected he'd simply decided—with good reason—that a romance between his research partner and his sister could affect their working relationship. The guy did have occasional flashes of insight, though. Maybe he had picked up on the fact that Anak found the topic embarrassing. He just told Joe that he didn't think of Claire *that way*, and neither of them ever mentioned it again.

That was just as true now as it had been back then. Yes, she was attractive. He wasn't blind, and while his host body was only *technically* human, it was—in the words of that android from one of the *Star Trek* shows—fully functional and adept at multiple techniques.

Anak's problem was the age gap. On Parda, Claire would still have several years of primary training left and would be very much off-limits. After training, there were no actual restrictions, but people still tended to form relationships with those born within a generation or two of their own. While he'd dated outside of his peer group a few times, his two commitments had been with partners fairly close to his own age. You simply had more in common with them than you would have with someone who had many more—or many less—lifetimes of experiences. His last commitment on Parda had spanned nearly four centuries on Earth, not counting the mandatory separations between commitment periods. He thought they'd lasted so long in part because he and Brinn wore the same generation mark on their forearms.

So, yes, he'd been relieved when it finally dawned on him the previous afternoon that Claire's repeated questions about his plans in New York probably weren't romantic in nature. She was a reporter, after all. Not an *investigative* reporter, but she no doubt had gained some ability to spot deception when interviewing sources.

Unfortunately, telling her the truth was out of the question. The best he could do was to avoid outright lies to the extent possible and hope it would be enough to quell her curiosity.

"It's just that you said you'd been putting it off for a while," she prodded after a few seconds of silence. "And to be honest, you don't really seem to be looking forward to it."

He shrugged. "Some of the others meet up a few times a year. I don't usually go. You know how these things are. People trying to one-up each other. It can get tedious."

All of that was true. Most of the others were now on sabbatical, so they had plenty of free time on their hands. He was fairly sure he was the only member of the Watch with an actual, ongoing assignment at this point. Unlike the others, Anak didn't have time to attend any strictly social gatherings.

This meeting, however, was a Conclave. You didn't miss it without a damn good reason.

"To be honest, I *don't* really know how they are," Claire said. "But I can imagine. I didn't bother with my high school reunion. I wasn't at the last school for long and barely had a social life since Kai was threatening to make me do an extra year if I didn't get into one of the colleges she wanted. Stanford had some sort of five-year thing last spring, but I didn't bother. Not living in the dorms meant that I didn't make many close friends, Wyatt being the obvious exception. His social circle was much larger than mine. I don't know … maybe we'll do the ten-year."

Anak felt his throat tighten at Claire's casual mention of future plans. Her ten-year reunion wasn't even four years away. At her age, making plans for four *decades* in the future wouldn't be all that odd. It was well within her expected lifespan, even without factoring in the extra decades—or more—promised by Rejuvesce.

But if that manuscript was right, there would be no reunion for Claire's class at Stanford. Long before the date rolled around, Stanford, Claire, and everyone else on this planet would be gone.

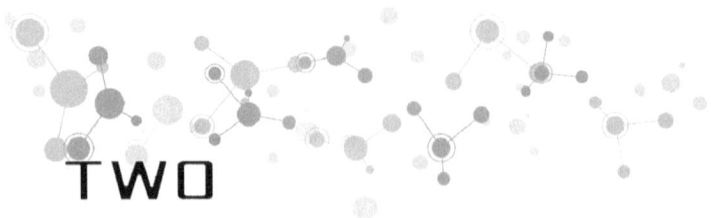

TWO

ANAK CLUTCHED the arm rest and took a centering breath. He didn't *know* anything. Not for certain. There was still a chance that he was misinterpreting all of it. He'd only translated about two-thirds of the manuscript, and he sure as hell wasn't an expert in ancient Ufretan. He was also seeing everything through the lens of Tobias Shepherd's memoir, which could still be a lie.

The only thing he felt he'd really eliminated at this point was his initial assumption. At first, he'd thought maybe the journal was written in a variant of Ufretan because there had been First or Second Alliance colonies on the planet and some group of Martians had wound up adopting the language as their own. It certainly wouldn't have been the first time that a colonized planet wound up speaking the language of their oppressors.

But that didn't really fit with the little that he knew about first contact procedures back then, and the more he read, the more it became clear that the manuscript had been written by an actual Watcher assigned to Mars. There were just too many similarities for it to be anything else. Not just the similarity in words, but also the customs that Das mentioned. It was probably written toward the end of the First Alliance or the beginning of the Second, but he had no way of checking the history at the moment. The author hadn't said one way or the other. Then again, would anyone have referred to it as the *First Alliance* at that point? That term probably wasn't used until long after the First Alliance ended and was replaced—eventually—by the *Second* Alliance.

Still, the fact that the author had entitled the manuscript *The*

Journal of Eberin Das didn't mean it was an actual journal. Eberin Das could be a character in some Watcher's lame attempt at dystopian fiction. While Anak couldn't quite make himself believe it, he clutched at the slender thread of possibility that some writer had been so desperate to get their deathless prose into the hands of readers that they'd protected their work by encoding it inside the DNA of the hardiest organism on the planet.

Because the alternative—that the manuscript was an actual diary—was simply unthinkable. The alternative meant that everything he'd been told was false. And not just what he'd been told about his mission here, but everything he'd been taught about the Alliance, about his entire civilization.

And it meant that Arbet had been lying to him for the past several decades. Okay, not lying in the strictest sense. They'd barely spoken since she moved up to the Triad after Uden's death. But with a secret this massive, her silence was the moral equivalent of a lie.

"Are you okay?" Claire asked.

"Yeah. Just … still a bit out of it, I guess. Not sure if it was the sun or just some bug I picked up."

It hadn't been either of those things. The red patch on his face, which he'd gotten due to a careless application of sunscreen, had been a bit uncomfortable, but otherwise, he'd felt fine when he went to pick Claire up at the hyperloop terminal. It was what she'd told him during the drive that landed like a punch to his gut, and he'd latched onto sun exhaustion to give him some time alone to work on the manuscript and try to figure out how he was going to handle the upcoming Conclave.

"Either way," he continued, as he searched inside his bag for his earphones, "it seems to be fully resolved. Aside from my sleep schedule being a bit off."

He located his earphones and was about to put them on when he felt Claire's hand on his wrist.

"Are you mad at me about something? Or at Joe?"

"What?" Anak shook his head. "No."

She'd seemed a bit hurt when asking the question, but then her expression shifted to realization, and perhaps a touch of guilt. "Wait ... you're not angry that he opened the files when you weren't around, are you? Because if so, that's *totally* my fault. *I'm* the one who didn't want to wait."

"No. I'm just..." Anak sighed and shook his head again. "I've got a lot on my mind. Plus, I'm feeling better, but still not a hundred percent, and ... as you noted, I only got a couple of hours of sleep."

"Sorry. I didn't mean to pry."

He could tell she wasn't entirely buying it, but he couldn't say more. Not without stoking her curiosity, and the very last thing he needed was her poking around this weekend. It was bad enough that she was going to be in the same city. He'd be much happier if she were safe in...

Safe in *where*, exactly? DC? She didn't even have a house there anymore. Maine? Even with the guards watching Bellamy House he was worried. If he'd known exactly what Claire would be bringing back from New Haven, he wouldn't have suggested that she invite Ro and Jemma. Not that they *should* be in danger, especially the child. He could imagine a few members of the Watch—Maela or Meeks, maybe, and yeah, Durav—killing a *youngling* to protect the mission or their fellow Watchers, but Jemma was little more than a baby. Surely even they wouldn't harm an infant. It would be...

The word that popped into his mind first was *inhuman*, which was actually kind of ironic. Many humanoids, on this planet and others, had no qualms about killing children in other countries or putting those in their own country in significant danger if they were born to parents with different skin tones, religious beliefs, or even economic status. He'd long thought that was something Earth would have to work on during their probationary membership. But for worlds in the Alliance, harming a child was the strictest taboo.

Well, harming *Alliance* children, at any rate. If his suspicions about their actual mission were correct, they'd been perfectly okay with annihilating every child on Mars and were gearing up to do the same to those on Earth. And the rumors of civilian casualties in the ongoing war in the Hodjeri system were one reason he'd opted for the much, much longer commitment with the Watch instead of a shorter service period in the military.

He squeezed Claire's arm and gave her the best smile he could muster. "It's okay. Really. But I do think I'm going to try to catch a quick nap if you don't mind? I've got a hectic day ahead."

"Oh, sure. I may try to do the same." She flashed him a hesitant look as she tucked a loose strand of dark hair behind her ear. "Before you go to sleep, though, I need to message Alice about Wednesday. What would be a good time for you?"

Anak had forgotten all about his promise to meet with Claire and the archeolinguist. He tried to wrangle his way out of it, noting that he wasn't sure how much use he'd be now that they had Shepherd's notes and copies of *Tales from the Aveezi Forest* in both languages. He couldn't even be certain he'd still be in New York in two days' time. In the end, he simply copied the translation software to Claire's computer and told her he'd try to make the meeting if she let him know when they had settled on a time and place.

Claire smiled and nodded, but her eyes narrowed slightly, and Anak could tell that she'd picked up on the lie. Before she could call him out on it, though, he jammed the earphones into his ears, closed his eyes, and pretended to sleep.

THREE

AS CLAIRE CROSSED the rooftop of the apartment building, Anak sent a message to Joe letting him know that he'd finally gotten her to agree to take the gun. There was a good chance that she'd taken the pistol only to placate the two of them and would shove it into a drawer the second she entered the apartment. And it could well be a moot point, anyway. A handgun wouldn't be much use if one of Durav's people was targeting her. But he felt better knowing she was armed, and he'd promised Joe that he would try. He owed the man that much, especially now that the clock was almost certainly running out on their friendship.

While he waited for the AeroLyft to get clearance to take off again, he checked his messages. The phone had buzzed twice while he pretended to sleep. He'd ignored it both times. If it was the investigator wanting to update him on his efforts to track down Drex and Stasia, that wasn't a conversation he'd wanted to have in front of Claire. And he definitely hadn't wanted her sneaking peeks over his shoulder if he had a message from Tobias Shepherd, since she'd have questions—entirely *justified* questions—about how he'd obtained the man's contact information.

The first message was indeed from Shepherd. And the delay apparently wasn't because he'd been laboring over a lengthy reply. It was just one word: *Deceased*. Still, it seemed to answer his question. If Shepherd hadn't recognized Uden's name, he wouldn't have said the guy was dead, right?

Anak closed his eyes and took a deep breath. With that single word, Shepherd had erased all doubt. There were a few things that didn't line up as neatly as he'd like, and he still had a ton of questions. But the tiny sliver of hope he'd been clinging to—the possibility that this was all a misunderstanding—was now gone. All he could do now was try to find a way to avert disaster.

No, that was painting the situation with far too small of a brush. It wasn't just a disaster. It was a global apocalypse. And if he was being honest, avoiding it entirely wasn't in the cards. Earth had no chance of defending itself against the Alliance. The best he could imagine was a delay. Convincing Joe and Kolya to hit the brakes might buy the planet a few decades. Maybe even a century or two, if they could throw sand in the gears of other curious entrepreneurs who decided to pick up the research.

The odds of achieving even this stopgap measure were incredibly slim, but they'd be nonexistent without allies.

He opened the message from the investigator, Mark Milner, and found a callback number. Milner picked up on the first ring.

"Well, the good news is that we had them. Unfortunately, we lost them again. I've got two people on it."

"So they *are* in the Bronx?"

"Yeah. Or at least they were twenty minutes ago. We placed cameras at every hotel in a five kilometer radius around Van Cortlandt Park, like you suggested. Located them at a place just off Henry Hudson called the Cortlandt Inn."

Anak had contacted Milner a few days earlier and told him to shift the search to the area around Riverdale, following a hunch that Drex might show up during the Conclave. No way they'd dare attend, but if she had recruited Stasia, it stood to reason that she might try to convince one or two of the others to join her if she could catch them before or after the meetings. And now that he had a better grasp of *why* Drex might have taken over the Flock, he thought that was even more likely.

"They've changed their appearance quite a bit," Milner continued, "so we weren't sure it was them at first. But we got a good enough image as they were leaving that facial recognition gave us a tentative match on the blond. Or rather the one who *used* to be blond."

The AeroLyft, which had finally received clearance, hovered above the roof of the apartment house briefly, then veered to the north.

"But there was another woman with her, right? And your guy gave them the message?"

"Uh, no. Like I said, we didn't get a positive hit until they were heading out of the hotel. He followed the car but lost it on the freeway. But at least we know what they're driving now. A blue Argo. I'm hoping we can pick them up again on the satellite."

"Okay. Keep me posted."

"We got a partial tag, too. Maybe we could call it in to the local cops? I mean, one of them *is* wanted in connection with those attacks on Mars, right?"

Not just one of them, Anak thought.

"No," he said. "If you track them down again in the next hour or so, call me. If you find them after that, just leave a message and I'll get back with you as soon as I can. I'll be out of pocket this afternoon, probably into early evening."

The flight to the Van Cortlandt Park helipad took less than five minutes. When the AeroLyft touched down, Anak keyed in the code to send the chopper back to Jonas Labs, per Joe's agreement with Kai. Then he pulled his bag from behind the seat and headed for the parking area.

Normally, he would have just walked from here. The cluster of houses that served as headquarters for the Watch was only a little over a kilometer from the park. But the idea of approaching on foot made him uneasy today and he was glad he'd decided to call a car. In fact, now that he was here, even the short walk over to the lot seemed risky. He felt eyes on him, and a tendril of dread clutched at his throat as he scanned the cars. The green single seater at the curb was his ride, but there were four other vehicles, including a silver Neon Pulsar that looked like one he'd seen in the courtyard at a previous Conclave.

This was stupid. If the Triad wanted to take him out, why would they do it here? They'd just order their sentry drones to attack him when he arrived. Or they'd have one of the *ipret-tai* strangle him in his sleep. Why risk drawing attention by striking him down in public?

Plus, if the Triad was truly some sort of dark cabal willing to wipe out errant members, would Drex and Stasia still be alive months after defecting? Milner had managed to find them, after all. Admittedly, only after he was given a tip on their possible destination, but the Triad had even more information about Drex than Anak did. If they hadn't found, hadn't *killed*, two outright defectors, there was no way they'd bother with him.

And finally, no matter what he might think about Durav and Sandjeel's willingness to resort to violence, did he really believe Arbet would be part of something like that? If she thought he was in any danger, she'd have gotten word to him somehow.

You're overreacting, he thought as he slid into his rental. *Pulsars are a dime a dozen in wealthy suburbs.*

He'd have felt a lot better about that thesis if the Pulsar hadn't pulled out of the lot behind him. It looked like two people inside, but the sun reflecting off the windshield kept him from making out anything beyond that. The car followed him onto Moshulu and turned left onto Fieldston when he did. So, instead of turning onto 250th Street as planned, he told the car to keep going.

When he turned a few blocks down, the Pulsar continued along Fieldston. Anak took the block a couple of times, but there was no sign of the other car. He breathed a sigh of relief, then circled back around onto 250th. A few minutes later, he pulled up to the curb about a half block down from Goodridge Avenue, the street that led into the Triad's neighborhood on the left and to a smaller cluster of other houses down a narrower road to the right.

Still nothing from Milner. It was nearly eleven-thirty, and the official opening event of the Conclave was a lunch that began at noon. It was a buffet, so he could push it out another hour maybe. He didn't want to draw extra attention by strolling in too late, but he wouldn't be able to take calls once he was inside HQ. Even if he could find a private spot (unlikely), and even if they weren't monitoring everyone's communications (even less likely), there was no reception in the Great Hall.

The Triad claimed this was because the hall was underground, but that excuse had ceased to be believable decades ago. They were obviously blocking the signal. Everyone knew it, but Anak had never assumed it was due to any especially nefarious motives. Outside communication had *always* been frowned upon at Conclave. The main reason for these events was to report on activities during the previous cycle, but a strong secondary reason was to provide a gentle reminder that the planet where they currently lived and worked was not their home. That was one thing that didn't seem to have changed during the many, many eons since Eberin Das held the job.

If he didn't get up with Drex soon, he would just have to claim he needed fresh air at some point during the afternoon and go back up to the surface to check his messages. It wasn't as if they locked everyone inside the gates.

Or at least they hadn't done so in the past. The Watch had just seen two defections, though. The odds that this would be a typical gathering seemed slim at best.

It occurred to him then that the sensation of being watched back at the helipad could easily have been his mind projecting forward to the rest of the day. Because every eye *would* be on him at the Conclave. His fellow Watchers would be hoping he was about to deliver news that would mean going home within the next few years, or possibly even sooner if the Triad decided to call the colonization milestone early. And the Triad almost certainly knew that he was in possession of information about the chambers at Icarus. They *might* not know what that information was, and they might not know Claire had given him the key that would allow him to translate it. But they must know he had *something*.

So the Triad would be watching him, too. Mostly, for signs that he was lying.

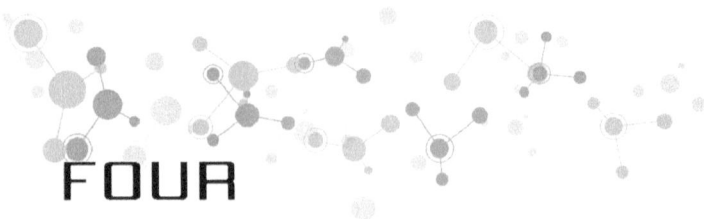

FOUR

ANAK HAD NEVER LIED at an official meeting. It would never even have occurred to him to do so. He'd always given a full and accurate accounting of progress toward the milestone in each of the five positions he'd held.

Lying had, in fact, been the thing that many Watchers found most difficult to master, but then it wasn't something that they'd had much practice with during their previous assignments. White lies and flattery were, of course, common enough on any Ufretan world. You couldn't really have a society without those. But when Anak first arrived, he'd been surprised at how routinely most people on Earth lied, even about the most trivial things. Maybe the tendency toward honesty came about as societies achieved longer lifespans. Keeping up with the lies you'd told was hard enough when people lived eighty or ninety years, but when you and everyone around you lived for millennia, it bordered on impossible.

Still, lying was an essential skill for Watchers. Their very identities were lies. They had to lie each and every day in their interactions with humans. And as with pretty much everything, most of them had gotten quite good at it after a few decades of practice.

The Triad, though? They must have been accomplished liars long before they left the Ufretan system if they'd managed to keep something of this magnitude a secret. Well, Sandjeel and Durav, at least. Arbet would have learned the truth about their mission the same way Uden did—after being promoted to the Triad. The knowledge had quickly driven Uden to suicide, but

Arbet must have found a way to make peace with the situation, given that she'd been living with it for forty years now.

That left Anak with some very conflicted feelings. He'd known Arbet casually at the Academy, but they hadn't become close until they found themselves in the same stasis environment on the trip to Earth. There were two options for mental stimulation during stasis. In Pod One, which was by far the most popular, you experienced virtual scenarios based on events and people pulled from your memories. Reenactments, if that's what you wanted, but you could also tweak the parameters a bit to improve on those experiences. Revive a failed romance. Travel to a new place with friends or family. The simulations were far from perfect. He'd heard many stories about how badly wrong they'd gotten some detail. But the virtual versions were generally seen as the less tedious way to deal with the long cycles they spent in transit.

In Pod Two, you were essentially left to your own devices. There was a library of generic virtual experiences and games that you could explore on your own or with other Watchers in the pod, but none of them tapped into your memories.

Anak was one of five who chose Pod Two. His reason was simple. It had only been a little over two cycles since his breakup with Brinn and his memories were still treacherous. On most Alliance worlds, couples committed for a set period of time. You could get out earlier if it simply didn't work, but pretty much everyone stuck it out until the end of the commitment, at which point you were required to live separately for a cycle. Basically, it was an extended separate vacation. At the end of the break, if both parties agreed, you recommitted. If not, you parted ways.

Parting ways was the most common outcome, but he and Brinn had beaten the odds. They'd lasted sixteen commitment periods, nearly four centuries in Earth time, and had even talked about applying to have a child during their last commitment. They were both on the young side for approval, but it occasionally happened. At the end of that last break, he'd come back looking forward to more time together—only to find that she'd met someone new.

All of his recent memories involved Brinn, so any personalized stasis environment would have made him miserable. He suspected that Arbet had similar reasons for avoiding Pod One, which she jokingly called "memory hell," but he never pried, and she never offered. They rarely interacted with the other three in Pod Two, who had clearly picked it for the purposes of an extended virtual *ménage à trois*, which unfortunately devolved into one couple and one pissed-off outcast before the trip even reached the halfway point.

Arbet was considerably older than most of the people Anak had hung out with on Parda, but they clicked. They had similar tastes in music and games, and a similar view of the world. There was a physical attraction, too, but after one rather awkward attempt to take the friendship to a different level, Arbet had shaken her head sadly and said, "It's okay. You're not yet ready to move on from your *amali-tai*. Maybe we can try again when it's just the two of us."

She'd been right. Even though he'd rejected "memory hell," Brinn's ghost seemed to have followed him into stasis anyway. And, unfortunately, you really needed to keep your head in the game during virtual sex. If your mind didn't stay in the moment, your avatar tended to follow suit.

So, he and Arbet had gone back to long, strictly platonic conversations over endless games of *padjit*, a traditional Noveran strategy game that she taught him. It was a bit like an extended chess match with an element of chance thrown in to keep it lively. He missed *padjit* and was disappointed that even though it was programmed into the stasis pods on the transport, it hadn't been included in the computer system at HQ. It would have been nice to play during Conclave, even though he hadn't been much competition for Arbet. She'd learned the game as a child, but he suspected that her mind was simply better at the sort of logic that helped you excel at the game. Her first advanced training had been as a legal advocate, and she still gravitated back to that profession every few rotations.

Arbet was assigned to the colonization milestone, so they never talked much about the specifics of the work ahead of them during the journey. But they had talked about the role of the Watch in general on many occasions.

Once, in the middle of a game, Arbet had summed up her philosophy about their mission. "We're like…" She fell quiet for a moment, and he'd been unsure if it was because she was deciding on her move in the game or merely trying to find the right word. Finally, she said, "We're like midwives."

He laughed at the comparison. That seemed to annoy her.

"I'm serious." She moved her game piece forward a few spaces before continuing. "A midwife guides a fragile being into the larger world. The infant probably has only a vague sense that there is life beyond the womb, but the midwife brings it out of the dark and into the light. Often, it happens naturally, but sometimes, they need a bit of coaxing. That's exactly what we're doing. The people here, for the most part, have even less notion of what lies beyond their world. Our job is to help bring them out of the narrow confines of that darkness into the light of the larger universe."

Anak had taken the job more as an escape and as a much needed change of scenery, so her analogy hadn't really resonated with him back then. But as he worked with scientists moving closer and closer to the milestone, he'd found himself thinking back to it often.

At Conclave, especially during those first decades, most of the meetings and activities had been organized around their specific milestones, although a few Watchers floated between the two groups. Since he and Arbet were on separate tracks, they never had much chance to converse during the day. She had surprised him, however, by showing up at the door of his assigned room on the final night of the second Conclave, a bottle of *evir* in hand.

"Are you alone now?"

He'd glanced around the obviously empty room, before realizing what she meant.

"I am."

"Would you like some company?"

"I would." And whether it was the passage of time or the fact that he was no longer dealing with a virtual body, Brinn's ghost did not trouble them that night or ever again.

They kept it discreet, maintaining a distance at the public events. Fraternization was frowned upon at Conclave—plenty of time for that during your sabbaticals—but they were far from the only ones sneaking from one room to another. At least one night during each Conclave, she would slip over to his room, usually asking that same question. *Are you alone now?* He'd been much more enthusiastic about attending Conclave in those days. They'd even managed to sync up their schedules for two brief vacations together. But all of that ended when Uden died, and Arbet was promoted to the Triad.

She'd given him a sad smile at dinner the night after Sandjeel made the announcement, and he'd known without a word that she would not be joining him that night or any other. Since then, they had done little more than exchange greetings.

He couldn't help but wonder if she remembered that long-ago conversation over the *padjit* board. Did the midwife analogy haunt her now? If she knew they were delivering this infant world straight into the hands of an executioner, how could it not?

He hoped she remembered it, because he had absolutely no chance if she didn't. While the Triad wasn't required to factor the opinions of the Watch into their decisions, they *were* supposed to listen if someone had a suggestion. Or a complaint. And since Arbet seemed to have some sway with Sandjeel, Anak definitely needed her in his camp.

But he would also need to pull in the other Watchers. Were there others, beyond Drex and Stasia, who knew the truth? Drex had disappeared from the scene shortly after she left her assignment at KTI, which everyone had assumed would be her last. She'd been in a highly visible role as Kolya's wife, so she would either need to have her appearance altered or lay low for a few cycles before taking on a new identity, and with KTI closing in on the colonization milestone, it seemed unnecessary. She hadn't even shown up for the previous Conclave. Absences did happen on occasion due to travel delays and so forth, but absent Watchers were always conferenced in. Sandjeel had simply said there was a problem with Drex's communications. The next time Anak had seen her face—or even thought much about her, if he was being honest—was when he discovered that she had deposed Tobias Shepherd as leader of the Flock.

Something had clearly happened to push Drex in that direction, and the most logical conclusion was that she had learned the true nature of their mission. Which led him to wonder if the Triad had told *all* of the Watchers once they were no longer working on one of the milestones. Was he the last to learn the truth? Maybe the Triad had passed along that bit of knowledge as each Watcher went off on their final sabbatical, as a gentle reminder to enjoy the sights of this planet while they still could. *Hurry, hurry. Last chance to see...*

He began running through names of Watchers who might have been as horrified as he was by the truth. Housen, for starters. Maybe Reese. He ticked off about a dozen others in his head, although he honestly couldn't be sure about most of them. He hadn't exactly been a social butterfly at the Academy, still too bruised by the breakup with Brinn to do much more than sulk, so he didn't know any of them on more than a casual level. Sure, they'd all been here for well over a century. Most of them would probably be appalled at the impending destruction. They'd be angry about being duped by the Alliance. But would it be enough for them to abandon ties back home? To risk their own lives? Because it could easily come to that.

Drex was still his most likely ally, given her defection from the Watch, but even there, he saw some major red flags. First and foremost among them was the fact that she'd taken in not just Stasia—which was understandable given that they'd been friends even before the Academy—but also the two people who set the bomb at Icarus. And before he could even consider trusting her, he needed to know why.

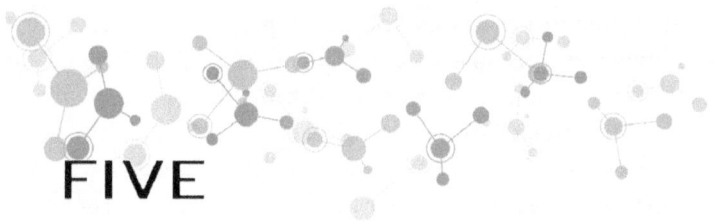

FIVE

AT TWELVE FORTY-SIX, an airport van turned onto Goodridge. Still no word concerning Drex, but Anak couldn't afford to wait any longer. He followed the van. At least this way, he'd be going in with a group. It was probably his only hope of fading into the background for a few minutes until he could get a feel for the room.

As his car rounded the corner, the towering row of cypress trees that separated the Triad's little cloister of six houses from the other half of the neighborhood came into view. The Triad's headquarters sat atop a slight hill to the left, guarded by tall, wrought iron gates. Ahead about thirty meters, the road ended at a smaller gate with a narrow sidewalk beyond that took you to the other houses. Three of them, including the two used by Arbet and Durav, were linked to the main headquarters through underground tunnels, but the other two were accessible only by foot. A brick retaining wall on the opposite side of the road kept the two families who lived down the road across the street from being too nosy, as did the dense patch of woods that surrounded them on two sides.

This was, technically, the third headquarters for the Triad, although the abandoned farmhouse in Arizona where they had holed up just after arrival in the spring of 1953 didn't really count. It was just a temporary location secured by the last of the small scout teams that had preceded them in order to lay the groundwork for their mission, gathering both the DNA samples to create their host bodies and the information they'd need to assimilate.

Their first real headquarters had been in Houston, near what was known at the time as the Manned Spacecraft Center. But the Texas location became risky during the secession crisis. Several European cities were considered, but moving Sandjeel—who, as leader of the Triad was required to retain his native form—was a big enough challenge within the US. They had opted for New York, instead, and had been here for more than forty years.

Finding a relatively isolated spot in New York City hadn't been easy, though. The biggest challenge with the move had been the renovations. Special permits from the city were required for the underground construction they needed to accommodate Sandjeel. He was much more sensitive to the higher temperatures on Earth, and it was easier to keep him comfortable below ground. In 1950s Texas, they'd simply purchased an old ranch about thirty kilometers out of Houston and hired a team from another state to custom build the place. An underground bunker wasn't all that weird in the era of "duck and cover." Sputnik had launched about two months before construction wrapped up on the place, so the locals had seemed to write the ranch off as the pet project of yet another rich nut who wanted a luxury bomb shelter in case of a nuclear attack.

In the end, the history of this area of Riverdale had provided the solution to their problems. Back in the early 1900s, the entire neighborhood had been part of a 12-acre estate owned by a religious group called the Outer Court of the Order of the Living Christ. The leader had built an opulent mansion on the highest point of the property to serve as the earthly residence of Jesus, whose return they believed to be imminent. The Christ House, as it was often called by the locals, remained unoccupied for decades, with the leader of the cult and a few dozen rank and file members opting to live in small shacks scattered about the property at the foot of the hill. Jesus never arrived to take ownership of the house, and when the cult leader died, most of the Outer Court's property was sold off to developers.

The Triad decided to revive the cult, at least on paper. Through one of their holding companies, they purchased the Christ House, which had changed hands and names numerous times over the years, along with six much newer homes at the foot of the hill. They also directed their attorneys to register the Outer Court as a religious corporation with the state of New York. After that, any questions about the underground construction were chalked up to the sort of weird quirk you might expect from a cult. They even got a tax break. And, in one sense, the spirit of the Outer Court lived on. Since only the Triad and their *ipret-tai* lived here full-time, three of the huge houses —plus the ancient mansion at the top of the hill—sat empty between Conclaves. They were mostly expensive window dressing for the underground complex.

The tall wrought iron gates of the main house swung shut behind the airport van just as Anak's car rolled up to the entrance. After transmitting the security code, he waited for the gates to open again, then proceeded up the brick drive to the circular courtyard.

He groaned out loud when he recognized the three people getting out of the van. They were all from Ufretas Prime. That didn't give them any special status—officially, at least. All worlds in the Ufretan Alliance were equal. Unfortunately, no one seemed to have sent that memo to any of the Ufretis that Anak knew.

One of the passengers, a guy named Graf, was at the back of the van, pulling bags from the luggage compartment and handing them out to his traveling companions. They all looked fit, rested, and tan. Anak wished, not for the first time, that he'd gotten a body with better sun tolerance.

He grabbed his bag from the seat next to him and sent the car on its way, thinking that he was probably better off just going in on his own at this point. But Graf spotted him as he was closing the luggage hatch.

"Anak! The last working man! How you doing?" He spoke in Ufretan, the common language of the Alliance that was used at all gatherings, but the Californian accent he had cultivated in the 1980s still managed to seep through in the cadence of his speech. He'd also kept the hairstyle—blond, shaggy, and constantly falling into his face. Arbet had once said Graf was clearly shooting for Kurt Cobain but looked more like David Spade.

"Not bad," Anak said. "Yourself?"

"Doing great, doing great. You got good news for us? Last time I spoke to Durav, he said your guy at JL was right on the cusp."

Graf delivered this news casually, as if it were no big deal for a member of the Triad to be passing on a bit of gossip. It didn't surprise Anak, though. Durav was also from Ufretas Prime, as was Maela, who had taken on the role of his unofficial assistant after the move to New York. The five of them were a tight little clique, often skipping out on larger social gatherings in favor of private events at Durav's residence where they were housed during Conclave.

Anak waved his hand in a *comme ci, comme ça* gesture. "I'm afraid Durav is overstating the case. We're not even in full *in silico* trials yet and ... one of the parameters is off. We've still got quite a bit of heavy lifting ahead."

The lifting ahead was minimal and the part about one of the parameters being off was a flat-out lie. But there were only a few hours left until the Conclave's official meeting convened, and he'd prepared two different reports. Since he was now sure that he was going to transmit the pessimistic version—that he was going to *lie*—it was better to sell their progress short from the get-go.

"You've got to be kidding me." Graf groaned. "Couldn't you nudge his ass a bit harder?"

"Yeah, right. You've obviously never met Joe Echols. The man is stubbornness personified. He doesn't *nudge*."

"Too bad, man." Graf slung the final two bags over his shoulder and began walking toward the house. "You've gotten cheated on the travel front. A bunch of us who are heading down to the West African shore for a few months after Conclave were just saying yesterday that it would be great if you could join us."

Anak managed to fight back the laugh, but it was a close call. He'd never known Graf to travel with anyone outside of his little Ufreti posse. Still, he didn't think what he'd just said was a total lie. All of the Watchers were probably hoping he'd be able to join them—or, at least, join *someone*—on sabbatical, since that would mean his milestone was achieved and they'd be one giant step closer to heading home. And if the Triad decided to call the colonization milestone early, it would be the *final* step. The Ufretan ship that relayed messages between Earth and home would be in communications range in less than two months.

"Not a big deal," he said. "I should have plenty of time for travel before we leave, since we're not going to make this window. But hey, even if I don't, I can always come back at some point, right?" He watched Graf as he spoke, hoping to gauge his reaction. "Wouldn't it be cool to see the changes they make here on Earth once talks with the Alliance begin?"

"Yeah, I guess?" Graf said as they headed toward the door. "It's a hellaciously long trip, but I heard they've upgraded the stasis pods in the new transports. If the ride home isn't too boring, I guess I could see coming back. Someday. Maybe."

Graf was obviously never coming back. He'd complained about the limitations of the stasis environment pretty much every time he mentioned the trip to Earth. But he *had* taken a moment to mull the idea over. Would that be the case if he thought the planet would be a barren rock in a few cycles? Anak didn't think so.

The guy could be lying, of course, but the reaction hadn't seemed calculated. And if the Ufreti crew didn't know the truth, Anak was fairly certain the rest of the Watch remained in the dark. Well, except for Maela. She clung to Durav like a tall red leech, happily flouting the rules against fraternization. Anything Durav knew, it was a safe bet Maela knew, as well.

"Durav is gonna be in a foul mood. He's been ready to head home since we were back in Houston and..." He lowered his voice. "Pretty sure this isn't common knowledge yet, so don't say anything, but the Triad is planning to call the colonization milestone. You're now the only roadblock, my man, and he seemed convinced that you were bringing good news. Said we should plan to stick around a few days extra, because they've got a big celebration ready to roll."

Anak felt the blood drain from his face. It wasn't a shock. Not really. He'd known it was a possibility as soon as he heard that Stasia was no longer at KTI. But he'd hoped that they'd try moving someone else into place. They were still at least a decade away from the final stage of terraforming Mars, so the odds Kolya would already be moving on to exoplanets seemed remote.

He took a deep breath and tried to get his emotions in check before responding. But he needn't have worried. The guy wasn't even looking at him.

"So now we're gonna be stuck in New York and..." Graf sniffed twice, wrinkling his nose in distaste. "You smell that?"

Anak nodded even before he picked up the scent, glad for anything that diverted Graf's attention. But he was right. There was a faint but unmistakable smell of decay somewhere nearby.

"A dead animal, maybe? Or I guess it could be something in the trash." He glanced around. No trash bins were visible, but they were probably near the garage across the courtyard.

"Yeah," Graf said. "In this heat, it wouldn't take long for something to go off. I'll have to tell one of the *ipps*."

As they stepped into the house, Anak heard an engine rev

behind him. At first, he thought it was the airport van leaving, but then one of the four garage doors began scrolling upward. A second later, a silver Pulsar—almost certainly the one he'd seen in the parking lot earlier—zipped into the courtyard. He couldn't make out the male passenger, but he recognized the long reddish-blond hair of the woman with him.

Maela. Speak of the devil.

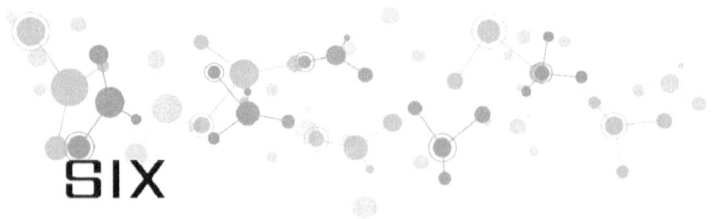

SIX

HE FOLLOWED Graf into the multistory foyer, which was large enough that it might better be described as an atrium. Light filtered in from the front windows onto the honeyed wood floors and curved staircase leading to the upper levels. Four luggage carts sat off to one side, painted gray, blue, green, and brown to match the trim of the houses where the Watch slept during Conclave. A long table next to the carts was piled with the robes that they wore, each in colors matching the insignia of their respective homeworlds.

One of the two female *ipret-tai* who served the Triad came forward to greet him. The women weren't physically alike, aside from being above average height and looking to be in their early thirties. Still, Anak always had a hard time remembering if the dark-haired woman was called Dora or Helen. He had a similar problem with the male *ipret-tai*. They all wore the same pale blue robes, the same pleasantly bland smile, spoke in the same dull monotone, and stared back at you with the same blank, expressionless eyes.

Anak had encountered *ipret-tai* on any number of Alliance worlds, but they still unnerved him. On his own homeworld, Parda, household servants were robotic. Form followed function, and they didn't look even remotely humanoid.

The *ipret-tai* weren't sentient. But they looked like they *should* be sentient. The group that served at headquarters had been created from the Earther DNA samples the advance teams collected, just like his own body and those of the other Watchers. But instead of transferring a full consciousness, complete with memories, emotions, and personality traits, *ipret-tai* were provided with basic programming to perform a set series of tasks. Some of these tasks were basic, but others were very complex. Two of the *ipret-tai*, for example, had medical training and were responsible for the surgical alterations that were occasionally required in order to change a Watcher's appearance.

The one feature that set them apart physically from the Watchers—aside from their zombielike affect—was the traditional servant symbol. A small black crescent was inked above the right eye of all *ipret-tai*, with an additional numerical designation added to the members of Durav's guard.

At first, the Earther *ipret-tai* had bothered Anak to about the same degree as the other humanoid versions he'd encountered at the Academy. Over time, however, he'd found them increasingly eerie. It wasn't that these *ipret-tai* had changed during the time they'd been on Earth. Their bodies had the same longevity tweaks as the Watch, so they hadn't aged. The only physical difference he'd noticed was that a few of them had put on a bit of extra weight over the years. And it certainly wasn't that they'd changed psychologically. They could be taught new tasks, but they seemed incapable of emotion or independent thought. No, it was more that his own expectations had changed. The more time he spent among actual Earthers, the stranger it felt to interact with ones who were essentially empty inside.

There had been eighteen *ipret-tai* when they first arrived. Nine were assigned as general servants for the Triad—two males and one female for each member. The remaining nine, all male, had been tasked with security. Over time, however, most of the security staff had disappointed Durav in some fashion and had fallen prey to his legendary temper. The female assigned to his house had also died under rather murky circumstances not long after the move to New York, although there were differing opinions as to whether she had died by Durav's hand or by Maela's.

Most of the Watch found the killings distasteful, but they

were within Durav's rights. While there were a few Alliance worlds where it was punished along the same lines as animal cruelty on Earth, Ufretas Prime had no laws against killing *ipret-tai* who displeased their owners. Generally, owners simply sent them in to be reprogrammed, since that was by far the cheaper option. But if you had the resources to waste on an entirely new servant, there was nothing to stop you from taking out your frustrations on the old one. The Ufreti seemed to view it pretty much the same as someone tossing out a broken vacuum cleaner. One day while walking through a neighborhood near the Academy, Anak had spotted a dead *ipret-tai* with the other trash outside someone's home, his eyes fixed sightlessly on the sky above.

The downside for Durav was that his temper had left him short on security personnel. The upside was that it made everyone on the Watch reluctant to cross him, and Anak was pretty sure that was exactly how the man liked it. He couldn't *really* kill them—with the exception of Sandjeel, their actual bodies were in stasis back home awaiting their return. He could, however, kill their current hosts, which would mean losing all of the memories accumulated during their time on Earth. Would killing a host body violate any laws on Ufretas Prime? No one was quite sure, but if so, it wouldn't be murder. And when Durav was angry, it was hard to imagine that the risk of a minor penalty would convince him to rein it in.

Graf and the other Ufreti were now piling their bags onto the gray cart. Anak was about to add his own bag to the brown cart, but the dark-haired *ipret-tai* tapped his arm. He was fairly certain she was Dora, the one assigned to Arbet.

"I'm sorry, Anak. You have been reassigned to Lavender House. Room number three has been prepared with your preferred amenities."

"Reassigned? Why?" He glanced over at the colored luggage carts. "And what the hell is Lavender House?"

"I don't know why you were reassigned, Anak," she said in

her usual cheery, but still oddly flat, tone. "Lavender House is the one with lavender trim."

He'd known that much. It was true for all of the houses. Headquarters was the only exception. They usually just called it HQ, possibly because the trim was white and calling it the White House would have seemed a bit ridiculous. But he couldn't remember walking past one with lavender trim and...

"There's no lavender cart."

"Oh, that's no problem. I will be happy to take your bag to your room."

"Okay. Thanks ... *Dora.*" He tossed the name out, hoping for confirmation. Because the room change was odd. He'd been assigned to room seven in Brown House since they moved to New York. And while there was nothing in the bag aside from his clothes, he would still have felt better about handing it over if he was certain she was the *ipret-tai* assigned to Arbet.

She continued to give him the same bland smile as she reached out to take the bag from his hand. No confirmation of her name but also no correction. Which wasn't really a surprise. *Ipret-tai* had no sense of self. She'd almost certainly answer to the other name—to *any* name, for that matter—without hesitation. Maybe that was why he had a hard time keeping the *ipret-tai* separate.

A shaft of sunlight filled the foyer as the front door opened again. Anak glanced over just in time to see Maela step through, followed by the man who was with her in the Pulsar. He still didn't recognize the guy. At first, he'd assumed it was one of the *ipret-tai,* but no. He'd never seen him before.

Bringing outsiders into the Conclave wasn't simply unusual. It was unheard of. He was sure that Earthers entered the various houses on the property from time to time to make repairs and so forth during the rest of the year, but not when everyone was assembled.

Maela strolled over to greet her fellow Ufretis, who were pulling on their *ligren,* the formal robes worn at Conclave. The stranger continued on across the foyer and pressed his palm against the wall next to the library door. It opened a second later and Durav, who was standing near the arched mullioned windows overlooking the back lawn, turned to greet the new arrival.

As second in command, Durav had gotten his pick of the host bodies. He could have opted for the tallest one, minimizing the awkwardness of those first few years as their brains compensated for legs and arms that weren't quite the right length. But the man had been a preening peacock back home and he was every bit as vain about his Earth form. The body he'd chosen wasn't much taller than Anak's, and as one of the younger Watchers, Anak had been near the end of the line. Instead, Durav had opted for the closest thing he could get to the male ideal on Ufretas Prime. A closely trimmed dark beard covered most of his face below bushy-browed eyes. The beard covered his neck as well, leading down to a mat of chest hair so thick it could provide shelter for a family of small rodents.

When the library door closed, Anak went over to collect the packet with his robe and his *rezlat*—a handheld device that fit neatly inside your palm. At the center was a small indentation for your thumb, with a tissue scanner to ensure that you were the only one who could open messages you received from friends or family. You added replies to be sent back home and then turned it in, along with your *ligren*, at the end of Conclave.

He was surprised to see that there were at least a dozen packets still on the table. Apparently, he wasn't the only one running late. He rummaged around for a moment, but his robe wasn't there. There were plenty of others, including two in deep orange to match the seal of Seset, Drex and Stasia's homeworld, but none in the deep blue and gold shades of Parda.

He turned around to ask the *ipret-tai* about the missing packet and discovered that she was holding it.

"Here you go. Enjoy the Conclave." As she spoke, she pressed the bundle into his hands.

"Thanks," he said, not even realizing at first that he'd spoken in English.

"You're welcome, Anak," she replied, also in English, still wearing the same dead-eyed smile.

Anak stared after her as she carried his bag toward the elevator. He'd never heard any of the *ipret-tai* speak anything other than Ufretan. It was perfectly logical that they'd be taught English. Their duties undoubtedly required them to interact with neighbors from time to time, or with the occasional delivery person or contractor. Still, it multiplied the creep factor considerably.

When he unfolded the robe, a small scrap of paper fluttered to the floor. He thought at first that it was a tag of some sort, but … that was ridiculous. The *ligren* had traveled with them from Ufretas, and they would have been cleaned in-house.

He bent down to pick the paper up, and found that it was a handwritten note, unsigned.

Caithfidh tú bréag. Muinín aon duine.

Any shred of doubt that the note was intended for him vanished. To the best of his knowledge, he was the only member of the Watch who had ever studied in Ireland. Undergraduate degrees had always been easy enough for the Triad to fake, but you needed connections and publications in your assigned name to get positions at top labs, so they usually spent a few years doing doctoral or post-doctoral work once they assumed new identities. As Noah O'Brian, he'd relocated to Dublin during the early 2030s, happy to be away from the civil strife going on in the United States. He'd emerged five years later with the credentials that eventually landed him the job at VersaBio.

It had, however, been nearly fifty years since Anak left Trinity College and he had only been back to that country once in the years since. His command of the Irish language had slipped considerably. Still, the first and last parts of the message were common enough phrases that he translated the words instantly. The first part was *you have to*. The second was a full sentence—*Trust no one.*

His mind caught on the missing word, *bréag,* until he remembered a lab partner at Trinity who claimed their professor reneged on his promise of publication credit for a project that she'd done most of the work on. Every time the man walked by, she would mutter under her breath that he was a *feckin' bréagadóir.* That meant *liar,* so…

You have to lie. Trust no one.

He quickly crumpled the paper inside his fist and slipped the tiny wad into the pocket of his pants along with the *rezlat.* Then he pulled the robe over his head and cinched the belt.

When he looked up, Maela was staring directly at him, her eyes narrowed into tiny slits under a narrow fringe of red-gold bangs.

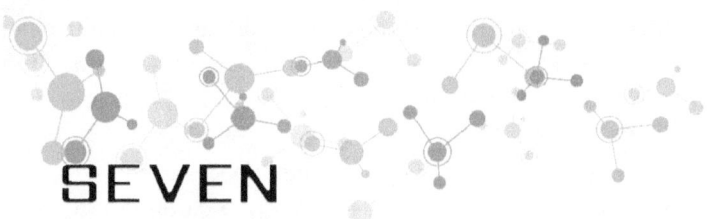

SEVEN

ANAK STEPPED out of the elevator into a near-perfect simulation of the main dining hall at the Academy. There were only two notable differences. The first was the corridor on the right that sloped gently downward to a sub-basement, which contained living quarters for Sandjeel and most of the *ipret-tai*, and beyond that, the tunnels that led to the other Triad houses. The second difference was that the buffet near the center of the dining hall was much smaller than the one at the Academy, and it contained more of the typical items you might find at any upscale corporate event on Earth, with just a small selection of replicated Ufretan delicacies on the side.

The replicator was one of the few pieces of advanced technology they'd been allowed on the mission. It was a necessity, since there were several key nutrients Sandjeel's body couldn't extract from Earth foods. But as Eberin Das had suggested, there were other motives, too. While the replicated versions weren't quite the same, the smells and tastes of home evoked a touch of nostalgia. So did the music and the shifting panoramas of natural wonders from the various Alliance worlds that were displayed on the wallscreens. Later, once everyone had time to separate out any private content on their *rezlats*, the wallscreens would be put to a different use as his fellow Watchers shared news stories, music, and other bits of information their friends and family had sent.

He fell into line behind two others, selecting the first few food items almost at random, although he couldn't help thinking of Das's journal as he added a small square of *braber* to his plate. There were plenty left, but then quite a few members of the Watch still hadn't arrived. And while *evir* might have flowed freely at the Conclaves on Mars, here they hoarded the hard stuff until after dinner. If you wanted a buzz before that, you had to make do with beer or wine.

Those who had already gotten their food were now seated outside on a stone patio that overlooked a picture-perfect recreation of the campus on Ufretas Prime where they had trained. Across the lawn was a smaller replica of the auditorium where they had attended plenary sessions and where they'd gather later in the afternoon for the general assembly.

It was an impressive simulation, overall. Occasionally, someone bumped into a wall and disrupted a holoprojector, but for the most part, the sounds, sights, and smells were a close enough match that he usually found it easy to forget that he was four entire systems away from Ufretas Prime. And that sense was only amplified once you started combing through your messages with news from back home.

Today, though, the wad of paper inside his pocket kept Anak's mind very much anchored to Earth. The *ipret-tai* had probably been the one to slip the note into his robe. After more than fifty Conclaves, at least a dozen of them at this location, there was an established rhythm for check-in. You dropped your bags onto a trolley, then collected your packet from the table. So, it was weird that Dora—again, assuming she *was* Dora —had handed it to him. Still, it wasn't the first time that one of the *ipret-tai* had been excessively helpful. Aside from those who were assigned to security, it seemed to be the overarching dictum of their programming.

Of course, the *ligren* were just sitting there in the open. At least a dozen of his fellow Watchers had collected their robes from the table before he arrived. He was the only member from Parda. Anyone could have figured out which packet was his and stashed the note inside. And it would have been easy enough for any member of the Watch, and definitely for any member of the Triad, to pull up his file and discover he'd studied in Ireland.

But it wasn't a given that he'd *know* the language. He'd learned Irish Gaelic more out of novelty than necessity. All of his classes at Trinity were in English. The only Irish he'd heard during his years in Dublin was in casual conversation, usually mixed with English to the point that it was easy to catch the gist. He'd simply found the language a fun little puzzle to tackle as he sat through classes that were far more basic than anything he'd studied at the Academy or during stasis.

Arbet was the only one who knew that he'd learned Gaelic. They had rarely talked about their work during those stolen hours together at Conclave. They generally didn't do much talking at all. But as they lay side by side in the moonlight one night near the end of his post-doc at Trinity, he'd told her a bit about Dublin and she laughingly attempted to master a few common phrases—*dia dhuit, sláinte, aon scéal*. It had just been a brief bit of pillow talk, a conversation that he might have forgotten entirely if it hadn't been their last night together before she moved up to the Triad.

The very group she was now telling him to lie to...

He'd already made up his mind on that front by the time he entered the gate and had sealed the decision when he told Graf that the rumors he'd heard about Jonas Labs were unfounded. Two other people had asked him the same question in the elevator coming down to the Great Hall, and he'd repeated the lie to them. *No, no, so sorry. We're definitely making progress, but it's taking longer than expected. Maybe by the next Conclave.* They'd grumbled, and then shifted back to whispered comments about Drex and Stasia's absence, which seemed to be the other topic *du jour*.

So, no. He hadn't needed Arbet's advice to lie. But he *was* curious as to why she had been willing to risk having someone pass it along. Wouldn't it have made more sense to contact him *before* the Conclave? Or was Durav watching her communications so closely that it was out of the question?

There was little possibility of her being around for him to ask, even if he'd been willing to chance it. Unlike Durav, Arbet and Sandjeel adhered to the rules—or maybe they were merely norms?—against fraternization. Everyone attended the formal dinner on the final night. A member of the Triad might also pop in briefly to deliver an announcement or perhaps to watch a few minutes of the *djvari* tournament, the only part of Conclave that Anak really looked forward to these days. But neither of them ever stuck around for long.

Tray in hand, Anak scanned the tables on the patio for an empty seat, hoping to find one next to somebody who had been around when he answered the question about rumors of the big breakthrough at JL. If he'd already burst their bubble, maybe they'd let him eat in peace. Or maybe he could find someone too preoccupied with their *rezlat* to be interested in chatting.

Before he could locate a suitable spot, a hand clapped him on the back. He stiffened. It was probably Maela coming over to ask him about the note. He should have made a side trip to the bathroom to flush it. The woman had no official authority to hound him about anything, but she had a firm grip on Durav's ear and, if the rumors were true, another appendage as well. If Anak didn't answer her questions to her satisfaction, she would happily trot off to tattle.

"Hey! How've you been, man?"

Anak's shoulders loosened at the voice. Not Maela, after all, but Reese, one of the few Watchers Anak had actually worked with for a while. About five years back, Jonas Labs had acquired the smaller biotech firm to which Reese had been assigned. He had stayed on at JL for a few years, eventually working among Kai's small army of assistants. Based on his reports at Conclave, his primary task had been translating the details of Joe's research into language that was more accessible to the public and—even more important for Kai's purposes—to their investors. Now that he thought about it, the work was quite similar to what Claire did at the *Atlantic Post* and no doubt the sort of role Kai had hoped her daughter would eventually assume at the company.

"I can't complain," Anak said in answer to his question. "How about you? Are you enjoying the easy life?"

Reese grinned. "Oh, hell yeah. You should try it sometime."

At the previous Conclave, the Triad had granted Reese's request for sabbatical. He'd argued that anything he was doing at JL was superfluous, given how closely Anak worked with Joe. At one time, that kind of redundancy would have been encouraged and even expected, but Anak had noticed a short-timer mentality seeping in over the past few cycles. It was obvious to everyone that success was on the horizon, and most of their minds had moved on to what they wanted to do when they got home. He'd even been guilty of that himself when he first began trying to translate Eberin's journal.

"Let's go find a table so we can catch up," Reese said, still grinning. "It's been way too long."

"Sure..." Anak said, even though he was thinking that Reese was being a little overly friendly. He was a nice enough guy, but they hadn't known each other all that well at the Academy. Reese had taken the Pod One option during stasis, and even though they'd both been working up on Olympus during the time Reese was at JL, they'd done little more than nod to each other in the elevator. That was partly because the Triad advised against them being too chummy in professional settings, and partly because Joe kept him too busy to socialize with anyone.

"As always, the one spot you can count on to be empty," Reese said, as he slid onto the bench of a table beneath a wide *usimi* tree at the edge of the patio.

It was true. At the Academy, they'd had good reason to avoid that table. While the shade was nice, there was a decent chance that your food or drink would be fouled by one of the many birds hanging out in the branches above. Their habit of steering clear of that table had carried over to the simulated version, even though this one was safe. You could still smell the ripe *usimi* fruits that attracted the birds and hear them chirping away over your head, but the holoprojectors mercifully drew the line at spackling the table with their droppings.

Reese immediately began tapping at something on his armscreen. For a moment, Anak thought he was playing some sort of game, but it would have to be one that didn't require a connection. That was fine with him. He wasn't actually disappointed at the prospect of a quiet, solitary lunch. But then Reese rolled up the screen, stashed it in the pocket of his purple *ligren*, and gave Anak another of those wide and not entirely sincere smiles.

"This one oughta be *fun*," he said, his tone clearly indicating that he meant the exact opposite. "Think it will top 2048?"

Anak gave a low chuckle. "Don't tell me you're still pissed about that?"

The 2048 Conclave had been tense. Nothing shook up a group of nearly-immortals like a death in their ranks, so all of them were on edge over the deaths of Djasa and Uden. Compounding that was the controversy over the Triad's choice for Uden's replacement. Instead of following protocol as they had after Djasa's death, they had opted to skip Reese and two other members who had seniority in favor of Arbet.

"I was never *pissed* about it. It's not like it was a pay increase or anything." Reese considered for a moment. "Okay, fine. I was *slightly* pissed at first. All three of us were. But after Sandjeel added the bit about the whole Triad being stuck at HQ? We all realized we'd dodged a bullet. I was surprised Arbet didn't put up more of a fight. I mean, travel is the main reason most of us took the Watch instead of the shorter term in the military." He lowered his voice. "But ... *come on*. We all know the reason they gave us was bogus. Sandjeel just wanted leverage against Durav, so he promoted someone from his own *korban*."

Anak was tempted to point out that Durav had to approve

Arbet's selection. It was true, however, that Durav and Sandjeel weren't exactly on good terms. He'd always gotten the sense that there was some bad history between the two, so the idea that one or both of them might have been tempted to play triangulation games in filling the empty seat wasn't out of the question. But Durav wasn't stupid enough to consent to anything that went against his interests.

The general consensus had been that Arbet's promotion was due to nepotism, since she and Sandjeel belonged to the same *korban*, which meant they traced their lineage to a common ancestor. A *korban* was a huge group, though, spanning not only multiple worlds in most cases but also many generations, sometimes going back to the Third or Fourth Alliance. And it wasn't like the two of them had an especially strong connection. Anak was fairly sure that Arbet and Sandjeel had never even met before she arrived at the Academy.

Reese was right, however, that the official reason for the decision—avoiding all three members being male—had made absolutely no sense. Sex had never been a consideration in the selection process for either the Watch or the Triad. They clearly hadn't considered it when they promoted Uden. And given the physical differences between the host bodies and their own, most of them hadn't worried too much about whether they were assigned a male or female host when making their selection. They'd been far more interested in getting *tall* bodies since adjusting to the smaller Earther frame had been the hardest part of training. Forty-three of the fifty-six host bodies were male, both because they'd had a harder time finding tall women when collecting DNA samples and because male Watchers were more practical when they arrived, since the vast majority of those employed in advanced scientific fields in the mid-twentieth century were men. They'd also been mostly white, which was why there was so little racial diversity in the Watch. Reese, whose host had South Asian features, was easily the darkest face in the room.

Anak caught a glimpse of Maela from the corner of his eye. She stood alone at the edge of the patio, now in the dark green *ligren* of Ufretas Prime, scanning the tables for an empty seat. Whoever her Earther buddy was, he apparently wasn't allowed in the Great Hall. Anak looked away quickly, but he could feel the woman's eyes on him as she approached. For a moment, he was sure that she was coming over to join them. At the last second, though, she pivoted to the right to join Graf and the other Ufretis.

"But yeah," Reese continued in an even lower voice, so low that Anak had to strain to pick up his words over the nature sounds above and the conversation at the tables around them. "Fairly sure this Conclave is going to be lively. I got here yesterday, and let's just say that there was a whole lot of talk over dinner last night. Seems like the very public defection of Drex and Stasia is raising far more questions than Uden's quiet suicide."

EIGHT

ANAK STIFFENED at the word *suicide*. It was the first time he'd heard anyone on the Watch suggest that Uden's death had been anything other than an accident. He hadn't even suspected it himself until he read Tobias Shepherd's memoir.

It now occurred to him that unlike everyone else he'd encountered since arriving, Reese hadn't asked about progress at Jonas Labs. He hadn't mentioned the place at all, which made it doubly odd, given that working there was something—really the *only* thing—they had in common. And that bit of fidgeting with his armscreen when they first sat down could have been a cover for starting a recording. Although, if it was, it must have been a last minute decision. Otherwise, why wouldn't Reese have set the recorder up before approaching him?

Anak decided to let the suicide comment slide for the time being and focus on the obvious fact that people were curious about the defections. "You're probably right. I picked up on some of the chatter about Drex in the elevator. So … no one has heard from either of them?"

"If so, they're definitely not talking about it."

Anak took a bite of salad, cursing himself for not framing the question more carefully. Reese's response could mean almost anything. It hadn't even ruled out the possibility that Reese himself was one of the people who was *definitely not talking about it.*

He tried again. "Guess we should have suspected something was up when Drex didn't conference in last time."

Reese raised an eyebrow. "Well, she really *couldn't* have,

given her assignment. I mean, it's not like she'd have been allowed a phone. Now that she's the leader, sure. But a few years ago, she'd have been just one of the sheep."

Anak frowned. What the hell was the guy talking about?

"I thought Drex was on sabbatical last time," he said after a moment. "Some wilderness thing."

"She might have taken a *few* months off after leaving KTI," Reese said around a bite of his sandwich. "Probably needed it, to be fair. The KTI assignment had been an absolute soap opera for ... what? At least three cycles before that?"

It was true. Early on, several different companies had been working on the colonization front, including KTI. Once Anton Kolya took over from his uncle, the company bought up or chased out many of their competitors, in much the same fashion that Kai had at Jonas Labs. The problem for the Watch was that Kolya was a notorious micromanager and more than a little paranoid. Under his leadership, KTI research was conducted in cells, with each lab working on some small piece of a larger project. They'd had no luck getting anyone inside Davina Monroe's lab on Mars or into Kolya's inner circle, which made it difficult to judge how close KTI really was to putting the various pieces together.

So, the Triad decided to assign someone to try a more personal approach. It seemed to work, at first. As Jenelle Tuller, Drex successfully lured Kolya into a whirlwind romance and marriage. She'd impressed him with her intelligence and in her first report, had seemed confident that he would include her in the business side of his life. By the next Conclave, however, Drex reported that Kolya wasn't interested in that sort of marriage, saying that it reminded him too much of his last relationship. Despite her best efforts to get him to talk about his work, he seemed to want nothing more than a carefree partner for late night dinners—and sex—after sixteen-hour days at work, with the occasional ski trip or walk on the beach. After three years together, Drex had less to report than Stasia, whom she'd gotten Kolya to hire for a top-level position in KTI's public relations department.

She began urging Kolya to delegate more, telling him that she was lonely, and suggesting that he promote Stasia. He actually listened to her suggestion about finding an assistant, but hired someone Macek recommended, instead. Drex found a way to sabotage the new guy—something that Macek suspected —and this time, Kolya took her advice about hiring Stasia. He still had almost no concept of work-life balance. On the plus side, that made it much easier for her to distance herself from the man, and once Stasia was fully established, she asked him for a divorce.

Reese was now saying that *a wilderness thing* was a decent description of being embedded with a Flock compound. "Most of the huts they sleep in don't even have running water. Anyway, I'm pretty sure Drex had been with them for about a year by then. It was definitely long enough for Maela to have gotten the boot, although I'd wager that she screwed up as fast as she could just to get out of there. She's never been one for rules and can you imagine her actually getting her hands dirty on one of the Flock's farms?"

Anak could easily imagine Maela getting her hands dirty metaphorically. The female *ipret-tai* assigned to Durav, who she was widely rumored to have killed in a fit of jealousy, was just one example. But Reese was right. The idea of her laboring in the fields was almost comical.

"Okay, though. Let me get this straight. You're claiming the Triad *assigned* Maela and Drex to the Flock? Did I miss a memo or something?"

"Keep your voice down." Reese cast a nervous look toward the other tables. "And kind of, I guess, although it's not from official sources. You've been in the lab, so you're out of the loop. But I've traveled with three different groups in the past few years. And you know how it is. You talk to enough people, and somebody heard this, somebody else heard that. Eventually, you piece things together."

And quite likely get it entirely wrong, Anak thought, *as one flawed inference leads to the next.*

"But why?" he asked. "If the Triad thought Shepherd knew something he shouldn't have, if they thought he was a ... security risk ... they'd have just taken him out, right?"

"Pretty sure that's what Durav *wanted* to do. But Uden put a kink in the plan."

"How? He was long dead."

"Sure, but he left behind a will. There was a big argument about it in 2048. I didn't pay much attention, mostly because I was..." He gave Anak a self-deprecating grin. "Yeah, yeah, because I was pissed about Arbet's promotion and grumbling to the others about it."

Reese wasn't the only one who had been distracted by Arbet's promotion, albeit for very different reasons. Anak's relationship with Arbet had always been casual, by necessity, but he'd actually been looking forward to stasis on the return trip, even letting his mind wander on occasion to a possible commitment period once they were back home. He'd been in a decidedly blue funk during that Conclave.

"Anyway," Reese said, "Uden left a will, in which he claimed the right of *ufrete* for some kid and his mother."

Anak had only the vaguest memory of them talking about Uden's will. From what he remembered of the discussion, however, it had mostly been focused on the distribution of property that Uden had accumulated during his eight decades on Earth. Even if Anak had considered the *protection* side of the right of *ufrete*, he wouldn't have been confident that it would be honored. The Triad supposedly decided all matters on the basis of consensus, but Durav was responsible for implementing security measures. Anak couldn't imagine him holding back on the basis of what he'd view as legal minutiae if he thought the Watch was at risk of being exposed.

"And…" Reese paused for effect. "Here's a fun little fact. That kid grew up to be Tobias Alvin Shepherd."

"Really?" Anak mustered up a look of mild surprise, even though he was beginning to suspect that he wasn't fooling Reese at all.

"From what I pieced together, Durav argued that the right of *ufrete* doesn't apply to Earthers. Arbet said there were no exclusions in the law that limited it by race or by the birth world of the beneficiary. She pulled up some case from Novera where it was extended to a representative from the Hodjeri system. Then they got into the whole debate over whether Earthers would be considered a different race or an entirely different species, and I'm guessing you can figure out who was arguing which side on *that*. The whole thing wasn't settled until after Conclave wrapped up, but in the end, Shepherd inherited Uden's house when he reached legal age and Durav basically got a hands-off notice from Sandjeel. Arbet must have won her *pranasi-tai* over to her side."

There was a bit of a leer in Reese's voice as he said *pranasi-tai*, a word that literally meant *elder cousin*, but was also a Ufretan slang term for something akin to a sugar daddy. Anak clenched his teeth, forcing himself to ignore the jab. It was far more likely that Arbet had won Sandjeel over through persuasion, logic, and a knowledge of Ufretan laws, skills that she'd cultivated during her many cycles as an advocate.

"Then, at the next Conclave," Reese added, "Arbet made that little speech saying that we didn't abdicate our rights as Ufretans when we joined the Watch, and we all got those forms telling us how to declare our beneficiaries."

"I do remember that part." It was true, even though he hadn't acted on it at the time. The only property he'd owned back then was his cabin, and there hadn't been anyone he particularly cared to leave it to. Nor had he been close enough to anyone that he was worried someone might end up on a Triad hit list if they'd managed to ferret out the fact that he wasn't who and what he claimed to be.

Because it was no secret that the Triad was perfectly willing to kill a few people here and there to keep the mission under wraps. Usually, the killings were due to something that couldn't have been avoided. It had been easier to fly under the radar during the first sixty years or so. But back in the 2030s, after a member of the Watch was in a car accident and wound up hospitalized, Durav had ordered two medical personnel killed for raising questions about oddities in the Watcher's DNA. That was a problem they'd never encountered during the early decades of their mission when genetic science was less advanced.

But Uden had *not* been the only one who slipped up by getting too close to someone. In the early 2000s, a Watcher named Housen fell in love with a young woman who must have overheard something and was worried that he was in trouble. When he left for one of the Conclaves, she followed him from their apartment in California. Surveillance footage at the Houston headquarters picked her up sneaking through the gate and one of the *ipret-tai* killed her on Durav's orders. Anak never asked Housen about it directly, but rumor had it that Durav made the poor guy drive deep into the property and bury the woman himself.

In another incident, friends of one of the female Watchers had overheard her arguing with her contact in the Triad, much the same way that Tobias Shepherd had overheard Uden. Curiosity got the better of them and they swiped her phone. Both of them became "accidental" victims of what the police believed to be a drug-related shootout a few days later.

And before all of that, there was Heaven's Gate, which ended with the deaths of nearly forty people back in 1997. Rumor had it that a Watcher on sabbatical in the 1970s experimented with acid and revealed a bit too much information to a sexual partner. The Triad never *officially* acknowledged getting involved but Anak wasn't alone in suspecting they'd played a role in the mass suicide.

All of these incidents were routinely held up as object lessons on why Watchers should avoid emotional entanglements to the extent possible. But after more than a hundred and thirty years on the planet, most of them had slipped in that regard at one time or another. Not to the point of getting someone killed—that was still pretty rare—but at least to the point where they worried about the possibility.

Anak probably would have forgotten about the form Arbet sent, though, if not for the fact that he received it a second time. Communication with headquarters had always been limited when Watchers were on assignment. Unless the issue was an emergency, you generally added any questions or comments to your report and discussed it in person at the next Conclave. That had been even more true since Arbet took over the administrative arm of the Triad. But just a few months back, he'd gotten another copy of the form, along with a note from Arbet, who claimed she'd been looking through the files and realized that some members of the Watch had never submitted it.

I do hope you'll take a moment to fill this out, Anak. I'm sure you'll agree that if we don't exercise the rights we're granted, it makes it easier for some people to justify taking them away—not just from you, but from the rest of the Watch, as well. It only takes a few minutes to protect them. Surely you have someone you can designate as legatee?

He knew that Arbet had probably sent the same message to half a dozen others who had failed to return the form, plugging their names into the slot in place of his own. But it was the closest he'd come to personal communication with her since she joined the Triad, and he couldn't bring himself to delete the message. He considered adding Joe or Claire, but neither of them needed his money or his properties. In the end, he decided to do some research and then leave everything to a few good charities.

The other aspects of the right of *ufrete* never even crossed his mind until a few days later when Claire showed up at the lab. Although he hadn't yet been aware of the discovery at Icarus, the Mars trip meant that Claire would now be connected to *both* milestones. That made him uneasy.

It only takes a few minutes to protect them. Arbet had almost certainly meant protecting the rights of his fellow Watchers, but maybe it was also a subtle reminder of the innocent people who'd been killed simply because they stumbled upon the truth. He still had a hard time believing Durav would play by these new rules if that happened, but it might at least slow him down. So, when Anak got back to his apartment that night, he pulled up Arbet's message and filled out the form with Claire's name. If nothing else, it saved him the trouble of researching charities.

"Did you send the form in the first time?" he asked Reese. "Or did Arbet have to nag you?"

"Nah. I don't remember Arbet nagging me about it, but I never saw the need to submit it. I make a point of spending my money and … I keeps meself to meself." He grinned theatrically on the last line, which Anak was pretty sure was a catchphrase from some comedy in the 2050s. Or maybe it was from a song?

They ate in silence for a few minutes, then Anak said, "What do you think changed her mind? Drex, I mean. She's assigned to find out whether Shepherd poses a threat to the mission and the next thing you know, she ousts the guy and takes over his cult. Doesn't make a lot of sense."

Reese peered at him over his drink. "I don't know. But you can bet your ass that question will be raised at the general meeting tomorrow."

"*Tomorrow*? I thought we were meeting after lunch."

"Nope. Eleven o'clock tomorrow. Arbet announced the change last night. Said we should take today to relax and reconnect. I mean, it makes sense, right? You're the only one who has much to report." He snorted. "Not like the old days. Remember the one in the 2010s that dragged on for nearly three full days?"

That had been the heyday, when almost everyone was assigned to one of the dozens of companies working on some element of the two milestones. Presentations had dragged on for a day and a half, and then they'd split up into working groups for more in-depth discussions. By 2076, though, it was just KTI, Jonas Labs, and another pharmaceutical company that JL swallowed up a year later. At the previous Conclave, only Anak and Stasia had delivered official reports. The others had simply relayed their travel plans.

"Oh, I definitely remember it," he said. "They ran out of coffee both days and I kept dozing off until the next time Sandjeel rang the bell between speakers. And yeah, I guess it makes sense. The official part shouldn't last much more than an hour if I'm the only one presenting."

Reese gave him a sly look as he tipped back his beer. "Given how averse they are to discussing the Drex and Stasia debacle, I'm pretty sure the Triad would have postponed the entire Conclave if not for those pernicious rumors that you were bringing us big news. You lured all of us back here for nothing."

Anak seriously doubted they would have postponed Conclave. They'd never done that, even during the secession crisis when travel had been a lot more complicated.

It wasn't a point worth arguing, though. He just said, "I didn't start the rumors. And I'd have happily shot them down if anyone had bothered to ask."

The first part was true. Aside from sending the beneficiary form back to Arbet, he'd had no contact with any of them since the previous Conclave. That last part, though? If anyone on the Triad had asked him a month ago, maybe even as recently as a week ago, he'd have told them that things were still on track. Rolling right along, full steam ahead. If pressed, he *might* even have been confident enough to recommend that they call the milestone early instead of waiting for the next communications window. It was going to happen within the next year or two, anyway. Why not go ahead and bring in the diplomats so they could begin preparing Earth to join the Alliance?

Which begged the question of exactly who had started the rumors. Reese seemed like the most obvious candidate. If he was still in touch with anyone from Kai's office, he might have some inkling as to how quickly they were advancing beyond the original projections for Rejuvesce. Joe generally played things close to the vest until they were at the testing stage, but Kai was pushing hard right now. One of her assistants could easily have overheard her attempts to badger Joe into announcing early and passed that bit of gossip along to Reese.

His poker face apparently needed serious work, because Reese shook his head and said in a low voice. "Wasn't me, man. Anyway … we've got the rest of the day ahead of us." He leaned back and popped a grape into his mouth. "The *djvari* tournament starts at two. We're both on Green. I think Meeks is heading up the Red team. Then tonight, during cocktail hour, they're showing a concert that should interest you. Bordis Fursa … aren't they from Parda?"

Anak nodded absently. He doubted he'd bother with the concert, but there was no getting out of the tournament. At least it would be a distraction for a couple of hours. Then he'd make some excuse and head over to his room for a few minutes. Check his messages to see if he had a response from Drex. Or maybe try to find Arbet.

"It's a new recording, too," Reese continued, seemingly oblivious to Anak's lack of interest. "Well, relatively new. Came in during the last comms window. So, there's *plenty* to keep you busy *right here* in the Great Hall." He dropped his voice again and held Anak's gaze as he carefully enunciated each word. *"No need to lounge about in your room."*

The words were clearly intended as a caution, and while he hadn't been especially clear about the exact nature of the threat, Anak got the point.

Stick to the public areas. Don't go off on your own.

Maybe his earlier thought about one of Durav's *ipret-tai* strangling him in his sleep wasn't so far off the mark after all.

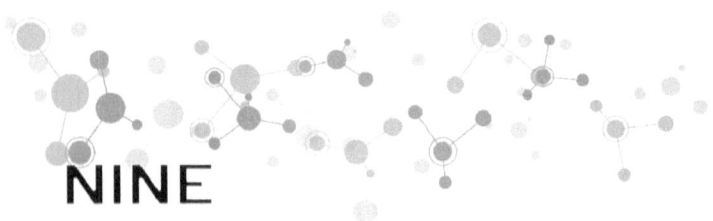

NINE

A DISAPPOINTED GROAN rose up from the bench on Anak's right almost as soon as the flat yellow disk blasted out of the chute at the end of the ramp. The others could already tell it was a crap shot. He'd come in too hard with the striker, and instead of rising at a gentle slope that might have carried the puck into the center square, it soared upward for a few seconds too long. It still landed in the middle box, so they were spared the full penalty, but it fell several meters short of the target. Which meant they were down another player now. Housen clapped him on the back and then headed over to join the dozen or so spectators. The rest had wandered back inside to share recordings they'd gotten from back home.

Sadly, it wasn't the worst shot Anak had made during the tournament. The real stinker had come several rounds back when he looked up just as he was about to swing and spotted Arbet standing inside one of the doorways.

He was always a bit distracted when she was in the room. It was partly a physical reaction. The body she'd chosen was definitely attractive—tall and graceful, with long dark hair and pale, almost translucent skin. He'd had far more direct contact with this body on the twenty-nine separate nights that they'd spent together at Conclave during those first decades. In his mind's eye, though, he still saw her other form, the one he'd first seen at the Academy. The one that they'd used to craft the avatar that he had watched for countless hours over the *padjit* board during stasis. A curvier body, covered with short, fine hair the color of caramel. It reminded him of this microsuede couch he'd owned when he was Noah O'Brien—it was smooth as silk when you rubbed it in one direction, but it tugged at your skin if you rubbed it against the grain. He loved that sensation. Arbet must have liked it, too, because she had arched upward against his hands. His palms still tingled as he remembered the feel of her during that first, breathless interlude before the memory of Brinn popped in to ruin everything.

Of course, both the encounter and his memory of it could have been purposefully amped up by the virtual environment. There was a reason so many people were addicted to virtual sex, often to the point where they were incapable of enjoying the real thing.

So, yes, Arbet's presence alone might have shaken him, but it was compounded by the fact that she was deep in conversation with Reese, who had gone inside after his last turn to fetch both of them another beer.

His curiosity about what they were saying distracted him to the point that he very nearly missed the shot completely. But the edge of the striker caught the puck, sending it into a wild tailspin. It landed at the very edge of the box, barely inside the line, and cost the Green team two players.

Anak was usually the best player in the Watch. Stasia was the only one who had ever given him any competition. Since she wasn't here, his teammates had expected an easy victory and were, understandably, a bit sulky. He'd been competing since childhood, and while he supposed you couldn't really call it *muscle memory* given that the muscles that actually learned the game were back on Ufretas Prime, his instincts usually kicked in as soon as he picked up the striker.

Not today, though. It was partly because he was out of shape. Since he started work at Jonas Labs, he'd had little time for sports aside from the regular table tennis matches with Joe. And it wasn't like he could practice the game. The closest thing he'd ever seen to *djvari* here on Earth was a game called *hornussen*, which never really caught on outside of its native Switzerland. It also had a defensive component that *djvari* lacked, where the opposing team swatted the puck out of the sky with paddles. He'd toyed with the idea of paying someone to program a hologame version of *djvari* but never got around to it.

The bigger problem today, though, was that he couldn't keep his head in the game. That had been true even *before* he saw Arbet. Maela was directly across the ramp from him on the Red bench, only a few feet away. In the past, she'd rarely paid him even the slightest attention, so the fact that she had been staring at him the entire game was unnerving.

Still, even with these distractions, he'd earned enough points to advance in each round, but it left him with far fewer points than usual to advance the weaker players on his team. The game had gone back and forth for the past hour, with both teams losing a member here and there and then earning enough surplus to buy them back into the game. With Housen's exit, Green was now down to three players again—Anak, Reese, and a guy named Merbis—which meant they would have only three chances to accumulate points while Blue would have four.

In regulation play, a tournament didn't end until one of the two teams lost all of its players, and that could take a long time. On Parda, tournaments sometimes went on for several weeks, with the teams packing up and going home, then reconvening a few days later to place new bets—it wasn't *djvari* without side wagers—and picking up again where they left off.

Conclave tournaments were time-limited, though, and he now had just under ten minutes to pull ahead—which explained why Meeks, who was currently the top scorer on Red, was taking his own sweet time making his way to the ramp. The longer the four remaining Red players dragged out their shots, the better their chances of a win.

The last Red player stepped up to the ramp as the buzzer sounded. Game over.

He leaned across for the Ufretan equivalent of a post-game handshake, tapping the base of his Guinness against whatever

Meeks was drinking. But before he could straighten back up, he felt a knee bump against his ribs and something cold and wet began seeping through the back of his sleeveless green jersey onto the shirt below.

"Sorry, sorry." Reese put his now empty bottle on the bench and began looking around, probably for a towel to clean up the mess.

"Not a big deal," Anak said, pulling the jersey over his head and using the dry part to dab at his shirt.

"No, man. It's soaked. You'll definitely need to go change before you put your *ligren* back on for dinner. You look like you could use the fresh air, anyway. But you should get moving if you're going to get all the way over to Lavender House and back by eight."

Anak shot him an annoyed look and tossed his wet jersey onto the bench, now certain that the guy had doused him on purpose. *First, you tell me to stay near the Great Hall and now you're pushing me out the door,* he thought. *Make up your damn mind.*

Reese was up to something. But maybe this was what he'd been talking to Arbet about earlier. Either way, it would give him an excuse to check his messages.

"Fine." He tipped back the last of his beer, handed Reese the empty bottle, and headed to the elevator.

He pushed the button for the ground floor, but at the last second, an arm shot out to keep the doors from closing. The heavy scent of cologne, the purple trim on the sleeve of the *ligren*, and the mat of dark hair on the back of the man's arm told him instantly that it was Durav.

Anak expected him to launch straight into some snide comment or to ask where he was running off to. Instead, he punched the button for the second floor, leaned back against the elevator wall, and watched him through slightly narrowed eyes for several seconds before speaking.

"We're all looking forward to your report tomorrow, Anak. My sources tell me you have very good news for us."

Judging from the man's sour expression, Anak was fairly sure that other sources had told him the exact opposite during the past few hours.

"Yeah, I wouldn't go that far. There's been *some* progress since the Rejuvesce launch, but Echols has hit a bit of a roadblock. We're looking at another cycle at a bare minimum." A faint ping indicated that they'd reached the ground floor. As the door opened, he added, "I *can* see how those rumors might have gotten started, though. JL's corporate office has been trying hard to spin things in a positive light to keep stockholders happy."

Durav gave a derisive snort as the door closed.

The table with the *ligren* was now empty, except for two orange robes bearing the Sesetan insignia. Everyone else had apparently arrived. Someone would need to tell the *ipret-tai* that Drex and Stasia weren't coming, otherwise the robes would likely be there until the next Conclave.

Unless, of course, this was the *last* Conclave.

Anak was almost to the front door when voices from the second floor caught his attention. He glanced up, expecting to see Durav. But it was Maela's human buddy, who seemed to have the run of the place, at least above ground. He was talking to two of the male *ipret-tai*. Or more accurately, giving them orders. While Anak couldn't make out the words, it was clear from the man's tone and body language.

He looked away quickly, not wanting to draw their attention. After stepping into the empty courtyard, he paused on the veranda to breathe in the early evening air. It was hot and humid, without the slightest hint of a breeze, but still better than the recycled air underground.

Or at least, that was his initial thought. His first deep inhale carried the same whiff of decay he'd noticed earlier. The memory of the dead *ipret-tai* he'd seen all those years ago near the Academy ran through his head and he glanced toward the garage again. From this angle, he could just make out the trash bins on the side. But there was no way Durav would toss a body into the trash here on Earth. He'd have one of the other *ipret-tai* bury it. And whatever the smell was, it was coming from the other direction.

With each step down the brick drive, the stench grew stronger. He eventually discovered the source just before he reached the gate. A fat, headless groundhog lay at the edge of the drive. Flies roamed lazily over the carcass. He scanned the area nearby and spotted the head of the unfortunate creature. It had rolled down a slight hill before coming to a stop at the brick fence, about a meter to the right of the gate.

Had the groundhog been clipped by a car? There had certainly been enough of them coming in and out earlier in the day. It was hard to tell in the fading light, so he held his breath against the smell and crouched down in order to get a closer look.

Definitely *not* a car. The cut was at a slight angle, but it was clean, and the fur and flesh around it was singed. A laser, then.

That was odd. He'd seen a few of the *ipret-tai* armed with handguns, but never with a laser. While it could be one of the sentry drones, that sort of equipment was illegal in all but a few states.

Anak carefully nudged the corpse off the drive with his shoe and continued toward the gate, casting a quick glance around for the drones. Not that he would have been able to tell anything about their armament from this distance. Then he pulled his phone out of his pocket to send the gate code. He was about to close the gate behind him when his phone service kicked in, buzzing several times in quick succession.

The streetlight above sputtered to life. As he was debating whether to read the messages or wait until he got to his room, his phone rang. He yanked it from his pocket again and checked the display, hoping Milner's people had finally delivered the message and it was Drex calling the number he'd told them to give her.

But it was Claire. He could ignore the call, but she'd probably just call again, so...

"Hey. What's up?"

"Sorry," she said. "I meant to text you but accidentally called instead. Um ... does three o'clock work for you on Wednesday?"

Her voice seemed shaky, and he fought the urge to ask if something was wrong. But the longer they spoke, the more likely he'd slip up and say something that aroused her curiosity. And if one of the other messages waiting was from Drex, he wanted to allow plenty of time for that conversation.

"Yeah. That should work. I'll message and let you know if anything changes."

Before he could end the call, Claire asked if everything was going okay.

"Sure. Going great." Something whirred in the trees on the other side of the fence. He glanced over his shoulder to see a large silver drone hovering about a foot above the gate. At almost the same instant, headlights turned onto the road partially blinding him. "Listen, I've gotta go. See you on Wednesday."

He hung up and flicked the settings to mute all calls as the car zipped past, heading toward the end of the road. But instead of turning onto the drive that wound through a stretch of woods to the two non-Triad houses on the other side of the street, as he had expected it to do, the car made a U-turn at the end of the road. Then it accelerated straight toward him.

TALES FROM THE AVEEZI FOREST

THE SNEAKY DJURTA

Translation by Nathaniel Everett

AS EVEN THE smallest child knows, the Aveezi Forest is a place that you should never, ever go. Dark and wild, the forest teems with creatures that snap and snarl. They will happily gobble up any youngling so foolish as to enter.

But even in the Aveezi Forest, light and dark must find a balance. Deep, deep inside the forest—where, I must again caution, you should never, ever go—there is a wide glade called Alestria, where gloom and danger may not tread. Here, the trees hang lush with ripe babda and usimi fruits, the waters flow sweet and cool, and the wind hums a soothing song. Here, the suns shine brightly in the daytime, the sky shimmers emerald and violet as they set, and the creatures live (mostly) in harmony.

It is here in lovely Alestria, on a bright sunny afternoon, that we find Motz and Tibbo—the very best of best friends—heading down the road toward one of the community gardens. Tibbo's tiny frame was perched on Motz's big blue shoulder. He would have preferred to walk after a long morning in the classroom with no activity, but Motz said his tiny legs could never keep up. That wasn't true. Motz walked so slowly that Tibbo could have run circles around him. But it was too nice a day to argue, with a warm gentle breeze that ruffled his orange fur.

It was also too nice a day to be stuck pulling weeds and searching for any sperza pods that had ripened early. That was their assigned chore for the day, however, and it was better than scrubbing the floors. A wrapped bundle of snacks was nestled inside the basket they would use to carry home the grain pods, so they could have a picnic when their work was done. And if they were quick about it, they might have time for a bit of fun before heading home.

When they reached the fork in the road, Motz's eyes turned wistfully to the narrower lane on the right that led downhill toward the lake. "It's still weeks until the harvest," she said. "The sperza pods will probably still be yellow. I'll bet we could skip today, and no one would ever know. Wouldn't you like to go for a swim?"

Tibbo loved the lake. Unlike the boggy water near the edge of the forest, the lake was crystal clear, and swimming was one sport where he outshone his big blue friend.

"Well, sure, but…" he began.

Motz veered immediately to the right and started trotting downhill.

"But we *can't!*" Tibbo added quickly. "You may be right about the sperza, but we also have to clear out the weeds. That's the most important part, even. Ossa said that someone spotted a patch of djurta weed in one of the other fields. And you know how fast djurta can spread."

Motz stopped and heaved a heavy sigh, but she didn't reverse course toward the main path. "I'm *hot*, Tibbo. I want to swim. And the field Ossa told us about was all the way on the other side of Alestria."

"I know you're hot," he said. And it was probably true. Motz's fur was much longer and thicker than his own. "But djurta weeds are carried by the wind. They could easily have traveled to this field, too. The entire crop would be ruined in no time at all."

Motz gave another, even more dramatic sigh and began lumbering back up the hill toward the main path. "I don't even like sperza. It's too gloopy."

Tibbo disagreed. He loved nothing more than starting out his day with a hot bowl of sperza porridge, sweetened with usimi syrup.

"But you do like the bread they make with it," he reminded her. "And the cakes, and the cookies, and the *popkins*..."

He emphasized the last word, and Motz did exactly as he'd known she would, fishing around in the basket for one of the popkins they'd packed. She broke him off a corner, and he was happy to see that it actually had a nice bit of mashed berry this time instead of being only the crust.

By the time they arrived at the field a few minutes later, the popkin was gone, aside from a smattering of crumbs that had landed on Motz's belly. They stepped inside the gate and surveyed the field of sperza stalks—twelve rows with twelve plants each, some of which were higher than Motz's shoulders. The top half of each stalk was ringed with dozens of spherical pods each about the size of Tibbo's head. And Motz was right about one thing, at least. There wouldn't be many pods to harvest today. Most of them still appeared to be yellow. And not even that golden yellow that's almost orange, but a pale, whitish yellow like the fur on Ossa's head.

They had worked this field together the previous year, so he expected Motz to follow their usual pattern, lumbering down each row of sperza with Tibbo on her shoulder, looking for pods that had turned from pale yellow to a deep reddish orange. Then, they would sit side by side, chatting and playing guess-my-secret as they worked their way from stalk to stalk, yanking the weeds from the damp soil.

But today, she placed him on the ground at the end of the first row. "I'll gather the ripe pods, since I'm so tall. You handle the weeds, since you're so tiny. We'll finish faster that way and maybe still have time for a swim."

"Fine," Tibbo said, although Motz probably didn't hear him, since she was already trotting off to the other side of the field. He supposed that her plan *did* make sense, although it didn't seem to him that it would be nearly as much fun as working together.

There were more weeds than he would have expected, given that this chore was assigned to someone in the village every third day. But he decided to make a game of it, singing an old harvesting song that Ossa had taught them last season and seeing how many weeds he could yank up before he reached the end of each verse. He pulled fat weeds, skinny weeds, prickly weeds, weeds that came up with the merest tug, and weeds that fought so hard that he fell over when they finally popped out of the ground, all the while keeping his eyes peeled for any hint of djurta.

Tibbo had only seen the plant once, three cycles back when Ossa still accompanied them on their afternoon chores. He had yanked up one of the broad-leafed weeds and found a tiny patch of color below. It was beautiful, with shiny, deep purple leaves and delicate pale pink flowers growing along a slender vine. Tibbo had been very surprised to hear Ossa gasp when they showed it to him.

"Oh, my," he'd said, craning his long, long neck down toward the plant. "This isn't good at all. Stand back, younglings. And don't touch it."

"Why?" Tibbo asked. "Will it hurt us?"

"No. But it *can* hurt the sperza, so we don't want it to spread." Ossa gently placed his handkerchief over the weed, then grabbed a trowel and dug it up, along with much of the soil around it. Then he tied his handkerchief around the bundle. "I'll have to burn this when we get back to the classroom. And we need to check the entire field extra carefully. You can never be too careful with djurta."

"But that doesn't make sense," Motz had said. "How can such a little weed hurt the sperza when its stalks are so much bigger?"

"It's true that the djurta is tiny," Ossa said as he stuffed the handkerchief into his pocket. "It doesn't seem like a threat if you consider each one individually. But djurta weed comes from deep inside the Aveezi Forest, and it is very, *very* sneaky. Remember those little tufts on the flowers? They're lighter than a starsprite feather. If you tug at the plant or even breathe too heavily on them, they take flight and spread to the next plant and the next and the next. And djurta weed grows extraordinarily fast. If we left this patch undisturbed, by the time the next shift arrived, there would be hundreds of new sprouts in this field ... and the vines of this tiny weed would be at least halfway up this stalk, sinking its barbs into the flesh and absorbing the nutrients. We'd have to burn it, maybe even burn the entire row in order to stop the spread. No, you have to catch it early. Careless weeding or foolish delight at the djurta's pretty flowers could put all of Alestria at risk."

Tibbo was glad that he hadn't spotted any of those purple weeds today. There were napkins in the basket—big, Motz-sized napkins—and he remembered the steps Ossa had taken to remove the djurta. But he was still quite concerned that a bit of that pink fluff would catch on the breeze without him noticing. And he definitely wouldn't ask Motz for help. She'd insist on doing it all herself, because she was older and bigger. That was, of course, true, but she could also be quite clumsy. The last thing they needed was for her to trip and send the weeds flying.

He moved on to the next row, and then the next. When he was halfway through with the fourth row, he realized Motz was back, sprawled out near the fence munching on the other popkin they'd packed. Tibbo had worked up an appetite pulling weeds, so he called out to remind her to save some for him.

"I put your share in the basket with the pods I picked. Hurry up, okay? I'm already done. At the rate you're going..." She yawned and stretched out on the grass without finishing the sentence.

"If you'd come and help me, we'd have lots of time to swim," he said. But he knew it was pointless. With Motz, sleep followed food like night followed day. It was just her nature. She rarely napped for long though, and he was happy that they'd at least be able to do the last few rows together when she woke up. And so he continued his weeding game, singing more softly now so as not to wake her.

By the end of the ninth row, his hands and arms ached with every pull. Even his backside was sore, as he'd found a large cluster of really stubborn weeds a few rows back and landed hard when it finally came loose. Still no purple djurtas, though, and that was a relief.

Motz began to stir a few minutes before he finished the tenth row. Soon, he heard the loud yawn she always made when she stretched at the end of her nap.

"You're *still* not finished?"

"No," he said. "And since you're in such a hurry, you could help me."

"But that's not fair! You agreed to do the weeding if I did the harvest. It's not my fault that you're so slow."

It was on the very tip of his tiny tongue to shout out that it wasn't *his* fault that Motz was so lazy. But she would surely complain to Ossa, who would scold Tibbo for being unkind. And it wasn't really laziness. It was just Motz's nature, as he'd been told many times. She simply needed more sleep than Tibbo.

"I'm going as fast as I can," he said. "I haven't even stopped to eat."

Motz cast a longing look at the basket, and he could almost hear her big blue tummy rumbling at the thought of the bit of popkin she'd set aside for him. To her credit, she didn't reach for it, but he still kept a wary eye on her as he moved on to the next stalk.

"Look at the suns, Tibs. We'll barely have time to get our toes wet. Just leave the last two rows. I pulled up the biggest weeds while I was harvesting."

"The biggest weeds aren't the problem. Ossa said—"

"I know, I know," she said. "Which is why I also looked for the djurta weeds. I pushed the others aside with my feet and there were no purple leaves beneath. No pink flowers."

Tibbo's heart caught in his chest as she spoke, imagining her big blue feet kicking a cloud of pink djurta fluff into the air. Thank the heavens she hadn't found any.

"Come on," she grumbled. "Let's just go."

He ignored her and kept working.

She watched him for a moment, then pushed herself up from the grass. "Well, *I'm* leaving. You can come with me and eat your lunch on the way to the lake. Or you can walk there alone."

Tibbo really did *not* want to walk alone. For one thing, he was tired and achy. It would take him twice as long to get there on his short legs. Even worse, the path to the lake ran by the wesselberry bog. The bog was barely a stone's throw from the forest, which was filled with all sorts of nasties who might be willing to risk a bit of daylight to swoop out and scoop up a tasty bite-sized snack. Like the vurga that very nearly killed him when he tried to save a starsprite. Or the murky green naidar that slithered in the bushes at the edge of the forest until they spotted their prey. Then they spit out a slimy naidar bubble that wrapped tight around your body, sealing off your nose and your mouth so that you couldn't breathe. After you stopped struggling, the naidar sucked you back into the woods and straight into its tummy. He'd only seen those in books, though —and in his nightmares.

He glanced at the last two rows of sperza. To his surprise, there were actually a few weeds piled up at the end of the last row. Maybe Motz had done some weeding after all. Then again, he hadn't really looked all that closely in this direction earlier. It was entirely possible that the pile had been there when they arrived.

But did it even matter at this point? If Motz was really leaving, he was leaving, too.

Sighing, he dragged himself down the row toward Motz and fetched his share of the popkin from the basket. It was a reasonable portion, given their size difference, but he'd been working very hard for the past few hours, and he wished it were larger.

What really annoyed him, though, was the number of sperza pods in the basket.

"Four pods!" he said. "That's all you picked while I pulled weeds for hours?"

Motz shrugged. "I can't help it if so few of them were ripe. And I still had to look for the ones to pick. That's hard work, too."

Tibbo didn't think picking four pods could be called hard work, but he climbed onto Motz's shoulder with his meager snack in hand, and she took off toward the lake with a loud whoop.

He was still quite angry with her when they arrived at the lake. She must have sensed this, because after a few minutes of splashing around, she rolled over to float on her back and told Tibbo he could use her belly as a diving platform, which was always fun. He was never able to hold a grudge against Motz anyway, and by the time they got back to Ossa's cottage, they were laughing and joking, and he'd all but forgotten how mad he'd been.

Motz dug the four sperza pods out of the basket and handed them to their teacher. "I had to look a long time to find even this many," she said. "But Tibbo pulled a lot of weeds."

"Very good," he said. "And you saw no sign of djurta weed, Tibbo?"

"No, sir." It was true, but he was still glad when Ossa's penetrating eyes moved on to something else.

The next day when Tibbo and Motz arrived at the cottage for

lessons, Ossa grabbed a large basket from the closet and announced that they would be altering their usual schedule. Instead of lessons in the morning, they would do chores first. This wasn't unusual. Depending on the weather and the assigned chore, they often changed things up a bit.

Still, Tibbo couldn't help but feel anxious as they headed off, in part because Ossa rarely accompanied them on chores now. But they were assigned to help in the storehouse. Rainy weather had resulted in a larger than usual babda crop, and babda fruits could go from barely ripe to nearly rotten in the blink of an eye. Almost everyone in Alestria would be putting in a few hours in the storehouse today to lend a hand, so Ossa was probably assigned there as well.

When they reached the turnoff to the storehouse, however, Ossa motioned for them to keep going along the path. Which was the very path he and Motz had taken the day before.

"I'm afraid we have another chore to deal with before preserving babda," Ossa said.

"What's that?" Motz asked.

"Oh, you'll see soon enough," Ossa replied. "Perhaps you should give Tibbo a ride so that we can make better time."

Tibbo was all but certain that he already knew. His tiny stomach was twisted into a thousand knots by the time they reached the field.

Even from the gate, he could see that several of the stalks in the far corner of rows eleven and twelve, which had stood straight and green the day before, now hung limp at the top thanks to the deep purple cloak that covered their lower halves.

"It is very fortunate that I took this route on my walk this morning," Ossa said, turning his sharp gold eyes toward Tibbo. "Usually, I prefer to walk around the lake this time of year, but a little voice told me to come this way. Had I not listened, the entire field might have been lost. I'll be coming down here later with three of the other elders. If we're lucky, we can contain the damage to just those four plants. But it might have been avoided entirely if you had done your job, Tibbo."

Motz sighed. "It's partly my fault, too."

Tibbo gave his friend a little smile of gratitude. He wasn't going to say anything—no point in both of them being in trouble—but he was glad that she decided to speak up.

"I rushed him," she continued. "It was hot, and I wanted to swim. It's just that he was working so slowly, and I'd been finished for ages."

He waited, expecting her to go on. She didn't.

"You *also* said you didn't see any djurta on the last two rows! So it's at least as much your fault as mine for lying."

"It wasn't a lie," Motz said. "I didn't see any djurta."

"Because you never looked."

"Now, now, Tibbo." Ossa shook his head in reproach. "Didn't you agree to do the weeding?"

He nodded, although Motz hadn't really given him a chance to *dis*agree. And would it even have mattered? Once Motz made up her mind, Tibbo had little hope of changing it.

"Well then, you can't really blame Motz for not doing your chores. But I do agree that she should have been more responsible, so both of you must be punished. What do you think that punishment should be?"

Tibbo always hated when Ossa asked that question. There was no good answer. If he was too lenient, Ossa would point this out and add something extra on top for not taking it seriously. And if he suggested a hard punishment, he always wondered if he could have gotten something easier if he'd dared to suggest it.

Before he could make up his mind, Motz spoke up. "This will mean we have less sperza in the storehouse this year, won't it?"

Ossa nodded. "Yes. I'm afraid it will."

"Then the best punishment would be to lessen the burden of

our mistake on the others. We should give up sperza porridge for breakfast. For an entire cycle."

Tibbo held his tongue, but it wasn't easy. That was no punishment at all for Motz. It was more of a reward.

"A wise suggestion," Ossa said. "But I think we could limit it to just a season if you can both tell me what you've learned from this mistake."

"Never to rush others when they are doing their chores," Motz said.

Never let Motz divide the chores, Tibbo thought, but did not say. Instead, he looked out at the damaged crop and said, "I've learned that failing to do my job carefully can put everyone at risk."

"Very good," Ossa said. "And here is a further lesson: we must be ever vigilant against things—and creatures!—who would harm Alestria or steal our resources. A lovely or benign appearance can disguise evil intent. Like the tiny djurta weed that seems too small to threaten the mighty sperza stalk, such poisons can spread rapidly, infecting the good and weakening our people. And this is *doubly* true of anything that comes from the Aveezi Forest…"

Tibbo and Motz filled in the rest. "Where we should never, ever go."

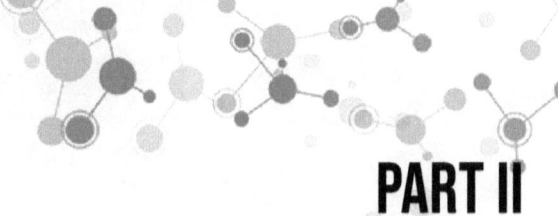

PART II

CLAIRE

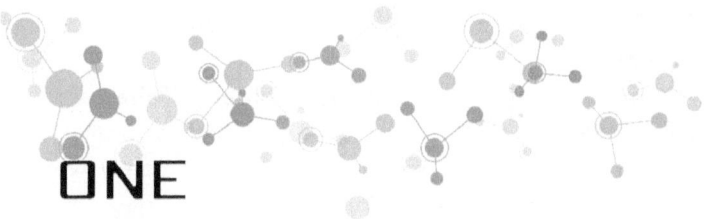

ONE

Wednesday, September 6 1:13 am

AFTER READING THE JOURNAL, Claire watched Beck's video message again. She had nearly thirty minutes left on the drive, and she considered skimming through the journal a second time as well to see if she'd missed anything. But what she really needed was to talk it through with someone. Wyatt was one option, since she'd transferred the files to him before she left New York. But there was no way he'd had time to get to them, given his late meeting with Macek. And he could only give her feedback on the story itself, not on the accuracy of the translation.

For that, she needed Alice. The downside of sending the journal to her was that her translation would then be influenced by Beck's version and two relatively independent translations would be much better, given that one thing she was worried about was how Beck's own experiences might have seeped into his translation. But Alice's work was already intertwined with Beck's to some extent, since his notes had been in the files that Claire gave her on Monday. Having Beck's version as a starting point would also speed up Alice's work on the sections he hadn't yet translated, and she really needed to get a better idea of what was in there. Not that she thought Beck would *purposefully* hold anything back, but…

Only that wasn't actually true, was it? She now *knew* that he'd been holding many, many things back.

Since it was much too late to call Alice, she sent her Beck's translation, along with Shepherd's memoir and a quick message asking her to call the next morning. To her surprise, Alice rang back almost immediately.

"I'm a night owl," she said, in response to Claire's apology for bothering her so late. "And my only class tomorrow is at eleven. I was actually going to message you before I went to bed, but ... where did you get this translation?"

"From Beck. Let's just say he has a closer acquaintance with the language—the modern variant, at least—than I originally thought. Which I know sounds insane, but..."

"I'm not going to argue the fact that it *sounds* insane, but if it makes you feel any better, you'll have company in the asylum, since it's something that I'd already considered. As I mentioned when you were here this morning—although I guess I should now say *yesterday morning*—there were idioms in those notes. Idioms are hard to translate even between similar languages. So, unless the notes were a prank of some sort, Beck had to have been relying on resources other than the ones you gave me. I've just finished going through both sets of notes from Shepherd for the *third* time and the word *philosopher* definitely isn't there. I also couldn't find anything that would have enabled anyone to interpret *the abeeda has a sweeter peel* as *a cloud with a silver lining*. The main reason I didn't call earlier is that you said Beck was a friend. I know he's missing, and I know you're worried ... and I couldn't really think of any explanation for this that wouldn't paint him in an unfavorable light."

"Well, that's even more true now. Have you checked the news in the past few hours?"

"No. I've been immersed in the translation. Why?"

Claire brought Alice up to speed on the bombings and everything else that she had learned about Beck. There was silence on the other end when she paused for breath. Thinking back over everything she'd just explained, she added, "Are you *sure* you still want to be involved in all of this?"

"Yes," Alice said. "Although I'll admit that the bombs make me nervous. I was just skimming through the last few sentences of Beck's translation as you spoke, and ... taking in the magnitude of this. He thinks this book is *real?* That this manuscript is describing what destroyed Mars?"

"He does."

"And you agree?"

"Maybe? I'm still not certain. But I'd feel a lot more comfortable answering that question one way or the other if you could compare this version to the one that you're working on and confirm that it's reasonably accurate. And maybe get a basic computer translation for the sections that are unfinished. You might also want to read the first few chapters of Shepherd's memoir to ... put things into context." She hesitated for a moment before adding, "And I'm going to send you a video. It's personal, so please don't share it with anyone else."

Beck probably wouldn't appreciate her sharing it with a stranger. But Alice needed to know exactly what she was involved in. And while pointing her toward the memoir and the video was probably the coward's way out, Claire couldn't really think of a good way to break the news that Earth might be in line for the same fate.

"Sure," Alice said. "I can do that."

"Thanks. I'm in Boston now, so I won't be able to meet tomorrow as we'd planned. Could you keep me posted by phone?"

A few minutes after they ended the call, the car pulled off the interstate onto the ramp for Audubon. She took several deep breaths, trying to brace herself, but the dark, skeletal remains of the biodome silhouetted against the night sky still hit her like a sledgehammer.

Power inside the buildings was apparently out. The only sources of light were a dozen or so security and emergency vehicles parked on the wide lawn and the string of bright orange police drones positioned around the campus to keep the curious at bay.

On the positive side, two of the buildings seemed to have

suffered almost no damage. Some sections of the main Jonas Labs building were still standing as well, although the extent of the damage to the top half would probably require it to be completely rebuilt. As Joe had said on their call, Olympus had taken a direct hit.

If the employee garage was still intact, it was almost certainly blocked off by the security drones, so Claire parked the car in the guest lot and messaged Joe to let him know she'd arrived. He didn't respond. She waited a few minutes. When there was still no response, she left a voicemail, grabbed her bag, and headed toward the building. Hopefully one of the security guards could give her an update, or at the very least, let her know if Joe had already left.

As she got closer, she discovered that about a third of the vehicles on the lawn weren't emergency workers as she'd thought, but news vans. A gaggle of reporters had gathered on one side, along with camera crews pointing their lights toward the center—where, to Claire's absolute lack of surprise, she found her mother.

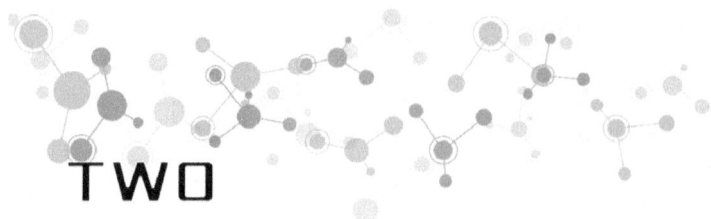

TWO

CURSING SOFTLY, Claire pulled her own press pass out of her bag and began moving toward the front, praying that Kai would stick to the current disaster rather than taking this opportunity to finish the speech she'd begun at the Ares Consortium dinner.

A woman was asking about casualties at the other two facilities when Claire reached the front. Kai's mouth tightened slightly when she saw her daughter, but she quickly returned her focus to the other reporter.

"Six fatalities in all," Kai said, "including a security guard who was killed at this location. We also have three employees dead in Bangalore, and two more at Lomas Verdes. Almost everyone else has been accounted for. There are a few dozen injured, but only three of those are serious, so we're hopeful that the others will pull through." She nodded toward another reporter. "Yes. Go ahead."

"Thank you, Dr. Jonas. I was wondering if you could fill us in a bit on the timing of the attacks. The video issued by the Flock last night claimed that they gave a fifteen minute warning to all of the targeted buildings. That was confirmed by a spokesperson for Kolya International, and your own head of security when I spoke with him earlier. The explosions happened at nine p.m. Eastern ... *but* we have three different sources who claim that the security alert for *this* facility was issued at eight thirty-eight. Why do you think you got an advance warning?"

"I'm afraid I'll need to refer you back to our chief of security, as I was not here at the time. And on that note…"

Several of the reporters began speaking over each other at this point.

"When these attacks happened you and Anton Kolya were appearing at the same event. Do you think that's a coincidence?"

"Ms. Jonas! What did you mean by your comment at the Ares Consortium about *unlimited lifespans*?"

Kai's eyes darted toward Claire and then back to the cameras. "I'm sorry. This has been a tremendous shock and I'm beyond exhausted. My office will issue a statement in the morning with any updates we receive overnight."

She turned quickly and headed toward the main entrance. Claire followed but was stopped by one of the security guards who had been flanking Kai during the press conference.

"I need to speak with my mother."

He looked confused for a moment, then glanced down at the name on her press badge and back up at her face. "Oh. Sorry, Ms. Echols."

Kai didn't slow down at all. But she was still in the heels that she'd worn to dinner and Claire had changed into flats, so she had no trouble catching up with her.

"We had an agreement that you would not cover stories about the business," Kai said, without breaking her stride. "That hasn't changed simply because we have a disaster on our hands."

Claire took a deep breath. "I'm not here for the story. I'm *here* to see Joe. Where is he?"

"I don't know. He may have gone home. We had words shortly after I arrived, and he stormed off."

"Can you blame him?"

Kai stopped then and turned to face her. "I was planning to tell him everything when he returned from his vacation. But you just couldn't wait, could you? Even knowing how upset he would be already over this attack. Over Beck."

Claire had actually messaged Joe *before* she learned about the bombings but there was no point going into all of that, so she focused on Beck. "Have they found him? Is he okay?"

"Wilson thinks he made it out, but we still don't know for certain." Kai said. "And from what I've heard, he's going to have a whole lot of questions to answer if he does show up."

Claire followed her mother's gaze and spotted Wilson talking to three security guards at the far edge of the biodome. Knowing that she'd get more answers from him than she ever would from her mother, she started in that direction, but Kai grabbed her arm and yanked her back.

"If you see Joe, do *not* make things worse. I just wish you'd had the good sense to leave all of this to me. I'm much better at handling his moods than you are."

"This isn't about *handling his moods*. It's about the research. *His* research. He didn't want it made public yet and he deserves to have some say as to when it is announced. Of course, I told him. In fact, I'm beginning to think I should go ahead and tell him *everything*. Maybe he could have avoided this betrayal or at least been a bit more prepared for it if he'd known you'd already done the same thing to Dad."

Kai pinned her daughter with an icy stare, her entire body rigid except for a vein twitching on the right side of her neck. Claire had seen this often enough during adolescence to know that her mother was fighting hard to keep her hand from darting out for a quick slap. She hadn't backed down as a teen and she didn't back down now, even though she was worried that Wilson would disappear before she could reach him.

When Kai finally spoke her voice was tight and flat. "I didn't *betray* your father. We had an understanding. Not that it's any of your business. Or Joe's. I still can't believe that Kolya told you."

"Kolya assumed I already knew. And I'm glad I found out. It kept me from making a horrendous mistake. Beyond that, though, you're right. What you do is none of my business ... unless it hurts my brother."

She started to add that Kai shouldn't bother waiting up for

Joe, but he still hadn't responded to her message about the hotel. Maybe he *had* gone home. And if not, she was perfectly fine with Kai pacing the floor half the night, trying to come up with the magic words to convince Joe that she had his best interests at heart.

THREE

TWO OF THE guards who had been with Wilson were gone by the time Claire weaved her way around the vehicles to the edge of building two. He was still talking to one of them, however, so she hung back far enough that they could finish their conversation in private.

Wilson waved her over a few minutes later. "Probably not the nicest thing to say to a lady, but you look dead on your feet, Miss Claire. You lookin' for Joe?"

"Yeah. Have you seen him?"

"He's going through the computer logs in the security office over in building four. It's on the main level and didn't take as much damage. Pretty clear that their main targets were Olympus and the labs in building two—those are completely destroyed—but they weren't taking any chances. They also planted explosives in the pump rooms at the top of the two waterfalls, which tells me they had fairly detailed knowledge of the biodome. Most of the grounds crew wouldn't even know how to get up there."

Wilson shook his head as he surveyed the wreckage. The waterfalls built into the walls of buildings one and three were now nothing but rubble. Dome panels were everywhere, including one that was draped across several trees in the eucalyptus grove. One section of the banyan tree had been shorn off by a piece of scaffolding.

"Come on. I'll walk you over. Probably best if we go around the back way, though. What a godawful mess. Crazy sonsabitches."

"Is there any word yet about Beck?"

"We think he got out, but he was definitely injured. They found blood and..." He trailed off, grimacing. "I'll omit the gory details, but he was last seen heading toward the garage so we're pretty sure the blood is his. I've got someone going through our backup footage that's stored offsite, and we should know soon. The thing is, I've known Beck for over a decade now, same as you and Joe, and I sure wouldn't have pegged him as the type who'd run off and leave us worrying about whether he's alive, you know? And ... I can't go into all of it given that there's obviously gonna be an outside investigation into the attack, but it's clear that Beck knows more about this than he let on. That's good in one way, because we got a heads up that allowed us to evacuate ... did your mama tell you about those kids?"

Claire's breath caught in her throat. "No. What kids?"

He held a hand up to calm her. "They're okay. Just gave us a scare. Brother and sister who were supposed to be playing inside the dome. Parents were out on a date night, told the sitter it was okay as long as they were inside by nine. We had people combing this place looking for them right up to the last minute. Someone spotted them two, maybe three minutes before the bombs went off, coming across the shopping center parking lot. They'd sneaked off for ice cream. Pretty sure that search was the only reason Beck was still inside. Like I said, though, there's going to be a full investigation, so if you've got any idea where he might be, you need to let me know, okay? I can't protect him unless he levels with me. There's a whole lot of things about this that don't add up. And Beck seems to be right in the middle of most of them, so people are gonna be looking for him."

Claire had a strong feeling that there was more than one set of people looking for Beck, but she nodded. "He called me just before the explosion. Said something about trying to save the biodome, but he thought he was out of time. That's the last..." She yawned widely. "That's the last I heard from him. I really don't know where he is now. But if he contacts me, I'll give him your message."

"Fair enough," Wilson said, although his expression made her suspect that he'd picked up on the fact that she hadn't agreed to call him if she found Beck, but only to pass along his message. "And ... what he told you about trying to stop them tracks with what I know from Sawyer. He's the guard I was just talking to, and he was the last one to see Beck. He spotted him on one of the security cameras in the dome. Says he thought Beck was going after the guy who set the devices, although we now know it was a team that did it. Looks like three people, in total. Your mama is still pitching the one fatality as a Jonas Labs guard because someone got a photo of the body and yeah, he's wearing one of our uniforms. But he's not one of my guys. Never even worked here from what I can tell. The one that Beck went after though—he used to be on staff. Worked with your mom, in fact ... and I still need to fill her in on that." He winced. "Pretty sure she's gonna lose it. I didn't really know the guy other than to nod at him in the hallway. Don't know if he was connected to the Flock back then, or if he lost his mind *after* he quit, but based on what Sawyer observed I'm thinking Beck must have known him when he was..."

Wilson trailed off when they spotted a beam of light approaching from around the corner. A few seconds later, Joe came into view, using his phone as a flashlight.

"Well, guess I don't need to walk you over to building four after all," Wilson said. "Did you find everything you needed, Joe?"

"More or less. I'm not done yet. You should go home, though. I'll be sure everything is locked up when I leave. Although..." He looked around at the destruction and gave a vague shrug.

"I think I'm gonna take you up on that," Wilson said. "It's been a bitch of a day. If I don't see you tomorrow, Miss Claire, don't forget what I said, okay?"

She blanked for a moment, then remembered what he'd said about telling Beck to call him. "I won't."

"Make her get some sleep," Wilson added over his shoulder. "She looks about ready to drop."

Joe raised his phone and looked closely at her for the first time. "He's not wrong, you know. You should have just gone straight to the hotel. There's nothing you can do here. When did you last sleep?"

She was tempted to argue that nobody looked good in the beam of a flashlight, but what was the point? "I got a few hours last night. And a few the night before. I came straight here because we need to talk. It's important."

"More important than all of this?" He tilted his head toward the empty spot where his lab had once been. "And it's not just the building. I have data backups offsite, and they've been deleted. Most of the information is still there, but it looks like I've lost at least five months of work. The *only* other person who had access was Beck. And Mom, too, I guess. But she sure as hell wouldn't have done anything to set the research back when she's out there overselling it. I'm working with someone at one of the sites right now to see if we can recover any of the data, so unless you know where Beck is and why he would do something like that ... anything else needs to wait."

"I don't know where he is..." It was what she'd told Wilson, and it was a true statement, for the most part. But Beck had said something in the video that pointed her in the right direction, assuming he'd made it back to Maine. She was planning to share the video with Joe, so she amended her statement slightly. "I *think* there's a chance that he's at his cabin, but I don't know for sure. I do, however, have a pretty solid lock on his motivations, although there are a lot of missing pieces. And it will take a while for me to explain. Probably twice as long given my lack of sleep. So yeah. Go back and finish with your data guy. We can talk in the morning."

FROM THE RED PLANET

TUESDAY, 538/69

FLOCK ATTACKS NEPENTHES LAB

(DAEDALUS CITY) A series of explosions caused major damage at a Kolya Terraforming facility near Doba early this morning. The Earth Watch Alliance (aka "the Flock") issued a fifteen minute warning to evacuate the main lab and several test domes that house ongoing experiments critical to future stages of the terraforming effort. Fourteen people were killed, and dozens more seriously injured in the explosion, which caused the collapse of two sections of the underground tunnels connecting the lab to the dome communities where scientists and their families reside. The injured were evacuated to the nearest critical care center in Elysia.

An unnamed engineer at the Nepenthes lab noted that the destruction went well beyond the group's stated targets. Large cracks have developed in the tridygel panels that form the domes over Doba, one of the two communities connected to the lab by the tunnel system. While there is no longer a risk of contamination from the *Azospira oryzae*, as was the case in the early months of the lockdown, the atmosphere outside the domes is still not conducive to human life. The engineer said that residents will be confined to biosuits while outside protected buildings until repairs can be completed.

We asked about rumors of an armed confrontation between Doba and Ehden, the second dome connected to the lab via the damaged tunnels. Our source declined to comment, suggesting that our questions would be better addressed to KTI security.

This is a developing story. *The Red Planet* has reached out to KTI for information and will post updates as we receive them.

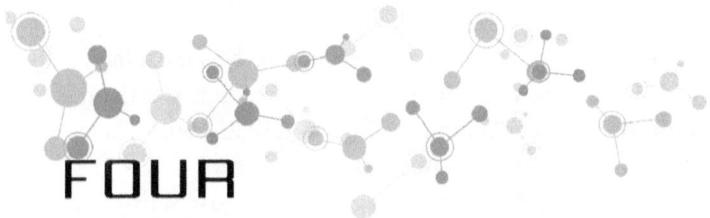

FOUR

CLAIRE WOKE to the sound of running water. At first, she thought it was the shower, but then she heard a bell—a microwave, maybe?—in the other direction, so the water was probably the kitchen sink. As she lay there, trying to muster the energy to move, the smell of coffee wafted into the room and pulled her out of bed. Joe knew her too well.

A quick glance at her phone showed that her promise that they would talk *in the morning* was no longer an option, as it was after one already. She had a voice message that Wyatt left for her a little before ten saying that he was going to get a few hours of sleep but would call around four. There was also a voice message from Paul Caruso saying that Kolya needed to talk to her concerning the attacks. That could definitely wait. She took a moment to scan a text from Alice as she pulled on a pair of shorts under the T-shirt she'd slept in. Then she splashed some water on her face and joined her brother in the main room of the suite.

"Sorry. I overslept."

"Pretty sure you needed it." Joe nodded toward a pizza box on the counter. "Leftovers from what we ordered for the emergency workers last night."

She grabbed a slice, picked off the mushrooms, and poured a cup of coffee before joining him on the sofa.

"I just talked to Wilson," he said. "They've cleared away the wreckage and there are no other bodies. The blood they found just outside the parking garage is probably Beck's, based on the footage. Or maybe the guy who was with him. There was a good bit of blood and … uh … part of a finger."

"What?"

"Yeah. But we know he made it out, so he's most likely alive. Still not answering his phone, though, which is worrisome. You should try. He seems more willing to talk to you." There was a strong undercurrent of bitterness in his voice.

"I've already *tried*. I'll try again. But I just sent a video to your phone. Maybe you should watch it before we talk."

He retrieved his phone from the other bedroom and opened the video Beck had recorded the previous day. When it ended, he tossed the phone onto the coffee table and sank back into the cushions.

"It's bullshit, Claire. Complete and utter bullshit. I don't know why he's doing this, what he stands to gain from it, but you can't actually *believe* he's telling the truth? You think he's one of these Sentinels that Shepherd talked about? I've worked with John Beckett every day for over a decade. Don't you think I would have noticed *something* during that time if he was an alien?"

"I had the same thought at first. But then I realized that if he's really been here since the 1950s ... well, wouldn't that mean he's had a lot of experience acting like a human? He'd have more experience than either of us. More than anyone who was actually born on Earth."

"*If* he's been here since the 1950s. But that *if* is doing some extremely heavy lifting. Do you have any proof to support it?"

"I don't have anything going back *that* far. But..." She spent the next several minutes walking him through the information that Wilson's daughter, Genni Chatterjee, had sent her from the archives at Jonas Labs, including the photograph taken in 2034.

He shrugged. "Everybody's got a doppelganger."

"Fine. I'll grant you that. And if it was the only odd thing, I'd be as inclined to dismiss it as you are. But there's also the manuscript. Do you remember back at Bellamy House, when you transferred the information on Shepherd's nanodrive to me? You included the work that Beck had already done on the translation. On the drive up here last night, I messaged Alice Dobroski, the linguist at Columbia University. She said there was information in those notes that Beck couldn't have gotten from Shepherd's files or through the translation programs. Things that only someone who knew the language or a close variant of it would have been able to translate. She's still working on the parts of the manuscript that Beck hasn't completed, but she messaged me this morning to say that what he's done so far seems accurate to her."

"So? That could simply mean Beck helped Shepherd create this bogus language. I still think it's far more likely that this entire thing is a hoax. Just never imagined that Beck would be part of it."

For nearly an hour, she laid out the evidence, and Joe batted it away. Which was exactly how she'd known the conversation would go. Joe had never been comfortable with concepts that he couldn't quantify or test. That was one reason he rarely read fiction, and almost never watched it.

"Everything you've told me so far is circumstantial," he said. "And to quote Carl Sagan, extraordinary claims require extraordinary evidence."

"Like what? A picture of Beck stepping off a spaceship? A video, even? Either way, you'd say it was altered. Or you'd shrug it off as another doppelganger. At a certain point, Joe, circumstantial evidence has to be enough. And the video Beck recorded—how is that circumstantial? That's a direct, uncoerced confession."

He fell into one of his characteristic silences. She didn't prod but instead took the opportunity to grab another slice of the pizza and a bottle of water from the hotel fridge. When she got back to the couch, he was watching the video again.

At the end, he asked, "So what exactly is the plot of this *Journal of Eberin Das?*"

"Some of it you probably surmised from the video," she said, ignoring his sarcastic tone and use of the word *plot*, with its not-so-subtle suggestion that the journal was fiction. "But it's basically diary entries from someone who held a monitoring position on Mars similar to Beck's here on..." She held up a hand to forestall his objections. "Sorry. Who held a monitoring position on Mars similar to the one that Beck *claims* to have been doing here on Earth, concerning the achievement of the two milestones."

"Which are?"

"One would be your work, obviously. Although I got the sense from some of Beck's notes on the journal that it's not simply extending life but achieving something close to biological immortality. The second seems to be expansion outside of our solar system."

"Which is Kolya's next big thing."

"Right. In the journal, Mars had decided that the higher gravity on Earth meant it wasn't a good candidate for ... martaforming? Or whatever the term would be. Their government was leaning toward colonizing exoplanets as a long term goal. Most of the entries revolve around Eberin's gradual rejection of what he views as his duty to the Alliance in favor of a moral duty to protect the Martian people. As I said, I don't have the translations of all the entries yet, but from what I've pieced together, he formed a resistance that attempted to take over the headquarters—the Triad. I assume they failed, and at some point, he decided that he could at least try to leave a message for some future civilization."

She considered for a moment, then added, "Maybe even explicitly as a warning for Earth. They knew there was life on the planet. Not advanced technological life, but if intelligent life eventually evolved, Mars would be the most logical first foray into off-planet colonization, just as Earth was the first choice for Mars. Even more so, since we have a much easier time handling the weaker gravity on Mars than they'd have had handling our much stronger gravity. As to why the Alliance chose to monitor those specific achievements—"

"It's because they're linked," Joe said. "If you extend lifespans, you're going to tap out the resources of the planet. That leaves you with two choices. Curtail births, which people are going to resist or encourage the expanding population to move off-planet. At that point, we become potential competitors for any other intelligent life out there doing the same thing."

"That's an excellent point," she said, not adding that it was one that had already occurred to her. If Joe was connecting dots on *her* side of the argument now, that was a good sign. "Come to think of it, it ties in with something that Eberin Das wrote in his journal. Do you want me to send the translation to you?"

He gave her a sour look. "Fine. Send it."

She did, but he didn't open the file. He just stared out the window, taking in the scenic vista of the parking lot and the highway beyond.

"So … you're convinced?" Joe asked after several minutes of silence.

"That Beck is one of these Watchers? Yes."

"No. About the journal."

"As convinced as I can be without the full translation. Which Alice is working on."

Another long pause. "And you know where Beck is?"

"I said I *might* know. Remember our first night at Bellamy House? After dinner, we sat out on that little balcony with the view of the mountains and watched the sun set over Mount Agamenticus. Earlier, Beck had mentioned to me that he has a little cabin over there. That's where he usually stays when he goes up to Maine for a few days. The challenge is going to be finding it, since there are probably dozens of dirt roads and rustic cabins. He pointed it out from the AeroLyft, so it's not *exactly* a needle in a haystack situation, but pretty close."

"Is Wyatt going with you?"

"Probably not. He said he was heading back to DC. I'm not worried about going on my own, though. Beck isn't going to hurt me."

"Not sure how you can state that with such assurance when we've just established that the man is an alien who has been lying to both of us for more than a decade."

She took a deep breath, carefully keeping her face neutral. This was as close as Joe Echols ever came to acknowledging that he was wrong. Slowly but surely, he just adopted your position as his own.

"I'll have a gun," she said. "*His* gun, in fact. But you're welcome to come with me if you're actually worried."

"Can't. I've got to deal with this … fiasco at the lab. Mom still doesn't know about the missing data, and we need to have it out about her stunt last night. Guess I've now got an extra incentive to keep her from overpromising to the stockholders. But … even if I could get away, I'm not ready to talk to him." He gave an annoyed huff. "*Nudging*."

"What?"

"Beck said that he and these other Watchers have been *nudging* researchers in the right direction. What the hell does that mean? He's my research partner, but I've always…"

"But you've always been the lead."

"*Exactly*. Only now I'm wondering how much of the research is *mine* and how much is the product of the advanced mind of an eleven-hundred-year-old alien who already knew all of the answers."

He added an unconvincing laugh at the end, trying to pass the question off as a bit of idle speculation, but Claire registered the fear beneath it. Joe had no concept of work-life balance. His work *was* his life. And even if he didn't seek the limelight, his ego was very much wrapped up in his accomplishments. He'd always been more than willing to share credit with Beck, but finding out that he might not have been the one in the driver's seat, that he might have been manipulated? That would be a massive blow.

"Seriously, Joe? When have you ever let yourself be *nudged* when it comes to your research? Even by Beck. Hell, I seem to remember Mom trying—and failing spectacularly—when you were in college." That seemed to mollify him a bit, so she added, "It's *your* work. If you hadn't already been heading in the right direction, Beck wouldn't have taken the job as your assistant."

"Maybe," he said grudgingly. "When are you leaving?"

"I'll grab a shower and then head north. If I don't have any luck before dark, I'll stay at Bellamy House and start again in the morning."

"Okay. Call me if you find him. I've got questions, some of which I'd really like answers to before I deal with Mom. I'm still not..." He shook his head. "I'm still not entirely convinced this is all real. I just can't think of any other reason Beck would destroy six months of work. It's baffling."

Claire thought that was far from the most baffling thing about all of this, but she nodded. "I have questions, too. I'll add that one to the list."

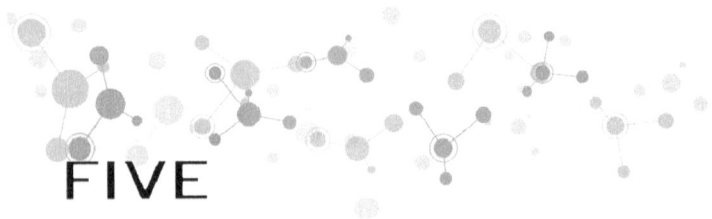

FIVE

THUNDERCLOUDS GATHERED in the distance over Nahant Bay as Claire's car pulled out of the hotel lot. She kept her eyes fixed on the ominous gray mass, rather than looking at the ruined hulk of Jonas Labs. The sight had been depressing enough last night. She had no desire to see it in the harsh light of day.

Rain began to fall in thick gray sheets shortly after the Aeris merged onto the highway, pelting the windows with such vigor that she was tempted to pull over until the storm let up. But given the snippy conversation about safety she'd had with the AI when she asked it to tail that car to Riverdale a few nights back, it would undoubtedly stop of its own accord if the conditions were too dangerous.

Wyatt called a little after four, looking tired and sleep rumpled. She expected to see the familiar disarray of his apartment in the background, since he'd said he needed to get back to DC. But he was at a hotel. A cup of takeout coffee and a half-eaten pumpernickel bagel were on the nightstand.

"I take it you're still in New York?"

"Yeah," he said. "I'm supposed to meet with Macek again in about an hour. Things were still a bit too chaotic last night for us to have a private conversation. And given that we've already uncovered several questionable people in his organization there could be others, so privacy seems like a good idea."

"You could have slept at the apartment, you know."

"I thought about it. But it felt weird without you there, like your mom was going to walk in at any minute. And yeah, I know she's in Boston, but..." He frowned into the camera, shaking his head. "Where *are* you? The lighting is awful."

"Driving through a freaking monsoon on the way back up to Maine. We still haven't heard from Beck but I'm pretty sure that's where he went based on what he said in the video."

He pressed his lips together for a moment, clearly fighting what he wanted to say, and then just blurted it out. "Would you please wait until I can join you? I can probably get away by early tomorrow. I'm really not keen on you going alone and Beck *did* suggest that I tag along."

"I really can't. Wilson thinks Beck is injured. They found blood in the area where the cameras last saw him. Quite a bit of it and ... part of a finger. I'd have left immediately after he told me, but I was running on fumes at that point. Unlike you, I've never really mastered the knack of sleeping in a car. And I needed to tell Joe about all of this. So, please *do* come up as soon as you can, but I need to find Beck ASAP. And ... he's not going to hurt me, Wyatt. If you watched the video, you have to know that."

"I did watch it. I also skimmed through the diary. Which is one reason I didn't get to sleep until the sun was up. Too damn many questions running around in my head. My concern is less about Beck than these other Watchers or Triads or whatever he called them. I got the sense that they may be hunting him now, and he made it sound like you could be a target, too ... although, what the hell is a right of *ufrete*?"

"I have no idea. That's at the top of my list of questions, assuming I find him."

"How did Joe take the news?" Wyatt asked around a bite of bagel.

"About Beck?"

He made an expansive gesture, to indicate not just Beck but everything.

"About as well as could be expected. I mean, he already knew something was going on based on Beck's behavior over the past few weeks. Plus, in addition to the damage to his lab, about six months of their work is now missing from the backups and Beck was the only one who had access. It took a while, but once I showed Joe the video and gave him a summary of what's in the Eberin Das journal, he seems to have accepted it. I think he was actually kind of ... relieved, I guess? ... even if he found what I told him hard to swallow."

"Relieved that the sword of Damocles is hanging over the entire planet?"

"No. Not that part. Just ... relieved to hear something that helped explain Beck's actions. After Kai's stunt at the Ares Conference, I think he needed to know that Beck at least was motivated by something other than greed."

They talked for a bit longer, and she promised to update him if she located Beck. After they hung up, she spent the rest of the trip scanning the satellite map, trying to match the images on the phone to the vague memory of the scene through the window of the AeroLyft when Beck tapped the glass to indicate the general direction of his cabin. The main road he'd mentioned had to be Mountain Road, since it was the only one that led up to Mount Agamenticus. She *thought* he'd said the turnoff to the cabin was about half a kilometer away from the trailhead. But she couldn't remember whether he'd said it was before or after. There were at least a dozen small roads snaking off on either side, and most of those were intersected by even smaller roads.

She had resigned herself to the unpleasant reality that she'd have to try them all when it occurred to her that Beck might have left a map or some other information about the cabin at Bellamy House. It made sense that the couple who ran the place might keep an eye on his other property, too. The bed and breakfast was only a few kilometers beyond Mountain Road, so she decided to check there before she began hunting. The odds weren't good—she thought it far more likely that sort of information would be inside their phones or the house computer system—but at least she could grab a cup of coffee and check in with Ro and Jemma before heading up the mountain.

She messaged ahead to see if Ro could poke around in the room where Beck had been sleeping or maybe inside the kitchen junk drawers for something with an address near Mountain Road. Ro answered a few minutes later.

> Beck's room is locked. There's a desk in the kitchen, but ... is this really something I should be doing? I mean, it's not my house. They've probably got security cameras in here.

> It's fine. I'll explain when I get there.

The storm continued through Massachusetts and New Hampshire, finally tapering off not long after she crossed into Maine. Ten minutes later, the sun emerged, and fine tendrils of steam began snaking upward from the pavement on the road ahead.

As the car approached Bellamy House, Claire spotted a flash of silver through the slats of the white split rail fence. It was one of the perimeter bots that Wilson had sent to help secure the place. A green light blinked twice as she passed, making her wonder if the bot had picked up a code of some sort identifying the Aeris as property of Jonas Labs.

The guard at the gate wasn't one of the two that had been on duty Monday morning when she and Beck left Maine. She checked Claire's ID, said to enjoy the rest of her day, and locked the gate behind her. The car continued up the gravel path, stopping on the right side of the gray stone house. Jemma came bounding around the corner, pulling up sharply when her bare feet landed on the gravel drive. Claire scooped the girl up, relieved to discover that her purple swimsuit was mostly dry.

"Wanna come in the pool with me?" Jemma asked as they headed for the covered walkway that led to the side entrance.

"Mommy wouldn't let me go in when it was thunderstorming, but it's over now. And I'm really *not tired*."

Her strong emphasis on those last two words was a dead giveaway that Claire's arrival had come in the middle of daily nap negotiations.

"I'm sorry, sweetie. I can only stay for a few minutes and then I have to go back out for a while. Can you give me a rain check for tonight or maybe first thing tomorrow morning?"

Jemma frowned and peered at the patches of sky that were visible through the ivy draping down from the railing above the walkway. "It's stopped *now*, but I don't know about tonight or tomorrow. Can't you do a rain check with your phone?"

Claire laughed. "When you ask someone for a rain check it means that you can't do what they want right that moment—"

"Because it's raining?"

"Well, sometimes, but…" Claire shook her head, realizing that she wasn't entirely sure where the phrase came from, and any explanation would probably just confuse the kid even more. "Never mind about the rain check. But I *will* try to get back for a swim after supper, okay?"

"Okay. But I'm really *not tired*."

"Of *course* you're not," Claire said as they stepped into the little alcove near the kitchen. "When have you ever been tired at naptime?"

She personally thought that five was a little old for a nap, and suspected Jemma wouldn't resist bedtime nearly as hard if the afternoon snooze was phased out. But that was Ro's call to make, so she just pressed a kiss into Jemma's hair, breathing in chlorine, sunscreen, and a faint hint of lavender from her shampoo.

And that was the trigger. That tiny whiff of lavender sent her into a tailspin, as the full weight of everything she'd learned in the past few days slammed into her chest.

SIX

MAYBE IT WAS the cumulative lack of sleep, or the fact that the evidence had stacked up slowly. Or maybe it was just hard for her mind—for anyone's mind—to tackle the magnitude of the entire planet being at *imminent* risk. It had been true in the vague sense for her entire life. Climate change, nuclear weapons, an asteroid that they didn't manage to deflect—you could argue that the planet was always *at risk* . The end of everything was always a possibility.

But now there was a timetable. Six months, a year or two at most.

It had taken the weight of Jemma in her arms, the achingly familiar smell of her shampoo—a scent that evoked countless baths and snuggles for bedtime stories—to bring home the simple reality that the end of everything meant the end of everyone she loved. If Beck was right, Jemma might make it to her sixth birthday. Her seventh, if they were very, very lucky.

"Claire?" Rowan's tone made it clear that this wasn't the first time she'd said her name.

"What?"

"I said *are you okay?*" She pulled a wriggling Jemma from Claire's arms and ferried the girl away to the living room, telling her she could play a game on her tablet.

Claire sank down onto the bench by the door, taking slow, deep breaths to ward off the looming panic attack. This onslaught of emotion wasn't helpful. She had to locate Beck, had to find out how she could help avert this disaster. He hadn't sounded particularly hopeful in the video, but destroying the labs couldn't be the entire plan, right? There had to be something more they could do. Some way to stop this.

"Okay, then." Ro dropped down on the bench next to her. "What's wrong?"

"I'm fine," she said, ignoring her friend's skeptical look. "Did you find anything in the desk?"

Ro shook her head. "Pens. Markers. Thumbtacks. A few pads of sticky notes that are probably older than I am. An ancient-looking key, but I checked, and it goes to that antique door to the walk-in pantry. No maps marked with an X or anything like that."

"Then I guess I'll be doing the needle in a haystack routine."

"What exactly is this needle you're looking for?"

"Beck's cabin. And Beck. Things have gotten ... weird."

"Things were already weird."

"Fair enough. They've gotten weird*er*."

"Is this connected to the bombing at Jonas Labs?"

"Yes, but there's more going on. I'll explain everything when I get back. If I go into the details right now, there's an excellent chance I'll freak out again. And I really do need to get a move on while I still have daylight. I'm just going to make some coffee for the road and then—"

"Whoa." Ro put a restraining hand on Claire's shoulder and pressed two fingers of the other hand to the side of her neck for a few seconds. "Yeah. Exactly as I thought. Your pulse is racing. No caffeine for you. I think I saw some chamomile..."

"Ick. No. But ... maybe you're right about the caffeine. I'll grab a seltzer."

"I'll get it," Ro said. "But you've got *me* freaking out now, so you need to at least give me the summary version."

"Trust me," she said with a shaky laugh. "The summary version isn't going to make you *less* freaked out."

"Now you're just plain scaring me."

"Okay, okay. But don't say I didn't warn you. Remember Tobias Shepherd's Sentinels?"

"Yes." Ro tossed the seltzer cap into the trash and handed her the bottle. "They're the aliens he claims are judging us for wrecking our planet."

"Well, the judging part is right, but it's more that they've been assessing our scientific progress to determine whether we're going to be a threat to something called the Ufretan Alliance. I can explain in more detail later, but long story short, they're real. Beck calls them the Watch. And their leadership tribunal is right on the verge of reporting back that we've crossed that threat threshold."

Claire gave her a brief overview of the two milestones, then paused to take a sip of her seltzer as she screwed up her courage for the next part.

"So what happens after they make their report?" Ro asked warily, clearly sensing that this was the part that had Claire on the verge of panic.

"The same thing that happened to Mars when the Ufretans decided *they* were a threat."

Ro's eyes grew wide and then drifted toward the living room, where Jemma was now asleep on the floor, her dark curls covering the tablet that was doing double duty as a pillow. "How long are we talking?"

"Beck seemed to think it would be a year or two at most. Maybe less than that."

"And he's trying to stop these ... Ufretans?"

"Yes. But he's also *one* of them. Like Uden—I mean, Professor Everett, the one from Shepherd's journal. These foot-soldiers, the Watchers who are out there working in labs assessing our progress, all believed we'd be welcomed into their Alliance. He said the Watchers viewed the assignment as sort of an interstellar Peace Corps."

"So ... the Watchers thought it was a first contact situation. Kind of like the Vulcans waiting to contact Earth until *after* we developed warp drive." She glanced at Claire's expression, then added. "That's from *Star Trek*."

"I *know* that. I was just trying to remember whether the Vulcans were the pointy-eared logical ones or the ones with the elaborate foreheads."

"The former. Just to be clear, though, are you saying that Beck is an alien? Or just that he's been *working* for aliens? Because he looks pretty human to me."

"No. He's one of them. There was some sort of consciousness transfer. His body *is* human, but it was cloned. An advance team collected DNA back in the early 1950s."

"So right around the same time as Roswell. Score another one for the conspiracy theorists."

Ro was about to push for more information, but Claire held up a hand. "I'll send you the files that Beck gave me. And the partial translation of the Eberin Das journal. It won't answer much, but at least you'll know as much as I do. Because I really do need to go."

"Okay." Ro pulled out her phone. "Where do you think his cabin might be?"

Claire relayed the minimal information that Beck had given her.

"And that's all you've got?"

She considered for a moment. "When he first told me about the place the other day, he said it was rustic. In the middle of the woods, which he liked because he could see the stars at night. He couldn't spot the place from the AeroLyft because there was too much tree cover this time of the year. And he's right. I searched the satellite map on the drive up and couldn't find anything that really fit the criteria."

"Well, it's not a *lot* to go on," Ro said. "But it would seem to eliminate any properties near the road or near other houses. If the car you're in has a decent AI, you might want to see if it can pull up some *older* satellite photos. Maybe one from winter months when structures would be more visible?"

"That's an excellent idea."

Ro gave her a weak smile. "I *do* get them from time to time."

SEVEN

"I'M SORRY, but this is *not* a road."

The tone of the Aeris's AI fell firmly into the category of *disapproving British schoolmaster.* And while it was probably Claire's imagination, it seemed to her that the car's disapproval had deepened considerably during the past hour since she left Bellamy House.

Ro's suggestion that she consult older satellite maps had indeed been a good one. The AI had quickly narrowed her search down to five properties that seemed to fit the information that Claire had about Beck's cabin. All five of them, perhaps unsurprisingly, were accessible only by dirt roads and none of them so far had met the Aeris's exacting standards for an acceptable thoroughfare.

Three children had been jumping on a battered trampoline in the backyard of the first cabin. Given the many, many things that John Beckett had lied to her about, she couldn't entirely discount the possibility that he had a secret family stashed away at his mountain retreat. It seemed unlikely, though, so she'd told the car to turn around and moved on to the next house on the list.

The second cabin sat at the end of a very long, very muddy road with an alarmingly narrow plank bridge near the middle. During that lovely little journey, she'd been informed on three separate occasions that the Aeris was not an off-road vehicle and that continuing the drive under such deplorable conditions would violate her warranty. When they'd finally reached the cabin itself, she'd discovered that the roof had long since been crushed by a fallen tree. She couldn't imagine Beck hiding out with the raccoon she spotted near the open front door, so she moved on to road number three.

Which, as the Aeris had just informed her, was not a road at all.

Strictly speaking, the AI was right. There was no road sign. Nor did it have a name on the map. It was little more than two tire tracks meandering through a clearing between the trees, with an irregular strip of grass running down the middle.

It was the grassy strip that caught her attention. The grass near the center was about calf-high, but something had flattened the blades along the outer edges.

"I don't care whether it's a road," she told the car. "And I don't need to hear your warnings again. Just shut up and drive."

The car's AI didn't respond. Claire was fairly certain that it gave her a disgruntled sniff, although that *might* simply have been the car's tires squelching through the mud.

An excruciating ten minutes later, the Aeris pulled up in front of a security gate that hadn't been visible in any of the satellite images. A red and black NO TRESPASSING sign dangled from one wire near the center of the gate. The lockbox was so ancient that the AI couldn't interface with it, and Claire wondered whether it worked at all.

When she got out of the car to inspect it more closely, she spotted a blinking red light next to an alphanumeric keypad. Beyond the gate she could just make out the corner of a weatherbeaten gray roof about a hundred and fifty meters down an even more overgrown path. The only thing that really marked it as a path were the muddy tire tracks ... which looked fresh.

She crouched down to examine the lockbox more closely, hoping to find a button that she could press to request entry. No luck, so she tried pushing the "0" key. After a few seconds, the box emitted a harsh buzz, and the message *Enter Eight Digit Code* scrolled across the black strip above the keypad.

Sighing, she went back to the car to retrieve her phone. She should send Ro an update and her location so that they'd have some chance of recovering her body if some disgruntled landowner shot her for trespassing, because she was apparently going to have to ignore the dilapidated sign and climb the fence. There was no way she'd be able to guess an eight-digit code.

When she opened her messages, her eyes landed on the text Beck had sent the night before with the two files, including the video with the numeric title—*27424866.*

Eight numbers. *The title is the code.*

She hurried back to the keypad. The number 2 button tended to stick so the first attempt earned her another raspy buzz. On the second try, however, the light changed to green, and the lock clicked open. She shoved the gate backward into the knee-high grass and told the Aeris to drive inside and wait until she closed it.

About a minute later, the Aeris pulled up behind a white car with Massachusetts rental plates. The door on the left was ajar. As she moved forward to close it, a dark cloud of flies rose up, revealing a pool of dried blood on the seat below. There was blood on the opposite seat, as well, but the flies continued to swarm across the surface, having apparently decided that she was too far away to constitute a viable threat.

She closed the door, fighting back a wave of nausea, and took two steps toward the house before stopping. If there was ever a time that she should have a pistol in her hands, this was probably it. Once she retrieved the gun from the Aeris's glove compartment, she flipped off the safety and then headed toward the porch, this time giving the other car a wide berth.

"Beck?" Her voice shook, almost unrecognizable. She cleared her throat and tried again. "Beck! Are you here?"

There was no response, so she moved cautiously toward the narrow porch, where several cement blocks had been pushed together into rudimentary stairs. An Adirondack chair and table sat to the left. Two reddish brown patches marred the wooden slats of the porch. Those could have been paint splotches, but there was no mistaking the mark on the doorframe of the cabin.

It was a single bloody handprint.

FROM THE JOURNAL
OF EBERIN DAS

(Translation by John Beckett)
22.07.507

I HAVEN'T WRITTEN MUCH LATELY, because I've been busy and on the move. What energy I've had for writing has been channeled into the articles I give to Navi. I'm currently hiding out with a family in Astoba. They are distant relatives of Navi, and while I can tell that their belief in my cause is not as unwavering as hers, they are not scientists. They haven't seen the evidence that I placed in Navi's hands to support my story about the Alliance. They have only her word that I am what I claim to be, so in many ways I find their willingness to believe, their willingness to risk their own safety to keep me hidden, even more touching.

Navi and her partner keep me informed of what's going on outside this room. They smuggle out my articles and organize meetings. I send recorded speeches urging members to contact their elected officials, to protest at the various government labs working on the two milestones. We even have a few local and regional government leaders who, while not active members, have been willing to meet. To listen. I've told them the rules, so the next step is to convince this world to abide by them.

I held off on approaching Bodae until I had a large enough following that I thought he—and at least a few of the other

Guardians—would be impressed. The Martian-Ufretan Union now has more than four hundred local cells in five of the six regions, with over thirty-five thousand members in all. It's been less than a year since the Conclave, and I had hoped that Bodae and the other Guardians might be encouraged by how much success we've had with minimal resources in a fairly short amount of time. I can't prove it, of course, but I believe that the M-UU had a strong influence on the government's recent decision to prioritize orbital habitats over colonizing exoplanets. And while research on longevity treatments continues, M-UU members are circulating petitions urging the government to either further restrain reproduction or to limit the treatments to ensure an extended, but not indefinite, lifespan.

I'd hoped that if we could get action on both fronts, the Triad would be persuaded to report back that Mars has abandoned the research and no longer poses a threat. Then, once our transport arrives, we could start a movement back home, to convince the Alliance Council that the people here are not the caricature that we were led to believe and that they would in fact be worthy allies.

In truth, I feared that the Triad would take action against the M-UU even before I met with Bodae. We took some precautions in terms of secrecy early on, but it's hard to lobby for reform from the shadows. When those first public actions brought no retaliation, no violent action against our members, I grew hopeful that I would be able to reason with them.

I learned today that I was wrong. We were nothing more than a buzzing insect to the Triad, a minor annoyance that could be ignored until we pissed them off enough that they decided to swat us away. This afternoon, nine members of the M-UU were killed and several dozen injured in an explosion at a local meeting in the very town where I'm hiding. Navi and her family are okay, but nine people are dead as a result of my actions. Twelve, if you count the three hosts I took.

A written message from Bodae arrived less than an hour

after the attack, making it clear that they know where I am. He informed me that the Triad has decided to ignore the Martian government's decision to step back from the threshold and delay colonization outside their system. When our communication window reopens, the Triad will be reporting that the milestone was achieved. They will, in fact, be reporting that the planet has achieved *both* milestones.

It's a lie, though. I know from Navi's contacts at the lab that they are at least a year from a treatment that would extend lifespans indefinitely.

So, I've only made it worse, only sped up the inevitable conclusion. Bodae says that if I come back now, the Triad will be lenient. There will, of course, be a trial once we're home, but he seems to think I can make a solid case that my aberrant behavior was due to a botched transfer to my current host. He says he will testify on my behalf, and that several others have offered to do the same. Even Eidjri.

I won't be taking their offer, but I have to be honest with the M-UU. They have two options. The first is to quietly disband and accept the inevitable. If we do that, I'm sure that there will be no further attacks on our members. But I know these people well enough to be sure that most of them will reject that option out of hand.

Our second option is to fight. Not the Alliance itself. This tiny planet stands no chance at all against a force that size. But against the Triad? Against the Guardians? We still have time before the communications window opens, when the transport ship makes its scheduled run near this sector. If enough people are willing, we can form an armed resistance to take headquarters and force them to send a different message.

It would not be a permanent solution, but it would buy time for me to convince the others. And if we presented a united front—Guardians and Triad alike—to the administrators at the Academy, perhaps they would be willing to reclassify Mars.

If I'm asked to give odds, I think we have a better than even chance of taking headquarters, although that will obviously depend on the size of our force.

Our odds of convincing the others, though? Much of the responsibility for that will lie with me, and after my experience with Bodae, I believe our chances to be very slim indeed.

But a slim chance is better than none. And when the other option is the guaranteed annihilation of more than four billion people, how can we not at least try?

ANAK – TWO DAYS EARLIER

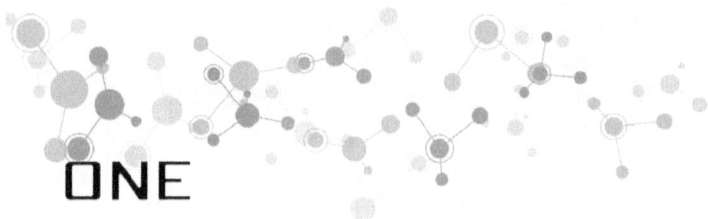

ONE

Monday, September 4 7:42 pm

ANAK JUMPED BACK, certain that the car would shift course and follow him. If it did, he had nowhere to go with the brick wall at his back. Instead, the car veered slightly in the other direction, pulling up parallel to the sidewalk. He felt a split second of relief, and then the right door flew open before the vehicle even made a complete stop. His hands went up instinctively and he had to back several steps from the curb to keep from being sideswiped.

A woman with dark blue hair leaned into the open door and yelled, "Get in!" He realized two things at almost the same instant. First, the woman was Stasia Ljubic. Second, the car was a blue Argo, which is what Milner had told him they were driving.

Drex was sitting on the other side of the car. Her auburn hair, which he was fairly certain she'd worn long the entire time they'd been on Earth, was now platinum, cropped so close to her head that it looked like a skullcap.

He took the empty seat next to Stasia. "What the hell? You guys nearly took my damn kneecaps off with that door."

"Sorry. We're in a hurry." Drex continued to gaze out the window as the car sped away from the house toward the main road. "You forgot to close the gate. Durav's going to be pissed."

"Durav is always pissed."

"Fair enough." She wrinkled her nose. "You smell like a brewery. What took you so long? And where are we supposed to meet Arbet?"

Anak took several deep breaths before speaking, both to lower his heart rate after the adrenaline rush of a car nearly crashing into him and to buy a few seconds to figure out what Drex was talking about. When he'd imagined this conversation earlier, he'd been the one firing questions at *her*.

"Okay, first, I haven't spoken to Arbet." He thought about the note in his pocket but decided to hold off on mentioning it until he had a bit more information from the two of them. "I did see her talking to Reese, though. And he's acting weird. Earlier, he cautioned me to stay inside the Great Hall, then a few minutes ago, he spills his beer all over my back and insists I go change before dinner. Although, he could also be working with Durav. I'm pretty sure he was recording our conversation over lunch."

"More likely he was jamming anyone else trying to listen in. Reese is with me. Has been for about a year now. He was actually easier to convince than she was," Drex added wryly, with a head tilt toward Stasia. "We haven't been able to reach him since he entered HQ, but he was supposed to arrange a meeting place with Arbet and send you out with the details as soon as possible. We've been driving by the gate each hour at twenty-past for the better part of the day. I really hoped we'd catch you *before* the general assembly, but..." She shrugged as if to say it was too late now. "What did you tell them?"

"Officially? Nothing. They've delayed the meeting until tomorrow morning, so I still haven't delivered my report. Unofficially, however, I've been telling everyone that the rumors of our success at Jonas Labs are greatly exaggerated."

"And are they?"

He opened his mouth to respond but then stopped. For the past few days, he'd constantly felt as if he'd slipped into a different timeline, into some strange new reality where everything he believed to be true was either entirely false or had been twisted beyond recognition. He *thought* he knew why Drex and Stasia had defected, but he'd been wrong about too many things lately. One or both of them could be reporting back to Durav.

And Arbet had said to *trust no one*. Despite the current gulf between them, he knew more about her character and trusted her far more than he did Drex, Stasia, or Reese.

"You first," he said. "If you want me to answer your questions, tell me why you left the Watch. While you're at it, I'd also like to know why you took a group of annoying but mostly harmless tree huggers and turned them into bomb-wielding terrorists. They damn near killed a friend of mine when she was on Mars, and now they've destroyed her house."

The car's AI interrupted at that point to request directions. Drex told it to turn right onto 250th and circle the neighborhood until further notice. Then, she leaned back into the seat. "First of all, I was not involved in either of the attacks you mentioned, so you'll need to direct any questions of that nature to Stasia. Or to Durav, in all fairness, since she was acting on his orders. And second, you should *thank* me. I'm the one who told Arbet that Claire had a very good chance of ending up in Durav's crosshairs and that you might take serious personal issue with that."

"What gave you that impression?"

"Just a hunch based on something her brother told me during my brief and rather disastrous attempt at seducing him. And apparently, his hunch was correct, given that you extended your right of *ufrete* to cover her."

Anak felt the blood rising to his cheeks and was glad that the interior light of the car had flickered out a few moments earlier, leaving the cabin in shadows. What the hell had Joe told her?

"It's not like that," he said. "Claire is ... she's little more than a child."

Stasia laughed. "I spent quite a bit of time with Claire onboard the *Ares Prime*. She doesn't look much like a child to me. Kolya didn't seem to think so, either."

"I guess we have different standards then. But ... since we've established that she *is* under my protection, maybe you'd care to explain why you keep trying to kill her?"

"I wasn't *trying* to kill her. And I had nothing to do with bombing her house. That's all Durav. As for the explosion at Icarus ... he *did* tell me that she was under your protection, but he also said that the information inside that second chamber could expose our mission. So my priority had to be destroying it."

"Which still doesn't make sense to me," Drex said. "I mean, yes, the symbols were clearly some ancient variant of Ufretan script, but we're the only ones who would know that, right? Anyone else would assume they were Martian. And there were plenty of symbols on the outer chamber, which everyone had *already* seen..."

"If you want the answers to those questions, you'll have to ask Durav." Stasia's tone made it clear that she and Drex had been through all this before. "All he told me was that failing to destroy the chamber could put the entire Watch at risk."

Now Anak wished the light inside the car was *on*, because it might have given him some other clues. Durav had clearly expected that the team Claire was on would find something incriminating inside the chamber. But these two? From everything they'd said so far, it didn't sound like either of them knew about the Eberin Das journal.

He turned toward Stasia. "So Durav tells you to blow up the chamber and you just happen to have a bomb lying around?"

"No, Anak. Some of the mercenaries Durav hired to replace his dwindling supply of *ipret-tai* have connections on Mars. He had one of them deliver the bomb to me before I left Nepenthes Station. And I swear to you ... we really did try to keep casualties to a minimum. Pax and Meadow were supposed to have the bomb go off in the early morning, but they were late arriving at Clark Crater and before they could finish setting everything up, the mining crews were already heading up to start work for the day. So they changed it so that the bomb would go off at ten minutes after noon, *after* the lunch whistle, when everyone would have been down on the crater floor. But that Kimura guy moved the bag early. No one told us there was a motion trigger after the bomb was set. So we wound up with multiple casualties and barely a dent in the chamber. Durav was already furious at me after Shepherd survived the drone attack. In the end, I just couldn't go through with it, so I expelled most of the neurotoxin beforehand. And it *still* nearly killed the man."

This part, at least, tracked closely with the story that Claire had told him and Joe about the attack during the debate. The doctor on the *Ares Prime* had said the amount of neurotoxin in the drone should have killed Shepherd instantly.

"I knew Durav would be doubly furious if I screwed up a second time," Stasia added. "But if he wanted an assassin, he should have assigned one of his *ipret-tai* goons. Or one of his human guards."

"Or Maela," Drex said darkly. "Pretty sure it wouldn't be the first time she's killed for Durav."

Anak steered them back on topic. "You still haven't answered my question, Drex."

She drummed her fingers against the empty seat to her left. He could feel her eyes on him as if she was trying to decide how much to tell him. Finally, she sighed. "I left the Watch because I learned that the Triad has been lying to us about our mission. Which I believe you already suspect, since Claire Echols has a copy of Shepherd's memoir. Stasia left because I finally managed to persuade her that—contrary to Durav's claims—I had not lost my mind while investigating the Flock and am, in fact, telling the truth."

Based on what Stasia had said a few minutes back, he thought she might have had another strong motivation. Yes, she and Drex had been close at the Academy, but it seemed at least as likely that Stasia was seeking asylum with the Flock because she was scared of how Durav might react to her repeated failure to carry out his orders. Durav didn't have as much latitude over members of the Watch as he had over his *ipret-tai*. If one of *them* failed him in any way, they generally didn't get a second chance, let alone a third. But he could still have made Stasia's life very difficult until, and maybe even after, they returned to the Ufretan system.

"As for *why* I've taken over the Flock," Drex continued, "I needed an army. I'm hoping they can help buy us some time. Durav tried to block me by funding another faction against Shepherd. Pax and Meadow, the two people who worked with Stasia in setting the bomb at Icarus were part of that group, although like Stasia here, they seem to have seen the light."

Stasia tapped her armscreen, ostensibly to check the time, but probably to change the subject as well. "I don't understand why Reese would send you out without letting you know the location," she said.

"Maybe because he couldn't talk freely. Maela was on the bench right across from us during the *djvari* tournament. And she was acting weird the entire time."

Stasia made a dismissive noise.

"Okay," he amended. "Weirder than usual. She brought a human into HQ. I'm almost certain they were tailing me when I left the helipad at Van Courtlandt. And then the guy strolled right through the foyer like he owned the place, before joining Durav in the library."

"Must be one of the mercenaries," Drex said. "It *is* a bit strange that he'd allow them to hang around during Conclave, though. And you're *sure* Reese didn't mention a location?"

"I'm sure. He didn't say anything that…" Anak stopped, thinking back to Reese's words before he left the Great Hall. "Except … he did say I'd need to get moving if I was going to make it all the way over to Lavender House. Which is odd, come to think of it, because I only learned I'd been reassigned when I arrived. And I don't remember mentioning it to him."

"What the hell is Lavender House?" Drex asked.

"That's exactly what I asked the *ipret-tai*."

"Unless…" Stasia began and then trailed off, thinking. "Could it be the older house, the one that the cult built at the top of the hill? Djasa lived up there for a bit right after the move from Houston. She thought it would be nice to have some space and privacy when she was here. But she moved down to Blue House after only a few weeks. She said the other place creeped her out. One of the Ufretis told me Sandjeel was annoyed because he had to stay hidden in his quarters for a full week so they could bring a work crew back in to dig another tunnel … after they'd already gone to a lot of expense to burrow all the way across the property."

From everything Anak had seen and heard, Sandjeel spent most of his time in his quarters anyway. It had been true when they were in Houston and even more true since the move to New York. He presided over the general meeting and attended the formal dinner, but otherwise he hid out in the sub-subbasement and left the work of running the Triad to the other two members.

Everyone pretended it was a comfort issue, and Sandjeel *did* overheat easily, but Anak had long suspected that the man suffered from depression. To be fair, being stuck underground for over a century would put anyone in a blue funk. There were, at most, three months out of the year when Sandjeel was comfortable outside, and then, only in the evenings. He couldn't venture beyond the walled-in areas of the grounds without the risk of someone claiming they'd spotted a sasquatch in the Bronx. But from what Anak remembered, Sandjeel's personality had been very much the same when he dropped in on their classes at the Academy. Then again, he'd known their true mission all along.

He pushed those thoughts aside and focused on the key question. "Does the older house have lavender trim?"

"I have no clue," Stasia said. "I'm mostly worried about the fact that it's on Triad land. Arbet can't seriously expect us to just waltz up to the front door."

It was a valid point. There were only two ways that he knew of to reach that house—through the tunnels or by foot on a road that went past the other houses and then narrowed into a winding path up the hill. Either way, it would mean spending quite a bit of time on Triad property.

"Pull up a map," Drex told her. "Maybe we can find a back route. I have no desire to be tranqed and hauled in front of Durav for questioning."

Or worse, Anak thought, remembering the headless groundhog.

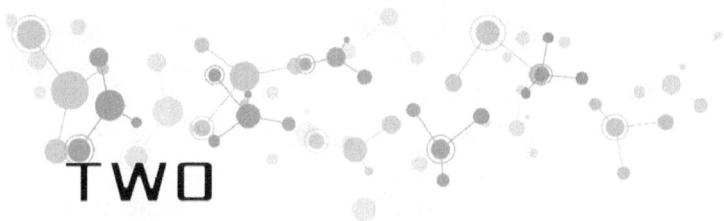

TWO

THEY LEFT the car at the curb on Delafield and began hiking up the hill along 253rd Street, following the map on Stasia's phone. Anak was unarmed. Drex carried a small handgun, and Stasia had a drone jammer, although he had serious doubts about its ability to bring down the sentry drones used by the Triad.

Stasia checked the map again. "Damn it. We should have been there five minutes ago."

There was a decided hint of accusation in her tone, and it seemed to be directed at him. "Hey, it's not my fault. I didn't know about any of this until half an hour ago."

"And *that's* not *our* fault," Drex said. "We've been trying to reach you for several days. I left a message for you at work, since I didn't have your personal contact information. Reese said you slept at the lab most of the time, anyway. But you never responded."

"I was..." Anak caught himself just short of saying *in Maine.* "Away. I took a few days off. I've been trying to get up with you, too. The guy I hired tracked you to your hotel this morning, but—"

"See?" Stasia gave Drex an *I-told-you-so* look. "Someone *was* following us."

"Anyway," Drex said, ignoring her, "when we couldn't reach you, we set this up with Reese. If it feels like we're winging it, that's because we are."

"Then maybe you should have planned this meeting the *last* time you talked to Arbet."

"What?" Drex stopped and turned back to stare at him.

"This is the first time I've met with her in years. My only other communication with her has been through vague notes that I had Flock members bribe delivery trucks to slip in with the weekly groceries. It was a risk, but Arbet's female *ipret-tai* is the one who handles most of those chores."

"So ... if you haven't actually spoken to Arbet about any of this, how can you be sure she's not going to turn you in?"

Personally, Anak didn't think there was a chance in hell that Arbet would do that. But Drex didn't know her as well as he did, and he wanted to hear her reasoning.

"Turn us in to Durav?" Drex snorted. "Not bloody likely. She hates him."

This was true. To be fair, most of the non-Ufretis in the Watch hated Durav, but Arbet's loathing of the man had been apparent even before she took the open seat on the Triad.

"And," Drex continued, "because she's the *reason* I was assigned to the Flock. The only reason I was able to piece all of this together. I didn't understand some of the argument between her and Durav over the issue at the time, but Maela tagging along was entirely his idea. He wanted someone who would report back to *him*, rather than to Arbet. And we weren't the first. Housen spent several cycles with the Flock before we were assigned. Durav seemed to think that Housen had kept him out of the loop or maybe just flat-out lied to him."

It was a reasonable assumption. After what the guards had done to the man's girlfriend back in Texas, Housen didn't have much incentive to be loyal to Durav.

"Anyway, between the time Housen was with the Flock and the time Maela and I took over, the group mushroomed from a few hundred people here in the States to more than ten thousand scattered across the planet. By then, they were too big to simply erase. It would no longer be an easy matter like Heaven's Gate. More like a dozen Jonestowns."

"Jonestown?" Stasia gave her an incredulous look. "That was thousands of people. You don't actually think Durav..."

"No," Drex said. "I was just using it as a size comparison. My point is that the Flock had gotten too big to kill off by the time we took over."

"So Housen is working with you, too?" Anak asked.

Drex shook her head. "Not … officially. He's been on sabbatical. But I'm confident we can count him as an ally. Housen hates Durav more than any of us … and I think those feelings may extend to the entire Alliance. If they don't now, they will soon. A few years ago after Conclave, he told me he wasn't in any hurry for Earth to meet the milestones because he didn't want to go home. He was planning to apply to be a liaison or an ambassador to Earth or something. That's one reason I put off getting in touch with him. He's not going to take the news well."

"True," he said, although something about her words struck a false note. It was nothing he could pin down, though. If he'd been asked to guess which Watcher might defect, Housen would have topped the list. Drex had just confirmed those suspicions, so it couldn't be that she was trying to protect the guy by distancing him from the Flock. Or at least, if that was her goal, she was doing a poor job of it.

A few minutes later, they veered off into a patch of woods that, according to the map, would take them into the backyard of the house. Traffic noises faded as they walked, giving way to a raucous chorus of katydids and the occasional mosquito buzzing past his ear. Eventually, they came to an overgrown fir hedge. Anak poked around a bit until he found a thin spot between the branches and then pushed through to the other side.

The ornate wooden gazebo a few meters ahead seemed on the verge of crumbling beneath a collection of spiderwebs that stretched between the latticework. It had probably been a nice spot back when the cult leader built the house, perhaps thinking that they could join Jesus there for a glass of water-turned-to-wine and enjoy the contrast of their bucolic surroundings against the distant backdrop of New York. While you could still see the city lights, most of the woods were gone now, with the valley below carved into carefully manicured lawns like the ones surrounding HQ and the other Triad houses at the base of the hill.

No drones greeted them, but Anak's scalp still tingled as the three of them continued on to the darkened house at the top of the hill. He scanned the trees around them for any blips of light. They hadn't spoken since they entered the property, but they were still making plenty of noise between their feet crunching against years of accumulated leaves and small branches, and the occasional muttered curse when they tripped on fragments of the old stone path beneath the debris.

The house itself appeared to be in surprisingly good condition. The *ipret-tai* may not have bothered with keeping up the grounds, but they must have been tasked with at least basic maintenance of the building. It was too dark to make out the color of the trim, but it *might* be lavender. A raised patio, complete with assorted lawn furniture, spanned the rear of the property. Behind that, the faint ambient light of the city reflected off the curved glass walls of a large sunroom, although he suspected that anyone who ever lived in a place this opulent would have called it *the conservatory*.

As they stepped onto the patio, Anak picked up the first hint of light from inside the house. Not from the sunroom itself, but a pale glow that probably came from several rooms back. He was about to point it out to Drex and Stasia when a rustling from the left of the patio caused all three of them to jump in unison. Drex raised the pistol and aimed it toward the sound.

"You can lower the gun, Drex," Arbet said in Ufretan as she stepped out of the shadows. "Most of Durav's guards are off on one of his outside projects. Only one of them is on the grounds tonight and I arranged a distraction for him."

"What about the drones and surveillance cameras?" Anak asked.

"The security cameras are transmitting info recorded a few days back and the perimeter shield is off. Our drones only circle by for about five minutes each hour up here, given that the house is empty. Their next patrol is at twelve after nine. That doesn't give us much time to talk, but it's the best my *ufrenai* could manage."

The word *ufrenai* took Anak by surprise. The literal translation was *people of my house,* but the root word was *ufrete,* so it conveyed a deeper sense of connection. You wouldn't call roommates or employees *ufrenai.* So, who exactly did she mean? Her *ipret-tai* seemed the most likely and maybe even the only candidates, but he'd never heard any member of the Triad—or for that matter, any instructor at the Academy—refer to them that way. It was always *my ipret-tai,* or even more often, *my ipps.*

"I'm afraid I don't even have that long," he told her, pushing his other questions aside for the moment. "Dinner at HQ is at eight."

"Reese is covering for you. He's going to say that you *claimed* to have a headache, but he thinks you're probably just hiding out after your disastrous performance at *djvari* this afternoon. And if you're worried about Durav, he's hosting the Ufretis at Gray House tonight. I doubt he'll realize you're not at HQ and if he does, I'll handle it. Dora left your bag at my house. I'm hosting two other members of the Watch, so we'll take the tunnel back when we're done here. Drex, I'd love to say that you and Stasia are welcome to stay *here* for the night, but I think it best if you are on the other side of those fir trees when the drones make their nine o'clock rounds." She slapped at something on her bare upper arm. "Let's move inside before we're eaten alive. They apparently don't bother with insect control on this part of the grounds."

The sunroom felt much smaller than it had looked from outside. It was crammed so tightly with marble statues and potted trees that Anak barked his shin against one of the many pieces of furniture as they wound their way through the darkened room. His shirt was now mostly dry, but the fabric felt stiff against his back as he bent down to rub his injured leg.

"Sorry about that," Arbet said. "The lights here are on a timer, just like the other unoccupied houses are when Conclave isn't in session. I doubt any security alarms would go off down at HQ if a light went on out of sequence, but I'd rather play it safe and stick to the usual schedule."

She led them through a door on the left side of the sunroom into an area with a massive mahogany bar, matching walls, and a gold leaf ceiling. An ornate mirror behind the bar reflected light from a dining room on the other side of the foyer.

The *ipret-tai* who had passed Anak the note earlier stood in the corner of the dining room. As they entered, she popped a square of chocolate into her mouth. Trays of sandwiches and fruit were arranged at one end of a long wooden table, along with a pitcher of lemonade and a small plate of the chocolates. A fireplace with a couch and several upholstered chairs sat on the opposite side of the room.

"We'll have lights here for the next hour and twenty minutes, give or take," Arbet said as they entered. "Thank you for setting everything up, Dora. Once you've taken food out to Dave and Denny, you should head back home and make sure everything is arranged for tonight's guests."

Dora gave Arbet a quick nod and then slipped through a door at the back.

After taking a seat at the table next to Stasia, Drex cast a cautious glance around the room. "You're certain that we're okay to talk here?"

"As certain as I can be. David swept the place twice for listening devices, and he has the same security training as Durav's guards, so he should have picked up any oddities. And I've used this building a few times in the past for conversations with them that I'd prefer to keep private. So far, it seems safe."

Anak wondered why conversations with her *ipret-tai* would

need to be kept private. But she was still talking, so he filed the question away for a later time.

"Either way," she said, "it's safer than phone or messaging would be. Durav screens everything going in or out. And this is really our only face-to-face option since I can't leave the grounds without clearing it well in advance." She tapped her left wrist.

He'd initially thought the pattern on her arm was a bracelet, but he could now see that it was a tattoo.

"Is that a tracking device?" Stasia asked.

"In part. Its primary purpose, however, is to make me feel like my arm is on fire if I leave the premises without it being deactivated. And it's a lot harder to remove than your subcutaneous trackers were. I still have that one, too." She gave Anak a sympathetic smile and pulled back her hair, then ran her finger across a slightly raised area on the back of her neck, near her hairline. "They're all just to the right of the spine. If we decide to take any ... subversive actions, you'll need to ditch yours pretty quickly after you leave Conclave."

"So you're saying we've all had these, from the beginning? And you've been logging our movements the entire time? Even on sabbatical?" It probably wasn't fair to lump her with Sandjeel and Durav. She hadn't been complicit in this from the beginning. But he was angry.

"I wouldn't say *logging*. It's more ad hoc. In case of emergencies, if one of you is killed or hospitalized, the Triad can pull up your exact location."

"Or in case one of us decides to defect," Drex added. "I can remove it for you once you leave the grounds. It's pretty close to the surface. And apparently, we should be grateful that it doesn't double as a punishment device."

He gave them a little nod of admission. "I knew they changed the rules so that Triad members weren't allowed to travel out of the city, but I had no idea you were restricted to the grounds."

Arbet pressed her lips into a thin smile. "Oh, the restrictions are exclusively for me. Durav comes and goes entirely as he pleases. He's often away for weeks at a time. And I *do* get to leave occasionally. I even made it over to Long Island for an afternoon at the beach this summer. But I'm required to have an escort any time the tattoo is deactivated, and Durav insists that the escort can't be one of *my* people. That leaves him or Maela or one of his guards … and frankly, their company pretty much ruins any outing." She gestured to the food. "Given that our time is short, we'll need to make this a working dinner. Go ahead and grab a sandwich. I ate earlier, so I'll talk first."

She caught Anak's gaze for a moment when the others turned toward the trays of food. Her eyes flashed briefly, an expression he interpreted as asking whether he'd gotten her note. Or maybe she was asking whether he trusted her. Either way, he supposed the answer was *yes*, so he gave her a quick nod. He didn't have much appetite, but he added an apple and half of a turkey sandwich to his plate and poured himself a glass of lemonade.

"Okay," Arbet began. "I'm going to assume that all of you are aware that our mission here is something very different from what we were told when we signed up for the Watch. I can't imagine that any of you would be here if that weren't the case. We could trade stories about how we came by this knowledge, but maybe we should save that for another time. What you may not know is that the Triad will vote tomorrow on whether to call the colonization milestone. I'm planning to vote no, but I already know that I will lose."

THREE

EVEN THOUGH ANAK had already heard this bit of news, his stomach clenched at having it confirmed. Judging from Stasia and Drex's expressions, they felt the same.

"Yeah," he said. "Graf mentioned that on the way in this afternoon. Doesn't it seem a bit premature to you? KTI hasn't even finished with Mars. The last report Stasia made indicated that it would be another three or four cycles. Maybe even longer."

Arbet tilted her head slightly in acknowledgement. "That's one reason among many that I'm voting no. But I *do* understand why, based on the previous reports, Durav and Sandjeel both believe it's inevitable. And Kolya's penchant for secrecy means that it could take years to get someone else into a high enough position at the company to keep us updated. Taking all of that into consideration, they see no alternative but to call the milestone early."

Drex exchanged a look with Stasia and then started to speak but Anak jumped in first. "That's only *one* milestone, though. The Triad can't send the signal until *both* are completed."

Arbet's expression was wary. "Yes, but—"

"Then we're fine," he said. "Jonas Labs is *at least* a full cycle away from completion. Probably two. Maybe even as many as three. Any rumors that Durav has been spreading to the contrary are from the smoke Kai has been blowing to appease her stockholders after the concessions she made during the initial rollout of the drug. The greedy bastards stand to make a massive profit on their investment, probably far greater than any of them ever dreamed, but they can't get past the fact that it could have been *more*. That's what I told Durav when he cornered me in the elevator and what I've told anyone and everyone who asked since I arrived at Conclave."

"And that's what you should *keep* telling them," Arbet said. "But Durav has other sources inside Jonas Labs. At KTI, as well. They're not Watchers and obviously not as well positioned as you are currently, Anak, but ... you can always get people to feed you information if you're willing to pay for it. So Durav *will* challenge you at the assembly tomorrow. He's convinced that you've learned the truth about our mission and believes that gives you reason to submit a false report. Triad guidelines urge us to push for consensus, but that's little more than a polite fiction. So unless you can lie more convincingly than you did just now, I believe Sandjeel will join Durav in calling *both* milestones early."

"As I was *trying* to say a moment ago," Drex said with an annoyed look in Anak's direction, "they're about to get confirmation of their decision on the colonization front. Kolya plans to announce his new initiative for terraforming exoplanets tomorrow night at Beekman Place, during a dinner for the Ares Consortium. They've had a list of viable planets for some time now, all of which are considerably more conducive to human life than Mars was. None of the worlds on that list will require the early stages like building an atmosphere or perchlorate remediation. He originally planned to wait until the Mars project was in its final stages, but when I dropped in on him yesterday, he told me that he's changed his mind."

"Did he tell you why?" Anak asked.

"No. But he did mention that the cost is minimal enough that he could easily fund it himself if he can't get investors. They'll basically be aiming packets of the recombinant biobots in the direction of these viable worlds and then waiting for signs that they've taken root. He also mentioned something about synergy. And having heard rumors about a new breakthrough at Jonas Labs, I assumed ..." She shrugged.

Anak ignored the inherent question in her last sentence and asked more of his own. "How did you just *drop in* on Kolya? With everything that's happened recently? How did the head of the Flock get past security at Beekman Place?"

"It was surprisingly easy. I knew Kolya was there, so I simply handed myself over to the first security guard I found and asked to see my ex-husband."

"That seems rather risky," Arbet said. "How did you know they wouldn't turn you in to the authorities? I mean, the *real* authorities. Your face—both of your faces—have been all over the news."

Stasia chuckled darkly. "You clearly don't know Anton Kolya. No one in his employ—not even Macek, who has been with the man for decades—would risk Anton finding out that they'd called the police on someone he cares about."

"Exactly," Drex said. "And this wasn't the only time I've visited him recently. Before Kolya left for Mars, I went to Minsk and begged him to cancel stage six of the terraforming. That first trip was obviously less risky, though, since it was before Anak's friend Claire outed me as the new leader of the Flock."

He debated correcting her, but she probably wouldn't see much difference in Claire having written the story and her having simply confirmed Wyatt's suspicions. "Given that we all watched the planet turn green a few months back," he said, "I assume you had no luck convincing him?"

"I did not. Which is why I decided that I had no choice but to put all of my cards on the table this time. I told him everything about our mission. Even offered to let me test my DNA, since the genetic alterations to this body would at least prove I was telling the truth about *something*. All I got from him was an agreement to let me leave the building instead of having Macek confine me in one of the hotel rooms until he could get me the psychological help that he thinks I need. So, no. I haven't convinced him *yet*. But I can. *We* can. We just need more time."

Arbet bit her lower lip and Anak had a flashback to their

stasis environment, watching her plan her next move on the *padjit* board. Those lips had been thinner and darker, set in a very different face, but the contemplative expression was the same.

"Reese and I didn't have much time to talk," she said after a moment. "He flashed me a look at this app that he apparently believes will keep anyone from overhearing our conversation, but he's underestimating Durav. I stopped him before he said anything too damning, but from what I gathered, you have a plan to buy this extra time you need?"

"We do," Drex said. "The most important work on Kolya's extraterrestrial projects is under the leadership of Davina Monroe at Nepenthes Station on Mars. We've gained access to KTI's data storage system for the project, so we should be able to destroy their backups, and I have a team nearby ready to hit her lab late tomorrow. The question now is whether Anak can do something similar at Jonas Labs."

He gave her a perplexed look. "When you say you have people ready to *hit the lab* at Nepenthes, you mean they're going to blow it up, right?"

Drex nodded. "We'd hoped to carry all of this out after the stage six lockdown was complete, since there would be less risk of unintended casualties. But given Anton's change of plans, we can't afford to wait."

"Well, I obviously don't have a munitions expert on call and wouldn't be inclined to blow the place up, even if I did. People *live* there, for God's sake. People with families. But I *do* have full access to Joe's current research and backups. So, yes, I could engineer a delay. Set things back at least six months, maybe as much as a year. I'd need to zap everything at once, though—the data on the lab computers at the same time as the off-campus backups—because he'll get a notification that the files have been changed. And he's absolutely going to know I'm the one who did it, but at this point..." He shrugged. "What I don't under-stand is why you also need a physical attack on the Nepenthes lab if you can wipe Monroe's data. Isn't that enough to slow things down? You could still deliver a substantial blow without worrying about these *unintended casualties*."

Anak shot a look at Stasia with the last two words. Claire had been on the casualty list—very nearly on the *fatality* list— the last time her people started blowing things up.

"It really isn't enough," Stasia said, after another of her silent, cryptic exchanges with Drex, which included the same *I-told-you-so* expression as earlier, so they must have anticipated that this would be his reaction. "Even at Jonas Labs, your research isn't entirely *in silico*, but that's even more true at Davy's lab. Her research is in the DNA hopping around in her test domes or hatching out in incubators. We won't get a second chance, so we need to put *everything* on pause long enough for us to reason with Kolya."

"And you really think blowing up his buildings—and quite possibly people—is going to help sway him?" Arbet asked Stasia.

Drex answered instead. "It will get his attention. It will buy us time. That's the important thing. And you need to remember … it isn't about money or power for Anton. He is an idealist at heart. This is about his *legacy*."

"She's right," Stasia said. "He wants to be remembered as the great visionary who ensured that humanity would survive for many millennia to come. If we can show him that his plans will actually do the exact opposite, he *will* stop."

Arbet turned to Anak. "What about Kai Jonas?"

He was quiet for a moment. "If you're asking whether she's an idealist, absolutely not. But I'm baffled as to why that matters. Even the most hardheaded, hardhearted realist would halt a project if they truly believed it would lead to the actual destruction of their own planet." He stopped and reconsidered. "Okay, I mean, that's obviously *not* the case when the destruction comes on gradually and from many directions. But an imminent threat that can be pinned to two very specific causes?

No rational actor would ignore that. The trick is going to be *convincing* them that the threat is real. And while I have no sway with Kai, I think I can get Joe to listen."

Personally, he thought it would be a lot easier to do without losing the man's trust by wiping out nearly a year's worth of research. Hopefully, he'd have Claire's help in persuading him. She was already piecing together bits of the puzzle on her own. And Joe was primed for the news to some extent since he knew about the Eberin Das journal—which Anak still couldn't quite bring himself to mention in front of Drex and Stasia, given Arbet's earlier caution to *trust no one.*

"Joe is the best person, maybe even the only person who stands a chance of convincing Kai," he continued. "But I could easily see her discounting any evidence we put before her as fabricated. And she's definitely not above handing off her son's research to a scientist with fewer scruples. I may not know Anton Kolya personally, but I would be shocked if he's not equally skeptical."

"That's why we need *time*." Drex shifted her gaze to Arbet. "I thought we'd have at *least* another cycle. But if they're really planning to call this before the comms window closes, that only gives us a few months to convince both Kolya and Kai Jonas. Stasia and I obviously can't risk going to the assembly in person. Which is why we need you to arrange a call with Sandjeel beforehand. Convince him to at least hear us out."

"And if he says no?" Arbet asked.

"My plan is to move forward either way with the attack against KTI," Drex said. "I've set things in motion that would be difficult to stop at this point. And maybe Sandjeel will change his mind by the time the communications window opens if we can make at least some progress."

Arbet glanced at Anak then, a question in her eyes.

"I agree. If he says no, we really don't have anything to lose by making a last ditch attempt. If I leave right after the assembly, I should be back at the lab in time to take care of everything tomorrow evening."

"Okay, then," Arbet said. "I'll try to arrange a meeting first thing in the morning. It probably won't be with Sandjeel alone, however. Durav *will* find out, which means Sandjeel will almost certainly insist on including him from the beginning." Her mouth twisted in a sour smile. "Perhaps we'll discover that there are better angels in his nature after all."

They finalized plans for the call and Drex asked for Anak's number so that she could let him know the exact time of the planned attack at Nepenthes Station. He wasn't sure that it was all that important that they sync things up given that the two attacks were happening more than two hundred million kilometers apart, but he gave her his number. Then Arbet walked Drex and Stasia back to the sunroom. Anak stood to follow them, but Arbet motioned for him to stay. He did as she asked for about thirty seconds, but that left him feeling a bit too much like a well-trained dog, so he cleared the table, including his own barely touched plate, and moved over to the sofa.

Arbet returned about ten minutes later carrying a tray with a flask of *evir* and two glasses. "Sorry I took so long. I had to find Dora so that she could deliver the message to Sandjeel about tomorrow's meeting." She poured a hefty shot for each of them. Then she kicked off her sandals and sat at the other end of the sofa with her now bare feet tucked under her skirt. "So," she asked with a wry smile, "how have *you* been for the past twelve cycles?"

He gave a short laugh, then knocked back half of the *evir*. "I was doing quite well until a few weeks ago when I began to suspect that my entire existence is a lie."

"Ah. So ... you're pretty much where *I* was the last time that we had a real conversation. I'm glad you remembered enough Gaelic to translate my note."

"Me, too. Did the *trust no one* part include Drex and Stasia?"

She considered her answer for a moment, tilting her drink to one side as she watched the pale yellow liquid swirl inside the curved glass. "I trust *Drex*. If I didn't, I wouldn't have assigned her to monitor the Flock. I'm less sure about Stasia. She's always seemed a bit more … malleable. More inclined to follow directives from Durav without question. I still think there's a chance she's reporting back to him. Not that it really matters at this point."

"It's possible. But Stasia was ordered to kill Tobias Shepherd, and she's apparently the reason he's still alive."

At Arbet's look of surprise, he told her about Stasia's reported sabotage of the drone.

"Then Durav must have someone else inside the Flock who's reporting back to him," she said. "Sandjeel says that he's been following Drex's movements for months now, even though she and Stasia both ditched their trackers long ago."

"So he knows the two of them are here?"

"Almost certainly. He probably even knows Reese is working with them. And I'd say there's a better than even chance that he knows I'm up here with you. He may even know the details of Drex's plan. He just doesn't see it as a threat."

"Do you think her plan will work?"

"I doubt it. It's worth trying, though. And either way, it's better than the last-ditch effort that I was contemplating."

"And what was that?"

"Killing Durav."

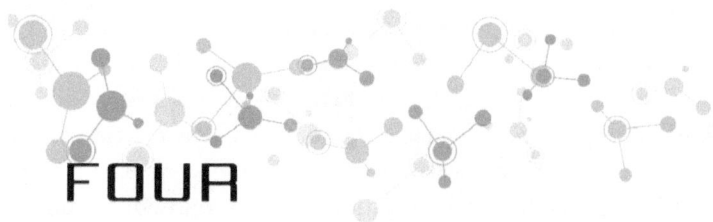

FOUR

FOR A MOMENT, Anak thought she was joking. Arbet's slightly twisted sense of humor was one of the things he had always liked best about her. But her expression right now was much the same as it had been right after she told him that Watchers were like midwives—her chin tilted slightly upward, one eyebrow lifted, almost as if she were daring him to laugh.

Nope. She was completely serious. Which had him wondering whether she might not have other, more personal reasons for wanting Durav dead.

He pushed that thought aside and focused on the merits of the proposition. If you left aside the fact that they were talking about murder, it wasn't a *bad* idea. Sure, Sandjeel would promote someone else to the Triad, but whoever took the job would be an improvement. Maela was the only Watcher he could think of who was anywhere near as odious as Durav, and she was almost at the bottom of the seniority list.

"I reasoned that if Durav were no longer in the picture, I could draw things out for at least a few more decades." Arbet grimaced, then took a sip of her drink, as if washing a foul taste out of her mouth. "He's like one of those cartoon devils, constantly whispering in Sandjeel's ear. *Why postpone the inevitable, old man? Aren't you ready for it all to be over?* I very nearly set my plan in motion last year, but he must have gotten wind of it because he abruptly left town. When he came back a few weeks later, he had those four mercenaries in tow. I think he may have hired a few others, too, because we've had visitors. Those four, though, seem to be permanent fixtures. They live with him over at Gray House, and one or two are almost always with him these days, especially Jason Boudreaux. You probably saw him today. He was skulking about HQ with Durav earlier."

"Yeah. I think he and Maela followed me from the helipad. How can hiring them…" He'd been about to ask *how can hiring them be legal,* but *legal* wasn't really the right word. There were definitely guidelines that the Triad was supposed to follow. Traditions that spanned several alliances, some of them going all the way back to the beginning. But with only a few exceptions, the Triad set their own rules of operation while on the planets they were surveying. So, he rephrased. "Why would Sandjeel allow Durav to bring in outsiders? It seems like that would compromise the security of the entire Watch."

"Durav *claims* they know nothing about the mission or our origins. They're just hired security, which he says were necessary to replace the *flawed ipret-tai* he was assigned." She hooked her fingers into air-quotes on the word *flawed.* They both knew the only flaw in any of the *ipret-tai* he'd killed was failing to get out of Durav's way when he was in one of his violent moods. "The man is bored. I think he's always viewed this assignment as a break from … I don't know. Laws? Morality? He's nearly out of *ipret-tai* to abuse and he can't risk drawing attention by venting his temper on the Earthers."

"True. I wouldn't be surprised to learn there was a string of unsolved murders in his neighborhood on Ufretas Prime."

"Me, either," she said, "And despite all of that, I'm not entirely sure I could have gone through with killing the bastard even if he hadn't upped his security. It would have put Dora at serious risk. I've been told that he makes one of his remaining *ipret-tai* sample his food now, so I'd need to come up with a new gameplan. And given recent events, our time is apparently limited. I guess it wasn't an entire loss, though. Planning that man's demise was the second most satisfying thing I've done during my time on the Triad."

"And what was the first?"

"Tweaking our last nine progress reports to the Alliance. Not *much,*" she added, clearly not wanting him to get his hopes up. "I had to keep it subtle enough that Durav wouldn't catch on. Which wasn't difficult, given that he generally just signed off on the reports. He's really not one to focus on the technical details."

Anak nodded. Durav's job within the Triad was security for the Watch. Well, security *and* logistics, technically, but aside from weighing in on assignments, he'd always handed off the actual work involved in getting Watchers placed at the various universities and businesses to Djasa, Uden, and then eventually, to Arbet. He'd never actually worked in any of the scientific fields involved in achieving the two milestones. It would have been easy enough for Arbet to downplay progress without raising alarms.

"But what about Sandjeel?" he asked, because Sandjeel should definitely have caught any changes she made. This wasn't, as they say, his first rodeo. One of the criteria for leading the Triad was previous service as a Watcher. Sandjeel had worked on the colonization milestone in that earlier post and had even taught a few seminar sessions during their last term at the Academy.

"If Sandjeel noticed I changed anything, he didn't mention it. More to the point, he didn't stop me."

"So you think he's an ally?"

She thought for a long moment. "I wouldn't say he's *eager* to see this planet destroyed, but ... he's also not convinced that it's worth saving."

Anak shook his head, frustrated. "The man has barely *seen* any of the planet. He sure as hell hasn't interacted with Earthers."

"Precisely. If you ask Sandjeel, though, he'd tell you he understands Earthers very well. After all, he's spent the past hundred and thirty years accumulating information through television, talk radio, and eventually the internet. These days, he's more into immersive experiences. He goes through phases.

From what Helen has told Dora, his latest obsession is fairly benign. Some animated game where he plays a warrior cat— and no, I don't want to hear any jokes about him embracing his furry side. Before that, though, it was an interactive reality group like that old show where they kicked you off the island. There was some murder VR where you never knew if you'd be playing the detective, the killer, or the victim until you were immersed in the game. Reenactments of famous battles and true crime, even though he knows damn well that most of those programs are ninety-percent fiction. So, yeah. Even though he's been cloistered away in his subterranean quarters since we arrived on planet, he considers himself an expert. And if all of *your* perceptions about Earthers were gleaned from his sources, I suspect you'd also hold them in fairly low esteem."

"I take it you've pointed out that he's drawing his inferences from a toxic information pool?"

"Yes. He disagrees. He says he sees them without their masks. And I don't know. Sometimes I think he's right. Either way, his views on Earthers are *not* the only…"

Arbet fell silent for a long moment, her eyes still aimed in his direction but staring through him, as the wheels turned inside her head. For the first time, he realized how similar her conversational style was to Joe's, filled with these extended pauses for reflection. Maybe that was why he'd grown attached to him so quickly. They'd slipped into a comfortable working rhythm almost from the beginning.

"I think the best thing at this point," Arbet continued, "might be for you to tell me what you know."

"Sure," he said, although he thought they'd established that fairly well at the beginning of the conversation. "I know that we're not here as an advance guard for diplomats who will welcome Earth into the Alliance. If Durav and Sandjeel actually use the beacon during this comms window, a ship will retrieve us and then they'll send in the military. Or more likely, they'll send in drone explosives like the ones they used to destroy that planet in the neutral zone a few cycles before we left. I'm now thinking the rumors that it wasn't a Hodjeri military outpost may have been true. And it's odd how little our weapons of mass destruction have changed over the eons, because judging from one of the entries in Eberin Das's journal, I believe it's the same type of weapon we used to wipe out Mars."

Arbet's eyes widened. "Not *exactly* the same, but yes, very similar. And I guess Durav was right. Your Claire did find something inside that chamber."

Your Claire. She seemed to have made the same assumption that Stasia and Drex did. And as tempted as he was to analyze her tone for hints of jealousy, he needed to focus.

"Yes. I didn't mention the journal to the others, but Eberin Das was a Watcher assigned to Mars. Probably during the Second Alliance. He inspired the locals to start a rebellion. I don't know if they buried him in the upper chamber or if it was just a memorial of some sort, but samples of bacteria were found in the chamber below, the one that Durav ordered Stasia to blow up. Claire brought samples back to Joe and we found that they had a document encoded in the DNA. The same was true for a few samples found on the surface during previous research trips, although they'd been seriously damaged by exposure to the blast. I've now translated enough of the journal to be reasonably sure that Eberin's Guardians were not the good guys, and I must assume the same is true for our Watch."

"It was the late *First* Alliance," she told him. "When those initial images from the upper chamber appeared in the media, Sandjeel and I both recognized the symbols as ancient Ufretan. He told me then that there were stories of a failed rebellion on Mars prior to cleansing the planet." She made an apologetic face. "Sorry, that's *literally* what the military calls it. Thousands of armed Martian natives stormed the headquarters, apparently planning to take over the Triad. One version of history—the one Sandjeel was taught on Novera back in the day—says that they very nearly succeeded. The version he learned at the Academy, however, claims the rebellion was put down in a matter of hours."

Anak spent the next few minutes telling her what he'd learned from the journal. "So ... I think the truth is probably somewhere in the middle. Either way, we know they lost in the end."

"True. Why don't you forward me what you've got so far when we get back to Blue House? Or the entire file, for that matter. I can run it through our system here and get a more exact translation."

He agreed, feeling a bit guilty about Claire's archeolinguist friend at Columbia wasting her time on the project.

"Anyway," Arbet continued, "after Sandjeel told us the story, Durav was convinced that the chamber was an existential threat to the mission—*his* words. So he contacted someone on Mars that Jason knew and had them deliver the explosive device to Stasia."

He stared at her, open mouthed. "You *knew* about that in advance? What the fuck, Arbet? People died. *Claire* nearly died—"

"No," she said. "*No.* I learned about the bombing after the fact, although Durav was more than happy to take credit when I confronted him. I don't even think Sandjeel knew ahead of time. And I'm *certain* he didn't know Durav ordered Stasia to kill Shepherd. Sandjeel has his faults, but he's a stickler for adhering to Alliance laws and..." She shook her head, looking a bit baffled. "He's also extremely superstitious about violating final wishes. I mean, that's not uncommon among his genera-tion, at least on Novera. One of my grands is the same way. But it's almost like he thinks Uden would haunt him if he didn't respect the terms of the will. And, I don't know. Maybe he does think that. He definitely feels guilty about Uden's suicide and believes he might be alive if they'd broken the truth to him more gradually. He was a lot more cautious when he told me. And since I was restricted to the grounds," she added with a tight smile, "he was able to make sure that I didn't do anything drastic."

"Did you ... actually consider doing something drastic?"

She finished her *evir* and poured both of them another shot before speaking again. "I'm guessing you've read this memoir of Tobias Shepherd's?"

It seemed like an abrupt change of topic. But he could see why suicidal ideations might be a subject that she'd prefer to avoid, so he let it go.

"I have. Claire obtained an advance copy from Wyatt Garcia —her colleague at the *Post* and also her *amali-tai.*"

It probably wasn't the smoothest way of dropping that bit of info into the conversation. He wasn't even certain it was true at the moment, given that Claire and Wyatt seemed to be in a constant state of flux between friends and lovers. But he hadn't wanted to leave Arbet's misperception about his relationship with Claire unchallenged.

"Shepherd's memoir was the other thing that helped me piece all of this together," he added. "The old professor he described was obviously Uden, although I think some elements of the story were a bit off."

"Yes," she said. "The timing, for one thing. I don't know if he compressed the timeline for dramatic effect or if his child-hood memories are simply a bit shaky, but Sandjeel told me that Uden was here at HQ the day before he died."

"Did he and Sandjeel argue?"

She shook her head. "Not at all. Sandjeel said he was in a better frame of mind than usual. It had him hoping that Uden was finally adjusting to his new role. His new reality."

"How did you get a copy of Shepherd's memoir?"

"Durav. He had his people snag a few copies before they burned the rest of them."

"They burned the publishers, too, you know. An elderly couple in Virginia."

"No surprise, I guess. But still..." She winced.   "Do you

remember what Shepherd said about Uden's last words to him?"

"Yeah. He said Uden told him the Sentinels would rescue the faithful. Take them away on the mothership if they truly did their best to save Earth. But he also thought there was a good chance that Uden was lying."

"Exactly. He believed Uden was trying to give him a thread of hope. Something to hold onto. That section really hit home for me because I've often wondered the same thing about Sandjeel. When he contacted me after Uden's death, and told me the truth about the Watch, he also told me that a small but growing group within the Academy, in the Alliance Senate, and even some within the military have been pushing for a change in how we deal with emerging worlds. They argue it's hypocritical to punish these planets for the very same things that Alliance members did when we were at a similar stage of development. This view has had adherents since at least the Third Alliance, but it's gotten a major boost due to our war with the Hodjeri."

The Hodjeri system—five planets with a common star and a handful of nearby exoplanets—had once been part of the Alliance. At some point, they began to balk at the way common resources were being allocated and eventually refused to bear their assessed share of costs. Not long after that, they began trading with non-Alliance partners and eventually pulled those partners in as allies. That marked the end of the Fifth Alliance and the beginning of the Sixth, which no longer included the Hodjeri.

"Anyway," she continued, "Sandjeel told me that if we could delay long enough, he thought Earth would fall under a new set of rules. It wouldn't include admission into the Alliance. The military thinks this planet is too distant for that to be manageable. But he said we might be able to avoid total annihilation."

"Only … you said you think he was lying to you. Trying to keep a bit of hope alive."

"I *did* think that at first. But … we've had many conversations since then, especially after I got him addicted to *padjit*."

Anak felt a totally unreasonable twinge of jealousy at this revelation. Not because he thought there was anything physical going on between her and Sandjeel. He had a hard time even imagining that. And *padjit* was a Noveran game. Why wouldn't two Noverans play it together? It was just that he'd always thought of it as *their* game. He and Arbet had spent far, far more time together over that game board than they had in bed.

"But you said the game wasn't in the computer system."

"It's not. I had to make a special request for it to be included in my stasis environment, and even then, they didn't bother with the traditional symbols on the markers and along the edges of the board because they're in Noveran script rather than Ufretan. But … I had plenty of time on my hands once I was added to the Triad, so I carved a board and markers. I knew that Durav wouldn't have the patience for strategy games in general and he'd be even less likely to learn a Noveran game, so it gave me a few hours each week to talk to Sandjeel alone."

"I guess that's another reason Shepherd's memoir struck a chord with you. It's pretty much the same thing he did with Uden."

"Yes. And like Shepherd, I learned quite a bit during our games." She laughed softly. "Although I have to give him kudos. I've had decades to extract information from Sandjeel. He had only months with Uden. How much do you know about Sandjeel's background?"

"I know he served a lot of time in the military. He also served as a Watcher at some point, otherwise he wouldn't be head of the Triad. I'm guessing he's one of the oldest people in your *korban*. Pretty sure he's older than anyone in my own line. Aside from that…" He shrugged. "I've never had a real conversation with him beyond answering questions in seminar and, later, during Conclaves. And even then, he seems kind of like he's checked out. Phoning it in, as Earthers used to say. But who can blame him? It's not like he can get out and enjoy the sights. I'm guessing he's been ready to head home pretty much since we got here."

"He's been ready for it to be *over*, yes. Although I think that feeling comes and goes. But..." She finished off the second shot of *evir*, clearly trying to work up the nerve to say whatever came next. "Sandjeel is a voluntary terminal. He won't be going home. *None* of us are going home."

Anak didn't respond—*couldn't* respond—and after a moment, she continued.

"The Alliance will send an unmanned fleet. They'll set up in the formation that the military calls a *naidar bubble*, like the monster in those children's tales."

"Because it wraps around the planet."

"Yeah. Then they nuke the hell out of it. And you were right. The weapons probably aren't all that different from what they used to destroy Mars. Destruction is easy, after all. Give Earth another couple of centuries and they'll likely be able to do the same. The only part you got wrong is that they don't intend to retrieve the Watch first. From their point of view, there's no reason. Sandjeel doesn't want to be rescued, and it's not like we have any use for these bodies once we're home."

"But how will they sync up our conscious...ness..." He stopped, realizing that this answered something that had been nagging at him for days. "That's how they've kept all of this secret for so long. They simply revive Watchers with their previous memories. No, wait. That would lead to too many questions. I'm guessing they add a little something to fill in the blanks?"

She nodded. "The Academy has the information from each Watcher's *rezlat*, which means they've seen every message transmitted to and from family and friends since we arrived—those messages are heavily, heavily censored in both directions, by the way. Thanks to the reports we've submitted each cycle, they also know everywhere we traveled on sabbatical. Every job we held, everywhere we studied. That makes it pretty easy to implant some simulated memories. Sandjeel says they also add a strong suggestion to keep you from asking specific follow-up questions about the planet to which you were assigned. For example, he has fond memories of the world where he served as a Watcher near the end of the Fifth Alliance, but he can't tell you the *actual* name of that planet. If he hadn't later risen to the upper echelons of the military, he'd never have realized that those memories were false."

"So you're saying the leader of *every* Triad is a voluntary terminal?"

"It's not that many in the grand scheme of things. We're only the fourteenth Watch to travel outside our sector during the entire Sixth Alliance. And in quite a few cases, the leader is only *technically* a voluntary terminal. The job is frequently offered to rebellious or even corrupt military or political leaders on member worlds as a way to avoid sanctions for their actions being levied against their entire *korban*. If the Watch under their leadership successfully completes the mission, it's considered evidence of their loyalty to the Alliance, which then purges all record of their crimes." Her voice dripped with sarcasm on the last word.

"What about Sandjeel? Was he coerced?"

She considered for a moment. "He would say no, but there was definitely some *indirect* coercion. Did you know he has a daughter?"

"No."

"She's a few generations older than I am. A member of the previous Watch. Or maybe it was the one before that. Sandjeel was never very clear about the timeline. He'd already learned the truth by the time she volunteered, and he tried to dissuade her. But she was bright-eyed and eager to help bring an emerging world into the Alliance. Her mission didn't drag on for quite as long as this one. When it was over, they revived her, complete with fake memories of her time away. And Sandjeel wasn't allowed to tell her the truth. I don't think he realized how much that would eat at him. How much guilt he would feel. He was terrified that he was going to crack and tell her everything. That would have been viewed as a violation of his military oath, maybe even treason. And it could have affected her and other members of his *korban*, as well. It probably wouldn't have had much impact on distant kin like me, but he couldn't stop thinking about it. He decided to apply for voluntary termination … and his request was denied."

"Denied? But they can't do that. It's a basic right."

"Wartime exception. Claimed it was for the good of the Alliance, citing his military experience and the rising number of war casualties. But I think they could see that he wouldn't be much use to them on the battlefield in his current state. So they offered him this assignment, instead."

"The war is going so badly that they'd refuse a request for voluntary termination?"

"From what I've gathered, yes. There are protest movements on every member world pushing for a negotiated settlement. And three Alliance planets have switched sides since we've been on Earth, requesting protection from the Hodjeri. One of those planets was Seset."

She was quiet for a moment, letting that sink in. If Drex and Stasia's homeworld was no longer part of the Alliance they'd be refugees when they were revived at the Academy. And that was the best case scenario. They might even be considered prisoners of war.

"And," she continued, "the Alliance didn't take that lying down, of course. Seset has been a war zone for the past few cycles. It's mostly under Hodjeri control, but there are half a dozen cities occupied by *ipret-tai* soldiers. In case you're wondering, Parda is still in the Alliance. So is Novera."

"It would almost make it easier if they weren't. Do they know? Drex and Stasia, I mean."

"I assume Stasia knows. Drex definitely does. I told her

everything a few weeks before we assigned her to monitor the Flock. That unauthorized field trip to talk with her was what earned me this little souvenir." She held up her wrist to display the tattoo. "I suspect the timing of my trip was also the reason Durav decided that Maela needed to join Drex inside the Flock. She lasted about six weeks, which was five weeks longer than I expected, to be honest. Maela is not my favorite member of the Watch by a long shot, but I'll admit I was worried about her safety when Durav found out she was in Spain with Graf and the other Ufretis instead of shadowing Drex."

"So when were you planning to tell *me* all of this?" Anak tried to keep the annoyance out of his voice, but it was there, front and center.

"At this Conclave, actually. Based on your last report, you thought there would be five to ten years between the Rejuvesce launch and any breakthrough that came close to biological immortality. Like you and like Drex, I thought we had more time. And maybe we would have, if they hadn't dredged up that chamber on Mars. But everything has snowballed now, and…" The lights in the room flickered out, leaving them with only the faint glow filtering in from the foyer. "And that's our cue to head back to my place."

FIVE

THEY TOOK the elevator down to the tunnel, where a motorized cart was waiting, along with the two *ipret-tai* who had been guarding the outside of the house. The four of them climbed into the cart. Just before they reached Arbet's house, they spotted Dora standing on the right side of the tunnel opening the door of a breaker box. A second later, the section of the tunnel wall just to her right slid open to reveal what looked like a maintenance or utility room.

Dora was about to enter, but then she noticed them approaching. She pressed the keypad again and the doorway vanished.

"What's wrong?" Arbet asked as they pulled up next to the girl.

"There is ... a thief ... in our house." The words came out in jagged bursts, as the woman's eyes traveled from Arbet's face to Anak's and then back again.

For a moment, he thought she was accusing *him*. But that was ridiculous. He hadn't even stepped foot in Blue House.

"It's okay," Arbet said. "Take a few seconds to calm down."

Dora took several deep breaths, then continued. "I placed Anak's bag in room number three, as you told me to do. When I went in to turn back the beds just now, his bag was no longer there. I'd already made up the rooms for the other two guests, and their bags are right where I left them."

"Okay. But what made you run to the..." Arbet trailed off. "Oh. You're worried that *Durav* is the thief."

"Yes. Because today you said not to let Durav see the note I gave to Anak. I didn't. I was very careful. But I thought maybe he found out anyway and stole the bag. And so I ran here to hide."

The idea of Durav doing anything so menial as swiping a bag himself when he could order someone else to do it was a stretch, but otherwise this was a fairly reasonable deduction. That was surprising, in and of itself. But for Dora to take the next step, to realize that she should hide, almost certainly meant that she'd been given explicit instructions to do so. *Ipret-tai* couldn't experience fear, but they could experience physical pain. Arbet must be concerned for the girl's safety.

"It was very smart of you to hide," Arbet said. "It may not have been Durav, though. More likely, it was one of his Earther guards. Or Maela. But you shouldn't trust *them,* either."

"The room *smelled* like Durav. His perfume burns my nose." Dora's face still wore the same blank expression as always, but her voice shook as she spoke.

"Yes. It stinks, doesn't it?" Arbet gave her a gentle smile, then squeezed closer to Anak and patted the seat next to her. "Either way, you're safe now. Close the electrical panel, okay? You can ride with us."

It was possible that the girl's voice quavered because she'd been running, but he was beginning to question some of what he'd been told about the *ipret-tai.* Most of his experience with them was from his time at the Academy. Maybe the idea that they were incapable of emotion was nothing but a convenient fiction. It no doubt made it easier to justify forcing a servant to work every waking hour if you thought of them as automatons.

About two minutes later, the cart pulled into an open elevator, and they ascended to the garage of Blue House. A faint chime sounded as Arbet's two male *ipret-tai* entered through the garage door. They made a quick sweep of the premises before the rest of them went inside. Dora told them that the other two Watchers who were staying at the house were still in the Great Hall, probably watching the after-dinner concert that Reese had mentioned.

Arbet's place was nearly as large as HQ, although it had a more modern layout, with at least half of the main floor occupied by a large central room that included an area for dining on one side and a sunken space for entertaining on the other. One wall was glass, offering a view of the patio, the pool, and the lawn beyond. The house was at least ten times the size of his own apartment. He'd only been with Arbet during Conclaves and on the two occasions they met up during sabbaticals, so he'd never seen any place where she lived when she was a member of the Watch. But this decor was far more formal and austere than he'd have imagined. Had her tastes changed that much? Or maybe she hadn't wanted to make the place feel like a home, given that it was really a glorified prison.

"Dora will take you up to your room," she said, nodding toward the stairs. "Was there anything *important* in your bag?"

Given her emphasis on the word *important*, he suspected that she meant the journal. "No. All of my data is on my phone. Nothing in the bag but clothes, toothbrush, and so forth."

"Okay. Hang tight, then. We'll find you some replacements." And then she left without another word.

Anak followed Dora up to the second floor. She opened the door to one of the bedrooms, gave him a quick nod, and scurried off. Maybe she was still picking up traces of Durav's cologne. He couldn't smell anything, but *ipret-tai* might have a more developed sense of smell. On the other hand, though, she could simply be rushing off to find him a spare toothbrush.

His room was spacious, with an adjoining bath, a king-sized bed, and two upholstered chairs with a game table in the center. A round *padjit* board sat on top of the table. It was the first physical version of the game he'd seen. This one, unlike the virtual game they'd played in stasis, had ornate gold markings etched into the sides of the wooden gameboard. Tiny symbols had also been carved into the top surface of the fifteen egg-shaped wooden markers, each polished to a high sheen, which were arranged in a circle on the raised shelf at the center of the board. Seven were finished in a light pine shade, seven in deep mahogany, and the last, which sat upright in the middle, was painted jet black.

He picked one of the markers up at random, running his finger across the gold symbol. It was Noveran script, from what Arbet had said earlier. Did she know what the symbols meant, or had she simply memorized them while learning the game? Parda must also have had some other language before they joined the Alliance, but he'd never seen it written. It wasn't taught in school, or as part of their history. There was just a brief mention of the times before, with the vague suggestion that lives in that era had been nasty and brutish, although apparently not short. Parda must have met the longevity milestone in order to be offered membership in the Alliance.

Now he had to wonder whether any of what he'd been taught was true.

He considered playing a solo scenario he'd used to practice when Arbet was teaching him the game but couldn't quite remember how to set it up. So he sat in one of the chairs, still absentmindedly tracing the symbol on the *padjit* marker with one thumb, as he checked his *rezlat* for news from home.

He ignored the financial messages, not really caring at this point how much his savings account and investments had increased or decreased this cycle. The packet of messages from his mother contained around a dozen links to news about Parda and the Alliance, and a hologram of her sitting on the balcony of her apartment recounting what she and her current *amali-tai* had been doing over the past cycle, along with some casual gossip about mutual acquaintances.

It was nice to see her familiar smile, but he couldn't help wondering how much of what she'd recorded was censored by the Academy. It didn't look as if anything had been altered, but would he be able to tell? Worse, his mind kept wandering to how they'd weave the various messages he'd received over the years in with his travels on Earth and the jobs he'd held here in order to concoct nearly a century and a half of memories for the Anak currently in stasis. It made him want to purge everything on his *rezlat*, but that would serve absolutely no purpose. They obviously had copies.

Still, they'd have to do a bit of creative work in his case, because he didn't keep up with many people on Parda. In the early years, he'd corresponded with a handful of friends from previous assignments, but those messages had tapered off over time. These days, the video from his mother was often the only visual communication he received. His father sometimes sent a hologram as well, and Anak looked forward to those. Some of his most vivid memories from childhood were the hikes they'd taken through the forest near his grandparents' home in the Fareem Valley, eating wild berries and hunting for the tree fungi that his grandmother liked. He could clearly recall the sharp, sinus-clearing aroma of the trees along the edge of that forest, much like the rainbow eucalyptus near the lake at the center of the Jonas Labs biodome.

Unfortunately, his father had never been the sort to remember dates or anniversaries, and he often missed the deadline to submit messages to the Academy. Sure enough, there was no hologram from him this year. He had, however, sent an interactive video file, almost certainly a *djvari* match. It was labeled *Parda/ER*. That last bit might be short for Ermonis, but that didn't make sense. The Ermoni team was in a different league, unless something had changed.

He was about to send the file to his lenses, but then he noticed another message just below. It was from Brinn. This wasn't the first time she'd contacted him, but it was the first message in a very long time. Had he heard from her at all since HQ moved to New York? He didn't think so.

It wasn't a hologram. Just a short note, asking about the lake property they'd owned together. It had gone to her when they split up, with the provision that he would have the right of first refusal if she decided to sell, which was what she wanted to do.

She explained that she had a child now, a boy who would soon enter his first primary training, and she wanted a vacation home closer to where he'd be living.

Anak sat with this news for a moment, mulling it over. Poking at it, expecting it to sting. But it didn't. All he could feel for her was pity. It was like that Earth philosopher's allegory of the cave. Brinn was stuck on the inside. She believed the shadows on the cave wall were the real world, believed the Alliance was a force for good in the universe. He didn't begrudge her this happiness, this sense of security, even knowing that she would pass that blissful ignorance along to her little boy. She would take him into her lap and read him stories of Motz and Tibbo, happy in their little glade of sunshine, safe from the evils that surrounded them in the vast darkness of the Aveezi Forest.

He wrote a quick reply, congratulated her, and waived his right to the lake house. But he couldn't bring himself to record a response to his mother. While this face and this body were not the ones to which she'd given birth, he'd sent enough messages while on Earth that she would probably pick up on his mood. Or would they edit that, too? Either way, he didn't want to smile and pretend that all was well with him right now.

Because it really wasn't. He couldn't stop thinking about the cave of shadows in which Brinn, his parents, and almost every single person in the Alliance existed. The idea of going back into the darkness, of no longer knowing the truth, absolutely terrified him. He couldn't fathom losing more than thirteen decades of experiences, all memory of his relationships with Arbet, with Joe, with Claire. And having them overwritten by pure fiction? That was tantamount to erasing his entire identity.

A tap at the door jolted him out of this burgeoning panic spiral. Thinking it was Dora returning with a toothbrush, he stashed the *rezlat* back in his pocket and told her to come in.

But it was Arbet. She tossed a silky black robe and a floral toiletry kit onto his bed. "This should hold you until we can locate your bag. Just leave your clothes outside the door when you go to bed, and I'll have them cleaned." She smiled at the wooden marker, still in his hand. "Care for a game?"

"Sounds good. Although given how long it's been, you may have to refresh me on some of the rules."

She took the chair next to the window and began arranging the markers on the lower level of the board. "It wasn't Durav, by the way. We checked the security footage, and the thief was Maela. Dora must have—" She stopped and then shook her head. "I was about to say that she must have imagined smelling Durav's cologne, but if Maela had been with him, Dora probably picked up the reek secondhand."

"She seems frightened of him. I didn't know that was possible."

Arbet nodded. "She had an unfortunate run-in with the man a few years back. I intervened and … since she's part of my household he backed off. Her programming told her to submit to his demands and she would probably never have questioned that if I hadn't been so insistent that she avoid him in the future. It was partly his history of violence against the *ipret-tai*, but … it goes beyond that. They shouldn't be used as playthings. It's just wrong. It's not like they're capable of informed consent. Sandjeel didn't question my right to tell Durav to leave her alone, but he clearly thinks I handled it badly. He says it's my fault she's so anxious around other people now."

They focused on the game after that. He was still no competition for her, which came as absolutely no surprise given that she'd been playing regularly with Sandjeel. But his memory of *padjit* hadn't atrophied as much as he'd feared. They slipped into a comfortable rhythm and some of the awkwardness he'd felt in their earlier conversation faded away as he watched her plotting her moves.

About an hour into their game, he tossed what he was pretty sure would be a conversational grenade into the mix. He didn't *want* to do it. He'd have been happy to pretend they were back in stasis, with nothing but hope for the future and plenty of time on their hands. But given that time was actually a scarce commodity right now, that sort of pretense would be essentially the same thing as hiding in that cave of shadows. Or taking the blue pill and slipping back into the blissful ignorance of the Matrix. He didn't want to do that, and he believed there were others in the Watch who would feel the same.

"Whatever happens at the meeting tomorrow," he said, "the others need to know the truth. It's only fair."

Her eyebrows shot up, but her gaze remained on the board. "You think that's *fair*? I could make an equally strong case that it's cruel."

"You told Drex, didn't you?"

"Yes. When I thought there was still time to stop it. To delay and to hope that Sandjeel was right that reforms are coming. Now, though? If Drex's plan fails, as it almost certainly will, we'd be condemning everyone in the Watch to six months, maybe a year or even more of angst as they wait for this world to end. Of watching the skies for those little blips of light as the drone ships move into formation around the planet. I just don't see what purpose it would serve when there's nothing they can do to help. They're not going to remember any of this when their bodies are removed from stasis. Like I said before, I don't think Durav can be convinced. And the odds of Sandjeel going against him on something this major are slim to none."

"But we're only asking for a delay. What would be the harm in granting that? Sandjeel doesn't like Durav. Never has. Why would he side with him against you?"

"You overestimate my influence. I'm just a lowly member of the Watch who got a field promotion." She moved another of her markers into the center circle, and then finally looked up to meet his eyes. "Durav is one of the original Triad, appointed by the Academy and confirmed by the Senate. Siding with me would not be in Sandjeel's best interests."

"So what? What does he have to lose at this point? You said

he's planning to die here anyway. And there are plenty of other ways to accomplish that without blowing up an entire planet. If he helps us and still wants to opt out, I'm sure we can find a compassionate form of assisted suicide."

"He's worried about his daughter. About the entire *korban*, for that matter. And hey, he's not alone there. All of our families would be punished."

"But what kind of punishment are we talking about, Arbet? Economic sanctions, right? It's not like the Alliance Guard is going to come through and start chopping off heads."

"It's economic punishment, yes. But it can be severe. Do you remember the Ufreti general who defected to the Hodjeri back when we were at the Academy? Thousands of people were affected by those sanctions. His immediate line had to forfeit everything and return to entry level positions. Some of them were nearly Sandjeel's age and they were reduced to barely above the *ipret-tai*."

"Listen to what you're saying, though. Thousands of people were affected. *Thousands*. And they weren't killed. Just *affected*. Personally, I'm willing to risk that to save billions here on Earth. And yes, I'd say that even if I was talking about my own *korban*. My own family, even. Has all this time around Durav convinced you that Earthers are subhuman? That their lives are expendable?"

Her eyes flashed and she pushed her chair away from the game table. He'd clearly gone too far. But he couldn't take the words back. And it was a fair question. How many Earther lives was she willing to sacrifice to avoid inconveniencing a few thousand people on her homeworld?

"You should get some sleep," she said as she headed toward the door. "I'll see you in the morning."

Anak sat there for a moment, going back and forth between mentally kicking himself and being convinced he'd done the right thing. If Arbet wasn't fully behind Drex's plan, what was the point of even having the meeting? They'd be better off going with her original idea of killing Durav. He didn't generally think of himself as the murderous type, but he was quite sure that he could live with that man's death on his conscience. You could even argue that it wasn't actually murder when he was going to be rebooted. Durav wouldn't even remember it when they pulled him out of stasis.

Of course, the Anak they revived wouldn't remember *doing* it, either. Nor would he remember anything else that had actually happened here on Earth. Which drove home the point that while the body they revived on the other end might bear his name, might resume his life on Parda, it wouldn't really be *him*.

One way or another, Anak Djurdin of Parda would die on this planet. And that was infinitely better than being stuck inside that false version of himself, never even knowing what they'd done to him.

Arbet was right about one thing, though. He needed sleep. He stripped down, dropped his clothes into the hallway outside the door as directed, and headed into the shower. The steam cleared his head a bit, and it was nice to rid himself of the lingering stench of Reese's beer.

Later, when he was in bed and very nearly asleep, he heard another soft tap. He pulled on the robe and opened the door to find Arbet. It was hard to be sure in the dim light of the hallway, but he thought she might have been crying.

"Are you alone?" she asked.

He glanced pointedly down at his borrowed robe, which ended around mid-thigh. "I certainly hope so."

She followed his gaze, one side of her mouth quirking upward in amusement. "I think it suits you. Would you like some company?"

"I'd like that very much." He didn't add that he would also like an answer to the question he'd asked that pissed her off so mightily. It was an important question, and he'd have to come back to it eventually even if he didn't like upsetting her.

Right now, though, he didn't merely *want* company. He

needed it. It wasn't just about the sex, or even mostly about the sex, even though it had been a while. More than anything else, he needed to be with someone who shared his reality. Someone who knew him. *This* version of him, his real self, and not the poor, clueless sap sleeping in the stasis bay at the Academy.

SIX

Tuesday, September 5 8:08 am

ANAK WOKE UP ALONE. No surprise there. It had been their usual pattern, and Arbet had merely been another Watcher back then. Given how blatantly Durav flouted the fraternization rules, he couldn't imagine anyone saying much about it if they were caught together, but he understood why she preferred to be discreet.

Even though he wasn't surprised at Arbet's absence, he still wasn't happy about it, for reasons that were entirely his own fault. He had fully intended to have a long, serious conversation with her. In fact, he'd lain in bed for several minutes afterward, their bodies spent and tangled, trying to think of a way to rephrase his earlier question that wouldn't be quite so abrasive. In the end, he'd thought for a bit too long, and the past few nights of subpar sleep had caught up with him before he arrived at the perfect conversation starter.

The clothes he'd worn the night before were now folded neatly on top of the dresser, along with his *ligren*, which someone must have retrieved from the Great Hall. On top of the clean clothes, he found a handwritten note.

> *Sandjeel has agreed to the meeting. Ten o'clock, Triad's Chambers. I'll be having breakfast with him beforehand, so I will meet you there.*
>
> *And you should know that Sandjeel isn't the only one with a child to consider.*

He sank back down onto the bed, cursing himself. When Arbet mentioned that his sanctions might also affect her family the night before, he'd translated that to mean parents and several generations of grands. But she *was* a good deal older than him, so it was entirely possible that she might have been granted a parental license. He hadn't asked when they were in stasis, in part because she said she was in Pod Two in order to avoid *memory hell*. He'd interpreted it as the same sort of hell he was going through—a nasty breakup—and had avoided questions about her personal life.

And that was a reasonable assumption. Parenthood wasn't the sort of thing you had to *ask* about. It was something that people told you without any prompting at all. He didn't know what the exact percentages were on Novera, but only about a quarter of applicants were approved on Parda. If you were one of the lucky few who received a license, it wasn't something that you hid. It was a status symbol. And even if her child was now fully grown—even if they were his own age or older, something he really didn't like thinking about—he was surprised that she'd taken an assignment like this that required such a lengthy separation. He'd never heard anyone else in the Watch mention having kids. The Watch was the sort of post you generally took only if you were uncommitted and childless.

A loud buzz from the right jolted him out of his thoughts. He glanced at the wallscreen, which was now flashing *8:15*. Arbet must have set an alarm for him before she left. He dressed quickly and arrived at the Great Hall about twenty minutes later. Heady aromas of bacon and coffee hit his nose before the elevator doors even opened, and his stomach, which had balked at dinner the previous night, growled in anticipation. That reaction seemed a bit hypocritical to him. The situation hadn't improved, and there was still an excellent chance that Sandjeel and Durav would send the signal before the comms window closed and Earth's final countdown would begin.

But the body wanted what it wanted, and right now it was demanding fuel. He loaded a tray with pancakes, eggs, bacon, and fruit, keeping an eye out for Arbet even though he was fairly sure she was already in her breakfast meeting with Sandjeel. He didn't see her. Didn't see Reese, either, but then it was still a bit early. He was actually surprised at how many people there were in the room, given that the Assembly wouldn't begin until eleven. Only a few were out on the patio this morning. Instead, they were gathered at the bar tables near the wallscreen, sharing videos and other items of interest they'd been sent from home. The one on the screen at present was a comedian, but not one that he recognized.

"You've gone native, Anak." Maela stood behind him with a mostly empty plate, apparently heading back to the buffet for seconds. "I mean, look at your tray. There's not a single item on it that you couldn't get from an IHOP."

He wasn't sure that IHOP still existed, but he couldn't argue her main point. "I drank a bit too much yesterday. Thought it might be safer to stick to the stuff I eat on a daily basis." The excuse had come naturally, before it occurred to him that he didn't owe her an explanation. "Instead of critiquing my dietary choices, maybe you could tell me why you stole the bag out of my room?"

She gave him a sly smile and a one-shouldered shrug, not even bothering to deny it.

"Never mind," he said. "Everyone knows there's only one reason you do anything—because Durav said to *do it*. I've known *ipret-tai* who have more free will than you do."

The comment had exactly the effect he'd hoped. She glared at him and stalked off, apparently forgetting all about refilling her plate. There was really nothing to be gained from pissing the woman off. It probably made it even less likely that she'd return his bag, but the only thing in it he'd miss was his earphones and it was worth losing them to get a rise out of her.

He took a seat at one of the empty tables and for several

minutes, he didn't pay attention to anything but the food. As his hunger died down, the chatter around him began to register. Several of the others groaned at what must have been a lame joke from the performer on the screen.

"Seriously, that's the best thing they sent you?" Graf said. "Your friends must absolutely hate you, Meeks. Pull it down. I got something way better." He pointed his *rezlat* toward the screen and blinked twice. The comedian was replaced by a *djvari* match. "Finals from the last Grand Tournament."

The tournament, which was similar to an Alliance-wide Olympics, was held once each cycle, and made regular appearances on the wallscreen during Conclave. Those who were not fans of the sport usually gathered at one of the other houses. The screens were smaller there, but they could avoid the chaos.

The consensus seemed to favor the game over the comedian, so Meeks gave in. "Do you at least have the game where Elbrazza broke the record for consecutive targets? *That* would be worth watching."

Graf shook his head. "Unfortunately, no. I'd like to see that, too, but they just sent the final game. We asked Durav last night if maybe they were holding that video back for the milestone celebration, but since we've apparently got another freakin' cycle or two before that I sure as hell hope not."

Anak poked at his food, ignoring the fact that half of the eyes in the room had now turned toward him.

"Personally, I'd rather watch the comedian," Housen grumbled. "We already *know* which team wins the final."

"Well, I *don't* know," one of the women said, indignantly. "And I don't want to know in advance, so keep it to yourself."

She was talking about the game, but her words echoed Arbet's comments from the night before. Was she right? Would it be cruel to tell them? Just because he wouldn't want to be kept in the dark, just because the thought of waking up in that body without his memories sickened him, that didn't mean the others would feel the same. Some of them might *want* to lose the memories of their time on Earth. Housen, for example. Would he want to hold onto the memory of digging a grave for the girl he'd loved?

Anak had to ponder that one for a moment, but in the end, he decided that Housen would want to remember. There was a time when he had wanted to purge every memory of Brinn from his mind. It had been brief, though. He could remember the good times now without feeling bitter, and on occasions of brutal honesty, even admit there had been a few warning signs during their last commitment.

But in Housen's situation? He wouldn't just want to remember the *girl*. He'd want to remember the man who had ordered her death. Who had ordered him to bury her. And if he ever got the chance, he'd want to make him pay.

Anak watched a bit of the game, trading a few good-natured barbs with the guy at the next table who didn't even play *djvari*, but still felt entitled to critique his lackluster performance at the previous day's game. Then, with eight minutes left until ten o'clock, he finished off the last of his coffee and looked beyond the patio toward Assembly Hall on the other side of the quad. Or, more accurately, the virtual façade of the auditorium that was projected onto a wall on the other side of this massive basement.

As he returned his tray to the cart, he had to fight the urge to smash it into the wall and take out a few of the holoemitters, just to remind everyone that none of this was real. But he didn't. He just pushed through the door to the patio and headed off across the fake lawn toward the fake building on the other side.

It was, as always, a beautiful morning at the Academy. He couldn't remember it ever raining at Conclave, even though Ufretas Prime had a long, bitterly cold rainy season. Had they included any of those dreary, gray days in the simulation, just to give Sandjeel some variety? Or was he stuck with the same, relentlessly sunny skies day in and day out?

Anak pulled on his *ligren* before entering the auditorium,

both because it was expected attire for formal Conclave sessions and because he knew he'd need the extra layer inside the building. Sandjeel could tolerate the warmer temperatures for short bursts, like when he dropped in on events in the Great Hall. But given how long the assembly sessions usually lasted, they kept the auditorium considerably cooler than most of the Watch found comfortable in order to accommodate him.

This version was much smaller than the real thing, but otherwise it was a decent facsimile. Six rows of benches were arranged in the shape of a wide *V*, with three on each side, facing a raised platform where the Triad sat during sessions. Along the walls were four doors, two of which led to the rooms they used for breakout sessions. One led to the restrooms. The door closest to the front of the auditorium, from which the Triad always entered, led to what was officially known as the Triad's Chambers, even though it seemed to be used primarily as Sandjeel's office.

Anak tapped on the door, but there was no response. After another try, he took a seat in the front row and waited. It was still five minutes until their meeting, so they might not have arrived yet. He considered recording a response to his mother's message, since the auditorium would make a more impressive backdrop than his room back at Arbet's place. But he was too on edge. Instead, he turned to the game file from his father. He'd thought that ER in the file name might be for Ermonis, but it could also be short for *Elbrazza Record*. Elbrazza played for Degarae, not Parda, but they *were* in the same league, so it was possible.

He switched the *rezlat* to personal mode and sent the game directly to his lenses. The file was a twenty minute highlight reel, and it was indeed a game between Degarae and Parda. Any doubt that it was the game where the record was broken was dispelled by the opening title—*Elbrazza Takes Trophy*. In the upper right corner, Elbrazza's total was displayed next to the current record, held by an Ufreti player named Rengar, who was up by a few dozen at the beginning of the game.

He'd watched a little over six minutes of the highlights when his attention was yanked back to reality by the sound of voices on the other side of the door. *Raised* voices. While he couldn't make out what they were saying, it was definitely Arbet and Durav. He paused the game and stuck the *rezlat* back into his pocket.

When he knocked this time, the voices quieted, and Arbet met him at the door with a tense smile. Her face was still flushed from whatever argument she'd been having with Durav. She wore a bulky gray cardigan over her *ligren*, and he understood why as soon as he entered. The auditorium had been chilly, but this room was downright cold.

He'd never been inside the Triad's Chambers, either here or at the actual Academy, and hadn't known what to expect. Aside from the frigid temperature, it was essentially the same as the breakout rooms, with a conference table and two wallscreens. A massive desk occupied most of the corner across from the largest wallscreen. An absurdly large chair sat behind the desk, with two smaller chairs facing it. The room itself was also slightly larger and had a refreshment center, as well as an extra door that led to the tunnels. That door was currently open, and he could see Sandjeel lumbering toward them, so the tunnel probably went directly to his quarters. He was dressed in his formal *ligren*, with narrow threads of light in the colors from each of the Alliance homeworlds against a jet black fabric.

As he approached the desk, Durav, who had already parked himself in one of the smaller chairs, nodded toward the conference table. "Pull up a chair. Or you could remain standing. I really can't see this taking more than a couple of minutes assuming Arbet ever manages to get our fugitives on the phone."

Arbet flipped him off, then turned to Anak and asked if he would get her a bottle of water. He went to the beverage station and took a bottle from the fridge. As he turned back, he noticed something odd on the wall next to the bar. It had three built-in shelves, each divided into three sections. Most of the shelves contained books, but the square at the center held a clear case about the size of a shoebox. Inside the case, on a small pedestal, was the *brelat*. He'd only seen it once before, back at the Academy. It was almost identical to the *rezlat* in his pocket, with two exceptions. First, it was a pale blue instead of white. And instead of a single cell scanner in the middle, there were two, positioned at either end of the palm-sized oval.

By the time he got back from the break area with Arbet's water, she had dragged a chair over for him and was tapping a number onto the screen on her arm. Apparently, the Triad didn't have their phones blocked below ground like the rest of the Watch.

His foot bumped against something as he leaned over to hand her the water. He looked down to find his missing bag on the floor, resting against the base of the chair. Arbet, who had taken the seat in the middle, gave him a furtive look, pressing her lips into a firm line, which he interpreted as a suggestion that he simply take the bag and not say anything about the theft.

Sandjeel dropped into the chair behind the desk, neither of which seemed all that large once the man was there to put them into perspective. He looked even wearier than usual this morning, and more than a little put out.

The Triad leader's native form was similar to Arbet's in that his face and body were covered with short, fine hairs. Anak had mistakenly referred to Arbet's body hair as *fur* on one occasion and she had curtly informed him that she was not an animal. Sandjeel's hair was longer, lighter in color, and slightly mottled, with flecks of ginger and light brown mixed in with the pale blond. He also wore a nasal cannula that connected to a portable tank attached to the back of his *ligren*. It emitted a slow stream of argon and extra oxygen to make the air he breathed closer to that of the Noveran atmosphere. Arbet had also used one of those at the Academy, along with about a third of the Watch. Meeks and one other guy had also needed pressure suits. Anak had counted himself lucky that Parda was a close enough match to the atmosphere on Ufretas Prime that he hadn't needed any special equipment or anything more than a brief period of adjustment.

After a short delay, Drex and Stasia appeared on the wallscreen to the left of Sandjeel's desk, both looking nervous. The hotel room in the background was definitely not an upscale establishment. Given the resources of the Flock, they could obviously afford something better, but then again, they were trying to evade both Durav's crew and the FBI. A hotel with water stains on the ceiling was probably more willing to take cash and not insist on official identification.

"Oh, my," Durav said in mock delight. "We've finally located our little lost sheep. Although I suppose Drex is fashioning herself as a *shepherd* these days. Stasia, I must admit that I expected this sort of behavior from *her*, but you? I thought you had a better developed sense of duty. Your mother will be very, very disappointed. I don't believe you were aware of this, Arbet, but Stasia's mother is one of the few Sesetan officials who opted to seek asylum within the Alliance instead of siding with the Hodjeri."

As the color drained from Stasia's face, Anak remembered thinking about the predicament that the two of them would be in when they were revived at the Academy. He'd never considered that Seset leaving the Alliance might also have been a *good* thing since it freed the two of them from worrying about repercussions against their families.

"No," Arbet said. "I hadn't heard that. And given your rather casual acquaintance with the truth, I'm not at all sure that I believe you. Did you know about this, Sandjeel?"

He shrugged. "Durav would probably have better information about military matters than I do. There were some Sesetan officers who asked for asylum, but as to whether one of them was her mother, I have no idea." He turned his dark eyes toward the screen. "We might as well cut to the chase. Arbet has already told me the general outline of your proposal, Drex. The answer is no."

Arbet's jaw dropped. "The only thing I told you was that she has a plan to halt further advances at Jonas Labs and KTI. If you'd already made up your mind based on that alone, why even agree to the meeting?"

"Because I felt that I owed *all* of you a personal explanation for my decision."

"And," Durav added, "this way, Arbet can make her apologies to Drex and Stacia in advance, since they will not be here for the general assembly, when she apologizes to the rest of the Watch and is formally censured for breaking her oath."

SEVEN

ANAK WASN'T sure what formal censure involved, but Arbet's original plan to simply kill Durav was sounding better and better. His guards weren't in the room at present and judging from Arbet's current expression, he was certain that she'd happily join in if he couldn't take the guy's doughy ass out on his own. Unfortunately, there was probably a panic button under Sandjeel's giant desk, and Anak thought there was at least a fifty-fifty chance that he'd feel obligated to push it.

He clenched his fists in frustration ... and that's when his thumb knuckle bumped against the *rezlat* in his pocket, which triggered an idea. He wasn't sure that he could pull it off, but...

Slipping his hand inside his pocket, he pressed his finger into the little divot to switch it on. But when the game highlights resumed on his retinal display, he didn't blink to start the video. Instead, he shifted his gaze to the right and selected the symbol to record.

He felt a momentary pang of regret for recording over the file from his father. Not because it contained any meaningful history, in his opinion, and he was sure his father would agree. They both thought Elbrazza was an egomaniac, a strutting peacock who had been playing twice as long as Rengar. And they both believed there should be a time constraint on *djvari* records—on all sports records—since the only things that kept you from playing indefinitely were the rare, unfixable injuries and eventual boredom with the game. He kind of hoped Rengar would jump back in and reclaim the trophy.

So, his problem wasn't deleting the file itself. It was because the file triggered memories of their many conversations about the game, and the hazy, distant memories of his father teaching him to play. That's what made the file meaningful, and he wouldn't be erasing those memories. But still, the *djvari* clip was almost certainly the last contact he'd ever have with his father. Maybe not the last contact his father would ever have with *him*, which hurt his heart and his head in equal measure, but at least he didn't have to worry that his parents would grieve his loss. They'd still have their son, or some portion of him. He just hoped they wouldn't suffer on Parda for what he was about to do here on Earth.

If this was going to work, though, he had to take control of the conversation. The only picture would be the lining of his pocket. That meant the audio not only had to tell the full story, but the first part had to be compelling enough to keep anyone from switching away from an apparently blank screen.

"Then give us your explanation, Sandjeel," he said loudly. Maybe a bit *too* loudly, so he reined it in a notch before continuing. "As someone who has been lied to about the nature of our mission not merely since I joined the Watch, but for my entire life, I'd really like to know why you're willing to condemn over ten billion people on this planet simply for having the same level of scientific curiosity that we did at their level of development."

Arbet clutched his arm. "Anak..."

He pulled away. "No. He said he had an explanation. Let's hear it. I'm sure Drex and Stasia want to know as well."

"Yes," Drex said. "Are you really so eager to commit genocide that you can't wait until the end of the communications window to render your judgment? That's all we're asking you to do!"

Sandjeel sighed heavily. "I'm far from eager. And I *might* have been willing to consider a delay if there was any hope of a permanent solution. But Durav is right. The current situation makes any other outcome impossible. This recent spate of defections by Seset and four other worlds from the Alliance have caused a rather harsh shift in the culture both within the Alliance government and the Academy."

Anak was fairly sure that Arbet had said Seset was one of *three* planets that defected, not one of five, but he didn't interrupt.

"I had some hope that the Alliance was moving in the other direction," Sandjeel continued. "Several members of Djasa's *korban* were in intelligence and she told me that even government members at the upper echelons had begun to openly suggest relaxing our policy on emerging planets. But with the war heating up as it has, if one were even to mention any possibility other than cleansing this entire world, it would be seen as sedition, as siding with the Hodjeri."

"As it should be," Durav said. "Arbet shouldn't simply be facing censure, as I noted earlier. She should face sedition charges upon our return to Ufretas Prime."

Anak glanced at Arbet, but she didn't meet his eyes. He'd been horrified enough at the idea of waking up with a false set of memories but hadn't even considered that those implanted memories could be weaponized. Any charges against her would be faked, since they couldn't tell the true nature of her so-called crime without revealing the actual mission of the Watch. What sort of memory might they implant? Would they even bother to revive her from stasis? And then there was the child she mentioned...

Sandjeel ignored Durav's interruption, directing most of his attention to the two women on the screen. "As I was saying, I must refuse your request because it's pointless. Let us say that you do manage to persuade these two scientists to halt their research. Maybe you even convince them to doctor their findings in ways that discourage others from following their lead. How long would this last? Earthers are a curious lot. Like that cat on the children's show." This drew a blank look from everyone else in the room. "Oh, never mind. But they *are* curious beings. You know this is true. It wouldn't be long before someone else picked up the torch and continued on. I do understand why this is hard for you. It would be far better if Arbet had never told you the truth…"

"Which, again," Durav interjected, "is grounds for a charge of sedition."

"That matter is settled, Durav." Sandjeel's gaze pinned Durav to his chair, and for the first time, Anak could actually envision the older man as a former general. "Unless you want my next message to the Academy to include a report on how you endangered our mission and the entire Watch by killing off more than half of the *ipret-tai* assigned to you, we'll have no more talk of sedition charges. Are we clear?"

After a brief standoff, Durav gave Sandjeel a curt nod, and the older man continued. "I take no pleasure in this and truly wish there were another way. But this is our mission. Even if your plan succeeds, at some point, the Earthers will reach those milestones. And when they do, they will be deemed a potential threat to our Alliance, at which point our military will act swiftly to neutralize that threat. How could I, in good conscience, ask your fellow Watchers to remain here when the outcome is inevitable? The only fair course of action is to let them return to their lives *now*. They're eager to return home. And who can blame them? We've been here far longer than planned as it is."

"Shouldn't *they* be allowed to weigh in on that decision, though?" Anak countered. "Yes, they're all eager to return, but would that still be the case if they knew that they were condemning this planet and everyone on it to complete annihilation? I'm guessing quite a few of them would be willing to extend their tour of duty a cycle or two. And it's … it's *immoral* not to tell them that these bodies we occupy will be destroyed with the rest of the planet. Don't they deserve to know that they'll awaken without any memory of this world, that they'll lose the past forty-three cycles of experiences? You are the leader of the Triad. These people are in your charge. Surely, they have the right to know that they're going to be revived at the Academy with a head full of false memories, just as you were, just…"

He'd been about to say *just as your daughter was,* but Arbet was in enough trouble without him adding the fact that she'd shared Sandjeel's family history.

"Just … forget it," he amended. "You've clearly made up your mind."

"I have," Sandjeel said. "We will inform the Watch at the assembly that we have decided to call both milestones. Why dim their happiness at reaching the goal that they've worked toward for so long? We will celebrate this achievement. And when the comms window opens in a few weeks, we will send the signal. We have no choice but to fulfill our duty."

"And I have no choice but to fulfill mine." Drex's gaze shifted to Anak for a second, silently reminding him of the commitment he'd made the night before, and then the screen went dark.

The room was silent for a moment, then Anak uttered a shaky laugh as he slumped back into his chair. "I should go. You obviously won't be using my report to the general assembly … and I don't know. Maybe you're right about the others. Why make them miserable for no reason? It's not like they're going to remember anything you tell them when they're taken out of stasis. For that matter, neither will I. I should just grab a bottle of *evir* from the dining area and get a head start on my final sabbatical. As Graf pointed out yesterday, I've been seriously cheated on the travel front."

Sandjeel sighed heavily. "That is true. Hold on…" He opened a desk drawer and offered Anak a red ceramic flask. "You might want to be careful with this one. We've been cutting the *evir* with local spirits for many cycles now. The stuff they serve in the Great Hall is barely half strength. It is a poor apology but the best I can do. I just wish Arbet had spared you."

Anak took the bottle but shook his head. "Arbet is *not* to blame in my case. She can give you the details, but I had already pieced most of it together before I arrived at Conclave."

Durav was now typing something into his armscreen. Anak suspected this was his cue to leave immediately, but…

He turned to Arbet. There were so many things he wanted to tell her. So many things he wanted to *ask* her. But there was no time, and this definitely wasn't the place. "Why don't you come with me?" he asked in a low voice. "I could use some company. We could travel a bit and then lie on a beach watching the skies until the *naidar* bubble arrives."

She gave him a confused smile. Her eyes clearly conveyed that she knew he was up to *something*, even if she wasn't sure what. But she shook her head, and then nodded down at the tattoo on her arm. "Even if I *could* leave, I have responsibilities to Dora and the others." She placed her hand on the side of his face. "Take care, Anak."

"You could have saved your goodbye," Durav said. "He's not going anywhere."

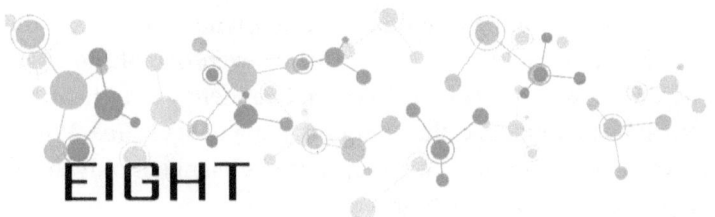

EIGHT

"THAT WAS a nice little speech at the end, Anak, but I'm not buying your sudden change of heart." Durav tapped the edge of his armscreen. "Maela is on her way to escort you to Gray House, since I don't think Arbet can be trusted to watch you."

"Just let him leave, Durav," Sandjeel said. "Maela can remove him from the premises so that he can't upset the others if you want. But having him remain here under some sort of house arrest would simply confuse and alarm the rest of the Watch. They're about to celebrate the culmination of more than forty cycles of work. Why spoil the party? If Anak wants to cast his lot with Drex and Stasia and go out with the Earthers, I say we let him."

Anak expected Durav to point out that allowing him to leave was only a temporary fix. There would be nothing stopping him—or Drex and Stasia, for that matter—from contacting the other Watchers when Conclave was over.

But Durav simply rolled his eyes in a long-suffering expression. "Have it your way, then. Maela will escort him from the grounds and make sure that he doesn't run his mouth to the others and as you say *spoil* the party."

Anak didn't plan to stick around long enough for them to change their minds. He gave Sandjeel and Arbet a quick nod and was halfway to the door when Durav pointed out that he'd forgotten his bag. He mumbled a *thank-you* at this unexpected and highly suspicious bit of courtesy and retrieved the bag from beneath the chair before joining Maela in the auditorium.

The bag *probably* didn't contain a tracker. After all, he already had one of those under the skin at the back of his neck.

It might be something as mundane as a listening device. On the other hand, it could be an explosive or even one of the nasty little drones that Stasia had sicced on Shepherd, ready to attack as soon as he unzipped the compartment and set it free. Which he definitely would not be doing, since he planned to ditch the bag as soon as he left the building.

As they crossed the lawn heading back toward the Great Hall, Maela embarked on a soliloquy of taunts about how badly he'd screwed up, accompanied by scattered threats of dire bodily harm if he did more than nod at any of the others in the Great Hall. He ignored her and pressed his finger into the hollow of the *rezlat*. When the video file appeared on his lenses, he blinked to rewind to the beginning. Everything in his central field of vision darkened slightly as he sped through the part he'd recorded over, and then he was back at the opening credits, with the large orange letters proclaiming *Elbrazza Takes Trophy*.

"Are you listening to me?"

Anak startled and pulled his attention back to Maela, who was now tapping a small stun device against her palm.

"Yes, I hear you."

"Good. Because I've got errands to run for Durav and I don't have time for any more trouble from you. Straight through the hall and into the elevator."

He nodded and kept walking. Did she know the truth about their mission? Probably. But he had to wonder if she'd thought through the full implications, especially in regard to her relationship with Durav.

Several people glanced in their direction as they headed toward the elevator. It was common knowledge that he and Maela weren't on friendly terms, so the fact that they were together was enough to arouse a bit of curiosity among the Watchers in the hall. It was now ten thirty-two, less than half an hour before the assembly, and most of the Watch was here. There were a few outside on the patio, but the majority were watching the game. Hopefully, a few more would tune in when the new video started. Housen had been watching earlier, but if he was in the room now, he was no longer with the cluster of people near Graf. And there was no sign of Reese. Too bad. It would have been nice to have someone in the crowd who already knew the truth.

He felt a wave of guilt. Arbet and Sandjeel were probably right that what he was about to do was cruel. But the upcoming milestone celebration wasn't commemorating the induction of a new world into the Alliance. It was the moral equivalent of dancing on the graves of more than ten billion souls. They had the right to know that. Maybe a few of them would be as horrified at that thought as he was. Maybe they would confront the Triad. Maybe their reaction would be enough to change Sandjeel's mind.

Maybe, maybe, maybe.

And maybe this was nothing more than him raising a firm middle finger to the Triad and the Alliance. But he had to do *something*. He had to try.

He pulled up the video while they waited for the elevator. When the doors opened, he turned and blinked twice to send the file to the main screen before stepping inside.

As the elevator doors closed, he could hear sounds of confusion, followed by a muffled cheer and Graf asking the others which one of them had been holding out.

Maela frowned toward the door as they ascended, clearly trying to piece together what she'd just heard. When she looked back at Anak, she jerked the stun device up to his chest. "Get your hand out of your pocket."

"Hey, hey. Take it easy. I'm just getting my *rezlat*." He slowly pulled the device out to show her. "I assume I should drop it into the basket on my way out as usual?"

She relaxed visibly, but kept the weapon pointed toward him as they exited on the ground level and crossed the foyer. The basket was normally next to one of the columns, but it wasn't out yet, so he stripped off his *ligren* and left it, along with the *rezlat*, on a table near the door.

His hand lingered on the *rezlat*, but only for a moment. In a perfect world, he'd have walked out with the device in his pocket, taking the holograms from his parents and other memories with him. But removing it from the grounds would almost certainly break the connection to the screen in the Great Hall. He wasn't even sure it stretched this far but hadn't been able to think of a way to leave it on the lower level without raising Maela's suspicions.

"My phone is in my back pocket," he told her, glancing pointedly at the stunner in her hand. "Is it okay if I call a car?"

"You can call once you're *outside* the gate. I've got better things to do than babysit you while you wait for your ride."

He had no intention of waiting here, anyway. His idea had been to get a head start on scheduling a car to meet him a few blocks from HQ, but he'd just have to make the call once he was outside. And did Maela's *better things to do* mean the errand for Durav she'd mentioned earlier or going back to the Great Hall to see what the rest of the Watch had been cheering about? He really, really hoped it was the former. If she was in the room, she would almost certainly message Durav as soon as the audio Anak had recorded began playing and any hope he had of this idea working required his fellow Watchers to listen for at least a few minutes.

He couldn't worry about that now, though. At the moment, he needed to focus on putting as much space as possible between himself and HQ before Durav figured out what he'd done. He picked up the pace as soon as they were out the door, relieved to discover that the air had cleared a bit. The stench of death had still lingered when he entered the building earlier, even though the actual groundhog was gone. He pitied the poor *ipret-tai* who'd gotten stuck with the nasty chore of carting the corpse away.

Maela waved one hand in front of the sensor as they

approached, and the gate swung open. "I guess we'll see you back at the Academy," she said with a nasty smile. "Or maybe not. Durav isn't sure they'll bother to revive the traitors. I mean, even if they wiped your memories of the time here on Earth, the seed of treason is clearly inside you. You'd probably betray the Alliance again eventually."

He was tempted to point out that Durav wouldn't give her the time of day once they came out of stasis given the difference between her status and his back on Ufretas Prime. That would almost certainly wipe the smile right off her face. But she might respond by zapping him with that stunner and the last thing he needed was to be incapacitated on the ground five minutes from now when his recording of the meeting with the Triad started playing downstairs. Instead, he gave her a little nod, walked through the gate, and picked up his pace the second it closed behind him.

As soon as Anak reached the corner, he paused long enough to toss his bag over the side of the fence. It might set off a security alarm inside HQ, but whatever Durav had stashed in there, he didn't want to leave it outside the fence where a kid or someone living on the street might open it and get a nasty, and possibly lethal, surprise. He heard a dull thud when it hit the ground, so his money was now on one of the nasty little bugbots that had been plaguing Claire rather than explosives.

He ran, keeping a cautious eye on the road behind him. About two blocks down, he paused long enough to call a car, then continued on, crossing the parking lot of an abandoned school. At ten forty, the car picked him up at the corner of Lakeview and Broadway, as the information bomb he'd dropped on the Watch should have been going off. If Maela wasn't in the room, he probably had at least a few more minutes before Durav found out.

He told the car to head toward Boston, then leaned back into the seat, struggling to catch his breath. Once they were a few miles out of the city, he'd stop somewhere. He needed to make a recording to send Claire. She deserved answers. So did Joe, but talking to Joe about all of this, even in a video that he would only see after the fact, was more than he could bear right now. Durav could go on all he wanted about treason and sedition. Erasing Joe's data felt like a far more traitorous act than anything Anak had done back at HQ.

But first, he needed to find a drugstore and a hotel. The sooner he got this tracker out of his neck, the better. That was mostly because he didn't see any point in making it easy for Durav to find him. But it was also psychological. That tracker was the one physical thing that tied him to the Watch. To the Alliance. To Anak Djurdin of Parda.

He wished his other self well and hoped that he would be revived from stasis without incident. Even more so, he hoped that any consequences the other Anak and his family might suffer from today's actions would be mild.

But he was no longer that man. Eberin Das had been right on that point. If he was going to cast his lot with the people of a planet that the Alliance had condemned for the grievous sin of curiosity, if he was going to die for their cause, he would not do so as Anak Djurdin. He would die as John Beckett.

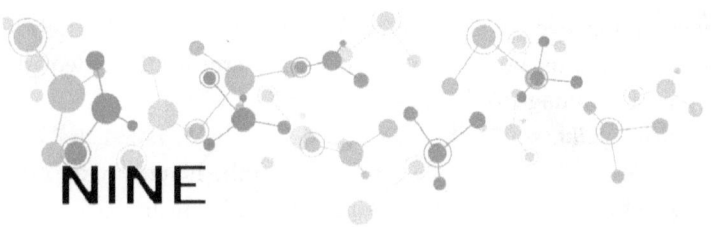

NINE

BECK BOARDED the hyperloop at the Stamford station at seven twenty. He'd hoped to be in Boston by midafternoon, but removing the tracker had turned into a multi-hour ordeal.

Once the car was well outside New York, he'd found a drugstore located next to a chain hotel in Stamford, both within walking distance of the Loop. He'd chugged several hefty shots from the flask that Sandjeel gave him before going into the store to purchase a set of cheap earphones—the only thing he really needed from his bag—along with an Exacto knife, a bottle of disinfectant, and some bandages. His entire purpose for leaving Conclave with a bottle of *evir* was that it would be one less stop he'd need to make during his escape from the city. Because there was no way he'd have the nerve to slice into his own neck if he was completely sober.

With everything else going on, however, he'd forgotten Sandjeel's warning about the strength of that particular bottle of *evir* until it was too late. He'd very nearly been *too* drunk to cut the tracker out by the time he made it to the hotel. Once he managed to extract the thing, he staggered back into the parking lot and tossed it inside the rental car. Then he changed his reservation to delivery mode and sent the car to a random address in Albany.

It was after one o'clock by that point. His plan had been to go back inside and clean up the bathroom, which now looked like a scene from a horror flick. After that, he would record the message to Claire and then head north on the hyperloop. Instead, he collapsed on the hotel bed, intending to just lie there for a few minutes until the room stopped spinning. He'd opened his eyes a little over four hours later, still slightly buzzed. He was, however, sober enough to record the video and repair the damage to the hotel bathroom.

Now *fully* sober, he regretted that he'd failed to buy painkillers. His head was pounding from the hangover, and the back of his neck throbbed with each beat of his heart.

As the train left for Boston, he wavered back and forth on the advisability of stopping at his apartment. If Durav realized he had removed the tracker—and he might, since Beck wasn't entirely sure how the thing worked—then the apartment was the first place they'd look for him. They might try the lab, too, but at least there were security guards there to keep people out.

He really wanted to stop and get his cat, though. Crichton was nearly thirteen and solitary by nature, which was a good thing given how often Beck crashed at the lab. The cat liked his routine of watching the cars come and go in the lot, and he didn't care for travel. That's why Beck hired a sitter to come in to top off the feeder and hang out for a bit on the rare occasions that he went up to the cabin for a few days.

This, however, was going to be more than just a few days. The odds were damn good that he wouldn't be coming back to the apartment. Maybe he could find a cat lover to take Crichton in. Or he could just pay the sitter to keep coming. He could certainly afford her services for the six months or so that Earth had left. But he'd miss the little guy. And he hated to think of him spending his final months mostly alone.

A quick check of the feed from the security cameras outside his apartment turned the decision into a no-brainer. Crichton had been lounging on his usual perch near the window at a little after four when something startled him and he shot off into the dark of the apartment, most likely sliding into his favorite hiding spot under the bed. This was the cat's standard reaction to someone at the door, so Beck switched to the doorbell camera and saw two men in the hallway. One of them was the mercenary he'd seen with Maela and Durav at HQ. The second guy, standing just behind him, was one of Durav's *ipret-tai*.

The two locks on his front door kept the men at bay for less than a minute. A break-in should have triggered an audible alarm and also alerted security at Jonas Labs. But they must have managed to disengage the system. Given how slowly the men were moving, they obviously weren't worried about being caught.

When Beck switched to his three interior cameras, he expected to see them setting up explosives. Instead, they began searching the place. The *ipret-tai* had a scanner that didn't appear to be Earther tech. He waved it over every surface, including the walls and the floor, while the other guy systematically tossed the entire apartment—dumping the contents of drawers, closets, and cabinets, and even slicing into pillows, sofa cushions, and mattresses.

What were they looking for? The only thing he could think of was the Eberin Das journal. But if that's what they wanted, they'd have taken his computer, and that was the one thing they hadn't even touched.

Well, the computer and Crichton. They either hadn't noticed or hadn't been inclined to harm him, because when Beck scanned forward about fifteen minutes, he saw the cat emerge warily from the bedroom to survey the damage, tail twitching and lips curled back as he sniffed the stranger-scent in the air.

They didn't appear to have left anything dangerous behind, although Beck had been watching at double speed so he couldn't be certain. He went back to the point where they entered and was a few minutes into a second viewing of the break-in when his phone rang.

It wasn't a number that he recognized but he answered anyway, thinking it could be Drex. Her number wasn't in his phone, and she'd told him the night before that she'd be in touch to let him know exactly when the KTI attack was happening.

"Where are you?" Drex asked.

"On the Loop. Maybe ten minutes from the lab."

"You still haven't purged the data?"

"*Lower your voice.*" He turned down the volume to the point where he could barely hear her talking. "And no, I haven't. As I explained last night, I need to handle both things at the same time, and it has to be done at the lab. Otherwise, Joe will get—"

"Then you need to go as soon as you're off the train. Sandjeel changed his mind."

"You're kidding. Do you know why?"

"A minor uprising among the other Watchers. Arbet seemed to think you might know something about that."

He decided to neither confirm nor deny. "And Durav is okay with the delay?"

"Of course not. He's pissed but he doesn't have much choice other than to accept it. We've been granted until the end of this comms window on the condition that we also take out three of Kolya's facilities and two more belonging to Jonas Labs. That includes the main headquarters buildings for both. And yes, we'll issue a warning to minimize casualties."

He grimaced, even though he knew it wasn't an unreasonable bargain. He'd agreed to zap the new Rejuvesce data just on the possibility that the action might make Sandjeel change his decision, and this would assure them a guaranteed reprieve for a few months.

"Okay. When?"

"At nine p.m."

"*Tonight?*"

"Yeah. That's why I said that you need to get moving."

For several seconds, he couldn't even respond. "How in hell could you get something that major organized in a matter of hours?"

A long, heavy pause followed. "I didn't. It ... it was part of the deal from the beginning, okay? I've had people in position for weeks now, ready to move in as soon as I gave the word and plant the explosives. Or rather, I've had them ready in all but one of the facilities."

"Which one?" he asked, even though he was fairly sure he knew.

"Yours. I had a woman from the Flock on the Jonas Labs maintenance crew, but then they put some new guy in charge of security. He did a much more thorough check of everyone's credentials than his predecessor and flagged some ... irregularities in her paperwork."

That part definitely tracked. When Wilson took over as head of security a few months back, he'd repeated the mandatory background search on everyone who had been hired in the past decade, arguing that his predecessor and the guy's second-in-command had been, in his words, *lazy sonsabitches*. Beck remembered breathing a sigh of relief that he'd been there longer than the cutoff and that Reese had already resigned. Their backgrounds were solid enough on paper, but any in-depth search that tried to track down family, close friends, high school records, and so forth, was likely to uncover a few red flags.

"At any rate," she said, "you won't have to get your hands dirty, if that's what you're worried about. I *think* we've got it covered now. If not, we'll just go with the other five sites, but you need to assume that the Jonas Labs HQ is coming down at nine with the others."

"Why didn't you tell me all of this last night?"

"Personally, I wasn't sure that we should tell you this part at all. Stasia and I were both worried you might try to stop it. I think you're too close to the people there to see the bigger picture and we need to send a *strong* message. Arbet even admitted we might be right to keep this part quiet given that you made it rather clear last night that you were squeamish about possible casualties."

"*Squeamish*? Seriously? Your *strong message...*" He'd been about to point out that it could kill hundreds of innocent people, but given the crowded train, he searched for more neutral words. "What about the occupants?"

"Like I said, they'll get a warning. Fifteen minutes. And we all assumed that would be enough time, but then I remembered what you said about families living in one of the buildings. The last thing we need is pictures of a bunch of dead kids hitting social media."

"Oh, yeah. Can't have that sort of *bad publicity.*"

Based on her sharp intake of breath and the pause before responding, she clearly picked up on his sarcasm. He could almost hear her gritting her teeth.

"That's not what I meant. And it's also why I'm calling you *now* ... well, that, and to make sure that you're out of there by nine. As soon as my people are out of the building, I'll message you so that you can call security and give them a bit of advance notice."

"And what exactly am I supposed to tell them?"

"How would I know? You're the one who works there. Find a fire alarm and pull it. Whatever you need to do in order to get them to start clearing the buildings."

Manual fire alarms were a thing of the rather distant past, but he supposed he could figure something out. He was about to sign off when he remembered that Claire was in New York covering the Ares Consortium and would most likely be at this dinner where Kolya was making the announcement. "What about Kolya's offices in New York? At ... Beekman Place. Is that one of the locations?"

"No. God, that would be a disaster. There are too many tourists there. Too many people in general. Especially tonight, with Kolya's big dinner going on. That's actually another reason we're doing it now—Stasia has a backdoor into KTI's system. We should have a captive audience of a few hundred people, including dozens of journalists. Probably including your Claire, if that's what you're worried about. It's also why we need these attacks to happen at the same time, so again, you need to be out of there by nine."

"Yeah. I got it. I'm almost at the station now. It's like a five minute walk to the lab."

"Wait for my signal, though," she said. "And don't do anything stupid. We have to present a united front. Sandjeel could still change his mind and signal the Alliance at the beginning of the comms window. And then all of this would be pointless, so—"

He hung up before she could finish her plea.

TEN

DRIVING to the lab from the station was much slower than walking. But since he'd almost certainly need to make a quick exit on the way out, Beck took the time to hail a car and waited impatiently as the car circled the hyperloop lot and took the access road around the shopping center where the protestors always congregated. Where some were *still* congregated, which meant that Wilson's negotiations with the owner of the center must not have been successful.

Most of the protestors had already packed it in for the day, but there were still about a dozen people clustered beneath the awning of the sleek white bus belonging to the Gates of Destiny cathedral. Two marquees hovered above the bus, their warning of God's imminent vengeance against Jonas Labs bright against the early evening sky. There was no sign of the Flock's smaller grass-green school bus with its Earth-eyeball logo. Drex must have her people operating in stealth mode.

The small gaggle of protestors perked up as his car slowed to turn into the lab. They didn't target everyone entering or exiting the lab—only about one car in every five—and they usually took turns, possibly to avoid mixed messages. But given the hour, there weren't many employees coming and going and four of them hurried across the grass divider between the properties to block his way. He was surprised that two of the protestors wore Flock T-shirts, given the absence of their bus. Apparently, the environmental crackpots had made peace with the religious crackpots in the interest of inconveniencing their common enemy.

What followed was a well-choreographed dance that he'd

been through dozens of times over the past few months. When the car detected the people in its path, it stopped, honked, and flashed its headlights a few times. Then it issued a vocal warning and continued inching forward as much as possible. The protestors generally didn't touch the car—that put them at risk of more serious legal charges—but would instead simply shout and wave their signs for two minutes until the car's AI gave a final warning, announcing that it had right of way and the police would be summoned unless all pedestrians cleared the road within one minute. At that point, they'd shout once or twice more, then head back to the parking lot just before the time was up, usually making the sign of the cross (Gates of Destiny) or raising their middle finger (the Flock) on their way out.

The policy at Jonas Labs was to simply ignore them unless they shoved at the car or threatened you. Give them three minutes to exercise their First Amendment right to protest and then you could continue on your way. But Beck didn't have time for their bullshit today. He cracked the window just enough to yell out at the guy closest to him who was one of the Flock. Surely Drex had given her people a heads up about what was going down in a little over half an hour?

"Let me through, okay? I have an emergency."

"The *planet* has an emergency, dickhead. We're not going anywhere until our three minutes are up. Deal with it."

Apparently, this guy hadn't gotten the memo. And since Beck couldn't alert security until he made it up to the lab and wiped the data, he simply closed his eyes and took a few deep breaths as the chanting continued.

When the car's AI announced the final one-minute warning, the protestors cranked up the volume of chants for about thirty seconds and retreated back to their own turf. The path now clear, Anak's car zipped through the lot. He was about to tell it the code to enter the employee garage when he remembered that parking in his assigned spot would be a very bad idea.

Security would probably block off the garage as soon as he raised the alarm. They might even block off the main entrance. Instead, he instructed the car to park at the back of a lot behind building four where the only thing separating the campus from the access road was the curb and about twenty meters of lawn. If all else failed, he could manually override the car's protocol and drive across the grass. It would incur a hefty fine with the rental company, but that was the least of his worries at the moment.

He entered the garage by the side door, surprised to find that all three of the assigned parking spaces in front of the express elevator were empty. Kai usually left the lab around seven, but Joe's car should be there. The last time they'd spoken, Joe had been determined to cut his vacation short and be back in the lab bright and early this morning. While he'd been known to ride in to work with Kai on rare occasions if they went out to breakfast or if she railroaded him into an off-campus meeting with a key stockholder, neither of those seemed likely given how tense their relationship had been during the past few weeks. It was possible that they'd patched things up, but they'd clearly been at an impasse a few days back. Kai was determined to announce the breakthrough to her disgruntled stockholders and Joe was equally determined to hold off until he had a larger group of subjects under the age of twenty-five scanned for the *in silico* testing.

As Beck stepped into the private elevator and pressed the button marked *Olympus*, it hit him that this was probably the last time he'd make this trip. It wasn't merely that he'd be banned from the premises. The lab—the entire building—would no longer exist.

If given a choice between losing an arm and losing his lab, Joe would offer up the arm in a heartbeat. Left arm, right arm … it wouldn't matter. This was going to gut him.

But it was too late to change anything. He stared down at the phone in his hand, willing a message from Drex to pop up on the screen informing him that her people had left the campus. It was already eight thirty-one.

He still had no idea what he was going to tell Wilson. *Hey, I think I spotted a mad bomber in the parking lot...*

The top floor seemed unusually quiet when he stepped out of the elevator. There was no guard at the station after seven, so that much at least was normal. But even if Kai had already gone home for the day, her end of Olympus was almost always still buzzing at this hour. The silence probably meant she was out of town, with at least part of her entourage in tow.

The lab was empty, too, although that didn't necessarily mean Joe wasn't here. He'd taken to wandering around the halls during his walking brainstorm sessions now that Wilson had locked the door to the roof due to sniper threats from protestors. In the evenings, he sometimes roamed the main building, but during the day he usually paced around building four. It was vacant aside from the bottom floor, which was leased for the next few months by another company. The upper floors were being renovated for Jonas Labs's use and were technically closed off, but no one was going to tell Joe Echols he couldn't walk around in his own building.

Maybe Joe had changed his mind and stayed in Maine? That was good on one level. With the lab empty, it would be much easier for him to do what he needed to and get out quickly. On the other hand...

His conversation with Drex had pushed everything else aside, but now Beck's mind was yanked back to the video of Durav's men searching his apartment. He'd been much, much more secretive about ownership of Bellamy House, hiding it under a shell company. But if Durav had archived logs from the tracker he'd removed, he might know about it. Hell, he might even know about the cabin.

That meant he needed to give Joe and Claire a heads-up and get them to pass along a message that the guards Wilson had assigned to the place needed to be on high alert. He called

Claire first, thinking she could contact Joe, but it went to voice-mail. "Call me," he said. "We have to talk."

Maybe it was for the best that he had to call Joe. At least he could make sure he wasn't somewhere else on campus.

As with Claire, though, the call went straight to voicemail. He cursed softly as Joe's voice greeted him. It wasn't the usual spiel—*Busy. Leave a message.* Instead, he said he was out of town and would respond when he got back. It was possible that he'd forgotten to change his away message. That almost seemed more likely than him extending his stay in Maine, given how adamant he'd been about returning, thanks to that accursed tally in his head of the lives that would be lost for every day he delayed his work.

The beep for Beck to record a message sounded as he was thinking. He hesitated for a moment, and then just blurted out what was on his mind.

"Hey. I'm sorry, okay? Sorry for ... being so weird for the past few months and for everything that's going down now. If you're still at Bellamy House—actually, even if you're not—can you tell security they need to be extra, *extra* vigilant? And you're probably not going to believe this after tonight, but I really do love you, man. Claire, too. You're *ufrete.* And there's nothing more important than that among my people. Take care of yourself, okay?"

Beck ended the call, and for several seconds he looked around the lab, taking one last picture for his memory files. Then he pressed his palm against the pad to log in. The system greeted him, automatically loading the last thing they'd been working on before they left for Maine. Virtual Claire appeared a couple of meters to the right. She was aged forward to ninety-nine here, but didn't look a day over forty. Hovering next to her holographic body was a list of various vital statistics.

He pulled up the local files, and a few keystrokes later he confirmed that he did indeed wish to delete them. Virtual-Claire flickered once, then reverted to her baseline form. The hologram hovering above the lab floor was now thirteen years old, several years younger than when he'd met her. Several years younger than she'd been when Martin Echols died, and Beck had stood at this window looking out at the pond near the center of the eight-acre biodome as she and Joe scattered their father's ashes.

The trees in the nearby eucalyptus grove had been smaller then. They were full height now, and you could only catch glimpses of the pond from this vantage point during the day. He breathed in, remembering the scent of those trees, so similar to the ones in the forest on Parda where he'd hiked with his own father.

It was now eight thirty-five. A surge of anger ran through him. Drex should have messaged him by now. And they should have told him the full plan from the beginning, even if they knew he wouldn't like it. As much as he hated the idea, destroying the lab was understandable. Taking down the apartments and the biodome, though? That was gratuitous. He supposed the shock value was, at least in part, what they were aiming for, but he could have told them that they'd have more luck persuading Joe and Claire, and maybe even Kai, if they opted for a surgical strike rather than blowing up a piece of their hearts.

But he couldn't dwell on that right now. Yes, the biodome was a living thing, but it was still a *thing*. And the clock was ticking on getting *people* out of these buildings.

Since Drex hadn't called him, he decided to call her. For the third time in as many minutes, he was kicked to voicemail. "Why the hell haven't you called?"

He paced around for another minute, tossed one of the ping-pong balls against the net in the center of the conference table a few times, then crushed it inside his fist.

Screw it.

Calling Wilson before Drex's people were gone could put them in danger of being caught. He was fairly sure at least one of them was a member of the Watch. But it was eight thirty-seven, now, and still no word from Drex. Her promised advance warning window was rapidly closing.

He turned back to the computer, logged into the remote server, and deleted the backups.

Then, as he left the lab for the very last time, he called Wilson.

ELEVEN

AT EIGHT FORTY-TWO, Beck stood alone in a small control room on the second floor, staring at a wallscreen divided into five sections. The surveillance footage on the top third of the display seemed to be trained permanently on the security checkpoint at the Jonas Labs main entrance. Below that, four smaller screens flashed almost imperceptibly every ten seconds or so before shifting to a different view. Labs. Offices. Hallways. One camera alternated different views of the lobby. Another showed mostly the biodome. And every time that view popped up, the thoughts that he'd had in the lab cycled through again.

The door opened and a thin, dark-haired guy who didn't look a day over twenty stepped inside, followed by Wilson. Before his recent promotion, Wilson had been assigned exclusively to Olympus. Beck had seen him five, sometimes six days a week for the past fifteen years. He genuinely liked the man, and the wary look on Wilson's face right now bothered him deeply. Not that he could blame him.

"This is Sawyer," Wilson said, nodding toward the younger man. "Tell him what you need, and he'll pull it up."

Beck nodded. Wilson gave him one last perplexed look and then headed back down the hallway.

Sawyer sank into the chair in front of the display wall. "How far back do you want me to go, Dr. Beckett?"

"It's just Beck. And half an hour?"

He yanked a chair from one of the other workstations. Adrenaline surged through his system, and the blare of the evacuation alarm wasn't helping matters. As soon as he sat down, his right leg began a rapid, rhythmic tap, a signal that his body wanted to be up again. Up and pacing, or better yet, on its way out of the building.

"What exactly are we looking for?" The kid's voice broke halfway through, and Beck fought back the urge to tell him to just go. But he needed a second set of eyes—could use a third or fourth set, in fact, given how little time they had.

"We're looking for a tall guy. Taller than Joe Echols."

Sawyer whistled softly. "So ... *freaky* tall?"

"Yeah. But thinner than Joe. Lanky."

"Hair? Skin?"

"Fairly dark, I think. Same for his hair. Pretty sure he was clean-shaven." Beck doesn't add that it might also be a tall, blond guy. There was even an outside chance that it was a very tall *woman*. And if they'd decided to send one of the Flock, even their height wasn't a given.

But he was pretty sure Drex would have sent Reese, since he already knew the layout. He might even still have employee access if he'd managed to leave a backdoor in the system like Stasia apparently had at KTI.

"What's he wearing?" Sawyer asked.

"No clue."

The kid shot him a baffled look, with good reason.

"The only thing that stood out was that he was *freaky tall*, as you put it."

"O...*kay*." There was a hint of skepticism in Sawyer's voice now, which was fair enough. But at least he stopped asking questions. After that, they just scanned the screens in silence.

The story he'd given Wilson was that he'd spotted a suspicious guy leaving the building with what looked like a rucksack when he arrived on campus. He'd added that he hadn't thought much about it until he got up to the lab and remembered something that one of the protestors had said when they blocked his car on the way in. *Let him go. Come nine o'clock, he'll be in pieces along with the rest of those scum.* It was a lie, of course, but if Wilson zoomed in on the external security footage from that side of the building, he'd at least see that the protestors had indeed blocked Beck's car. Hopefully, he wouldn't be able to tell what they were yelling. If the protestors hadn't cleared out yet, some hapless member of the Flock was probably going to be hauled in for making a bomb threat, but Beck wasn't going to lose any sleep over that.

Wilson's only question had been why he had waited until he got up to the lab to call it in, given how specific that threat was. He'd immediately started evacuating the buildings but asked Beck if he'd be willing to risk staying in the building a few minutes longer so that he could look through the security footage and see if he could find the guy he'd noticed outside. If someone had actually set a bomb, maybe they could locate and disable it. Beck was fairly certain that it was more than a single bomb, but the story he'd given Wilson didn't cover that, so he'd simply agreed, mostly because it would have seemed odd if he didn't.

He'd considered giving a false description when Sawyer asked, rather than scanning for Reese. But then he wondered if maybe there was a middle ground that would confine the damage to the lab and put fewer lives at risk?

At eight forty-six, Wilson stuck his head in. "We just got confirmation. A recorded message from Corbin Drexel, leader of the Flock, stating that multiple explosives throughout the campus will go off at exactly nine p.m. We've cleared everyone but security out of the buildings, except for the apartments, which we're still working on. But … we've got a babysitter claiming two kids are missing out in the biodome."

Beck winced. "How old are they?"

"Seven and five. Brother and sister. I'm headed down to help search." He glanced at the clock. "You have *nine* minutes. Then both of you are out of here. Understood?"

"Yes sir," Sawyer said, keeping his eyes on the screen. He currently had all six feeds running at about ten times the normal speed, but there really wasn't much to see yet. Even after rolling the footage back, there were only a handful of ambitious souls working late in the labs. Occasionally, a blur of movement would prompt Sawyer to slow down the video, usually to discover it was a security guard. The vast majority of activity came from the robo-mop zipping around in the lobby.

"And we have action." Sawyer nodded toward the display, where the timestamp read *20:39*, which was about a minute after the time when Beck called Wilson with the advance warning.

Everything on the screens was now happening all at once. Red lights flashed in the hallways. The remaining lab techs dashed toward the emergency exits and the dozen or so security personnel who were on duty—including Sawyer—converged on the security desk in the lobby. Shortly thereafter, Wilson came through the entrance from the biodome. Beck appeared on the screen a few seconds later, and then the security team dispersed. Most headed into the biodome, which was the quickest path to the other three buildings on the campus, but a few headed back up to double check that the labs and offices were clear.

The wailing alarm that had been sounding stopped abruptly and Wilson's voice boomed out. "Samantha and Jeremy Kurnetsov. If you're playin' hide and seek in the biodome or inside one of the other buildings, please exit immediately. This is an emergency evacuation. Like a fire drill at school, okay? You are *not* in trouble, but you need to get out. Mandy is waiting for you on the lawn outside."

"You should switch the screens to the biodome to help search," Beck told Sawyer when the message ended. "They probably have footage backed up offsite, and I can go through it later."

Sawyer held up a hand. "This isn't the only room with surveillance screens. I'm sure Wilson has someone using the others. He said to look for nine minutes. We've got just over five left … and look… I spy a freaky tall guy." He tapped a key and one of the lower screens now filled the entire display.

It was Reese. Six minutes earlier according to the timestamp, so about four minutes after he called the warning in to Wilson. "What floor is he on?"

"He's on four," Sawyer said as he restored the other screens. "But are you sure this is the guy you're looking for? He's JL. That's a maintenance uniform."

"He's not an employee. Or at least, not a *current* employee. He worked here a few years back, but he was one of Kai Jonas's assistants. Follow him."

"He hit the up button. Probably going to Olympus." Sawyer switched the view to the sixth floor, but Reese never got out. "Okay, I guess it's five." He switched the view to the fifth floor and rolled back a few seconds. Sure enough, Reese exited, turned, and tapped in a few numbers to open a door to the right of the elevators.

"Is that … a janitor's closet or…"

Sawyer frowned, then pulled up a security map on the top screen. "No, it's the pump room for one of the waterfalls. Looks like there's a ladder going down to the other floors and eventually into the biodome."

A few seconds later they picked Reese up again coming out of a door camouflaged to look like the rock wall.

"That was a little over a minute ago," Sawyer said.

"Can you unlock the maintenance door on this floor?"

"Sure." He tapped a couple of keys. "Should I call Chief Wilson?"

"No," Beck said. "We're closer and they need to focus on finding those kids. I don't suppose you have a gun?"

"*What?*" Sawyer looked appalled. "No. I'm cybersecurity, not *security* security. All I've got is this. You want it?" He pointed to a stunner on his belt. It looked like the smaller, much weaker brother of the one that Maela had pointed at Beck earlier in the day.

"Yeah. Better than nothing." Beck shoved the stunner into his pocket, pulled out the new earphones, and grabbed a pen. He jotted a number down on a notepad near the keyboard. "I'm heading down. This is my number. Keep tracking him and let me know where he goes. And be sure you're out of here by eight fifty-five, like Wilson said."

He jammed in the earphones and took off running toward the elevators, answering his phone as he went. As Sawyer had promised, the maintenance door on the right was unlocked. The light flipped on as he stepped inside what looked like an equipment storage closet. He ran over to the ladder they'd seen in the video and started down. Wilson's voice broke into the alarm again to repeat his plea to the kids, this time sounding on the verge of panic.

"Can you still see him, Sawyer?"

"Yeah. But probably not for long. Looks like he's headed straight across to the other side of the biodome."

Beck reached the ground floor and threw the door open. It was full dark outside now, but there was plenty of light from the solar lamps that illuminated the walking paths.

"He's near the middle now. Walking at a steady clip but not running."

Beck ran toward the other falls, keeping to the paths as much as possible to avoid stray roots and branches. About a minute later, he spotted Reese stepping off the path into the woods about fifty meters ahead. "Sawyer? I've got eyes on him. What time is it?"

"Eight fifty-four."

"Okay. Thanks for your help. Now go find those kids."

Beck picked up the pace even more. When he was a few meters away, Reese turned around. "You just couldn't wait, could you? Two more minutes and we'd have been done. Instead, I had to hide under a lab table until there was enough of a break in the chaos for me to get out of the building. Have you seen Housen? Last I heard, he'd just finished up, but then the alarm went off and my phone stopped working. We've got one of the Flock guys in here, too, but you wouldn't recognize him."

"I haven't seen Housen," Beck said, thinking that Wilson must have started jamming communications when he set off the alarm. He'd had no issues with his own phone, but it was probably on a white list.

Reese turned back toward building two. "I'm going to check the—"

Beck grabbed his shoulder and spun him around. "You need to shut this down, Reese. You heard the announcement, right? We've got two missing kids—"

Reese's face fell. "Yes. I heard it. And I hate it. But the bombs are on a timer set to go off in less than three minutes. I couldn't shut it down even if I wanted to. Just try to keep in mind how many kids we'll save if this—"

"Bullshit. Drex even said if you couldn't get everything in place in time, they'd go with just the other five buildings. I don't believe she'd send you in without any way to cancel it."

"I don't care *what* you believe."

"Just give me the damn detonator." He shoved hard, and Reese stumbled back a few steps.

Reese's fist shot out and caught Beck in the stomach. His first instinct was to punch back, but he didn't have time for this. He pulled out the stunner. Reese spotted it and tried to knock it out of his hands, but the move came too late. The pellet caught him in the chest, and he tumbled backward.

A thwack sounded as Reese's head smacked into one of the rocks at the base of the waterfall. Beck had hoped to immobilize him for thirty seconds or so, just long enough to search him for the remote detonator. Instead, he was out cold.

He crouched down next to Reese and checked his pulse. It was strong, and the cut on his head didn't seem too bad. He began searching through his pockets. Nothing. He was about to move on to the bag he was carrying over his shoulder when Wilson's voice came over the speakers.

"We found the kids. They're safe. Everyone clear the premises immediately."

There was nothing in Reese's bag, either. In a last ditch effort, he pressed Reese's forefinger to his armscreen and scrolled through the most recent apps. Nothing.

With no other options left, he pulled Reese into a fireman's carry and headed for the closest exit, which was through the employee garage. He didn't know how much time was left and wasn't sure he wanted to know. God, he had screwed this up so badly.

When he slowed to catch his breath, he tapped the phone in his pocket and called Claire. He fully expected to be kicked to her voicemail again since she was almost certainly at the Ares Consortium dinner that Drex had mentioned. To his surprise, she answered. Her voice was hushed to the point that he couldn't even make out the words. Someone was giving a presentation in the background. It sounded like Kai, but that couldn't be right.

"I *know* you can't talk." He was actually having a hard time talking himself as he ran down the path with Reese on his back. "I just need you to ... listen. You were right, okay? It's a warning. And if you've already listened to the ... other message, you don't need to worry. I just talked to Joe. He stayed in Maine a ... few extra days. He's fine. Ro and Jemma are fine. Wilson is increasing their security."

That was a lie, and she'd find out it was a lie when she eventually talked to Joe. But he didn't want her to worry. He was *almost* certain Joe was still in Maine, and they did have security guards and perimeter drones at Bellamy Place.

He was in the garage now, only a meter or so from the side exit.

"I tried to save the biodome but ... I think I'm out of time, Claire. I'm sorry. You're safe where you are. Beekman Place is *not* on the list, but I suspect you're about to be in the middle of a panic. If I make it out of here, I'll be at my quiet place." He stepped through the door and turned toward the lot where he'd left the rental car. "But I don't know whether—"

Before he could finish, everything behind him exploded. He was airborne, with Reese still on his back, as debris rained down around them.

PART III

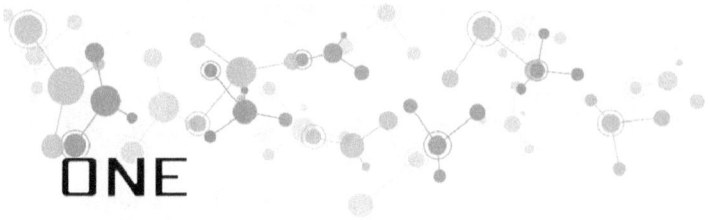

ONE

"BECK?" Claire knocked softly at first, then louder when he didn't respond. When he still didn't answer, she tried the door handle. Locked.

She called his name again, pounding with the side of her fist so hard that the door shook. When she stopped, she heard a barely audible voice inside.

"Hold on, hold on. I'm coming."

Two locks clicked, and then the door opened. Claire stepped into a dimly lit main room, with a couch and chair on one side and a miniscule kitchen on the other.

"Sorry. I ... didn't hear you at first." Beck closed the door and leaned back against it. He was wearing dark gray chinos and a plain white T-shirt, clean except for a widening splotch of crimson on the right side. A clumsy bandage, also bloody, was wrapped around his right hand.

"My god, Beck. Sit down." She placed the gun on top of the small desk just inside the door. "You look like you're about to collapse."

"Wouldn't be the first time this morning." He nodded toward a braided rug in front of the sofa, its varying shades of brown now marred by a dark red patch near the center.

"You do know it's *way* past morning, right?"

He let out a soft hiss of pain as he shifted his weight onto her.

"On second thought," she said, "you need a hospital."

"Couch. Hospital isn't an option. And even if it was, Reese needs it a lot more than I do."

"Who is Reese?"

"One of the guys who set the explosives at JL. A fellow Watcher who worked in Kai's office for a few years. He's in the bedroom. I think he's concussed. He may have other injuries, too. Which is my fault and—"

"Why is the hospital not an option?"

"Because they'd call the police. And because Watchers have to avoid our DNA being on record for obvious reasons. I just need some more bandages and something to seal the cut on my side."

"News flash. You left DNA all over that rental car outside," Claire said as she lowered him onto the couch. "And between the car and the state of your rug, I'd say that in addition to bandages, you're going to need a few liters of blood."

"Some of it is from Reese. And I doubt blood is something you can pick up at the local drugstore."

"If you'd let me know you were hurt this badly, I could have brought medical supplies with me. I've been calling you. So has Joe. And Wilson, for that matter."

"I don't know where my phone is. It's probably somewhere in the car. Unless I dropped it when I was trying to get Reese out before the parking garage collapsed, but I'm pretty sure I had it after that. To be honest, though, I wouldn't have answered unless it was you. I couldn't risk the call being used to trace my location."

"So why tell *me* where to find you?"

"Because you're the only one I trust right now. The only one I thought might believe me. Because if *you* weren't willing to give me the benefit of the doubt between what you already knew and the evidence that I sent you last night, then…" He shook his head almost imperceptibly. "Then we don't have any chance at all. Might as well let them find me."

Claire wanted to press the point, to ask whether the vague

them he referred to was the police or the Triad or the Flock. But it could wait. He was deathly pale and obviously in pain.

"If you won't go to a hospital, at least come back to the B & B with me so that Ro can take a look at you. She might even be able to prescribe something, although I don't know what the rules are since she's outside the state where she's doing residency."

"Not with security there. At some point, I will tell Wilson everything, but too many other lives are on the line at the moment. And I don't just mean from the Alliance. Durav—"

"Dammit, Beck!" The name Durav seemed vaguely familiar, but this wasn't the time for him to go off on a tangent. "You're not going to be able to help anyone if you bleed out. What if I bring Ro here?"

"How much does she know about all of this?"

"She knows you're an alien. And she knows the end of the world is right around the corner, courtesy of your galactic empire. When we have more than five minutes to talk, I plan to tell her everything else, just as I did with Joe and Wyatt. I'm done keeping secrets from the people I love. Is this Reese guy conscious?"

He sighed heavily. "I'm not even sure he's alive. We were set to arrive around ten last night, but I didn't wake when the car pulled up to the gate. I finally came to just after sunrise. I ... got us inside and got Reese into the bed—which started my side and my hand bleeding again. He woke up enough that I managed to get a bit of water into him. After that, I was going out to see if I could clean up the car enough to send it back, but I didn't even make it to the door. What time is it now?"

"Around six."

"Damn. That's at least ten hours ago. I need to go check on him." He started to get up, but Claire stopped him.

"No. You stay put. I'll do it."

The last remnants of sun filtered in through the blinds, providing just enough light for Claire to make out a long shadowy lump on the bed in the corner. There was no light switch, but she spotted a lamp on the dresser and waved her hand over the base three times before realizing it was too old to be equipped with a sensor.

While she didn't really *need* the light to check the man's pulse, she couldn't quite bring herself to approach him in the dark. He wasn't human—not really—and while that was true of Beck as well, she knew Beck. Plus, if this was one of the men who bombed Jonas Labs, she had no reason to trust him.

She was about to ask Beck how to turn on the light when she finally located a switch on the electrical cord. It had an odd little thumb wheel on the side. She gave it an experimental spin, and the lamp flickered on.

The man on the bed looked vaguely familiar. He was exceptionally tall with olive skin. Long, straight black hair was pulled tightly away from his forehead into a ponytail that fanned out onto the pillow beneath his head. The left side of his scalp was caked with matted blood from a jagged cut that ran from a few inches above his temple to the hollow of his cheek.

It took a moment for her to place where she'd seen him before. At first, she assumed she might have run into him at Jonas Labs. She didn't visit the lab all that often and hadn't been on her mother's side of Olympus in well over a decade, but she could have seen him in the hallway or on the elevator.

Then it clicked. He was one of the first Watchers to arrive at the meeting in Riverdale, along with a guy with a square jawline and a slightly hooked nose. Those two were among only four or five faces she'd seen clearly—and she'd remembered them mostly because Reese was the only person she'd seen go into the building who wasn't obviously Caucasian.

Now she was wondering what this guy's actual body, the one in stasis somewhere, looked like. Beck, too, for that matter. Were they humanoid? Reptilian? Images of the various aliens she'd seen in movies flashed through her mind.

Maybe that's where the bug monsters are hiding, Claire.

She shook Jemma's words away and focused on the decidedly *human* body in front of her, pressing a hand against the side of his neck. Her fingers brushed against dried blood near the back of his head, suggesting a second injury. He was alive, though, with a rapid, thready pulse, his skin hot and clammy against her palm.

She pulled out her phone. "Call Rowan."

Ro answered a few seconds later. "Glad to see that you made it. Is Beck there? Is everything okay?"

"He's here. And … no. Not really. Any chance you could make a house call to stitch up a couple of aliens?"

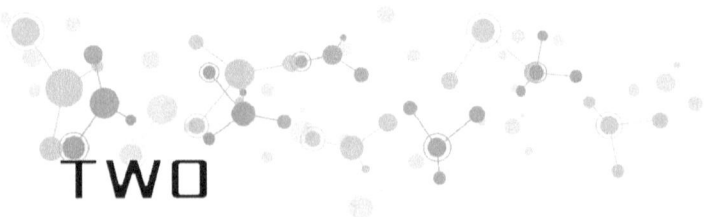

TWO

CLAIRE OPENED the door about forty minutes later to find Ro on the porch, a bright red medical bag slung over one shoulder and Jemma's drowsy head resting on the other.

"Oh. Jemma's with you."

"*Yes*, Jemma is with me," Ro said. "Where else would she be? Did you think I was going to leave her alone at the B & B with the security guards?"

"No, of course not. I'm just not thinking straight. Hold on a sec."

Claire stepped back inside, moved the pistol from the top of the desk into one of the drawers, and glanced quickly around the room. She'd dragged the stained rug out back and wiped most of the blood from the floor while she waited for Ro, but she'd have done a much more careful job if she'd considered the very obvious fact that Jemma would be coming, too.

"Okay," she said, opening the door again. "All set. What did you tell them? The guards, I mean."

"I said we were meeting your brother in Boston for dinner."

"But that's something they can—"

"Check. Yes. Which is why I called Joe and asked him to cover for me. I think I woke him up. I didn't give him all of the details, but he's a smart boy, so I'm sure he can fill in the missing pieces. All I said was that you needed me to help an injured friend and that I needed the access code for the boat Beck rented." Ro tapped the strap of the medical bag. "The first-aid kit at the B & B was little more than Band-Aids and antiseptic. Boats almost always keep decent emergency supplies on hand." She looked over at Beck, who was dozing on the sofa. "I'll check the guy in the bedroom first. What did you say his name is?"

"Reese. But he's not responding."

"Okay." Ro handed Jemma to Claire and headed for the kitchen sink to wash up. "If he's got any food here, she's hungry. You called just as I was about to heat something up for dinner."

Claire carried Jemma, who was beginning to wake up now, over to one of the stools at the kitchen counter. "Let's see what Beck has in his cupboards. I'm guessing not much, since he just got here, but maybe we'll find hidden treasure."

Jemma was uncharacteristically quiet. It could just be from dozing off in the car, but Claire also wondered how much she'd overheard in the past few days. She gave the girl's stool a little jiggle as she went by, knowing from past experience that a swivel stool would keep her entertained for at least a few minutes. It worked, although the spins weren't quite as vigorous as usual, nor were they accompanied by the normal giggles.

Beck's refrigerator was empty, aside from a bowl filled with takeout condiment packets, a jar of kosher dills, and a massive jug of spring water. She located an unopened box of crackers and a jar of peanut butter in the little pantry, along with some canned peaches and instant hot chocolate. No veggies and way too much sugar, but it covered all four food groups, more or less.

Jemma stopped spinning as Claire pulled the pop-top from the peaches. "Mr. Beck is all bloody. What happened to him?"

"He and his friend were in an accident. Hopefully, your mom can get them all patched up."

She was quiet for a bit, then said, "I don't like it here. It smells funny. When can we go home?"

"Soon," Claire said, unsure whether Jemma meant Bellamy

House or their actual home. Ro had told her about the fire, but how much of it had actually stuck?

And she was right about the smell. Beneath the disinfectant odor, you could still tell that the cabin had been empty for a while. It needed a good airing out.

"Just breathe in while you drink your cocoa," she said. "Then everything will smell like chocolate."

Beck was now waking up, so once Claire had Jemma settled with her makeshift dinner and the WonderKitties on her tablet, she poured a glass of water and took it over to him. He drained it. She had just returned with a refill when Ro came back into the room, shaking her head in dismay.

"I sealed the jagged cut on his head and the very *clean* cut—which, in fact, appears to be an incision—at the nape of his neck. But aside from—"

"That's where his tracker was," Beck said. "I had to remove it. Mine, too. I was working in the mirror and barely sober when I did my own, so I don't think I did as good a job."

He leaned his head to the side and Ro pulled back the bandage to reveal a messy cut at the base of his hairline.

"You definitely did *not*," Ro said. "As I was saying, though, aside from patching up his cuts, there's really not much I can do for him here. I'd hoped that the fever Claire mentioned was just from the concussion, but his abdomen is swollen and tight. That almost certainly means there's internal bleeding. I'm fairly sure he's got broken ribs and one of them could have punctured an organ. We have to get him to a hospital *now*, otherwise..." Ro trailed off as Beck shook his head.

"No. No hospital. Too many red flags."

Ro glanced over at Jemma, who was staring at the screen but probably still listening. She lowered her voice to an angry hiss. "Did you not get what I just said? The man is *dying*."

"I heard you." Beck took the glass of water from Claire. "And I truly appreciate your efforts and your concern. But Reese would tell you the same thing if he were conscious."

"Except … he is *not* conscious. And even if you were a family member, which I assume you're not, I can't allow you to refuse emergency care on his behalf."

He cursed softly as she pulled out her phone. "Wait, okay? Give me a minute to explain. I *get* why you think you need to do this, but as I believe Claire has already told you, that's not Reese's actual body. It's sort of a … composite clone. Human DNA that was altered for longevity, for resistance to certain diseases, quicker healing, and to accommodate minor differences between our native physical form and yours. Reese's *actual* body is in stasis."

"So what? He's inside *this* body. If it dies, then—"

"His *body* is in stasis," Beck repeated, "along with the original version of his consciousness, which was mapped prior to the transfer. So, it's not death as you know it. If this body dies, Reese will lose the memories that he's accumulated during this assignment, but the Alliance doctors will…" He trailed off, eyes widening slightly.

"But they will what?" Claire prodded.

Beck was quiet for a moment, then shook his head again. "Nothing that matters at this point. A lot of things are up in the air." He looked back at Ro, who was still very clearly debating whether to make the call. "The one thing I know for certain is this. If Durav, the Triad member in charge of security, discovers that Reese was taken to a hospital, the lives of the people who treat him will also be at risk. It wouldn't be the first time that he's killed innocents in order to keep our mission under wraps. I removed Reese's tracker, but if you use his ID, Durav will most likely find him."

"I'm thinking you should have *led* with that," Claire said.

"Yeah. It would have been nice to know all of this when I walked in the door, before I treated him. Before he became my patient. My responsibility. And what did you mean by *quicker healing*?"

"Nothing too dramatic," Beck said. "Our cells just regenerate a bit more quickly. I also injected him with something the Triad has us keep on hand in case of emergencies. Part of the whole avoiding hospitals thing."

"What's it called?" Ro asked.

He gave her a weak smile. "I only know the name in Ufretan. It works similar to a wound-homing peptide, but ... better."

"Does that mean there's a chance that his internal bleeding stops on its own?" Claire asked.

He shrugged. "Maybe?"

Ro glanced toward the bedroom. "I don't suppose you have more of this magical mystery serum lying around?"

"Unfortunately, no. There's another syringe at my apartment, but I only kept one here and Reese clearly needed it more than I did."

"That's only a little over an hour away," Claire said. "Maybe I should drive down and get it."

Beck shook his head. "Too risky. A couple of Durav's guys broke into my place earlier, and I'm not sure it's safe. I was going to stop in and pick up my cat but decided to check the security cameras first. Crichton is fine, but they turned my place upside down searching for something. And no," he said, anticipating Claire's question. "I don't know what they were looking for. I thought it might be the Eberin Das journal, but they didn't touch the computer."

Ro heaved a resigned sigh. "I'll see what I can get from the local pharmacy. But let me check you out first. What hurts most?"

He nodded toward his left hand. Claire fetched a bowl of water for Ro to use as a basin and had to fight back a wave of nausea when she returned to find that the outer edge of Beck's hand looked as if someone had shaved away most of the skin as well as the tip of his pinky. That definitely wasn't something Jemma needed to see, so she left the bowl with Ro and headed back into the kitchen to keep the girl distracted and to give Beck some privacy while Ro cleaned and rebandaged his wounds.

About ten minutes later, Claire heard Ro on the phone with a pharmacist. When she finished the call, she joined them in the kitchen. "I've called in a couple of prescriptions that may help Reese," she said as she washed up in the sink. "Also something for Beck to help with the blood loss, since he's all out of his alien miracle drug. I need to pick up a finger splint for his pinky, too. He's lucky he didn't lose it entirely. I sealed the cut on his side and gave him one of the painkillers I had left over from my tooth extraction a few months back so he should at least rest a bit more comfortably now."

"Is this going to cause problems with your supervisor at Johns Hopkins?"

"Most definitely. Everything is prescribed to *myself*, and Dr. Breyer is going to have a ton of questions about that when I get back. But given the end of the world scenario you mentioned earlier, a professional reprimand is pretty far down on my list of worries." She grabbed one of the peanut butter crackers from the plate. "The pharmacy closes at eight, so I have to get moving. Jemma, hon, I need you to stay with Claire while—"

That drew an immediate wail of protest. "No, Mommy. I want to go with you! It smells funny here and there's blood and it's scary."

"It's okay, Jemma," Claire said. "You haven't even finished your hot chocolate. Maybe we can search for a new game for you to play while you—"

"No, no, *no*. I *don't want* to stay here."

Ro, who would normally nip a tantrum like this in the bud, glanced over at Beck. His bloody shirt was now gone, but there was still a red splotch on the arm of the couch. All of this was undoubtedly nightmare fuel for a five-year-old. She gave Claire a resigned look, then swung her daughter up from the stool and onto her hip in one smooth motion.

"Plan B, then. Check on Reese and call me if there's any change, although I have no clue what I would tell you to do for him." She nodded her head toward Beck. "And make him eat something. Those meds aren't great on an empty stomach. In fact, I should pick up something more substantial for all of us, if there's a drive-thru nearby. I'll call when I'm headed back this way."

FROM THE MOHAVE COUNTY MINER

MAY 27, 1953

SAUCER FEVER STRIKES AGAIN

KEEP your eyes on the skies, folks.

This past Friday, word began to circulate that the Martians or Venusians (or insert your favorite alien species) are back, and this time, they skipped Roswell and decided to pay our own fair state a visit. Not just a single ship, but three or four flying hubcaps, hovering over the desert up near Pleasant Grove. According to two young eyewitnesses, at least one of those ships crashed out in the desert. The kids came back into town for a camera, but before they could get back up there and flash their Kodak Brownies at the wreckage, the military swooped in and cordoned off the area.

Now anyone who knows me will tell you I enjoy a good yarn as much as anybody, but I ain't buying this one. That could be because I spent this past Saturday afternoon with my own two kids at the State Theater, watching the new movie "Invaders from Mars," where—you guessed it—an alien ship comes crashing down into the desert.

I'm going to go out on a limb and predict that over the next few weeks, people here in Kingman will start acting really strange. By which I mean, stranger than usual. Then we're going to find this odd octopus-looking alien with his head in a jar and...

Well, I won't spoil it, just in case you haven't seen the movie.

THREE

AFTER RO LEFT, Claire made another cup of the instant cocoa and some more peanut butter crackers, then carried the food into the living room. She let Beck eat in silence until he pushed the plate away.

"I have questions."

He gave her a wry smile. "I'd be shocked if you didn't. And as I said in my message, I'll answer anything you want. But first…" He motioned with his head toward the bathroom door.

"Do you need help?"

"I do *not*." He started to push himself off the couch and winced. "Okay, I take that back. A little help getting up would be appreciated. And you could fetch me a clean shirt from the closet. Otherwise, I'll manage on my own."

She helped him over to the door and once he was inside, went into the bedroom for another T-shirt. When he returned, they eased him into the shirt, taking care to avoid the various bandages, and he collapsed back onto the couch.

"So what do you want me to call you? Anak?"

"It's pronounced An-*knock*, not An-*knack*," he said. "But I'd rather you called me Beck. That's what it says on my ID, and since I won't be going back to Parda … I guess I might as well embrace my future, however brief it may be."

"Beck it is, then." She glanced toward the bedroom, thinking again of the man on the bed. "What do your people look like? I mean, your *actual* bodies?"

He huffed out a little laugh. "Not all that different from you. There are minor variations between the member worlds in the Alliance, but we're all mammals. Two arms. Two legs. Two eyes.

Our physical frames are a bit larger, which is why they opted for taller bodies when collecting DNA."

"Isn't it a bit odd that you'd be so similar?"

"Don't get me wrong. We couldn't pass for natives. That's why we need the clones. But convergent evolution isn't all that surprising, given that our worlds are similar. If they weren't, the Alliance probably wouldn't see Earth as potential competition for resources."

It seemed a rather simplistic explanation to Claire, but she had too many other questions to belabor the point. "What happened to your spaceship? Is it in Area 51?"

"Nope. Area 51 is in Nevada. If the military is hiding anything there, it wasn't from our ship. Area 52 is in Arizona, but nowhere near our landing site. We did attract a bit of attention, though. Our ship was designed to self-destruct on entry, except for the transport module. A few sections didn't behave as expected, possibly due to some nuclear tests going on around the same time. Those sections were recovered by the U.S. military. Some leaked accounts claimed there was a small, brown body in a silver suit nearby. Again, not one of ours, so that part is clearly fiction."

"What happened to your transport module? Did it also self-destruct?"

"Stashed in a defunct mine near a ghost town outside of Kingman. We stayed at an abandoned ranch a few miles away for a little over a month while we adjusted to being in our new bodies. Eventually, the Triad purchased that land and set it up as a tourist attraction."

Claire stared at him. "A *tourist* attraction?"

"Not the section with the transport module. That's walled off—it's actually where the Triad's backup communication device is located. If someone sees the module, though, it looks quite a bit like an antique school bus. Sometimes, it's safer to hide in plain sight. The Triad pays the people who run the place a salary that would make them reluctant to ask too many questions. A Watcher assigned to the West Coast acts as the owner, and they stay there part of the year to keep an eye on things."

"Okay, let's move on from the distant past to more recent events. In the video, you told me you were heading to Boston to keep your end of the bargain. Or something like that. Did you already know that they were going to bomb the lab?"

"No. They left that part out because they were worried that I'd try to stop it. I *did* know that they were planning to target one of Kolya's labs on Mars. Davina Monroe's lab, in fact."

Claire frowned. She hadn't realized that one of the six buildings she'd seen on the screen at the Ares Consortium dinner was the lab at Nepenthes. But then she'd never seen the lab itself, just the test domes. And, to be honest, she hadn't paid attention to anything else once she spotted the familiar lines of the Jonas Labs campus in the top right corner of the screen.

"My assigned task," Beck continued, "was to wipe Joe's more recent data. His stretch goals, or basically everything we've been working on since we got the final approval on Rejuvesce. The idea was to set the research back a few months and buy us some time to convince Joe not to move forward. And hopefully, to convince your mom not to move forward without him."

"So the Triad agreed to hold off? In your video, I thought you said they voted no."

"They *did*, at first. But we had decided in advance that if they didn't give their approval, I would move ahead with the data wipe anyway as a last ditch effort. Drex would do the same with the attack on the Nepenthes lab. Our hope was that if we could show some progress before the communications window opens in a few weeks we might be able to persuade Sandjeel to reconsider. On the hyperloop back to Boston, I got a call from Drex saying there was a bit of an uproar among the rank and file of the Watch after I left. Which was my doing. I recorded a meeting that was supposed to be private and shared it with my fellow Watchers on my way out. At any rate, Sandjeel then agreed to wait until the end of the comms window if we followed through on the more drastic plan of action, which she'd actually been planning all along. But Drex remembered there were families living on the Jonas Labs campus. She decided I should give them a bit of advance notice since fifteen minutes might be cutting things a bit close. And it was. Did Wilson tell you about the kids who were missing?"

"Yeah."

"Okay. I spotted Reese through the security cameras and chased him down, trying to get him to disable the bombs or at least delay them until the kids were found. He said he couldn't, but ... I didn't believe him. We fought. He fell and clipped his head pretty hard on one of those boulders near the waterfalls. Knocked him out cold. Then Wilson came over the comm system saying the kids had been located and that everyone needed to get the hell out of there ASAP. But I couldn't abandon Reese. I mean, I might have disagreed with their methods, but he's on the right side, you know? He's not willing to simply give Earth over to its fate. So I flung him onto my back and took off for the closest exit. We made it out, but one of the devices went off about two seconds later and we were both hit by debris from the biodome. There was another Watcher inside. Housen. I don't know if he got out. Also a member of the Flock who was working with them."

"There was one body in the wreckage," Claire said. "Wilson told me the guy was wearing a maintenance uniform but wasn't a lab employee. I have no idea which one of them it was, though."

Beck nodded. "After that, I managed to get Reese into the rental car and gave it the location of the cabin. I have a vague memory of extracting his tracker and tossing it out of the car, but I don't remember much of anything else. Not until I woke up outside the gate this morning."

"From what you said in your voice message, it sounded like you were late getting out of there because you were trying to save the biodome. And yes, I hate that it's gone, but as Ro keeps reminding me, it's just a thing. And things can be replaced."

"Saving the dome *was* a consideration, although not the main goal. And yeah, it was partly because I knew how much it meant to you. And to Joe. I mean, it kind of felt like they were blowing up your family cemetery. But to be honest, I wasn't doing it *entirely* for you. I used to go down there a lot, especially when Joe was in one of his moods. The place actually reminded me a bit of home. Those rainbow eucalyptus trees are like a species in the southern region of Parda where I lived as a child. I don't have many vivid childhood memories, but I do remember the scent of those trees as I walked with my father in the woods near my grandmother's house. The smell wasn't quite as sharp as the ones in the biodome, at least in my memory. But it was similar. And I had just learned that I'm never going back to Parda, so … losing those trees felt a little like losing a connection to my own family, too. I probably need to stick to shorter answers or I'm going to doze off before you're finished."

"Okay. In the video, you said something that puzzled me. I forget the exact words, but something like it had been millions of years since anyone called the place anything other than Mars. But from what we know about the planet, that doesn't make sense. You meant *billions* of years, right?"

"Nope. Mars was habitable more recently than your scientists believe. We're still talking many millions of Earth years, but not *billions*. An easy enough mistake, though. They logically attributed the destruction to natural causes, and the Alliance's weapons—even many millions of years ago—were far more efficient than anything nature could dish out. Oddly enough, there was a physicist around the turn of this century who claimed Mars was destroyed by a series of nuclear explosions in the atmosphere. He was considered to be a bit of a flake overall, and his research received a thorough drubbing by the scientific community. But he was actually onto something with that theory."

"Okay. I'm looking forward to the day when I can pass that information along to Ben Pelzer. I suspect it will answer some questions about the chamber that have been plaguing him. Next. What exactly is this right of *ufrete* that you mentioned in the video?"

Beck was quiet for so long that she started to repeat the question, but he held up his hand. "I'm just trying to figure out exactly how to explain it to you. It's a way of extending the protection of the specific laws of your homeworld to an outsider. The Alliance is ... well, it's an *alliance*, obviously, of sixty-three planets. We share a common ancestral world, so we're similar in a lot of ways. We also share some overarching legal constructs that are required of all member planets. But we remain separate in many respects. Say you're from Parda, my own homeworld, and you go to Ufretas Prime or one of the other Alliance worlds. You can get a temporary travel or study permit, but if you want to stay longer than a few weeks, you're taking a major risk. Visitors aren't automatically granted rights on the other worlds to things like emergency shelter and food, or healthcare. You also have no right to work. No right to a fair trial, no protection against summary execution for trespass—and yes, that's a thing on some Alliance worlds. You simply have *no rights* under their legal system. But if you have a citizen to sponsor you, you are considered part of their *korban*—basically, their very extended family. Sort of like a Scottish clan. You then have the same rights as anyone else, and any act against you is an offense against the entire *korban*. The number of outsiders you can sponsor depends on your resources. Sometimes, the sponsor is an employer. Sometimes, a friend or romantic partner. Those rights extend after your death, too, and they can include transfer of resources. Uden—Professor Everett in the memoir—left everything he'd acquired during his time on Earth to Tobias Shepherd, claiming the right of *ufrete* for him and his mother. There was some dissent within the Triad, but in the end, Arbet convinced them—or at least, she convinced Sandjeel—that nothing in Ufretan law precluded extending the right to people outside the Alliance." He stopped, eyebrows raised in surprise. "In fact, I'm guessing she was the attorney who visited Shepherd on his eighteenth birthday. It didn't even occur to me to ask."

"But ... Uden isn't really dead, is he? I mean, based on what you told Ro about Reese. Even if the body he was using here is dead, he'll just lose the memories from his time on Earth, right?"

He considered for a few seconds, then shook his head. "I don't know for certain, but I believe Uden is really dead. Did you read the section in Eberin's journal that talked about voluntary terminals? All worlds in the Ufretan Alliance respect the right to die ... although there are a few notable exceptions I've recently learned about, so I guess it's possible. But if Uden made it clear in his will that his death was intended as a suicide, and if that information was transmitted back to his *korban* during the next communications window, I think they would have respected his final wishes."

Beck's words were beginning to slur a bit, but she pushed ahead with one more question.

"When did you extend your rights to cover me?"

"After I learned that you were going to Mars. That put you at the nexus of both milestones. Which made me nervous, especially given that you're a reporter and I knew you'd be poking around. I'd never used the right in the past. Never had any need. So I'm not sure I'd have thought of it if not for the reminder I received a few days before. It didn't mention you specifically, of course, but Drex told me that she'd contacted Arbet and suggested she give me a nudge after learning that you would be part of the team for the Mars trip."

Claire gave him a skeptical look. "That doesn't make much sense. Even if she wasn't responsible for the attack that nearly killed me on Mars, Corbin Drexel doesn't know me. Why would she be concerned about my safety?"

"Because she knew that *I* would be concerned about your safety. And because she needed me on board for her plan to work."

His eyes were closed by the end of the sentence, and she thought he had drifted off. She was about to get up when he spoke again.

"She's not a bad person, Claire. That's true for most of the Watch, actually. Our chances of success are ... miniscule, but if not for the work Drex has done, we wouldn't have any chance at all. And Arbet, too. I just ... I hope..."

But whatever he hoped for was lost to sleep.

FOUR

A FEW MINUTES BEFORE EIGHT, Claire's phone signaled an incoming message. Two short buzzes, which meant it was Ro.

> Finishing up at pharmacy now. There's an In-N-Out across the street. What do you want?

Beck was still asleep, but he'd probably be hungry when he woke up, so she messaged Ro back with an order for both of them.

> Got it. Should be back by eight thirty.

But eight thirty rolled around with no sign of Ro and Jemma. At eight forty-five, Claire called to make sure everything was okay.

No answer.

Still no answer five minutes later, although she did get a call from Paul Caruso, no doubt following up on his earlier text saying that King Kolya had requested an audience to discuss the attacks. She let it go to voicemail and tried Ro again. After two more failed attempts, she put the call on repeat, so that it would keep pinging Ro's number until it got a response.

Just after nine, she went in to check on Reese. Beck's alien super-drug didn't seem to be helping, or at least, not helping enough. A faint, high-pitched whistle accompanied each of the man's shallow breaths. The sensor clipped to Reese's finger showed oxygen at eighty-seven percent and his fever was just below a hundred and three.

Her phone vibrated on the nightstand. She snatched it up, realizing as she did that it was Wyatt's signal—one long buzz. His message, however, was short. Just a single question mark. But she knew that it stood in for a whole host of queries. *Did you find Beck? Are you okay? Why the hell haven't you called yet?*

She tapped to start a video call, feeling too on edge to deal with the back and forth of messaging. And she really needed to see Wyatt's face right now. When he appeared on the screen a moment later, a city street was in the background. He was in a line of some sort, with two people behind him. A woman's voice said something would be thirty-two dollars and fifteen cents.

"Hold on just a second, Claire."

She had a view of his pants leg for a moment, as she listened to the rustling of a paper bag and an exchange of *thank-yous*. Then Wyatt was back, walking away from the food cart.

"Sorry," he said around a bite of what looked like a knish. "I haven't eaten since this morning. I'm following something big, which we definitely need to talk about, but I wanted to wait until you located Beck to get his feedback, too. When Ro messaged me—"

"She messaged you? Thank god! Where is she? I've been trying to call. They should have been back here half an hour ago and I've been..." She trailed off as she watched an anxious frown settle onto Wyatt's face.

"She messaged me about *three hours ago* to ask if I could rescue Siggy from the kennel."

"Oh. Damn it." She sank down into a straw-backed chair next to the dresser.

"I told her I wasn't back in DC yet, but I'd get Kes to take care of it tomorrow. What I was *about* to say was that when she messaged, she told me you had narrowed down a few possible locations where Beck might be. What's going on, babe?"

Once she had him up to speed, she said, "I've been calling and calling, but she's not picking up. I need to go out and see if I can find them. Maybe she had car trouble. The roads leading to this place are really crappy. And maybe she left her phone at the pharmacy and couldn't call or..."

He didn't say anything, but Claire could read his expression. If Ro had lost her phone, she would have used the car's AI or Jemma's tablet.

"I know, I *know*. I'm grasping at straws. But what the hell else can I do?"

"It's okay. I get it. Go find them. But promise you'll check in with me every fifteen minutes."

"I will. Love you."

He smiled, but his eyes were still worried. "Love you, too. And I mean it. *Every fifteen minutes*."

When the call ended, she went back into the living room and crouched down next to the couch where Beck was sleeping. He didn't respond the first time she said his name, and she debated just leaving him a note. But her bag was in the car, so she'd either have to go out and get it or else track down paper and a pen here in the cabin. She tried again, this time giving his uninjured arm a gentle nudge.

His eyes fluttered for a second, then flew open. "What? What's wrong?"

"It's nine twenty. Ro and Jemma should have been back nearly an hour ago. I've called repeatedly, but she's not answering her phone and that's really not like her. I'm going out to see if she had trouble on the road. I'll be back soon."

"Wait. I'm going with you."

"No. You're not. You need to rest. And someone has to stay with Reese."

But Beck had already pushed himself off the couch. "I'm *going*. There's nothing either of us can do to help Reese if he takes a turn for the worse."

She was fairly certain that Reese had already taken a turn for the worse but stating that probably wouldn't help her case. The more pertinent issue was that Beck was more likely to slow her down than to help in his current state. But arguing about it would also slow her down, and he was already halfway to the door.

So she followed, remembering at the last second to grab the pistol from the drawer where she'd hidden it. It sat on top of a pad of paper, next to a pencil. Too bad she hadn't noticed them earlier. She could have left the damn note and avoided Beck tagging along.

The air outside was heavy with condensation. It felt almost like stepping into one of the hydrosonic showers on the *Ares Prime*. She helped Beck down the porch steps and onto the over-grown lawn, giving the rental car a wide berth as they headed toward the Aeris.

As the car turned around in the clearing, all she could make out was the gate, which was closed. About halfway down, the Aeris rounded the slight curve in the drive and its headlights bounced back from something beyond the gate.

"That's her car," Claire said, her throat so tight that the words were barely audible. Technically, it was Beck's car, the one he'd left at the B&B when they went to New York, but he knew what she meant. Her mind flashed to the rental car he'd been using instead, its seats spattered with blood. She squeezed her eyes shut against the memory and the horrible possibility that this car could be in a similar state. "No. No, no, *no*."

As soon as the Aeris stopped, she was out and running. She heard Beck open the door on the other side, but he was moving much too slowly for her to wait on him.

"Ro? Jemma?" The interior light was on. Even though she could see that there was no one inside, she called out again.

As soon as she reached the gate, she scaled the three metal rungs and dropped down to the opposite side. She landed awkwardly, and pain rocketed up from the pin in the ankle she'd injured on Mars. It barely registered, though, because she could now hear music. A chirpy chorus that she'd heard so many times that it was a perpetual earworm. *Anytime there's trouble, whether near or far away, call the Wonderkitties, they'll always save the day.*

One of the doors was slightly ajar. Jemma's tablet lay face up in the grass just outside, casting a bright prism of moving colors on the side panel of the car as the music played on. Claire picked the tablet up and switched it off without even thinking, as she'd done at least a half dozen times a day for the past three years.

There was no blood, thank God, but also no sign of Ro or Jemma. Well, no, that wasn't true. There were plenty of signs that they'd been in the car. Jemma's tablet. A half-eaten chicken strip on the floorboard in front of her car seat. A spilled bottle of apple juice. The medical kit Ro had swiped from the boat, which now had a white prescription bag sticking up from the side pocket. An In-N-Out bag with the food Ro had ordered hanging from the parcel hook.

But no Jemma. No Rowan.

They were gone, and—

"Someone was waiting for them."

Claire startled at the sound and looked over to find Beck approaching from the other direction.

"Another set of tire tracks just off the trail," he said flatly. "Wider than these. Looks like an offroad vehicle. And there are no other houses on this road. Just a pond about a hundred meters down."

"This is my fault." Claire's voice sounded foreign to her own ears, high and strained, on the edge of panic. "All my fault, all —" She stopped and amended that. "No, it's *your* fault, too. What about your stupid right of *ufrete*? You said—"

"I said *you* were safe, Claire. But ... they *won't* hurt Jemma. There's no way they'd hurt a child. It goes against ... against *everything*."

She could barely see Beck's face in the faint glow of the light from inside the car, but she could hear just fine. He *wanted* to believe what he'd just told her, but there was doubt in his voice. As there damned well should be. This monster Durav was apparently planning to kill everyone on the planet, kids included. Why would he draw the line at killing one of them a bit early?

"And what about Ro?" she demanded.

"They won't hurt her, either. This is Durav's work. He wants me to turn myself in."

"If they wanted *you*, why didn't they just climb the fence and come get you? Why not send in some of his drones and fire-bomb your cabin like they did my house? It doesn't make *sense*, Beck. You have no connection to Ro and Jemma aside from the two of them staying at Bellamy House for a few days. Why would this Durav person assume that you—"

"Why would he assume I would turn myself in rather than allow an innocent child to be harmed? Because I told him point blank that I'd rather die along with everyone on this planet than be part of its destruction! Because I walked *out* of the Conclave. And because I made sure every member of the Watch learned the truth about our mission on my way out."

Claire hugged Jemma's tablet to her chest and leaned back against the car. "But you said they *agreed* to Drex's plan. Durav was outvoted. So why is he coming after you now?"

Beck shook his head. "I don't know. Durav is probably acting on his own. The man has a vindictive streak. He's killed off half of the *ipret-tai* just for looking at him wrong."

"Half of the *what*?"

"The servants. And security guards. There were nearly two dozen at one point, but..." He pulled in a deep breath, then winced from the pain in his side. "Durav probably blames me for Sandjeel's change of heart. As I think I told you earlier, I recorded our conversation and transmitted it to the rest of the

Watch. I can't really see what difference it makes at this point, though. None of them will be taking the memories home."

"What does that even—" She stopped midsentence when her phone buzzed, remembering that she was supposed to check in with Wyatt. Had it been fifteen minutes already?

And then it buzzed again. Two *short* buzzes.

It was Ro.

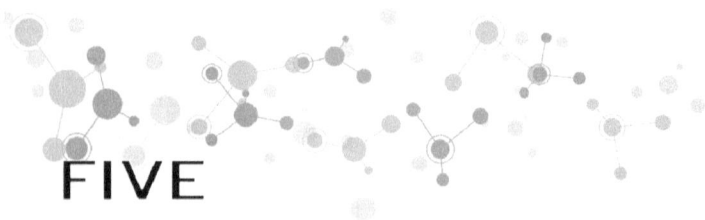

FIVE

CLAIRE YANKED her phone out so fast that it tumbled from her hands. She scooped it up from the ground and stared at the screen. The message was indeed from Ro's phone, but it was definitely not from Ro.

> I propose an even trade. Anak and the brelat you took from Uden's house, in exchange for your two friends. If you wish them unharmed, come alone.

She shoved the phone toward Beck. "What are they talking about? What the hell is a *brelat*?"

Beck stared at the message so long that Claire was about to ask if he needed her to read it to him. Maybe the pills Ro gave him had left him too loopy to focus.

He shook his head slowly. "It's from Durav. Or someone working with him. The *brelat* is the signaling device the Triad uses to inform the Alliance that both milestones have been met. The word means beacon. The signal is relayed from the comms ship directly to our military, or maybe even straight to the drone ships that form the *naidar* bubble."

She had no idea what a *naidar* bubble was, and really didn't care at this point. "Do you have it?"

"No. That's what has me baffled. I saw it in the Triad's Chambers yesterday. It was in a display case on the shelf. But even if something had happened to that one, there's supposed to be a backup device in the tunnels at our original drop site in Arizona." He stopped and drew in a sharp breath. "That's what they were looking for at my apartment. Durav must have thought you gave it to me, since he's under the impression that you took it from Uden's house in New Haven."

"But I didn't *find* anything there. No papers, no beacon, nothing. If Shepherd left anything in that house, whoever got there before me took it. The only things I found were a dead body and the warning messages scrawled in the guy's blood. And from everything you've said tonight, I assumed Durav was responsible for that."

"He almost certainly was. Well, not personally, but he ordered it. He's hired a bunch of mercenaries to replace the *ipret-tai*..." He held up his hand. "I'll explain everything else on the way to New York. For now, just answer him. Tell him ... tell him that you don't have the *brelat* with you, but you can get it. We need to buy some time, so tell him it's in DC or something and we'll deliver it by ... let's say three p.m. tomorrow."

"Okay, but why are we going to New York? Shouldn't we go to Arizona and look for the backup device? Even if you turn yourself in, do you really think he's going to release them if we only have half of what he's demanding?"

"No. I'm sure that he won't. But I'm also pretty sure he'd have had someone check for the other beacon before he resorted to kidnapping. Whoever took the one at HQ must have gotten hold of the backup as well. I need to get in touch with Arbet. Hopefully she'll have at least some idea what's going on." He looked over at the empty car. Its interior lights were the only illumination on the dark, foggy road. "Let's get this car inside the gate. I have to grab a few things before we leave. And I need to see if I can find my damn phone in the rental car."

"What about Reese?"

He ran a hand through his hair, looking miserable. "We leave him. I mean, what else can we do?"

As Claire rode back to the cabin in the Aeris, she messaged Wyatt.

Just checking in.

She hesitated for a moment, then added that there was no news. That she was still looking. As much as she hated lying to him, she really couldn't see any alternative. If Wyatt knew for certain that Ro and Jemma had been abducted, he wouldn't be able to stay on the sidelines. And Durav's message had been crystal clear. *If you wish them unharmed, come alone.*

While Beck searched the rental car for his phone, she grabbed the medical bag and went inside the cabin to check on Reese. He seemed about the same, which probably wasn't surprising given that she'd checked on him only a few minutes earlier. It only *felt* like that had been hours ago, days ago, in the before-times when she was merely worried and not absolutely terrified. She hated to leave without doing anything more for him, but she had no clue how to administer the medicine Ro had picked up. For that matter, she didn't even know which was intended for Reese and which was for Beck. Her high school first aid training hadn't even come close to covering this scenario.

And, in addition to a human-alien hybrid on death's door, the rental car outside the cabin looked like it had rolled in from the set of a slasher film. Beck could try to extend the rental period, but it wasn't a given. If someone else had already reserved it, the company would send a signal for the car to return to their nearest location. It wouldn't be able to follow those orders if it was inside the fence, but how long would it be before they sent someone here to retrieve it?

They needed help, and Joe was the most logical choice. She wouldn't risk telling him about Ro and Jemma, at least not yet. But he had people in his employ who could handle the situation here at the cabin. People he paid well enough that they could keep a secret. Maybe not forever, but it would give them some breathing room.

Joe's phone rang five times. She was rehearsing in her head what to say in a voicemail, but he picked up at the last second.

"ClaireBear. What's up?" He sounded groggy.

"I'm sorry to wake you, but … I found Beck."

"Yeah, I kind of figured that from what Ro told me when she called to say I was her cover story with the guards. Is he okay? Are *you* okay?"

"I'm fine. And Ro was able to patch Beck up. He's lost some blood and he's pretty weak, but that's the least of our worries at the moment. We've got problems and you're the only person I can turn to."

"What's wrong?" he asked, fully awake now.

"Okay, I can't give you the entire story at the moment. I just need you to trust that what I'm asking you to do is important. Lives are on the line."

"I really don't like the sound of that."

"Neither do I. Will you help me?"

"*Obviously*. I'm not going to pretend that I *like* being kept in the dark, but yes. Whatever you need."

"First, can you have security go check Beck's apartment for booby traps? Someone broke in today and trashed the place. And we need to be sure it's clear before we stop by in about an hour to pick up some medicine."

She then moved on to the rental car and the injured alien. As she was finishing explaining the situation, Beck came into the room. He didn't say anything, just collapsed into the chair next to the dresser and fixed her with a bleak stare until she ended the call.

"Durav told us to *come alone*," he said. "And while I'm not planning to enter through the front gate, we can't risk taking anyone else with us. We're already going there without the beacon. I still don't think they would harm…" He trailed off, leaning his head back against the wall. "Screw it. Who am I kidding? I have no idea if Durav would draw the line at killing a child. He clearly doesn't view Earthers as fully human. Even Sandjeel seems to consider it an open question."

"*Earthers?*"

"Yes. Would you rather be called Earthlings?"

"No. I'd rather be called *humans*."

"Okay." He looked a bit flummoxed. "It's just not a very precise term. I mean, all members of the Alliance are bipedal mammals. Primates. Which means we're … human, too."

"Fine, then. *Earthers*. Earthlings. What-the-hell-ever. And I didn't tell Joe *anything* about Ro and Jemma. I'm not telling Wyatt the full truth, either, although it's going to mean lying to him every fifteen minutes. I'm not entirely sure that I can pull that off. He believes I'm out searching right now, and I can't think of anything I could tell him that will keep him from heading up here to join the search. The reason I called Joe is that we need someone to handle the situation here at the cabin. We can't just leave Reese."

"I already *told* you. No hospital. No police."

"Which is where having a *private* security force comes in handy. Jonas Labs Security doesn't report to anyone but Wilson, and he reports to Joe and Kai. Give me the rental info for the car and I'll pass it along to Joe. He said he'll have someone try to clean it, but if that's not possible, he'll buy the car and have them dispose of it. We also have people at JL with enough medical training to either help Reese or if he's beyond help, at least keep him comfortable. And having Reese there might make it easier for Joe to convince Kai. The same oddities in Reese's DNA that make involving a hospital unwise will help show that he is, in fact, not…" She'd been about to say *not human* but decided to amend it. "Not an *Earther*. I know getting anyone else involved is a risk. But Joe is already part of this. And we don't have much choice." She could tell from Beck's expression that he still didn't like it, but he didn't argue. "Did you find your phone?"

"Yeah." He patted his pocket. "Under the seat. I was planning to wait and turn it on once we were on the road just in case it's being tracked, but I guess I no longer have to worry about giving the location of the cabin away."

"You can't actually expect me to apologize for that. Not

after..." Claire squeezed her eyes shut, warding off tears at the thought of Jemma's tablet on the ground. The spilled drink. Jemma would have screamed when they yanked her out of the car. And when she did, nothing in this world could have stopped Ro from diving in to protect her. And did Durav really need two hostages? Ro might not even still be alive.

"No. That's not what I meant at all." Beck's voice was soft as he leaned forward to squeeze her hand. "All I meant was that Durav has obviously already found the place. You don't owe me *any* apologies. I am so, so sorry, Claire. For all of this."

She wanted to scream at him. To yank her hand away. But she knew her rage was misplaced. Beck was just a convenient outlet for her anger. He hadn't known what the Alliance was planning. When he learned the truth, he tied his fate to that of Earth, turning his back on his own people. Whatever he'd done to piss Durav off had been part of an effort to save the entire planet.

Plus, Ro and Jemma had almost certainly been targets of opportunity. Durav's people wouldn't have battled security guards and perimeter drones at the B & B to nab a couple of hostages. If Ro hadn't shown up here when she did, they would almost certainly have attacked the cabin and grabbed Beck directly. Claire, too.

But the kicker was this. Beck hadn't *asked* her to call Ro. She'd made that colossal mistake all on her lonesome. Now she just had to pray it wasn't too late to fix it.

SIX

BECK BARELY SPOKE on the drive down from Maine. He just leaned against the side of the car, closed his eyes, and played his texts and voice messages aloud. Claire didn't know if he'd lost his earbuds or if he was merely signaling that he was an open book, but she heard multiple messages from Wilson and Joe, plus the texts that she'd sent to Beck during the dinner at Beekman Place, and a furious screed from Kai informing him that no matter what Joe might say to the contrary, his ass was fired. There were also two text messages that she thought were from Corbin Drexel, telling him that some guy named Towson or something like that had made it out safely, but the Flock member who had accompanied him had not. Drex was clearly angry about that, but also worried, asking if Beck was okay and if he'd heard anything from Reese. He didn't answer any of the messages, just tossed the phone onto the seat next to him when they were over, cradled his newly splinted hand in his lap, and appeared to doze off.

For her part, she watched the clock, dreading each quarter-hour update to Wyatt. The first time, she told him that they had Jonas Labs Security combing the roads around the B & B, hoping he'd take the hint that they had plenty of boots on the ground. He responded a few minutes later that he had a couple of things to take care of, but he'd catch the hyperloop up to join her as soon as he was finished. She told him there really wasn't much he could do and that he should at least wait until morning. He pushed back for a bit but then seemed to accept it. After that, he just sent short responses to each of her texts.

Beck roused himself when the Aeris pulled up to his apartment complex shortly before eleven. "This may be a total waste of time," he told her. "It's entirely possible they took the medicine when they broke in. Durav's mercenary wouldn't have known what it was, but the *ipret-tai* would definitely have recognized the container."

Claire still didn't have a firm grasp of what an *ipret-tai* was. Beck had told her they were servants, but were they humans that the Triad had hired, or had they brought household staff with them from the Ufretan system?

"Well," she said, "we're here, either way. We might as well go in and check."

"*I* will go in and check," Beck said, as he opened the door. "*You* stay in the car."

"Nope. We're going together." She opened her own door and was on his side of the vehicle before he managed to drag himself out of the car, even though she was moving more slowly than usual herself, thanks to her shaky landing when she scaled the gate back at the cabin. "Wilson told Joe that the place is clear. And you can barely walk."

It was true. The pain medicine Ro had given him was clearly wearing off because even though the Aeris was an extraordinarily smooth ride, he'd flinched at every rough spot in the road for the past half hour. If his alien superdrug had been stolen during the break-in, she could probably find something at her mom's house. The woman had an entire pharmacopeia of potent pain and sleep meds. But that would mean dealing with Kai. Judging from the voice message, Claire thought there was a very real chance that her mother would simply shoot Beck on sight. Even if she agreed to help, anything Kai had to offer would almost certainly leave him feeling loopy. Unless the plan was for him to simply walk in and hand himself over to Durav, that was the last thing they needed.

The apartment was every bit as trashed as Beck had suggested. A large gray cat yowled as they entered, obviously pissed that his owner wouldn't bend down to greet him properly and, most likely, annoyed at the indignity that his house had suffered. Drawers and cabinets had been emptied, their contents scattered in all directions. Every piece of furniture was slashed, and mounds of white stuffing covered the floor.

They located the syringe in the bathroom, still sealed, under an assortment of bottles and tubes. Everything had been tossed into the tub, along with the medicine cabinet itself, which they'd yanked out of the wall, probably so that they could search the space behind it.

As Claire followed Beck into the bedroom, she couldn't help thinking that this was a far cry from the fantasy her younger self had occasionally indulged in when she was crushing on Beck. He sank down onto the slashed remnants of his mattress and tugged gingerly at the edge of his shirt. It looked much better than it had earlier in the day, but blood was again seeping through the bandage that Ro had applied.

"Would you mind?" He held the unwrapped syringe toward her. "You just need to inject it into the muscle right below the cut. I could do it, but it's more effective if it's closer to the wound."

She took the syringe reluctantly. The cat leapt onto Beck's lap, tail twitching as he watched her.

"Didn't you tell Ro that your hand hurt more than your side?"

"Yeah, but my hand feels a lot better since you applied the splint back at the cabin. It's not my dominant hand, and the injury won't affect my mobility. That's my key concern, at the moment, because as I said earlier, we're not going in the front gate and that means we're in for a bit of a hike."

She grimaced, as much at the thought of how slowly they'd need to move due to Beck's injuries and her own aching leg as at her wariness to use the syringe. "You're sure the stuff inside is still good?"

"Yes. Just do it." He tensed as the needle entered his skin. Once she pulled it out, he added, "What I'm more worried about is whether Durav's guys swapped it for something else while they were here. I don't have security cameras in the bathroom, so I couldn't check."

Claire stared at him, mouth open. "Don't you think you should have mentioned that *before* I gave you the shot?"

"No." He smiled, although she had no idea what he found amusing. "For one thing, it was a very slim chance. You might have balked at giving me the shot if I mentioned it and I'd have ended up injecting it into my side. If it *was* some toxic substitute Durav planted, I'd be just as dead in either case. And this way, I'll get the most benefit from the drug by having you inject it closer to the wound."

"Or you could have healed the old-fashioned way instead of risking death and making me an accomplice," she shot back, even though she knew he was right.

"Well, the good news is that you're almost certainly in the clear. Durav doesn't do subtle. If he'd replaced that with something deadly, I'd already be foaming at the mouth like Shepherd was on the *Ares Prime*. He would have died, by the way, if Stasia hadn't drained off most of that drone's neurotoxin."

"He very nearly died anyway." She shuddered, thinking back to the man convulsing onstage. "And she could have simply not released the drone at all. Same for the explosion at Icarus. Stasia doesn't get a pass for trying to minimize harm when she could have simply refused to carry out Durav's orders. People died at Icarus because she didn't have the guts to say no."

Beck winced slightly at her words. While it could have been nothing more than a twinge from one of his injuries, she suspected her criticism of Stasia had hit too close to home.

"It's a bit more complicated than that. Stasia didn't know the truth at that point."

"You said that Drex told her *before* the Mars trip."

"Well, yeah. But she didn't believe her. It was pretty hard for me to accept at first, too, and I had the Eberin Das journal as evidence. All Stasia had was Drex's word."

"This other Triad member, though. Arbet. Why didn't *she* tell you? She's known for decades, right?"

"Yes." His voice took on a defiant note. "She *knew*. And she spent that time submitting doctored reports to the Alliance, hoping that maybe the resistance inside the Academy would grow and Earth would get a reprieve if she stalled long enough. Arbet also saw to it that Shepherd had the resources to start the Flock, which was another attempt to slow progress toward achieving the milestones."

Beck pushed himself up from the bed and grabbed a gym bag from the closet. "I need to pack a few things, since I had to abandon my bag at Conclave. See if you can find the cat food among the mess in the kitchen and fill Crichton's autofeeder. And the water dispenser. I'm going to call the pet sitter to cancel for tomorrow, since I can't think of a good way to explain the chaos here."

He hadn't answered her main question, but she decided not to press the point. If he and Arbet were friends, or more than friends, as she was beginning to suspect, the fact that she hadn't told Beck about their true mission—had, in fact, quite likely lied to him—probably bothered him as much as his own lies bothered Claire.

Instead, she did as he asked, eventually locating the bag of dry food under the kitchen table. There was a jagged split down the center and Crichton seemed totally disinterested in what she was doing, so she suspected the cat had already helped himself from the partially open bag.

Either the drug or the placebo effect was already kicking in, because Beck was moving much faster by the time they headed back out to the Aeris. He flinched slightly when he tossed his bag on top of Claire's in the cargo hold but otherwise seemed only a little stiff as he slid into the car for the drive to New York.

Once they were on the highway, Claire sent her regularly

scheduled update to Wyatt. He didn't answer this time. She left a voicemail, and while it was something of a relief not to have to lie to him directly, it bothered her. Was he angry? Or suspicious that she was hiding something from him? More likely both, at this point.

When she looked up, she saw that Beck was checking his own messages. After a few seconds, he tossed the phone onto the seat and closed his eyes.

"You're worried about her, aren't you? Arbet, I mean. That's why you keep checking the phone."

"Yeah. I'm hoping the reason she hasn't contacted me is simply because Durav confiscated her phone. But ... she has this tracking tattoo that causes a burning sensation if she leaves HQ without permission. If Durav goes on a rampage, she and the *ipret-tai* are the only ones who can't get away. Well, Sandjeel, too. But Durav isn't going to hurt him. If he wants to use the beacon, he needs approval from two of the three Triad members and Arbet wouldn't..." He sighed, shaking his head, then looked back out at the lights zipping past on the freeway.

Claire gave him a minute, but when it became clear that he was planning to leave it at that, she pressed on. "You're not sure she's on our side, are you? You think there's a chance she'd agree to support Durav."

"No, it's not that. Arbet *is* absolutely on our side. It's just..." He sighed again. "She and Sandjeel both have family members —offspring—who could be punished if it's discovered that they didn't carry out their duties."

"What about you?"

A twinge of pain crossed his face. "They could target my parents. A few generations of grands, too. But at least I don't have a child to worry about."

"They're not kids anymore though, right? Given the amount of time that you've been on Earth, they'd be adults by now."

"True. But do you really think the *age* of the child would change a parent's calculation?"

She shrugged. "Depends on the parent, I guess."

"Maybe. Either way, I couldn't let family ties factor into my decision. They'd only face financial penalties, like the loss of property and job opportunities and we're talking about billions of Earther lives that might be saved. I'd like to think that at least in the case of my parents, they'd be willing to take that tradeoff no matter how serious the economic sanctions. At least ... I *hope* it's still only economic sanctions. Tensions are on edge right now due to the war."

"The Alliance is at war?"

"Yeah. A long-running dispute with a neighboring system. The conflict has been going on in some fashion for as long as I can remember. Things heat up every few centuries and then they cool off again. They're in one of the hot periods now. There was one Alliance world that defected to the Hodjeri side back when I was in primary training, but that's the only case I can recall before we left for Earth. Recently, though, there have been others. Arbet told me that six planets have now switched sides, including Seset, which is Stasia and Drex's homeworld. Their policies have always been closely aligned with those of Parda, my own world, so ... it might only be a matter of time."

"What are they fighting over?"

"The same thing countries fight over on Earth. Resources. Differences in ideology, too, I suppose, although I couldn't really tell you much about Hodjeri society. Or maybe I should say *societies*, since I think their union is considerably looser than our own. They have multiple languages, for example, while all Alliance worlds speak a common tongue. Did you read that children's book? *Tales from the Aveezi Forest*?"

She nodded. "I read a few of the stories. Haven't finished it, though. To be honest, I got a bit tired of poor Tibbo getting the shaft."

"Yeah," he said with a dry chuckle. "I think that particular aspect of the stories may have been stressed a bit more in Uden's translation, although it's been so long since I read the originals that I couldn't really say for sure. The book itself was written not long after the Hodjeri war began, early in the Sixth Alliance, but some of the stories existed much earlier and were modernized. As a child, we listened to Motz and Tibbo tales the same way Earther children listen to Mother Goose or Winnie the Pooh. It was only as an adult that I realized those stories were … well, I guess you'd call them political propaganda, although I'd have been reluctant to use so harsh a term until recently. Looking back, though, it's pretty obvious that their safe little enclave of Alestria represented the Alliance and the Hodjeri Union was the dreadful forest into which we should never, ever go. And I can now understand exactly why they worked so hard to drill that message into our heads."

"Why is that?"

"Because if we did venture out into the Aveezi forest, we might find out that the true monsters were back in Alestria."

SEVEN

CLAIRE JOLTED awake to find the Aeris parked on a dark, treelined street. She hadn't fallen asleep in a car in ages, but the last thing she remembered was crossing over into New York. Beck was awake on the opposite side of the car, again checking his phone.

She sat up and ran her fingers through her tangled hair. "Where are we?"

"In Riverdale. There's a path through the woods over there that leads to the backyard of one of the houses at the edge of the Triad's property."

"How long have we been sitting here?"

"About twenty minutes."

"Have you heard anything yet?"

"From Arbet? No. I've also been trying to get in touch with Drex. The number I have is the one she used to call me yesterday, but she's not answering. I'm getting a little worried that Durav caught up with them before they left the area. My investigators managed to track them down, so..."

Claire sat silently for a moment, looking out the window at the vacant lot as she finished the last of a latte, now cold, that she'd grabbed from a self-serve kiosk a few hours earlier. "You're not planning to wait here until one of them messages you back, are you? Because we don't even know that they will, and at some point, we'll have to—"

"No. I mean, obviously, I'd feel much better about all of this if I could talk to someone who knows exactly what's happened here over the past thirty-six hours or so, but I know we can't just remain on hold. We're waiting here because the house we need to enter through is only about a ten-minute hike from here. The Triad's security drones patrol the area around Lavender House for about five minutes beginning at twelve after the hour. Assuming they haven't changed the schedule since Monday night, that is."

The clock on the dashboard showed that it was just after three a.m., which was about thirty minutes after their projected arrival. She felt around the seat for her phone. "Wyatt is going to be worried. I haven't checked in with him for over an hour."

"It's okay. I messaged him not long after you dozed off. Told him the police were continuing to search, but I'd convinced you to take a sedative so that you could get some sleep. I said you'd contact him when you woke up."

"Did he send a reply?"

"Yeah. Just a thumbs up. If you're going to respond, you should probably do it now. Once we're in the tunnels, you won't have a signal. They've got something down there that jams communications."

Claire grimaced and stared down at her phone, fighting the urge to call, if only to hear Wyatt's voice. She had no idea what they were about to walk into and really didn't want the last thing she ever heard from him to be a response that almost certainly meant he was annoyed at her. But given the late hour, he was probably asleep now. And if she called, she'd have to lie to him yet again about where she was and what she was doing. Probably best to wait.

There was also a voice message from Joe and a text from Alice Dobroski. The timestamp on Joe's message was just before two, so it would have come in not long after she dozed off. He said that Reese had been stabilized and airlifted to, of all places, the house next door to the one he shared with their mother. It made sense, once Claire thought about it. When she asked for Joe's help, she'd been in such a state of panic that she hadn't been thinking clearly. Some sections of the Jonas Labs campus were still standing, so she'd assumed they would simply take

Reese there, but she hadn't factored in the number of police and
reporters who would be hanging around after the bombing.
Their neighborhood, on the other hand, was gated, with full-
time guards, and completely empty now that Kai had bought
out the other houses. They had plenty of room to hide a few
doctors and an injured alien—one whose face had almost
certainly been caught on their security cameras just before the
attacks.

Alice's message had come in only a few minutes earlier.
She apparently wasn't kidding when she said she was a
night owl.

> Read first part of Shepherd's memoir as you
> suggested. Also discovered something I think
> you'll find very interesting in the Das journal.
> Maybe your alien friend isn't quite as alien as
> we thought.

Well, that was cryptic. Claire made a mental note to call her
in the morning—assuming, of course, that she was alive to call
anyone in the morning. With that cheerful thought at the fore-
front, she decided to message instead.

> It may be a while before I can call. Middle of a
> crisis. Will explain later. Stay safe.

Alice's response came back instantly.

> You, too. I'll send file in a few. Read then we'll
> discuss when you're free.

Claire was about to show Alice's message to Beck, but he
was rummaging around in the cargo area behind him.

"Do you still have the gun I gave you?" he asked as he
pulled the bag from behind the seat and into his lap. It was a
smooth movement, with no sign at all of his earlier pain or even

stiffness. The wonder drug must be working much better on him than it had on Reese.

"Sure." She removed the pistol from the Aeris's console, assuming he wanted it back. But when she turned around, he was pulling a second gun from the gym bag he'd packed before they left his apartment. She also spotted a couple of passports inside, along with stacks of money. It was more cash than she'd seen in at least a decade, all in one place. Where did he think they'd be going that still took cash?

"What about your drone zapper?" he asked.

"In my pocket. Do you have one?"

He shook his head. "Nothing that could destroy them. Just the app on my phone that will halt them if they enter my personal space. To be honest, I doubt your little zapper can actually kill the security drones that the Triad uses, but it might be enough to confuse them. Hopefully, we can just avoid them entirely, because I'm pretty sure they're equipped with lasers. I found a headless groundhog on the drive near the gate."

Claire shuddered, thinking both of the groundhog and the man she'd seen die in the courtyard of that house when she was watching the video footage for Wyatt. The drones that killed him had belonged to Kolya International, but someone inside the Triad's compound had intercepted the signal and turned them on Macek and his team.

"Wait," she said. "Did I even tell you about that?"

She thought back over the past few hours and realized that she'd asked Beck a lot of questions but hadn't told *him* much of anything that had happened to her while she was in New York.

Beck raised his eyebrows, waiting for her to go on.

"Remember when I called you on Monday night to set a time for the meeting with Alice? I was watching when you answered, through cameras Wyatt had Kes set up in two locations outside that house. I'm guessing you arrived at the same time as several others, because I never saw you enter. But I was pretty sure I recognized you when you came out the front gate and I called you to double check. Then I saw that car nearly hit you. I thought you'd been abducted."

She spent the next several minutes telling him about her conversation with Kolya at Beekman Place and about the attack on Macek's team that happened the next afternoon.

"Why exactly was Macek on the Triad's property in the first place?" Beck asked.

"Same reason Wyatt had cameras set up to observe it. Wilson sent both of them a tip that Drex and Stasia might be there. Macek blamed them for the bombings on Mars and I guess the FBI wasn't moving quickly enough for him. Speaking of the FBI, remember me telling you about the bogus agent who questioned me when Dr. Leffler was killed?"

"Yeah."

"Well, I saw her break into the building where Alice works, along with another guy. Alice set off the alarm and the two of them left before the campus police arrived. I checked Wyatt's video cam when I got back to the apartment and that same car pulled into the drive of the Triad's headquarters about twenty minutes later. It was—"

"Let me guess. A silver Pulsar? And the woman has long red hair?"

"Reddish blonde, yeah. With super short bangs."

"That's Maela. Durav's ... well, I'm not entirely sure *what* she is to Durav, but anything she does is on his orders. Hold on a sec." He pulled up a video on his phone. "From my doorbell cam. Is this the guy you saw with her the other night?"

Claire glanced at the screen. The image was a little blurry, but she nodded. "That's him. He works with one of the militias Wyatt has been investigating. Is he a member of the Watch, too?"

"No. Just someone Durav hired after he killed off most of his security *ipret-tai*. The other guy, the one standing behind him in the video taken at my place, is one of the two or three left of the original security force. We may run into some of the others once we're inside. You can spot them by the symbol inked above their eye. The ones assigned to Arbet can be trusted, but the others..." He shook his head. "Just stick close to me. And ... we should probably get going."

Claire instructed the car to stay in position and then opened her door.

"I'm sorry," the Aeris replied, "but this is not an approved parking space. I cannot violate the local traffic code."

"Except you've been parked here for the better part of an hour," Beck countered.

"No. I was not parked. I was *idling*. And the code applies to *un*attended vehicles. I am currently carrying two passengers."

"Okay," Claire said. "Then stay here *unless* you spot the police. In that case, leave, and then circle back to this location as soon as it's clear."

"By the time I am aware of police in the area, they will have recorded my signal. If they order me to drive to the impoundment lot, I will have no choice but to comply."

Claire gritted her teeth. "Fine. Circle the neighborhood until I page you. Stay within a three minute recall radius." She expected the AI to come up with some other objection, like a law against loitering. Instead, it gave her a crisp affirmative, waited until they were outside, then made a U-turn to head back toward the main road.

They hiked along the road for a couple of minutes. Aside from a dog barking and sirens wailing faintly in the distance, everything was quiet. After a couple of blocks, they veered off into the woods. She'd taken some over-the-counter painkillers shortly after they left Maine, and was now realizing that she should have taken another dose before the Aeris left with her bag. The uneven terrain wasn't helping matters, nor were the brambles tugging at her bare calves. If she'd had any idea that this was Beck's definition of *a path through the woods*, she'd have changed clothes. Although come to think of it, the only thing she had in her bag aside from shorts was the suit she'd worn to the Ares Consortium conference and the blue dress that she'd worn to the dinner.

Beck stopped as they neared a bank of fir trees a few meters ahead. "Almost there," he said in a low voice. "Are you okay?"

"I'm *fine*," she snapped, more than a little annoyed that she was struggling to keep pace with a man who only a few hours earlier had been so weak she'd had to help him across the room to use the toilet. She cleared a spiderweb from her shirt, then followed him through a gap in the trees.

They emerged into a small clearing about three-quarters of the way up the hill. The view was picturesque, with the lights of New York twinkling in the distance and a cluster of houses with well-manicured lawns in the foreground. Everyone seemed to be tucked in for the night, with only a few lit windows. The house on the far left was the one that she'd watched through the surveillance cameras on Monday.

Beck tugged at her arm, and they continued uphill toward the house at the top. This one was clearly older than the homes down in the valley, with architectural features that reminded her a bit of Allen House, the old Victorian in New Haven where she and Alice had found Devin Shepherd's body. The place was dark, with the exception of a light in a narrow window on one of the upper floors. There was also a faint green glow emanating from the patio. As they drew closer, she realized that it came from a security panel next to the sunroom that stretched across most of that side of the building.

"Do you have the code?" she whispered.

"No. But I shouldn't need one. Unless Durav has gotten around to blocking my access, in which case we'll need to move on to Plan B."

"Which is?"

"I have absolutely no clue." He gave her a brave smile, then pressed his palm against the panel next to the door. There was a delay, just long enough to make her nervous. Then the panel flashed twice, and the door gave an audible click.

"These lights are on a timer and the house is supposed to be empty," he said. "I don't want to set off any alarms, so we'll need to proceed in the dark. Stick close to me."

Claire followed his instructions. She'd had no intention of wandering off in the first place, given that Beck was the only one who had any idea where they were headed.

Her earlier thought that the place reminded her of Allen House vanished as soon as she crossed the threshold into the sunroom. The house in New Haven had been empty, aside from broken glass, graffitied walls, and the dead body. This place was a maze of statues, potted plants, and furniture, all jammed in so tightly that there was barely room to walk.

Once they entered the main house, they rounded the corner into a small L-shaped room with dark paneled walls and an ornate wooden bar. Two or three steps in, her peripheral vision caught a flash of movement to the left. She pivoted quickly, then lowered the gun when she spotted her reflection in the mirror behind the bar.

A streak of moonlight slashed across the marble tiles in the foyer, supplementing the pale glow of Beck's phone light. They turned left again, and proceeded down a narrow hallway, eventually arriving at an elevator.

"Shouldn't we take the stairs instead?" she asked as Beck reached for the button. "I mean, if someone is paying attention to when the lights go on and off, wouldn't the power surge from the elevator alert them, too?"

He considered for a moment, then shook his head. "It might, but it's a long way down. The tunnel is about two stories below ground level and that's measuring from the *base* of this hill. We're several stories above that and we'd be in the dark the entire time aside from our phones. Also, this is a very old house. I have no idea what condition the stairs are even in."

Claire thought they should be equally wary about stepping into the *elevator* of a very old house. But her leg was bothering her enough that the idea of that many stairs, even going down, was not appealing.

When the doors opened nine floors later, they stepped out into a tunnel maybe six meters in diameter. A line of circular lights on the ceiling stretched off into the distance, then appeared to vanish around a curve.

Beck surveyed the area near the elevator, then huffed in annoyance. "I was hoping we'd have transportation, but I guess there's no logical reason a cart would be here given that no one was inside Lavender House. We'll have to walk."

"Where exactly are we going?"

"Blue House. That's Arbet's place."

It was getting really hard to shake the feeling that Beck's main purpose for this trip was to find Arbet. She took several deep breaths, trying to wrestle down her frustration before speaking. "Do you think she'll know where Durav is keeping Ro and Jemma?"

"I doubt it. But she probably knows why Durav believes you have the beacon. And she'll almost certainly know why he's looking for it in the first place, given that Sandjeel overruled him and agreed to the delay. And without knowing either of those things, we'll be going in blind."

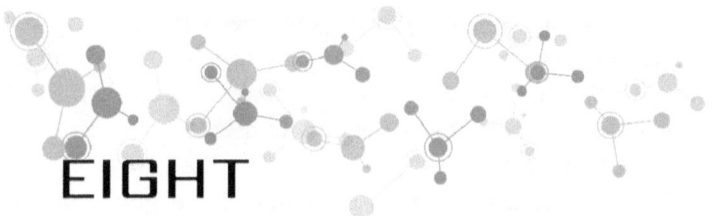

EIGHT

THE ELEVATOR to Blue House came into sight sooner than Claire expected, just as they rounded the curve in the tunnel. Her leg was still throbbing, but the walk had been shorter and far less grueling than their hike up the hill to Lavender House.

Beck pressed his palm against the security panel. Claire felt a twinge of uneasiness as the cobalt blue door slid open and they stepped inside. It felt like a trap. From everything Beck had told her, Durav wasn't an idiot. He knew they were coming. She doubted he'd be fooled by the fact that they'd arrived twelve hours early and were coming in through the back door. He was probably tracking their every move.

The garage on the other side of the elevator doors must have been equipped with a motion sensor, because the area lit up as soon as they entered. Beck cursed under his breath, then moved quickly toward a second security panel. It blinked green when he held his palm against it, and a gentle chime announced their arrival when the door opened, and they stepped inside.

They paused in the entryway as Beck surveyed the house's large, open living area. Claire didn't see anyone, and there wasn't really any place someone could hide. Still, she had the sense that they were being watched, although that could be because the entire back wall of the room was glass.

"I don't think she's here," Beck said. "If she were, one of her *ipret-tai* would have greeted us. We still need to check, though."

"It *is* after three in the morning. Maybe they're asleep?"

"Maybe, but the *ipret-tai* don't actually need much..." He stopped, then continued when she gave him a questioning look.

"I was going to say that *ipret-tai* don't need much sleep, but recent events suggest that I don't know nearly as much about them as I thought. We don't use cloned servants on Parda, so I haven't had much direct experience with them."

"*Cloned* servants?"

He gave her a quick nod, then pulled the gun from his pocket and motioned for her to come with him before she could follow up with more questions. They checked the kitchen and a small office but found no one.

Next, they went upstairs. It was dark, so Beck again employed his phone light, running the beam over a sitting area with a couch and coffee table. The light reflected back from two tumblers, drained to the dregs, next to a red flask like the one that she'd seen in Beck's video. Closed doors with the numbers 3 and 4 in the middle were on the right side of the room, and a hallway with additional doors stretched off to the left.

Beck opened door three. In the faint glow from the abstract pattern playing on the wallscreen, Claire could see that the bed was neatly made and there was a game board of some sort in one corner. No one was inside, however, so they moved on to room number four. It was dark and apparently occupied, judging from the long huddled figure in the bed.

Beck peered inside for a moment, then frowned and backed out, heading instead toward the hallway on the other side of the room where there were four more doors.

"Why didn't you wake that guy up?" she hissed. "Maybe he could tell you where Arbet is."

"Or maybe he's one of Durav's guys and he'd sound the alarm?"

He opened the first door on the right. Empty. She nudged him and nodded toward the second room on the opposite side, where a thin line of light was visible under the door.

"Looks like someone's awake," she whispered.

Instead of tapping on the door, as she'd expected him to do, he flung it open and swept the muzzle of his gun across the bedroom. Again, the figure in the bed appeared to be asleep, which seemed odd with the overhead light on. It seemed even odder when she got close enough to see that the man's eyes were wide open.

Beck took a step back toward the wall. "Oh my god. It's Meeks."

"Is he one of Arbet's *ipret-tai*?"

"No. Like I said, they have a tattoo above their eye." He bent over to check the man's pulse, but it was obvious even from several paces away that he was dead, and had been for at least a few hours, given the bluish tinge of his skin. "Meeks was one of the other members of the Watch. I didn't realize he was assigned to this house for Conclave. We just played against each other in the *djvari* tournament."

His voice shook on the last words. Claire stepped closer, intending to console him, but he was already backing out into the hallway, barely seeming to notice she was there. By the time she joined him, he'd already thrown open the next door, apparently tossing stealth and caution to the winds.

All of the other rooms were empty. She followed him back to the first occupied bedroom. Upon closer inspection, that man was dead, too. His eyes were closed, one arm flung over his chest, with his right hand resting on his neck. Something about the pose nagged at Claire. As with the other body, there was no sign of struggle and no blood, although it was hard to tell for certain with only the light from their phones.

"Where to now?" she asked, as they hurried back down the stairs.

Beck didn't answer. At first, she thought it might be because he was tired. He *should* be tired, given the amount of blood that he'd lost earlier in the day. But by the time they reached the bottom of the stairs, she was fairly sure his silence was due less to exhaustion than uncertainty.

"Maybe we should head toward the Great Hall," he said after a moment. "She could be with Sandjeel."

He was talking about Arbet. Again. Claire fought back the urge to remind him that they were here to save Ro and Jemma, which meant their main goal was finding *Durav*. Maybe Beck was right. Maybe Arbet could provide them with useful information. But if they didn't find the woman soon, they were going to have to come up with an alternative plan.

They returned to the tunnel and had been walking for only about a minute when they saw a fork veering off to the right, and just beyond that, a small white passenger cart.

"It's from Arbet's house," Beck said.

"How can you tell?"

"The blue trim." When they reached the cart, he leaned over and pressed his palm against the panel on the center console and said something in what she assumed was Ufretan. The cart responded and Beck stepped back.

"The last passenger was David, one of Arbet's *ipret-tai*. That's not good. There's no way he'd have abandoned it here if given a choice."

Beck motioned for Claire to get into the cart, then issued another command. The cart responded with a cheerful chirp, executed a three-point turn and proceeded in the direction they'd been walking.

Shortly after, the tunnel curved to the right with a narrower offshoot continuing straight ahead. The cart turned to follow the main passageway, but immediately screeched to a halt, decelerating so quickly that Claire and Beck both pitched forward.

After two shrill beeps, the AI began talking, presumably telling them to move whatever was blocking its path. Beck fired back with what she strongly suspected was an Ufretan obscenity, then got out of the cart, motioning for Claire to stay inside. She did, but moved over to the opposite seat so that she could get a better look.

The obstacle in the roadway was a woman with lank, shoulder-length blond hair, dressed in a long beige tunic. She was taller than average, but otherwise unremarkable aside from the black symbol inked on her forehead, just above her right eye. It looked a bit like a sixteenth note, except the bottom was jagged and irregular.

Beck crouched next to the woman and pressed two fingers against her neck. "She's dead. It happened more recently than the others, though. Her body is still warm."

"What do you think could have killed her?"

"I don't know. There's no blood. No sign of violence. My best guess would be poison of some sort."

As Beck began pulling the woman's body out of their path, a tiny blue light zoomed up behind him. It blinked once, twice, then hovered about a meter away. The pattern and the color weren't the same as the drones that had attacked Shepherd and followed Claire on Mars, but she had seen enough varieties of bugbots in the past few months that she had no trouble identifying the things.

Her mind flashed back to the video of Professor Leffler, standing in front of a CVS only a few miles away, slapping frantically at her neck as she felt the sting of the nanodrone's injector. No wonder seeing the dead man's hand on his neck back at Blue House just now had given her a chill.

She placed her pistol on the seat and fumbled in the pocket of her shorts. By the time she got her hand around the bug zapper, the drone was retreating. Still, this one wasn't nearly as far away as the bugbots in the cul-de-sac had been from her kitchen window. Three quick taps of the button on the side of the device sent the tiny blue light spiraling down to the floor of the tunnel.

Beck gave her a quizzical look as she slipped out of the cart.

"We have company." She nodded toward the spot where the drone had fallen, and he followed her over to inspect it. The light was still on, blinking steadily. She sent the kill signal again and the light sputtered but quickly resumed. "It stopped just outside your privacy zone, so I guess your app worked. Too bad I didn't bring my—"

Before the words *gas mask* could leave her mouth, Beck raised his foot and crushed the tiny drone beneath his heel.

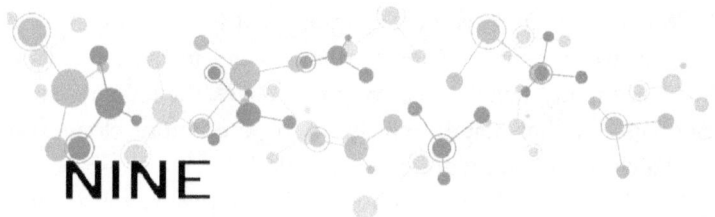

NINE

"DON'T BREATHE!" Claire said, at the same instant that Beck inhaled. She grabbed his arm and pulled him back toward the cart, away from the shattered bugbot.

She waited as long as she could, then tugged the neck of her shirt up to cover her face as a precaution and took a hesitant breath. As much as she hated the idea of using Beck as her personal canary in the coal mine, he seemed fine.

"You just said the woman over there was probably poisoned," she explained, in response to his raised eyebrows. "That drone could easily have been what killed her. Kes told me not to take any chances, because some of the poisons used in these things are aerosolized."

"I know. But you saw the lights. It was obviously communicating with whoever owns it, which almost certainly means Durav's security team. I had to disable it."

"If it was sending a signal, it went out long before I zapped it. It's not as if the thing transmits in Morse code."

"Fair point. Either way, though, we need to get moving."

Once they were inside the cart, he instructed it to resume their previous course. It maneuvered slightly to avoid the woman's body and continued down the tunnel.

"She was one of the *ipret-tai*, right?"

"Yeah. Her name was Helen, and she was assigned to Sand-jeel. Which means the Triad is down to only one female. They had three when we arrived."

"You said earlier there were several dozen in all. Why were so few of them women?"

"Most of the *ipret-tai* were programmed for security. And to be clear, we were mimicking Earther society in the 1950s. You didn't see many female security guards back then. Or research scientists, for that matter, which is why the bodies cloned for the Watch were also predominantly male."

"Really? I would have guessed the opposite, or at least assumed a fairly equal split, based on the ones you've mentioned and the ones I've encountered. Stasia, Drexel, Arbet."

He shrugged. "You've mostly encountered those who are fighting the system. Maybe life as an Earther woman tilted them in that direction."

Claire was about to counter that theory with the example of Baby Bangs, but the cart was slowing now. She caught a faint whiff of food as they neared the end of the tunnel. The smell wasn't appetizing, even though she'd barely eaten anything since the leftover pizza at the hotel more than twelve hours ago. This was closer to the stale funk of a school cafeteria or a roadside diner, heavy on old grease and overcooked vegetables.

A second fork on the right dipped sharply downward, but the cart continued along the main path, coming to a stop a few seconds later on a charging pad just beyond the point where the string of overhead light panels ended. They got out and continued on foot for about forty paces, then rounded the corner at the tunnel's end and saw nothing but blackness. She was reaching for her phone light when Beck drew in a sharp breath and stepped back, holding out a protective arm to keep her behind him.

Claire didn't break the silence, even though she really wanted to ask what had startled him so badly. She hadn't heard anything. She certainly couldn't *see* anything. For the third time that night, she found herself simply following blindly. There was enough light filtering in from behind them that she could make out Beck standing next to her and the floor for maybe half a meter in front of her feet. Beyond that, though, it was pitch black.

Beck uttered a low stream of curses as he turned his head slowly to take in the darkness.

"What's wrong?"

He gave her an incredulous look. "What do you mean what's wrong? They're *dead*. They're all dead."

Claire's heart gave a panicked jolt as she fished in her pocket for her phone. "Who's dead? And how can you even tell? I can barely see beyond my feet."

"Oh, right." Beck reached out for her arm with his unbandaged hand as he continued scanning the area around them. "Sorry. I have lenses that pick up light from the holoemitters…"

She stuffed the pistol back in her pocket and flicked on her phone light. There was no way she'd be able to hit anything in the dark, anyway. The flashlight didn't help much, but she could now make out a couple of serving stations against one wall. Moving to the left, she spotted several clusters of tables and chairs scattered around what looked like a roughly carved cavern.

And yes, there were bodies. Fifteen, maybe twenty, dressed in the same long tunics in a variety of colors, which they wore over street clothes. Some of the bodies were draped over chairs. Others were on the floor. One sat with his back propped against the end of the buffet station, head lolling to the side. He looked to be in his early thirties, with a deep tan and shaggy blond hair that fell across his face and the front of his green tunic. His long legs were splayed into a wide *V* on the floor and a small white device rested in the hollow of his open palm. It was oval, almost but not quite round, about an inch thick with a little dip in the center. It reminded Claire of the thumbprint cookies Grandma Echols had baked each Christmas. There had always been a separate box of them under the tree for her dad because they were his favorites.

This definitely wasn't a cookie, though.

"Is that a weapon?" she asked Beck, nodding toward the object.

"No. It's a *rezlat* ... a recording device. We use it to exchange messages with people back home. Not instantaneously," he added in response to her look of surprise. "The Triad only has contact with the Ufretan system when one of our ships enters the comms window every couple of years. That's when they get the messages. Families and friends send us music, books, news stories. We share some of it with the others and record our responses during Conclave, and then they're transmitted back to the Academy during the next window. Heavily edited, according to Arbet."

"If they have these other communications devices, why does Durav need the beacon? Couldn't the Triad just send a message back using one of those?"

He shook his head. "The *rezlats* connect to the Academy. The beacon summons the military. And it takes two members of the Triad to use it, which is why it has two of the little divots on top with cell scanners for identification."

Claire couldn't really see why that was a major distinction. Surely this Academy would pass important news along to the military and they could contact the Triad to confirm it. She supposed it might take a little longer, though. Maybe Durav was in a hurry to be back inside his own body.

Beck was now moving from one Watcher to the next, checking for signs of life. Claire continued scanning the room with her flashlight, praying that Ro and Jemma would not be among the dead.

Thankfully, she didn't find them, but she felt a rising sense of anxiety and something else, too. Something close to grief at being surrounded by so many bodies. Even though she didn't know these people, even though she knew that some version of them would be revived back on their homeworld, it was still horrible. How did Wyatt cope with this when he covered terrorist attacks and other mass casualty events?

And the bodies that Wyatt saw were undoubtedly in worse condition. Most of these looked like the people they'd seen back at Blue House—simply *dead*, with no sign of violence and no discernable cause of death. Probably poisoned, as Beck had noted. It must have been a quick-acting poison, too, because they all looked peaceful. It was as if they'd simply collapsed in unison.

All but seven, that is. Seven men at the very back had been seated against the wall. Four were dressed in the same beige tunic as the female ipret-tai who was killed in the tunnel and two wore similar tunics of dark gray. All were shot cleanly through the forehead, just to the left of the symbol inked above their eye. The two in dark gray also had a second, smaller symbol next to the one that reminded Claire of a musical note.

"Eight and Three," Beck said when Claire asked. "They were part of Durav's guard. He didn't bother to name them. The *ipret-tai* just before Eight is David."

The final man at the very end of the line was an anomaly in more ways than one. First, he was dressed in a standard black uniform, instead of a tunic. Second, he was considerably shorter than any of the others and seemed slightly bloated, so she thought he'd probably been dead for a while. His death wasn't nearly as clean, either, with one shot to his neck and another just above his jawline.

"He's not an *ipret-tai* and not a member of the Watch," Beck said. "I'm guessing he's one of the mercenaries who did something to piss Durav off. Although the other one I saw wasn't in a uniform. Just jeans and boots."

"He seems familiar, though. Maybe I saw him in one of the photos of militia members that Wyatt showed me." Feeling a bit ghoulish, she snapped a picture of the man so that she could check later. "But … as for the others, why would they use poison on the Watchers but shoot the *ipret-tai*? And what about the bodies we found at Arbet's house? Why weren't those Watchers here?"

"I don't know. Maybe they left early. This is only a little over half of the Watch, so there could be bodies at the other houses. And they didn't shoot all of the *ipret-tai*. The drone killed Helen … the woman we found in the tunnel. Maybe that's also how they killed the other Watchers. As for the ones here, my best guess is that they put the poison in some of the food. A little something extra in the *crestah* and *braber*. Or more likely they added it to the *evir* since it seems to have hit everyone pretty much at once. They could have been making a toast to finally going home. The *ipret-tai* wouldn't have been included in that. They're on very basic rations. They get two nutrient bars a day with the optimal…"

He trailed off and was silent for several seconds.

"What?" she prodded.

"Nothing. Just … the *ipret-tai* are *supposed* to eat only these meal bars that provide optimal calories and nutrition. One of the Ufretis at the Academy said he took a bite of a bar on a dare during primary training and claimed it was like biting into a *flodjes*…" He sighed. "Sorry, um, I guess the closest Earth equivalent would be something like *eating wet cardboard*. But the other night when we were at Blue House, Arbet had Dora—one of her *ipret-tai*—take a tray of sandwiches out to the two who were standing guard. And I saw Dora sneak a piece of chocolate. Or I *thought* she was sneaking it. For all I know, Arbet may allow her people to eat whatever they want."

Claire gritted her teeth as Beck worked his way through the tangent, reminding herself that he was upset. These people were his coworkers. He'd known them for longer than anyone on Earth had been alive. Some of them were undoubtedly his friends. And she wasn't the only one worried about people she cared about. Even if he hadn't come right out and admitted it, the man was clearly in love with Arbet.

"But *why*, Beck? Why kill any of them now if the Alliance is planning to leave them here when they destroy Earth?"

"That … might be my fault. They could have sent them out

for one last vacation, but after I told them the truth? Maybe Durav didn't want to deal with a few dozen angry Watchers. They'd just be on edge, watching and waiting for the *naidar* bubble to surround the planet." He shook his head. "Or maybe this was their plan all along. I don't know. Come on. We need to check Sandjeel's quarters."

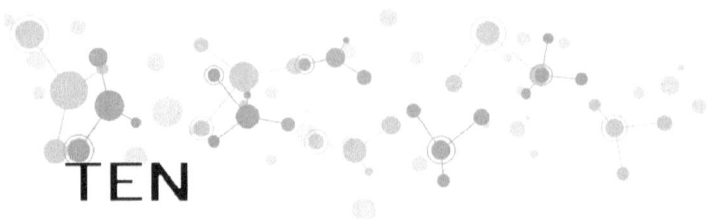

TEN

THEY REVERSED COURSE, walking back toward the tunnel. The panels on the ceiling hadn't seemed especially bright to Claire earlier. Now, after several minutes with only the light from the phones, she had to squint after rounding the corner so that her eyes could adjust to the glare.

At first, she thought they were heading back to the cart. But Beck continued on, past the charging pad, turning at the downward sloping branch she'd noticed on the way in. The temperature also dipped, plummeting at least ten degrees before they reached the end of the tunnel. It dropped another ten degrees once they stepped through the door, which was slightly—and to Claire's mind, ominously—ajar. Once again, she was plunged into complete darkness and had to resort to the light on her phone. It shook in her hands, causing the beam to jitter as she scanned the frigid room.

"Why is it so cold in here? It's like a f-freakin' … refrigerator." She'd very nearly said *morgue*, before realizing that the word might be a little *too* on the nose after the scene in the dining area.

"Sandjeel requires lower temps. You'd understand if you saw him. He's stuck in a fur coat 24/7. He gets very uncomfortable if he spends more than a few minutes at anything above six or seven degrees Celsius." He shook his head as he looked around the place. "I've never been in here. Sandjeel has rather odd tastes in personal décor."

She ran her phone light around the room. It was large and plain, with a large, plain gray sofa and a few other large, plain pieces of furniture in matching fabric. Absolutely nothing to see, or at least nothing that *she* could see. Which meant she had no idea what Beck was talking about, but at this point, she really wasn't interested in asking him for color commentary.

For the next few minutes, she tagged along behind him, waiting in the hallway as he searched the smaller rooms and walking in place to keep her legs warm. She wasn't normally afraid of the dark, but this was beginning to freak her out.

On the plus side, they'd found no dead bodies. But they'd also found no *live* bodies, so this detour had gotten them precisely nowhere.

"Where to now?" she asked when Beck joined her in the hallway after searching the last room.

"The Triad's chambers, I guess. It's the only other place at HQ where the temperature is kept within Sandjeel's comfort zone."

"Fabulous," she said, without the slightest hint of enthusiasm.

Beck glanced at her short sleeves and then downward, seeming to notice her bare legs for the first time. "Hold on."

A few seconds later, he came back with a bundle, which he shook out and handed to her. At first, she thought it was a blanket, but judging from the fabric—a thick, plush terry—it was probably a massively oversized towel. She wrapped it around herself like a serape and it still fell nearly to her ankles.

When she finished, Beck gave her a rueful, slightly amused expression. "Sorry. I just grabbed what was on top of the stack. If you want, I can find you something else."

She looked down at the towel. "It's warm. And all I see is *gray*. If you see something else, I don't want to know. Let's just get out of here."

"Okay. There has to be another exit somewhere around here that leads to a second tunnel. That's how Sandjeel came into the chambers when we met the other day."

Claire sighed. They seemed to have moved from looking for Arbet to looking for Sandjeel, and to the best of her knowledge, neither of them had abducted Ro and Jemma. Her frustration mounted steadily as she followed in Beck's wake yet again, phone light in hand, searching for this tunnel entrance in the same set of rooms they'd just searched for bodies.

A few doors down, they entered what appeared to be a home theater or gaming suite. The first time around, her gaze had been drawn to the right side of the room where a reclining chair, much too large to be anything other than custom-made, faced an enormous, curved screen that took up two walls from floor to ceiling. This time, she focused on the other side of the room and noticed something odd. She flipped off her phone light to confirm, then nudged Beck. "We need to go that way."

"Why? I thought you couldn't see in here?"

"I can't see the holo images. But actual *light* is coming from that direction. And the only place with lights since we came out of the elevator at Arbet's house was the other tunnel."

Claire took point now, moving down the corridor toward the glow. When she entered the kitchen a few moments later, she found a door rimmed in light on the opposite side of the room.

Beck chuckled as he opened it. "And the blind shall lead..."

She held her arm up to ward off the brightness. "I'm blind *now*, that's for certain. Really wish they'd make up their mind one way or the other about the hologram thingies. I'm going to end up with a migraine from all this switching back and forth." Even to her own ears she sounded whiny and petulant, like Jemma when she was overtired and hungry. Both things were true at the moment, and her leg was throbbing like crazy, but she needed to rein it in.

"Space was limited on our transport," Beck said. "Holoemitters are a scarce commodity. Light panels, on the other hand? Those could be purchased anywhere, even back in the 1950s."

"I don't see why they even bothered with the holoemitters,

since they seem to be using the tech mostly for interior decorating. You could buy paint and throw pillows in the 1950s, right?"

"True, but it's not just interiors. The area between buildings looks like the grounds of the Academy where we studied together. It takes a lot of emitters to create a seamless illusion. They also use them on the walls to show images from each of the member worlds—natural wonders and so forth. As Eberin mentioned in his journal, one of the goals of Conclave is to remind us that this planet is our assignment, not our home."

The tunnel was considerably shorter than the one between Arbet's house and HQ, and they arrived at the Triad's chambers a few minutes later. She'd imagined something spacious and grand—and perhaps it did look more impressive through Beck's holographic lenses. From her perspective, though, it was a basic conference room aside from the giant-sized desk and chair in the far corner. It had a refreshment center almost identical to the main conference area on her floor at the *Atlantic Post*, apart from a different collection of snacks and cups on the shelves. The room was as cold as Sandjeel's quarters, and the air had a crisp, almost metallic tang.

Beck pulled in a sharp breath. "What the hell?"

She followed his gaze to a shattered glass box on the counter next to the sink. One of the palm-sized devices like the one she'd seen in the cafeteria sat in the middle of the shards.

"Durav has completely lost his mind," Beck said. "The *brelat* is *right there*, just like it was during our meeting. I mean, it was *inside* the case and on one of the shelves then, but…"

Claire fished the object out of the rubble, being careful to avoid splinters. "Are you sure? It looks identical to the thing the dead guy was holding back in the cafeteria."

"No." He took it from her. "See? There are two indentations on this one."

He placed his thumb at one end of the device, frowned, then moved it to the other. Finally, he swiped across the smooth surface to the middle, where his thumb slipped into the little hollow. "Okay. That's bizarre. I definitely *see* two, but... What color is it?"

She moved her phone light a bit closer. "It's white. Or maybe off-white. Just like the other one. Why? What color do *you* see?"

"I see blue. Son of a bitch. Someone swapped it out for their *rezlat*. And then reprogrammed the holoemitters to hide the theft, which means it could have happened pretty much at any point since the move from Houston."

"When was the move? And who do you think would have done it?"

"We relocated HQ during the secession crisis. As to who might have done it, there are only three people with that level of access. No ... wait. Three now, but there were five people in all, if we count Uden and Djasa, the two members of the Triad who died. But it's really only *four* possibilities, since we can obviously eliminate Durav. I think it's safe to say he wasn't aware that someone switched the *brelat* until a few hours ago, since he seemed to think you have it."

He slipped the device into his pocket and nodded toward the door on the other side of the room. They'd only taken a couple of steps in that direction when they spotted the bodies.

There were two of them, both women, one flung sideways on top of the other. Despite a dramatic change of hairstyle and bruising around her face and neck, Claire recognized the woman on top as Corbin Drexel. Someone had beaten her badly, but that wasn't what killed her. A single, neat bullet hole marred the smooth, pale skin of her forehead. The exit wound, however, was far less neat, judging from the amount of blood on both the floor and on the body lying beneath her.

"God." Beck winced and turned away, gripping the edge of the conference table. "I was really hoping she and Stasia made it out of the city, but when I messaged her back about Reese, and she didn't respond ... I think I already knew. And in their case, dead is dead. Now that Seset is out of the Alliance, I can't imagine that anyone at the Academy will bother reviving their original bodies."

At first, Claire made the same assumption that Beck seemed to have made, thinking the second body was Stasia. But when she moved around to get a closer look at the other woman's face, there was no mistaking the fringe of red-gold hair just above the gunshot wound.

"Baby Bangs."

"What?"

"The second woman isn't Stasia, Beck. It's ... I can't remember what you called her earlier. The fake FBI agent. I didn't know her name and she kept popping up, so I just called her Baby Bangs. Because of...?" She motioned to her own forehead.

Judging from Beck's blank expression he'd never heard the term, but he nodded. "Her name was Maela." He placed a hand against the woman's neck. She hadn't been beaten as badly as Drex, but one vivid bruise slashed across her right cheek. "I think they've been dead for a while. At least four hours. Maybe longer, given how cold it is in here. Probably longer than the bodies at Arbet's house or in the Great Hall."

"But why would Durav kill her? I thought you said she was on his side."

"Could be for the same reason they killed the others. Just to get them out of the way and spare them the wait for the end. Although that blow to her face would suggest otherwise."

"Do you think maybe she was working with Drex?"

"No. Absolutely not. I think it far more likely that Durav was angry over his discovery that the *brelat* was gone and Maela just happened to be in range of his fists. Like I said earlier, he has a nasty habit of taking out his anger on others. Usually on the *ipret-tai*. In Drex's case, though, he was clearly trying to get information from her. And I think he succeeded."

Claire was about to ask why he made those assumptions when he lifted one of Drexel's hands to show three bloody crescents where fingernails had been. A fourth nail was bloodied and dangled by a thread of skin, while the fifth remained intact. Definitely torture, and Durav didn't sound like the sort of guy who would quit unless he'd gotten what he wanted, so…

She turned away and fought back a wave of nausea, taking deep centering breaths. It was becoming very hard to keep her panic in check. As awful as it was to see Drexel and yes, even Maela, in this condition, a traitorous voice in her head kept reminding her that it could have been Ro and Jemma. Might still be Ro and Jemma in a similar state around the next corner.

"What do we do now?" she asked, once her throat loosened enough to speak.

"We check—"

BWEE BWEE BWEEAHM BWEE BWEE BWEEEAHM.

Claire jumped back, nearly tripping over a chair as an alarm, blaring from every corner of the room, drowned out whatever Beck had been about to say. After the first few blasts, a woman's voice—almost certainly automated—came over the comm system. She spoke Ufretan, although two of the words sounded like *Grosvenor Avenue*, which Claire had seen recently on the map. It was one road over from Goodridge, where she'd watched cars going in and out of the Triad's headquarters.

As soon as the woman stopped talking, the earsplitting klaxon fired up again. She tried to ask Beck what the voice had said, what it was in fact now repeating after another round of the siren, but it was impossible to hear anything over the noise.

Beck grabbed her arm and pulled her toward a door on the other side of the room. It opened into a large, cavernous space with a raised platform at the front facing out toward several rows of benches. Except for the platform, it reminded Claire of a rustic Quaker meeting house she'd seen in a movie a few years back. That place had been peaceful and quiet, however, which was totally at odds with the current level of noise.

He flung another door open, and they stepped out into a black void. Her phone light bounced back from the ground beneath them, but when she raised it to look ahead, it didn't make even the slightest dent in the sea of darkness.

They'd only gone about twenty steps when the alarm stopped abruptly. After catching her breath, she asked the question she'd been unable to ask earlier.

"What was the voice saying? And why make the alarm so damned loud?"

"That's an intruder alert. And the noise level has to be a little higher on any sort of alarm because of Sandjeel. Initially, he was the only one living here full time, aside from the *iprettai*. And Novera—that's his native planet—has a different atmosphere. Colder, denser air, with a slightly altered mix of gases. Sound carries better there. They have slightly higher gravity, too, so their atmosphere pushes the sound waves harder. His ears are built for *that* environment—not for Earth's thinner, warmer air."

Claire thought it would have made a lot more sense for whoever designed the system to give the Triad leader a hearing aid rather than risking permanent hearing loss for everyone else, but she focused on the more relevant point for their current situation.

"So the guards know we're here." Her voice sounded faint, the alarm still ringing in her ears.

"They might, but the alert was automated, including the location. Someone entered the grounds near Red House."

"Which is on Grosvenor Avenue, right? That's the only thing I was able to make out from the announcement."

"Yes. The property backs to Grosvenor." He looked around nervously. "Let's just hurry and get back to the Great Hall. I don't like being out in the open like this."

"In the open?"

"Not literally. But in the simulated environment, this is the lawn between the auditorium we just left and the Great Hall. There are buildings—and windows—all around. I know it's not rational. If they're watching us, it's from cameras, which could be anywhere. But I'll still feel better once we're inside. Keep your flash trained on me and let's pick up the pace."

Claire wasn't inclined to argue, but her leg was in a less agreeable mood. She kept up for a bit but soon began to lag behind. Just as she was about to tell Beck to slow down, he spoke.

"We're almost—" He looked back at her, surprised. "You're limping. What happened?"

"Nothing. I landed weird on the ankle with the pin in it when I jumped the fence back at the cabin. I'm fine."

"You're clearly not *fine*." He kept walking but at a slower pace now. "Why didn't you say something earlier?"

"Because it's not *important!* The only important thing at this moment is finding Ro and Jemma and getting all of us out of here. If I'm moving too slow, maybe you could go fetch another syringe of your magic healing elixir. It seems to have worked wonders on you."

"It did. But I'm almost certain it would be toxic to you, given that your body hasn't had the same genetic tweaks as mine." He gave his hand an experimental flex. Aside from the pinky finger still being in the splint, you wouldn't even know it was injured. "I could probably carry you piggyback."

The hesitance in his voice suggested that he already knew what her answer would be, and he was right.

"No. Just don't make me jog again."

"Sure. Like I said, we're almost there."

As if on cue, the beam from her phone bounced back from something that looked a bit like a picnic table. She braced as they entered the cafeteria, certain that the alarm would start blaring again. But the room remained eerily silent. Her eyes had gotten so used to the dark that she could now make out almost everything in the room from the ambient light filtering in from the tunnel. Unfortunately, with dead bodies sprawled across almost every surface, she wasn't inclined to count that as a positive.

Beck was slightly ahead of her again, moving toward the tunnel. As he rounded the corner, he let loose with an impressive stream of obscenities. At least, she assumed they were all obscenities. Only the first few were in English.

She squinted against the tunnel lights. As soon as she was able to make out what the problem was, she mentally seconded everything he'd just said. The cart, which they'd left on the charging pad, was gone.

"Well, I guess we're hoofing it," he said.

She was surprised to feel a laugh bubble up. "How the hell did we not realize you were an alien sooner? Seriously, who even says that? And what was the other one you used last week? Something about Elvis leaving the building. Those were outdated before my grandparents were born. And I'm fine walking. It's not that far. To be honest, I'm less worried about that than I am about who stole the damned cart. Do you think it was Durav?"

"Maybe. But I think you can also send a recall signal from the home charging platform. I think we should check Blue House again before we try the other three. It's on the way … more or less."

Given his tone of voice, Claire suspected it leaned toward being *less* on the way, and she still thought it far more likely that Durav or one of his security guards was the culprit. But she didn't want to extinguish the hopeful note that had crept into Beck's voice at the possibility that someone from Arbet's house —maybe even Arbet herself—was alive. So she simply nodded, and they began trudging up the hill.

Halfway up, she was seriously reconsidering his offer to carry her piggyback. But then the tunnel began to level off, and she could see the turn leading to Blue House about twenty meters ahead. Her leg had been singing a full-fledged aria, but the pain began to recede and by the time they reached the smashed nanodrone, it was closer to a persistent, throbbing bass line. It was warmer now, too, and she tied her towel serape around her waist. She was tempted to just drop it, but who knew when Beck might decide to drag her through another walk-in freezer?

They passed the body of the dead *ipret-tai*, then veered left at the fork toward Blue House. As soon as they stepped into the intersection, the missing cart darted out of the narrower tunnel to the right, picking up speed as it headed toward them.

ELEVEN

CLAIRE FELT A SURGE OF PANIC, before remembering that the cart had braked when it spotted the body of the dead *ipret-tai*. It wasn't going to hit them. Assuming, of course, that the person—no, make that *people*—inside hadn't found a way to override the safety.

One of the two passengers was slumped against the interior wall. As the cart drew closer, Claire realized not only that he was dead but also that he was the *same* dead guy she'd seen on the floor of the cafeteria with his back resting against the buffet station. He must have lost the device he was holding somewhere along the way because his right hand now dangled between the seats next to the control pad.

The second passenger had shoulder-length hair, roughly the same shade of blue as the trim on the cart. And while the hair color suited her, Claire would never have imagined Stasia Ljubik wearing a faded hoodie and sweatpants. Even during her downtime onboard the *Ares Prime*, Kolya's second-in-command always looked like she'd stepped out of an ad for yacht club casual wear.

Stasia nodded toward the empty seats and barked at them to get in. Beck muttered something about déjà vu but followed her orders.

Claire, however, held her ground. It wasn't the dead body—okay, it wasn't *just* the dead body. The bigger problem was that she had trusted Stasia once before and very nearly died as a result. Three other people in that cave at Icarus Camp had been even less lucky.

Stasia gave her an impatient look. "Fine. *Don't* get in. Feel free to continue on foot, if you prefer. Although you don't seem to be making very good ... time." She trailed off, her eyes softening as they drifted down to the scar on Claire's leg. "I understand why you don't trust me, okay? But I don't know how much longer Durav's guards are going to be distracted by the disturbance outside. And I have no intention of letting them catch me again." She glanced over at the body. "I didn't kill him, if that's what you're thinking. He's just here because I needed his handprint to operate the cart. And I didn't kill Sandjeel's *ipret-tai* either, although I was with her when the drone attacked. It was awful."

The tunnel floor rumbled faintly beneath Claire's feet. Beck and Stasia didn't seem to notice, possibly because they weren't standing and the cart no doubt had shock absorbers. The shaking stopped after a couple of seconds, but it made Claire uneasy, and that tipped the scales toward joining them inside the cart.

"Yes," she said as she took the seat next to Beck. "I've seen the effects of those bugbots up close and personal. Why do you think they attacked the *ipret-tai*, but not you?"

She thought it was a fair question given the woman's history with deadly drones, but Stasia's mouth tightened. Then again, her expression might have been because she was pressing a dead man's hand against the console.

Or maybe it was both. As soon as the cart resumed course, Stasia turned to Claire and yanked up her sleeve to show an armscreen. "I *assume* I was spared for the same reason you were. I have an app that keeps the damned things at bay. Unfortunately, Helen didn't have a phone. None of the *ipret-tai* do. And..." She bit her lip. "We were moving quickly. Running, actually. I got a stitch in my side and slowed down for a second, otherwise my security app might have protected her, too. That thing came out of nowhere. Helen didn't even want to come with me. She kept mumbling that Twelve would find out she was gone. I think he's one of the *ipps* who is still loyal to Durav. But I'm no longer in the security system and my palm won't open any of the doors. That meant I needed her help. After the drone killed her, I hid in one of the maintenance tunnels for a while. I saw the cart go by, but I was too far away to tell that you were the ones in it. I kept thinking about all of the bodies we'd seen when we came through the cafeteria, and that's when it occurred to me that ... that I might be able to use someone else's hand to get into Blue House." She glanced over at Beck. "Although I guess we could have left poor Graf back there with Helen, since they apparently never got around to removing your prints from the system."

"Why were you going to Blue House?" he asked.

"Helen told me Arbet's *ipret-tai* had taken Sandjeel and some others there. Trying to hide them from Durav."

Claire felt a surge of hope. "Was it a woman with a child? Durav has my roommate and her daughter."

"The little girl whose pictures you showed me on the *Ares Prime*?" The look of genuine horror on Stasia's face went a long way toward redeeming the woman in Claire's eyes. "My god. She's just a baby. But no. Helen didn't mention anything about a child, and I assumed she was talking about members of the Watch. Of course, the *ipret-tai* don't tend to offer anything beyond what you ask and the only person I asked about was Drex. Helen told me she hadn't seen her, but ... it was the weirdest thing. I'm almost certain she was lying, and I didn't think *ipret-tai* could do that."

"Arbet seems to have been teaching a few of them some new skills," Beck said. "When did you last see Drex?"

Claire shot him a sideways glance, surprised that he hadn't told her that Drex was dead. It seemed kind of cruel not to let her know. He knew the woman better than she did, though. If he thought it was better to wait, she would simply follow his lead.

"I think it was a little after eleven. Two of Durav's Earther guards grabbed us near Trenton this afternoon. We had just pulled up to a diner where we were planning to switch cars. Drex thought they'd have video of the car we were using since it was the same one we were in when we picked you up outside HQ on Monday night. They brought us back here and locked us in the library. When they came back a few hours later, they said Durav had questions for Drex and that he'd be calling for me next. That was about four hours ago. I didn't see anyone else until Helen unlocked the door and we came down here to the tunnels. She said Durav left with about half of his men a little after midnight. I'm guessing Maela is with them, too."

Claire and Beck exchanged a look. Maela definitely *wasn't* with Durav, but had he taken Ro and Jemma? Beck looked like he was about to say something, but Stasia kept talking.

"I think there are only two or three of his people still here. A mercenary named Jason and the *ipret-tai* guard I mentioned. Maybe one other. They ordered Helen to keep an eye on me while they were up on the surface dealing with some sort of disturbance. The alarms keep going off."

"Like the one we heard a few minutes ago?" Claire asked.

"Yes. They've sounded three times now. They seemed to think the first time might be an animal tripping the sensor. That Jason guy said something about Durav widening the security range because of an attempted break-in on Tuesday. But..." She shook her head. "Why do you think Durav abducted your friends?"

"He discovered that the *brelat* in Sandjeel's office is a fake," Beck said. "And he thought Claire might have taken it from the house in New Haven where Uden lived. He told us that he'd trade Ro and Jemma for me and the *brelat*. I'm guessing he's unhappy with my decision to share the truth with the rest of the Watch. We told him that we knew where the beacon was and would make the exchange. That was a lie, of course. We don't have it. But you already know that, right?"

Stasia was quiet for several seconds. "Drex is dead, isn't she?"

Claire was clearly missing something. Why had Stasia jumped to that conclusion?

"Yes," Beck said. "I'm sorry. We found her body, along with Maela's, in the Triad's chambers. And I'm pretty sure she told him whatever he wanted to know."

Stasia winced, her eyes bright with tears.

"From what you've just said," Claire said softly, "Durav probably left here not long after she died. I'm worried that he may have taken Ro and Jemma with him, so if you have *any* idea what she told him or where he might be going, please tell me."

"I don't know. I swear. There was a time when Drex and I had no secrets, but lately … she didn't tell me everything. Maybe if I'd believed her from the beginning it would have been different, because I think she understood my reasons on a rational level. When Seset left the Alliance, her family was safe. My mother…" She sighed. "Long story short, Drex and I were still working on rebuilding trust. I really and truly do not know where the *brelat* is hidden. As she pointed out to Anak the other day, Reese believed her before I did. If she told anyone, it was probably him." She glanced from Claire to Beck. "He's dead, too, isn't he?"

"No," Claire said. "Last we heard, he was in pretty bad shape, but still alive. Beck gave him some of your alien super serum, which seems to have done a stellar job on his own injuries, and we have one of the Jonas Labs physicians taking care of him, so we're hoping he'll make it."

"If Durav now knows that you don't have the beacon," Stasia said, "why would he bother taking your friends with him? Maybe they're in the safe room Helen was trying to take me to."

Claire shook her head. "We were at Blue House less than an

hour ago. The only people we saw were two Watchers. They were both dead. If there was a safe room, we didn't see it."

She turned to Beck, but he was staring blankly into the distance, brows raised, looking very much like he'd had an epiphany.

When he realized she was watching him, his lips curled into a bemused smile. "Dora's safe room. I can't believe I forgot. And it's not in the house. It's in the tunnel just past Arbet's place."

Claire frowned. She was sure that he'd mentioned Dora before but couldn't remember if she was another Watcher or one of the *ipret-tai*.

"We'll literally be there before I could explain." He nodded toward the blue elevator door, just a few meters ahead, then said something in Ufretan. Instead of stopping at the house, the cart continued, slowing to about a quarter of its previous speed.

Just beyond the elevator, Claire felt the same rumbling she'd noticed before getting into the cart. It was stronger this time, reminding her of an earthquake she'd experienced when she was at Stanford. Again, though, it passed quickly.

"Did you feel that?" she asked Beck.

He nodded, but didn't take his eyes off the tunnel wall.

"I felt it, too," Stasia said. "And I don't think that safe room is going to be safe for long. I smell smoke."

Claire took a deep breath through her nose but didn't detect anything.

Beck ordered the cart to stop and jumped out, heading toward what looked like a breaker box, positioned about a meter above the ground and painted the same industrial gray as the rest of the tunnel. He yanked the panel door open to reveal several rows of switches, and below that, a security scanner like the ones she'd seen at the two houses they entered earlier. When he pressed his hand to the scanner, the section of wall immediately to his right began to slide open.

A split second later, the light panels in the tunnel flickered once, twice, and then went out completely. And as Claire reached yet again for the flashlight on her phone so that she could follow him, she realized that Stasia was right. That was definitely smoke.

Then everything else faded into insignificance as she heard a small, achingly familiar voice inside the safe room. "Mommy? What happened to the lights?"

TWELVE

THE POWER SURGE or whatever it was that took out the tunnel lights stopped the safe room door on its tracks, leaving an opening well under a meter wide. Claire squeezed through the gap and stepped inside. It was cool, at least fifteen degrees below the temperature in the tunnel. Goosebumps promptly resurfaced on her bare legs and arms, making her wish she hadn't left the giant towel in the cart.

She spotted Beck first, almost directly in front of her, embracing a tall woman with long dark hair and a bandaged wrist. A few notes of cheery music wafted in from the right. She followed the sound and found Jemma, her face illuminated by a screen built into the arm of the fuzzy chair in which she was sitting. Her right hand moved back and forth against the blanket wrapped around her. That rubbing motion—against a blanket, one of her stuffies, or the shirt of the person reading her bedtime story—had been one of Jemma's self-soothing mechanisms for as long as Claire had known her.

The fuzzy chair moved then, and Claire realized it wasn't the arm of a chair at all. It was an actual arm, with an armscreen, belonging to someone who could only be Sandjeel. He reminded her a bit of pictures she'd seen of yetis only with shorter body hair and less simian features. No fangs—his mouth was small with neat, even teeth and narrow lips a few shades darker than the rest of his face. The most alien feature was his eyes, in part because they were larger than normal, but mostly because they reflected green in the light from her flash, much like a cat's. He was dressed in jogging shorts, a T-shirt, and sneakers, all in the same plain gray as the towel Beck had taken from his quarters. His other arm was bandaged a few inches above the elbow. A nasal cannula extended from his nose to the large backpack at his feet.

"Claire!" Jemma broke into a wide grin, but it faded quickly as she glanced over to the right where her mom, also wrapped in a blanket, was seated on a large crate. Ro gave the girl an indulgent nod, and she scrambled off her perch next to Sandjeel and ran to Claire, who scooped her up, ignoring the twinge in her leg at the added weight. Jemma was okay. Ro was okay. Getting them out of here safely was the only thing that mattered.

Jemma buried her face against Claire's neck. "I'm so, so glad you found us. Those men were scary. And loud noises keep waking me up. I like Mr. Sandjeel, though. Did you know he's from someplace even *farther* away than Mars? It's colder there, so that's why his skin is all furry." Her voice dropped to a whisper, which still echoed clearly in the small room. "Mommy's mad at you."

Ro sighed and came over to make it a group hug. "I'm not mad. I was scared, just like you were. But it's going to be okay."

Claire could read her friend well enough to know that she was both scared and mad, and no doubt giving serious thought to making sure things *stayed* okay by getting her child as far away from the insanity surrounding Claire as possible. And really, who could blame her?

Arbet and Beck were talking in Ufretan. The two other people in the room, a man and a woman, stood nearby. Claire thought they were probably *ipret-tai* but they weren't dressed in the beige tunics, so she couldn't tell for certain without shining the light directly in their faces. They listened intently to something Arbet told them, then nodded and went straight to the exit.

As they were leaving, Stasia, who was still in the tunnel, called out. "It's getting stronger, Anak. We need to go *now!*"

From behind them, a very deep voice asked something in

Ufretan. Beck answered loudly in the same language, shaking his head at the end. The only thing Claire picked up was Stasia's name, but she didn't need an interpreter to figure out what Beck had said.

"She's *right*, Beck. It's smoke. I smelled it, too. I don't know if it's in the tunnels or up above, but I think it was coming from behind us."

"That's what I was afraid of when I felt the room shaking just now," Arbet said, shifting to English, as she motioned everyone toward the door. "They've started the self-destruct protocol. Head toward Lavender House. I just hope the power comes on before we get there. The backup generators should have kicked in by now. Rowan and Claire, you're in the cart with Jemma and Sandjeel. The rest of us will follow on foot."

Ro squeezed through first. Claire handed Jemma through the gap, then joined them in the tunnel. Someone had flipped on the cart's auxiliary lights, so she stashed her phone back into the pocket of her shorts. Thankfully, the dead Watcher was no longer inside. Not that Jemma would be likely to notice at the moment, anyway. Her head was already on Ro's shoulder, eyes blinking slowly as she teetered on the edge of sleep.

"Are you okay?" Claire asked Ro. "Did they hurt you?"

"Physically? No. Scared the hell out of me, though, especially when they switched us over to an AeroLyft. I kind of freaked out at that point, thinking there was no way anyone would be able to find us. But they said you stole something that belonged to their boss and all they wanted was to make the trade. Did they mean the manuscript?"

"No. It was the beacon they use to call the Alliance military. And I'm pretty sure they now know I never had it." Claire nodded toward Jemma. "She seems to be taking it in stride."

"It will probably hit her later, but yeah. I think mostly because she was so mesmerized by Sandjeel. You'd think she'd be scared of him, but..." She shook her head. "We were in a room with just him for about an hour, and then we were rushed out to that cart over there by one of the other servants. He did a good job of keeping her distracted while I removed a tracking tattoo—although it might better be called a torture device—from the arm of the dark-haired woman. Arbet. She says it's configured to cause severe nerve pain if she leaves the premises. I just hope I managed to extract all of the fibers." She sniffed the air. "That's *definitely* smoke."

"Yeah," Claire said. "This place has multiple, very loud perimeter alerts … but no smoke alarms? Doesn't make sense."

"Which means someone probably disabled them."

"Right. Probably the same person who set the explosions. That might explain why the backup power didn't kick in, too. Beck and I found a bunch of bodies in the various buildings we searched. And there were about two dozen more at the other end of these tunnels. Both Watchers and *ipret-tai* … the servants, including the one who was driving the cart. Which means there's a lot of evidence in these tunnels. What better way to get rid of it than to torch it? At the very least, it will stop anyone from looking too hard for other causes of death."

"That might also be why they left us alone with just one of the servants as a guard. They didn't figure we'd get very far before…" Ro shifted Jemma higher on her hip and shot a nervous glance at the tunnel door. They could hear voices inside, but no one else had come out. "What's taking so long? We need to *go*."

"Get Jemma into the cart." A moment earlier, Claire had been glad someone moved the dead guy but now she was wishing he was still there so they could use him as their designated driver. "I'll see what's keeping the others."

The two *ipret-tai* and Stasia were now standing at the door of the safe room, apparently listening to Beck, Arbet, and Sandjeel who were still inside. The argument—and it definitely *was* an argument—was entirely in Ufretan.

"What's the hold-up?" she asked Stasia.

"It's two-fold. Sandjeel's tank doesn't fit through the opening. But he doesn't want to come with us anyway. And I can't say I blame him."

"Seriously? He'd rather asphyxiate?"

"Asphyxiation would be a kinder end than what could happen if the public gets hold of him."

"But Beck told me Sandjeel was a voluntary terminal. Maybe…" She was hesitant to come right out and say it, but the man *wanted* to die. He'd apparently been willing to let everyone on Earth die, and they needed to get the hell out of this place. So why were Beck and Arbet putting all of their lives at risk trying to change his mind?

Stasia shook her head. "They're arguing that we need him. And I think they're right. Sandjeel is the clearest evidence we have that our story is true. I mean, sure, there's some evidence if they check the DNA of any of us who are Watchers. But they only have to *look* at him."

It was a good point, but Claire wasn't entirely convinced it would work, at least not outside the scientific community. Within a matter of hours, someone would probably claim Sandjeel had been created in a lab, like the ones Davina Monroe ran for KTI. And before the day was out, half the country would believe the lie.

Beck and Denny were now trying to widen the gap in the wall. They managed to eke out another centimeter or two, but it still wasn't enough to yank the backpack through, due to the size of the air tank it housed. Something Arbet said must have finally gotten through to Sandjeel, however, because he strapped the thing on his back, motioned them away, placed one hand on the door and one on the wall, and shoved. The door opened wide enough that, aside from ducking his head, he was able to walk straight through. She'd been thinking of him as a weak old man, and that was obviously not true. Old, yes. Vulnerable, too, given the differences between his planet and Earth. But definitely not weak.

Beck came over to where Claire was standing and handed

her a black key. "You'll reach Lavender House before we do. If the power is out, use the stairs. This is an *ipret-tai* master key. It should open the doors at the top and bottom. We have Denny's key, so close the door behind you to minimize the smoke. And could you keep an eye on Sandjeel? He's going to overheat very quickly, especially if he keeps pulling stunts like he just did with the door."

Claire stashed the key in her pocket and took the seat next to Ro, who was watching Beck hurry off to join the others.

"He seems remarkably improved. As much as I'd like to credit my medical wizardry, I'm guessing you found another syringe of that serum?"

"Yes. We stopped by his apartment on the way down."

"I used the same stuff on Arbet. Hopefully, it will work as well on her. I guess Reese's injuries were just too severe."

"He's still alive. Or at least he was a few hours ago. Joe has him at the house next to my mom's in Everly Estates. When the protests started over Rejuvesce, she bought out the other—"

"I know. Joe told me the other day that she purchased the entire neighborhood. He offered to let me and Jemma stay in one of the houses for a while since they've got fulltime guards, until we get things sorted out from the fire."

"Really?" Claire was surprised that Joe had suggested it, but it wasn't a bad idea. "What did you tell him?"

"I said I'd heard too much about your mother to want to be her tenant. But..."

Sandjeel wedged himself into the seat across from them. He placed his backpack on the other seat, hunching slightly over it to keep his head from bumping against the top of the cart.

"I knew I should have put that arm in a sling," Ro said. "You've reopened the wound."

"What?" He frowned at her, speaking in the too-loud tones Claire remembered from the period before her grandfather admitted he needed a hearing aid.

"Your *wound*," Ro repeated.

Sandjeel glanced down at the bandage, which now bore a tiny blossom of red near the center. He gave a dismissive snort. "It will be fine. I don't even feel it."

He pressed his hand against the console and issued directions in Ufretan. As the cart took off, he turned to Claire, a challenging look in his coppery eyes. "Anak tells me your family has the means to grant me the right of *ufrete*, as he did for you."

Their cart was passing the group on foot now, and Claire shot Beck an annoyed look. He could at least have given her a warning. Because she wasn't entirely sure how she felt about helping Sandjeel. Stasia was probably right that it would be good to have him as a … witness? Exhibit? But she found it hard to forget that the man had been on Earth for one hundred and thirty years, and unlike Arbet or the members of the Watch, he'd *known* the fate awaiting them the entire time. It was hard to imagine him doing something as horrific as what Durav had done to Drex, but that still didn't make him a good guy. At the very least, she would say that Sandjeel—and maybe Arbet as well—were in a moral gray zone.

"We don't actually have that *specific* custom," she told him. "But … if you're asking whether my brother and I have the resources to protect you, the answer is yes. My mother also has some degree of political influence, which she *might* be persuaded to use."

"I thank you, Ms. Echols. Anak and Arbet seem to believe that I can be of use in the effort to save this world, but I would have preferred to…" His eyes fell on Jemma, as if he were hesitant to talk in front of her. When he saw that she was asleep, he gave a single nod and continued at a slightly lower volume. "I wanted to remain in the storage area. A simple twist of the dials on my air tank is all it would take. Not an *entirely* painless end, but it would be quick. And it would certainly be preferable to the scenario I witnessed in *E.T.*"

"*E.T.*?" All that Claire could dredge up was a vague mental image of an alien with a big head and a glowing finger. She glanced at Ro, who also seemed to be drawing a blank. Too bad Beck, the bottomless pit of twentieth century trivia, wasn't in the cart.

"I'm referring to the extraterrestrial's fear of winding up with those men in white lab coats," Sandjeel said, apparently registering that they were at a loss. "I've seen many other shows that cover that scenario, as well, so I don't think it's an anomaly. I know how animals are treated in your labs, and there will be some who think of me that way."

Claire shook her head. "If the other shows you mentioned were like *E.T.*, Mr…" She hesitated, unsure if Sandjeel was his first or last name.

"It is just Sandjeel. There's also a numerical designation for legal purposes, but I don't think anyone here will be confusing me with some *other* Sandjeel. Or with anyone else on your planet, for that matter."

"Okay. Sandjeel. And I'm Claire. I was just going to stress that those shows are fiction, even though I'll admit that there's usually a bit of truth in them. But there's been a *lot* of progress in the past century. My brother relies on *in silico* testing. Despite some of the propaganda that the Flock and others insist on spreading, Jonas Labs hasn't experimented on living creatures for decades now. You can ask Beck. Anak, I mean."

"Oh, I believe you. I've read Anak's reports on your brother's research. But there are other labs, including ones run by your world's various governments. I'm far less certain of their ethics. I think E.T. had good reason to worry that he might be tortured, killed, and eventually dissected. To be honest, I don't actually mind the last two parts. What happens to this body after I am done with it is of no concern to me. But I *am* a bit of a coward when it comes to pain." He sighed. "Perhaps a bit of a coward overall. Which is why I'm requesting the right of *ufrete*."

"*E.T. phone home*," Ro said, finally making the connection.

"Yes," Sandjeel said. "That's what the missing *brelat* was for.

But since phoning home will hasten the end of your planet, let's hope Durav doesn't locate it."

"He can't use it on his own, though," Claire said. "He'll need your consent—or Arbet's—in order to signal the Alliance's military ships, right?"

"There are two cell scanners on the *brelat*. If the military receives a DNA signature from two of the three Triad members while our ship is in communications range, that's their cue to begin the cleansing protocol. So yes, technically, Durav can't activate it without consent from one of us. But..." He tapped the bandage on his upper arm. "Given that he left here with a sample of my blood, I'm fairly certain he intends to forge my consent."

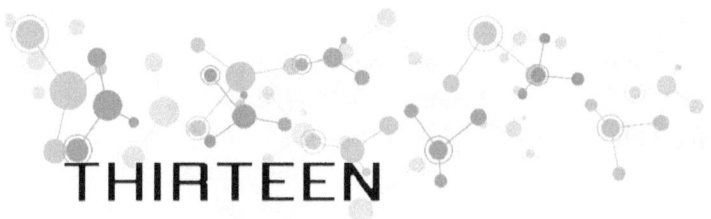

THIRTEEN

CLAIRE HAD to jiggle the master key several times, but eventually it caught. She swung the door open just long enough for everyone to step inside, then closed it quickly behind them. The stairwell was already dank and musty. No need to make it worse by flooding it with smoke. It would soon be seeping in through the cracks anyway.

"Well, we might as well get started," Sandjeel said, tilting his head back to survey the dark stairwell. "It shouldn't be more than four or five flights."

"I believe it's actually nine." Claire had debated keeping that bit of information to herself, not wanting to disillusion him at the start. But he was already breathing heavily due to the temperature being outside his comfort zone. Maybe from the smoke, as well. He needed to pace himself, which meant he needed to know the actual distance.

She had a sudden vision of Sandjeel passing out halfway to the top and tumbling down the stairs, his massive frame mowing the rest of them down in the process.

"Maybe you should go first, Ro? I'll hang back so that I can help carry Sandjeel's oxygen tank if he needs it."

Ro, who had just finished tying Jemma to her side with a makeshift sling made from the giant towel, took the key from Claire. "Okay. We're all going to need a hit of that oxygen if this smoke gets any thicker."

"It's not just oxygen." Sandjeel waved a hand for Claire to follow Ro. "And I can ... carry it on my own."

Claire hoped he was right. The tank was obviously heavy,

and given her aching leg, she wasn't particularly enthused about dragging even her own body weight up nine flights.

Ro flipped on her phone light, then tucked the bottom edge of the phone into the folds of the sling holding Jemma, leaving one hand free to grab the railing. Under normal circumstances, Ro could have sprinted this many steps, but not with a preschooler on her hip.

As for the stairs themselves, they were in surprisingly good shape. When Claire remarked on this fact as they began to climb, Sandjeel told her that the *ipret-tai* cleaned the old house a few times a year.

"The house is unoccupied. Has been for at least ... fifteen cycles. So they don't need to clean it ... regularly. But when they do ... I would assume they also ensure ... the stairwell is in good repair ... and not overrun with insects."

Claire shuddered slightly at the last word, thinking of a gazebo she'd seen outside Lavender House, covered with a patchwork quilt of spiderwebs. Since Sandjeel's breathing was already labored, she decided it might be best to avoid further conversation. They continued on in silence to the second floor landing where he stopped and leaned against the wall for a moment. A low chuffing sound filled the air, startling her for a moment. Was he having some sort of attack? But there was a smile on his face when he glanced up.

"I should have ... exercised more. I had ... all the time in the world here. Nothing else to do. But I think there's ... less incentive when you're ... a terminal. Voluntary or involuntary. You know that ... your body ... is going to give out ... eventually. Same on ... Ufretas Prime. Those bastards... run their bodies ... into the ground."

She wanted to ask *why* they would do that on Ufretas Prime. Everything Beck had told her suggested that all member worlds in the Ufretan Alliance had met the longevity milestone long ago. And based on the name alone, Ufretas Prime seemed to be a key planet, if not *the* key planet, in their system. But Sandjeel's hand was already on the railing, hauling himself to the next step. Her questions could wait. They were barely a quarter of the way up and he clearly needed to conserve every breath.

They stopped again on the landing between the fourth and fifth floors. This time, she helped Sandjeel remove the backpack so that he could adjust his airflow. He'd just finished hoisting the pack onto his shoulders again—still refusing to let Claire carry it for a flight or two—when Ro's voice echoed down.

"I'm at the top. I smell smoke, but I don't think it's coming from inside the house. Probably just drifting uphill."

"We're about halfway. We'll meet you in the foyer. Just head toward the moonlight."

Sandjeel grunted. "You're going to … wake the baby."

"Ha. Not likely. If your alarms were normal volume, she would have slept right through." Claire was about to add that Jemma had gotten accustomed to blaring alarms when their house was targeted by Durav's barrage of bugbots. But Sandjeel would probably feel the need to defend himself, and from what Beck and Stasia had said, she doubted that Durav was the type to clear his security operations with his superior. "As a heads up, though, Jemma is *five*. She considers that practically an adult and she will be highly insulted if she hears you call her a baby."

Another deep chuckle. "That's also true … of infants on—" An explosion cut him off in midsentence. The stairwell shook slightly, but the sound was muted, more like the first distant rumble she'd felt standing outside the cart in the tunnel. Of course, they were now five stories off the ground. It might not be all that distant after all.

"Sounds like the one … at Blue House went up. Hope the others … are all right."

"I'm sure they are—" Claire began automatically and then considered what Sandjeel had said. "Wait. You *knew* there were explosives at Blue House?"

"Yes. Plus the … Great Hall and … other houses. I didn't …

authorize Durav to … use them but it was … our failsafe, in case…"

"In case someone outside the Watch breached your security?"

"Yes."

"What about Lavender House?"

He shook his head. "That's our exit route. But there's one between here … and Blue House … that caves in this stretch of … the tunnel. Shouldn't go off for another … fifteen minutes."

His pauses for breath were getting longer and longer.

"Maybe we should sit for a minute or two?" she suggested.

Sandjeel shook his head, and they kept going. Maybe thirty seconds later, Claire heard coughing below, followed by a slamming door and feet pounding up the stairs.

"Claire?" Beck yelled.

"Yes. We're almost to the fifth floor. Ro and Jemma are already at the top."

The others caught up quickly. Sandjeel handed the air tank over to Dora without complaint and allowed Denny to help him up the stairs.

"You doing okay?" Beck asked, glancing down at her leg.

"Yes. Not so sure about Sandjeel, though." She stopped for a moment and listened. "Are those sirens?"

"Could be. Arbet said Durav had disabled the systems that automatically notify emergency services in case of a fire, but by now, someone in the neighborhood has probably called it in."

"Isn't that going to complicate our exit?"

He grimaced. "There's some distance between this place and the others. They'll *probably* be too focused on the houses currently on fire to notice us sneaking down the hill with an ailing alien in tow."

Claire thought that was a rather optimistic view of their situation, but didn't challenge it because her phone was now buzzing like a hornet's nest. Thirteen missed messages. Most were from Wyatt and her brother, but there was also one from

Kes and one from her security service for the house in Maryland. Given the extremely early hour, they probably weren't simply checking in. On the other hand, they'd already told her that the house was a complete loss. If something else had happened there, it wasn't her top priority at the moment.

"Can you call Joe?" Beck asked when he saw her looking down at the phone. "See if he'll send one of the corporate Aero-Lyfts to the Van Courtlandt helipad. With a medic. Sandjeel is going to need treatment for heat exhaustion."

She shot him an annoyed look. "Should I have him send a lawyer, too? Hopefully, he can find one who knows how to draft a right of *ufrete*."

"Arbet can help with that. We'll need to call another car, too. I'd do it, but it's probably not a good idea for me to draw attention to the fact that I still have the one at the cabin. And you might want to make it a van. I'm not sure we can fit Sandjeel into the Aeris and he certainly can't walk the full mile to the landing pad. At least not without attracting unwanted attention, even at this hour. Just getting him down that hill is going to be hard enough. It's in the mid-eighties out there, warmer even than it was in the stairwell. And we've got about twenty minutes before the security drones come by, assuming they're on their usual schedule. The only question is whether we go now or wait here until—"

"We go *now*," Arbet said as she pushed ahead of them into the foyer. "There's another incendiary device between here and my place, designed to collapse this end of the tunnel. I don't know how structurally sound this place will be after that."

The foyer of Lavender House looked different than it had when Claire entered earlier with Beck. At first, she thought it was because Ro and Jemma were there. Jemma was stretched out on a small sofa against the wall. Ro was already up and headed toward Sandjeel, asking if someone could fetch ice, water, and towels.

But it was more than that. Something about the light

filtering in from the windows, which was the only light in the house at present, had changed. When she came through with Beck, it had been only moonlight reflecting back from the white tiles, but there was another source now, brighter and flickering in a persistent pattern.

Before Claire could figure it out, Stasia called for her and Beck to come into the library on the other side of the foyer. She was standing at one of the large windows that looked out over the patio and, beyond that, to the Triad's cluster of houses at the bottom of the hill, now bathed in light from the emergency drones that encircled the compound. As Claire drew closer, she could see flames dancing in the windows of four of the six houses. Rescue vehicles were now lined up along the brick wall opposite HQ and a small black e-copter—which she now recognized as the source of the bright, flickering light in the foyer—hovered nearby.

"See that chopper?" Stasia asked.

"Yeah," Beck said. "Kind of hard to miss. Why?"

Stasia shoved her phone into his hand. "Zoom in on the logo."

He started to do what she asked, seemingly on reflex, then changed his mind. "Or maybe you could save time and just *tell* us?"

"Fine," Stasia said with a touch of annoyance. "It belongs to Kolya."

Claire already had her phone out, so she aimed it at the helicopter. It was a piloted model rather than the smaller, fixed-route AeroLyfts preferred by Jonas Labs. And Stasia was right. A gold diamond logo with the words *One Beekman Place* was emblazoned on the side.

"What I actually wanted an opinion on—*Claire's* opinion, specifically—is the man talking with the firefighters on the street in front of HQ." Stasia pointed to a spot near the end of the cul-de-sac. "I can't see his face, but—"

Claire couldn't see his face either and might not have been

certain if not for the logo on the helicopter. There were, after all, plenty of men built like refrigerators.

"Yeah. It's Macek."

The person who caught Claire's attention, however, was the shorter guy standing a few meters away. He was leaning down to talk to someone in a white car, so his face was partly in shadow, but she'd seen him in the half-light of her bedroom window more nights than she could count. She'd even slept in the T-shirt he was wearing a few times.

"Wyatt is with him."

She pulled up the last message he'd sent and tapped out a response.

> In house at top of hill.

Stasia snatched her phone back from Beck. "I have to get out of here." Her voice was tight, on the very edge of panic.

"We *all* have to get out of here. And maybe they can help us." Beck looked at Claire. "Do you think Kolya can be trusted?"

Stasia didn't give her a chance to answer. "Kolya isn't the one I'm worried about! If Macek finds me, he won't wait for orders. He'll just kill me."

Claire could understand her anxiety. Stasia had been Kolya's right hand, and she had betrayed him. It wasn't unreasonable for her to fear that Kolya's *left* hand might be planning a little retribution. But...

"I don't think Macek will hurt you. When I spoke with Paul at the ACon dinner the other night, he said that everyone, even Macek, was baffled at your sudden change. They blamed Drex, because they were both convinced that you were one hundred percent behind Kolya's work. Kolya said the same thing when I talked to him. They're going to want some answers, but I don't think—"

"You don't *think*?" Stasia stopped in the doorway. "I've

known Macek a lot longer than you have, Claire. He has a very short fuse. And since this is now the only body I have, I'm not inclined to risk it testing your theories on Macek's personality."

With that, she took off toward the front of the house. Claire thought that Beck would go after her. Instead he repeated his earlier question.

"Do you think we can trust Kolya? In general, but specifically in regard to Sandjeel."

She considered for a moment. "I don't think Kolya would harm him or turn him over to anyone who would, if that's what you're asking. He might even help us hide him. From our conversations, I've gathered that he has a deep and abiding distrust of government. And I suspect Kai will tell him all of this anyway, so..."

"Anak!" It was Arbet. "We have a visitor."

Claire realized then that she had heard the door open, but she hadn't heard it close. They ran out of the library to find everyone's eyes on Stasia, who stood frozen on the threshold. A flat black drone with a body roughly the size of a dinner plate hovered on the porch at eye level. As they watched, two more drones appeared, settling about ten meters back, near the circular driveway in the center of the front yard.

"Do you think they're armed?" Stasia spoke quietly, remaining completely motionless.

The question was probably aimed at the others, but Claire suddenly realized why the man in the cafeteria—the one who Beck said wasn't a Watcher or an *ipret-tai*—had seemed familiar. It wasn't from the photos that Wyatt had shown her. The guy was one of Macek's security officers. She'd last seen him bleeding out in the brick courtyard outside HQ, courtesy of drones exactly like these.

"Yes," she said. "The drones are lethal. They belong to Kolya. And unless they've been hijacked again, I think we're about to test my *theories* on Macek's personality."

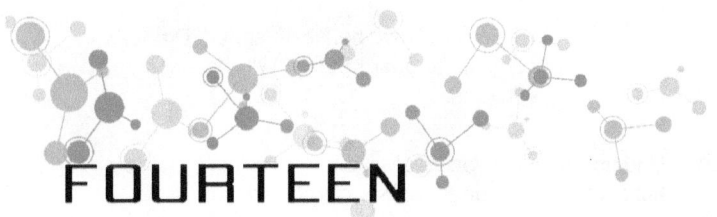

FOURTEEN

FOR A GOOD THIRTY SECONDS, everyone stayed in place, watching Stasia and the drones. Then Ro, who was crouched on the floor next to Sandjeel, muttered a curse and grabbed the bucket next to her, dousing her patient with the contents. He didn't react.

Neither did the drones.

After a moment, Stasia took an experimental step back toward the door. All three drones matched her movement precisely.

"I could try the zapper, but..." Claire shook her head. "I don't think it's a good idea."

"Neither do I," Beck said. "Even if it does disable them, one might get a shot off before it hit the ground."

Claire's phone buzzed. Keeping a wary eye on the drones, she lifted it slowly to read Wyatt's response.

> On my way. With Macek and a security team. He has visual on you, Beck and Stasia. Are Ro and Jemma still in the tunnels?

She frowned. How did he know about the tunnels?

> Both here. Both OK. You can reach us by a path from 253rd Street. Can you ask Macek to call off his drones? Another bomb is expected to go off shortly in tunnel. House may become unstable.

Wyatt's response came a few seconds later.

> He says to leave house if needed. Drones will continue to guard Stasia. Will incapacitate if she runs.

> Understood. Can you ask Macek whether his helicopter pilot is under an ironclad NDA?

> Weird question, but I can answer. Pilot is Paul Caruso. Why?

Claire really wanted to ask how he and Macek had wound up here, with Paul circling above them in a helicopter. But that could wait.

> I've promised the intergalactic equivalent of diplomatic immunity to head of Triad. He has heatstroke. Need help getting him to Boston ASAP.

There was a brief pause, and then her phone rang. Wyatt's number showed on the screen, but it was Macek's voice that boomed in her ear. "*Intergalactic*? I have zero patience for alien bullshit right now. Kolya and I had more than our fill of that when Janelle showed up the other day."

"Everything she told Kolya was true. I have proof. At least, for some of it. And … she's dead, Macek. Her body is down in the tunnels that are on fire, along with that of your team member. I saw them both."

Macek fell silent, probably thinking about how he was going to break this news to his boss.

"Would you call Kolya and ask if he'll help me?"

"I *can't*. He's … not available at the moment."

"Then will *you* do it on your own? We need to transport an … *individual* with heatstroke to my mother's house near Boston. My roommate is a doctor, so she and her daughter have to travel with him. I was going to contact my brother but waiting for help from Jonas Labs will take twice as long. Do you have a hoist or something similar in that helicopter that can lift..." She glanced at Sandjeel and did a quick mental calculation. "About a hundred and fifty kilograms?"

"No," Macek said, in a tone suggesting that it was a stupid question. "It doesn't have a hoist at all. It's a commercial transport, not search and rescue. But..." He cursed softly. "Hold on."

She went to update Beck while she waited, but he was on the phone. He paused to look at her, mouthed the word *Joe*, as a relieved, almost giddy smile spread over his face. He clearly hadn't been exaggerating his worry over losing their friendship. Knowing Joe, patching things up would take time. But at least they were talking. That was a good sign.

The flickering lights outside grew brighter, illuminating the porch. A few seconds later, Macek was back on the phone. "Caruso says it will be tight, but he thinks he can land on the front lawn up there. There's room for three so he should have your *alien* friend in Boston in a little over an hour."

Macek's voice dripped sarcasm on the word *alien*, making it quite clear that he didn't believe her. She was very much looking forward to seeing his face when he met Sandjeel.

"Thank you."

"Don't thank me yet. In exchange, we need a favor from you."

"What sort of favor?"

He ended the call without answering. Typical Macek power play. Not that she was in a position to refuse at this point.

Beck was still on the call with Joe. She gave him a thumbs up to indicate that they wouldn't need them to send an Aero-Lyft, but he could probably already tell that it was unnecessary. The skids of the helicopter were now visible through the open doorway. Its engines were nearly silent, making less noise than the rustling of trees at the edge of the clearing, as the twin rotors atop the craft sent leaves and small branches flying.

Claire crouched down next to Rowan, who was still tending

to Sandjeel. He was conscious now, so she seemed to be making progress.

"That was quick," Ro said, glancing toward the chopper.

"It belongs to Kolya. They've agreed to transport Sandjeel to Boston, to the house where Reese is being treated. Beck is arranging everything with Joe. There's room in the chopper for you and Jemma, too. Paul Caruso is the pilot. I trust him. Joe will be there to meet you, and I'll join you as soon as I can. There are protestors outside the gates most days, but Kai doesn't take chances with her personal security. The neighborhood is locked down. I know you're worried about getting back to work and you obviously can't trust any promises I make about your safety at this point, but..."

"But we don't have anywhere better to go. Sending Jemma to her dad isn't an option. He barely pays attention under normal circumstances. And to be honest, as worried as I am about our short-term safety, all of us may be dead in a matter of months unless we find a way out of this. I'll deal with the impact on my career if we manage to avoid being annihilated. Until then, if you can promise a roof over our heads and food to eat, I'd rather spend that time with Jemma."

"I can absolutely promise that. I'll also ask Kes to spring Siggy from the shelter and bring her up. And I think every one of those houses has a pool, so Jemma won't be bored. Hopefully, you won't be either."

Ro glanced down at Sandjeel. "Boredom won't be a problem if tonight is any indication. I've handled nearly as many emergencies in the past ten hours as I would on a shift at the hospital."

The helicopter was on the ground by the time Claire returned to the front door. Paul got out and stood next to the chopper, an entire host of emotions waging war on his face as he stared at Stasia. Once the rotors were no longer churning up debris, he pointed her toward a small bench at the edge of the lawn.

"Sit there until Macek arrives. And move *slowly*. Otherwise, you're going to take a tumble—and a chemically-induced nap—courtesy of your spooky little shadows."

Stasia gave him a curt nod and began inching toward the steps. The drones followed.

Paul turned to Claire, keeping one eye on Stasia's progress. "I'm glad to see that you're safe. You had us worried. I spent over an hour flying in circles around this neighborhood, tracking your signal. Then when Macek and Wyatt finally cornered your car and forced it to stop, there was no one inside."

"What do you mean, tracking my *signal?*"

"One of the little recording devices you were helping Wyatt plant at the ACon dinner. They're controlled remotely, so he had some friend of his sending us your coordinates."

Claire's eyes widened. She'd completely forgotten about the recorder. It was still in the pocket of the blue dress, which was in her overnight bag along with pretty much everything else she owned.

"Where is the car now?" she asked.

"Still driving around the neighborhood, I imagine. Wyatt said the AI was threatening to call the police if they continued to block the road."

"I distinctly recall you saying that Wyatt was an enormous pain in your ass just the other day. He must have moved up a few notches in your estimation if you and Macek agreed to help him track me."

Paul gave her a slightly offended look. "Well, *I* agreed because he said you were in trouble and I'm just that good of a friend. Macek's motives may be a bit more complicated. Also, you may not have noticed, but I contacted you twice today. It's a time-sensitive matter, so when you still hadn't responded when I left the office around one a.m.—yes, it's been *that* kind of day—I pulled up Wyatt's contact information and messaged to see if he knew how I could get in touch with you. I assumed I wouldn't hear anything until morning, but he got back with me maybe twenty minutes later saying the tracker showed you were somewhere in Connecticut, heading south, even though you claimed to be in Maine searching for your roommate and her daughter. I woke Macek—not something I'd recommend to the faint of heart, by the way—and half an hour later, we were airborne. I'm still not entirely clear why they reached the conclusion that you were headed *here*, but I believe it has something to do with a member of Macek's security team who was killed earlier in the week."

Claire nodded. "His body is in the tunnels."

Stasia finally reached the bench. She sat down slowly, fixing Paul with a baleful glare as her three drone wardens gathered in triangle formation around her.

"She's terrified, you know. Of the drones, but even more so of Macek. She thinks he's going to kill her."

"Oh, I'm sure he'll be tempted. But he won't do it. For one thing, Kolya and I would never get answers to our questions if he did. Is Janelle actually dead? Or Drexel, or whatever name she's using this week."

"She's dead. Beck and I saw her in the tunnels, too."

His mouth tightened, but he didn't say anything. Claire wasn't entirely sure what he was thinking. Stasia hadn't just been his boss. They were friends. And the last time Claire had spoken with Paul on the subject, he'd made it clear that he held Drex largely responsible for Stasia's actions.

"I'm sorry about not responding to your messages," she said as they entered the house. "I did see them, but it obviously hasn't been a normal day. What did you need?"

"To schedule a meeting with Kolya. He needs a favor." He held up his hand. "I'll let Macek explain the rest of it. He and Wyatt should be here any minute."

"I'm surprised Macek isn't stuck down there answering questions about the fire. You'd think the authorities would be suspicious if he was there when they arrived."

"We're the ones who called it in. Said we spotted it from the chopper. Speaking of which, let's get your undocumented friend onboard."

"My ... what? *Oh.*" She gave a short laugh. "I'm guessing that's not the *exact* phrase Macek used."

"No, but he can't actually have meant..." Paul fell silent as he took in Sandjeel, now more or less awake, with his back against the wall and several wet towels draped over his body. Arbet and Beck were crouched next to him, showing him something on Beck's phone.

Sandjeel was drenched from head to toe, and with the hair now clinging to his body, he looked a *bit* less alien. His eyes, however, were still too odd for anyone to mistake him for an Earther.

"I was really hoping the phrasing was just Macek being his usual rude self," Paul said. "Are you telling me that man is an actual ... alien?"

"Yes. So am I and everyone else here aside from Claire and her roommates." Beck retracted his phone screen to pocketsize, got to his feet, and extended his hand to Paul. "John Beckett, citizen of Parda, currently serving as a Watcher for the Ufretan Alliance. This is Sandjeel, citizen of Novera, leader of the Triad that oversees our Watch. We are both now the property of Jonas Labs. And as soon as I can get signatures from the others, they will be, too."

Claire stared at him, dumbstruck. "What? Jonas Labs can't *own* people. That's slavery. And last I checked, it's illegal."

Sandjeel groaned—not, apparently, in response to her comment but because Denny and Dora were helping him up. He looked extremely shaky on his feet, but they began moving him toward the door.

"I would generally agree," Beck said. "But Jonas Labs isn't a government. They can't offer asylum. As a corporation, however, they *can* protect their property from other individuals or governments. Arbet says it's as close as we can get to the right of *ufrete*. If this goes public, you'll have plenty of people claiming that aliens don't qualify as humans, anyway, and Jonas Labs has enough lawyers to tie things up in court for a while."

"Okay, I get why you'd seek this for Sandjeel. But do you seriously trust my mother enough that you're willing to become *property* of Jonas Labs?"

Beck gave her a tired grin. "Have you seen Kai's employment agreements? It's really not that big of a change. And no, I don't fully trust her. But I *do* trust Joe."

"Holy mother of God." The voice came from the doorway. Claire turned to see Macek standing in the same spot where Stasia had been a few minutes earlier. "What is that?"

"*He* is an alien." Ro shot a glare in Macek's direction as she scooped up Jemma, still wrapped in the oversized towel. "He is also *my* patient. And if everyone has finished gawking at him, I need to get him into a cooler environment ASAP." She turned to Paul. "How low can you get the temperature inside that chopper?"

Everyone was now heading for the front door, except Wyatt, who squeezed past Macek and the others to reach Claire. He wrapped his arms around her, pressing his face into her hair, as he pulled her close.

"I'm sorry," she said. "I didn't want to lie to you, but I knew that if I told you—"

"You were right. We'll talk when we get to the car. I'm just glad you're safe."

FROM THE MOHAVE COUNTY STANDARD

SEPTEMBER 9, 2084

TRIPLE HOMICIDE SHOCKS MINING TOWN

KINGMAN, AZ—County authorities are investigating the deaths of three individuals found dead inside the gift shop of the historic Paradise Valley Mine, a tourist attraction located outside Kingman.

The victims have been identified as the owner, 39-year-old William Dell, and two employees, Elena Mendoza, 74, and Kenny Quince, 28. According to the sheriff's department, the bodies were discovered early Thursday morning by a local resident. All three had sustained gunshot wounds.

"This doesn't look like a robbery gone wrong," said Sheriff Carla Ruiz. "Nothing taken, so far as we can tell, and there were no signs of forced entry."

Paradise Valley Mine has been a family-run operation for generations, founded by Dell's great-great-grandfather in the mid-20th century. The attraction is known both for its tours of the abandoned mine and more offbeat tours of the nearby desert where locals have long claimed alien ships crashed in the 1950s.

"Will was a good man," said local shop owner Mark Wiest.

"He usually spent a few months out of the year here. And Elena's run the place her whole life. I think she was hired by Will's granddaddy. Kenny was a sweet kid, too. A bit of an odd duck, to be honest, but the Dell family always went out of their way to find jobs for people with special needs. It's just a shame."

Surveillance footage from the premises is currently under review. If you have any information, please contact the Mohave County Sheriff's tip line.

FIFTEEN

AFTER GETTING Sandjeel onto the copter, a long argument over the group's immediate destination ensued as they trekked back down the hill. Claire tuned most of it out. She was tired and her leg wasn't any happier about going down this hill than it had been about going up. Plus, she already knew that she would be staying in New York to meet with Kolya. Wyatt was staying with her. She had assumed that everyone else would be heading north to the accommodations Joe had offered at Everly Estates, or as Beck was now calling it, Camp Ufrete. But Macek wasn't willing to release Stasia, at least not until she'd answered his questions about the attacks on Mars. Arbet, knowing the other woman's fears about Macek, was unwilling to go without her. And Beck clearly wasn't going anywhere without Arbet. Neither were her *ipret-tai*.

In the end, Macek suggested that they should all be guests of Kolya's Hotel Mir for the night. Or, more accurately, for the day, given that it would soon be dawn. Maybe it was for the best. They were all exhausted. And thanks to the rapprochement between Kai and Kolya, Macek was more likely to respect the fact that the Watchers and Arbet's *ipret-tai* were now officially the property of Jonas Labs.

A second argument arose over seating arrangements when they reached the Aeris and the company car that Macek had waiting at the curb on 253rd Street. Claire let them hash it out while she grabbed her bag from the car and dug around in search of the pain medicine. By the time she found the bottle and washed two of the pills down with the last bit of her latte, they'd decided that Dora and Denny would ride in the Aeris with Claire and Wyatt, something that clearly made the *ipret-tai* uneasy.

Wyatt didn't seem entirely enthused about it either. It could be that their odd behavior made him uncomfortable—which she completely understood. Or it could be because having strangers in the car meant they'd have to wait to discuss Claire's decision not to tell him the full truth about Ro and Jemma's disappearance—which was a bit of a relief.

The two *ipret-tai* stared out their side windows as the car left the neighborhood and drove through the Bronx. Claire had the strong sense that they hadn't spent much time outside the Triad's compound. They seemed mesmerized by the lights. Maybe a little overwhelmed, too, because as the car merged onto the highway, Dora tapped Denny's hand. Without a single word passing between them, they rested their heads against the back of the seat and appeared to fall asleep instantly.

"I'd be tempted to follow their lead," she whispered to Wyatt. "But I'm not sure a fifteen minute nap would do much good."

"Probably not." He pulled her closer and they rode in silence for a bit. Every minute or so, he seemed to be on the brink of saying something, but then he'd glance over at the *ipret-tai* and change his mind.

After three rounds of this, Claire turned to face him, eyebrows raised. "Again," she said, keeping her voice low. "I'm *sorry*. Durav said to come alone. He had Ro and Jemma. What else could I do?"

"No, no. I get it. That's not what I wanted to talk about." He looked again at Dora and Denny. "We may have a chance to talk in private before the meeting with Kolya. If not, just follow my lead, okay?"

"Okay... Do you know what this favor is that he wants?"

"Yeah. I kind of set the ball rolling, based on information from that new source I mentioned when you called last night."

"I didn't realize it was a new source. You told me you were

following an important lead and..." She frowned, remembering something she'd forgotten in all of the chaos. "You said you wanted to get *Beck's* feedback."

"It would have been nice, but I had to move ahead without it. What I'm worried about now is making sure that we're *both* included in what I've hopefully set in motion. I'm guessing you haven't had a chance to check the messages from Kes and your security service?"

"No. I saw them in the list, but..." She shook her head. "What else could anyone do to my house?"

He opened the app they used to submit their work to the *Post* and showed her a draft article.

Suspects in Rural Virginia Murders Apprehended

The piece was relatively short, under the byline of a junior reporter who had worked with Wyatt a few times on the militia investigation. Claire skimmed it quickly and learned that two men, one of them a former member of the Southern Sons militia, had been taken into custody in her neighborhood in Maryland around dusk the day before. The men were wanted for questioning in an arson case that had killed the owners of a small publishing house in Culpeper—the couple that had been preparing to release Shepherd's memoir, although that detail wasn't mentioned. According to the article, a surveillance camera had caught the men using what appeared to be a metal detector to comb through the ashes of a second house that had burned to the ground the previous week, which was obviously Claire's place.

Wyatt pressed his lips against her ear. "We'll talk about it later. But I'm pretty sure they were looking for the beacon."

She pulled back and stared at him. How did he even *know* about the beacon?

———

FAINT LINES of color streaked across the horizon by the time they entered the gates of One Beekman Place. The explosion of sound and light jolted the *ipret-tai* awake and they pressed close to the windows, their expressions full of childlike wonder. Even at five forty in the morning, the casino next door to the Hotel Mir was going strong, the music every bit as loud as it had been when Claire left the hotel after the bomb scare two nights earlier. She felt sorry for the people who lived nearby. As long as there were places like this, New York's reputation as the city that never sleeps would not be in danger.

As they pulled up to the curb, Claire placed her pistol in the Aeris's glove compartment and gave Wyatt a questioning look. He pulled out the pocket-sized Smith & Wesson he'd bought a few years back after the first death threat hit his inbox and added it to her own. The *ipret-tai*, who had already seemed skittish, practically bolted out of the car, looking anxiously for Arbet.

"She'll be here soon," Claire said, hoping to reassure them. But they looked even more alarmed, their eyes darting toward the Aeris, which was pulling away to find a parking space.

When the second car arrived, Macek got out with Stasia, her hands now clasped in front and discreetly bound at the wrist by clear restraints. Arbet was the last to exit, fumbling with a phone that Claire was fairly certain was Beck's. She motioned for the *ipret-tai* to follow her into the lobby, then picked up the pace to catch up with Macek and Stasia.

"Here's proof." Arbet shoved the phone in front of Macek, apparently picking up an argument they'd started in the car. "I handled all legal matters for the Triad, something I could not have done without being currently licensed to practice in New York."

"Unfortunately for you, that's entirely irrelevant. This isn't a *legal* matter. Given that she never formally resigned, Stasia Ljubic is still an employee of Kolya International. I'm simply planning to conduct an *exit interview*." Macek gave her a shark-like grin and led Stasia across the lobby.

Arbet countered with something about serving in lieu of a union representative.

"That doesn't apply in this case," Macek said. "As I suspect you know."

The members of Macek's team who had been with him in Riverdale followed the group to the elevators. Apparently, they would have an armed escort.

"So much for being *guests* of the Hotel Mir," Claire whispered to Wyatt.

"The fact that you're Stasia's employer does not give you the right to physically detain her," Arbet said, continuing the argument with Macek. "And in case you weren't listening in the car, we are all officially the property of Jonas Labs. I doubt Kai Jonas will take it kindly if Stasia is mistreated."

Either the mention of Kai gave him pause or Macek was just tired of the argument. "You know what. I don't care. You can wait in the room with Stasia if you like. You can even be there while I question her. It may be a while, though. I need to have a conversation with the three prisoners my team brought back from Riverdale as soon as Claire and I finish meeting with Kolya."

Claire's shoulders sagged. "We're doing that *now*? I don't suppose there's any chance I could get a few hours of sleep first?"

"I'm afraid not. This is an … urgent matter." One side of Macek's mouth quirked upward, as though he found the words incongruous, although Claire had no idea why.

"Fine," she grumbled, as she entered the elevator. "Might as well get it over with. At least then I can sleep without wondering what sort of Faustian bargain I've made."

Macek stared at the two *ipret-tai* as they filed into the elevator. "What is the significance of the tattoo on your foreheads?"

Neither of them answered. They just took a step closer to Arbet, almost in unison.

"It's ... similar to a caste symbol," Arbet said. "It shows that they are servants to the Triad."

"Do they not speak English?" he asked. "One of the three men we apprehended has a similar mark, so I'm wondering if I may need one of you to translate."

"They all speak perfect English," Arbet told him, "although they're obviously more accustomed to Ufretan. I believe the one in your custody is called Twelve."

"Like the number?"

"Yes. And you won't learn anything from him. *Ipret-tai* have a limited skill set. If he's been ordered not to talk, nothing you can do will break his programming."

"Programming?" Macek sniffed. 'You make it sound like they're robots."

"Training, then, if you prefer. They're not robots but they're also not entirely ... autonomous. They do as they're directed. They can't be held accountable for their actions."

"Like hell they can't. If this Twelve turns out to be the one who turned those drones on my team—"

"He couldn't have made that decision," Beck said. "Nor could he have refused to carry it out. Punishing one of them is the moral equivalent of punishing a child for a crime their parent committed. And, just as a heads up, the others you brought in will try to pin everything on him. They work for Durav, and they know that Durav considers *ipret-tai* expendable. If the local police decide to dig around the grounds near the Triad headquarters, they'll find the bodies of several *ipret-tai* who died by his hand."

"So I've been told," Macek said. "But why do these two cower like that? I haven't threatened them." He sounded almost hurt.

"Not directly," Arbet admitted. "But earlier tonight, Durav either killed or had someone else kill their ... brother, I suppose would be the closest term. You bark orders in much the same fashion that Durav does, and I have trained them to be wary of such men. It's probably the only reason they're still alive. And they can tell that Stasia, who seems to know you well, fears that you will hurt her."

"*This* again." Macek sighed. "As I said in the car, Stasia is not afraid of *me*. She's afraid of being held accountable for her actions."

"I'm afraid of you taking me back to *Mars!*" Stasia said. "There are people there who blame me for those attacks."

"Why restrict it to Mars? I'm fairly sure there are at least three people right here in this elevator who blame you for the attack at Icarus." He patted his own chest, then nodded toward Claire and Wyatt. "And that's without even getting into the more recent casualties at Nepenthes."

"That was *Drex*. And she tried to get Kolya to listen, but—"

"Would you rather I turn you over to the FBI?" Macek asked. "I believe they are also seeking justice for the murders at Icarus."

Stasia flinched at the word *murders* but then lifted her chin. "I'd rather face the FBI than what passes for justice on Mars."

Macek's expression softened. "If there are *truly* mitigating factors for what you did, as you have claimed and as others seem to suggest, then you should seriously rethink that decision. Especially if you are actually one of these aliens. That seems like something that would be detected when the FBI adds your DNA to their files. On Mars, you'll be under Kolya's protection. He has a better chance of keeping you safe there than Kai Jonas will have keeping the authorities at bay here on Earth, regardless of whether or not you are her property. On Mars, you would also be under *my* protection. And since Kolya has decreed that *I'm* not allowed to kill you, I'm certainly not going to give anyone else the pleasure."

SIXTEEN

CLAIRE SHOT MACEK AN ANNOYED LOOK. This wasn't the time for gallows humor or sarcasm. Dora and Denny clearly couldn't grasp such conversational nuances, and his words had unnerved them to the point that they were now pressed against Arbet's side like mismatched bookends.

An automated voice announced that they had arrived at the thirty-sixth floor. Once the two guards stepped out, Macek waved the others toward the exit. "These gentlemen will escort you to your rooms and remain in the hallway to make sure that you are not disturbed."

Arbet rolled her eyes, clearly interpreting Macek's last few words the same way that Claire had—*to make sure that you don't leave.* Once she was out of the elevator, she turned to Beck. "I'll be in the room with Stasia for the next hour or so. Can you make sure Dora and Denny are settled?"

"Not a problem."

Claire grabbed Beck's arm as he got out. "I'll message when I'm done with Kolya and see if you're awake. I don't know if I can sleep yet, so maybe you can grab a drink with me and Wyatt."

"Um … sure." Beck had looked like he was going to say no until he caught her slightly raised eyebrows and realized she had something to tell him. Macek probably picked up on that, too, since he was staring straight at them. Which meant that if Beck's room wasn't already being monitored, it would be soon.

"Or better yet," she said, "we can go down to breakfast. I'm starving."

Macek looked like he wanted to object, probably to say they

could have breakfast sent up to their rooms. But he didn't. Maybe she was being paranoid. The guards might only be intended to keep Stasia from running. Given that she was wanted for murder on two planets, it wasn't an unreasonable restriction.

Claire turned to say goodbye to Wyatt and found him still in the elevator.

"Macek agreed to let me ask a few questions of the two Lone Star members."

"Once I am *finished* with them," Macek said.

"Understood. And I'll be sitting in on the meeting with Kolya. Not participating. Just … tagging along."

Wyatt's casual tone seemed off to her. The man was a good actor. He had to be in his line of work. But she had known him for far too long. The meeting with Kolya had him very much on edge, and she really didn't think it was because of their brief mutual flirtation.

"Well, this is an intriguing little mystery," Claire said in a mock whisper. "A few days ago Macek is threatening you with bodily harm and now you two are thick as thieves."

Macek snorted and punched the button for the next floor. She'd assumed the meeting would be several stories higher up, in the penthouse. That's where she'd met Kolya the last time she was here. But maybe he didn't want everyone traipsing through his apartment.

"No mystery," Wyatt said. "Just cooperation in areas where our goals overlap. And I've already made it clear that if they want you to go, I'm part of the package." He added a casual shrug that was totally at odds with the exceptionally firm squeeze he gave her hand when she opened her mouth, planning to ask the obvious question—*go where?*

"I doubt either of you will be going. Kolya can be very persuasive." The elevator stopped, and Macek motioned them toward a hall on the right. "And none of this makes sense. Yesterday, Shepherd was perfectly willing to negotiate with

Kolya remotely. Even though we haven't made it public yet, he is well aware that we tentatively promised leaders of the other colonies that the stage six lockdown will end on the thirtieth, a little over a month ahead of schedule. That's twenty-four—no, twenty-*three*—days from now. Shepherd also knows we need this standoff to be over *before* lockdown ends. I'm not willing to risk opening back up until Davy's team runs their tests and gives the all-clear ... and the soonest we could be at Nepenthes is the fourth or fifth of next month."

Wyatt gripped Claire's hand all through Macek's rant, nodding either in sympathy or agreement at various points. Since he'd told her to follow his lead, she nodded a few times, too, trying to keep the confusion from showing on her face. The one thing she could absolutely agree with Macek on was that none of this made sense.

When they arrived at the conference room, Macek motioned for them to have a seat. Then, he made a video call and clicked to send it to the wallscreen. The KTI logo appeared above a spinning blue circle. Claire had seen this before on the few occasions when she tried—and almost always failed—to connect to outside sources during her stay in Daedalus City. She hoped he wasn't trying a video call with Shepherd. Even with voice-only, the lag would be so severe that she'd have a hard time staying awake between exchanges.

"We're not going to wait for Kolya?" she asked.

"No. We're *calling* Kolya. He arrived at Tranquility Base about thirty minutes ago. I was supposed to join him in the morning, but then we got this information from Wyatt's source, and I now have a host of other problems, including what to do with the three men in my holding cell. Or two men and ... whatever the *lawyer* called the other one."

He said the word *lawyer* as if it were a foul word, which Claire found rather amusing given that Macek was an attorney himself.

"I believe Arbet is telling the truth," she said. "Beck told me

Durav has killed most of the *ipret-tai* they brought with them when they arrived on Earth in the 1950s. I saw six—no, seven—of them who'd been executed down in those tunnels tonight, along with more than a few dozen Watchers."

"*Watchers.*" Macek narrowed his eyes. "You sound like Shepherd with his Sentinels. Please forgive me if I hold out for actual *proof* on whether they are aliens."

"But ... we *both* saw Sandjeel," Wyatt said.

"So what? Freaks *are* born right here on Earth from time to time. And this Sandjeel didn't seem very bright to me. Maybe they found a..." He made a little circling motion with his hand as he tried to come up with the word. "My grandmother called them *almasti*. Other places, they call them horrible snowmen. That seems at least as plausible as him being an alien."

"*Abominable* snowmen," Claire said. "Yeti. Sasquatch. Bigfoot. And yeah. He's a big, hairy guy. But you saw him only minutes after he regained consciousness. I talked to the man when he was fully lucid. He's as intelligent as you are. And no, that wasn't meant as an insult." She decided to shift to a different subject, given Macek's dour expression. "I thought Kolya was heading to Minsk tomorrow. Why the sudden change of plans?"

And ... that was the wrong question, judging both from Wyatt's increased pressure on her hand and Macek's raised eyebrows.

"*Obviously* the fallout from the Flock's attack on Nepenthes has to take precedence. We'd like to prevent any additional casualties, although that's not going to be easy with both sides armed and occupying connected domes that have suffered considerable damage. And now, with Shepherd making demands ... well, it's a powder keg. But yes. We'd originally planned to return to Minsk for a few days."

"How much does Kolya know about all of this?" she asked.

"I told him everything that you've told me. He knows about

Janelle. And he knows that Caruso is currently transporting—"
Macek broke off when his boss's face appeared on the screen.

Claire had never seen Kolya looking so haggard, or for that
matter, so old. An open bottle of liquor was on the table next to
his chair. She couldn't see the label, but based on the color and
on past experience, it was almost certainly krambambula.

As frustrating and annoying as Kolya could be, she felt a
surge of pity. He'd made it clear the last time they spoke that he
still cared about his ex-wife. And despite everything she'd
done, despite the fact that he must now realize their entire relationship was a lie, he had obviously been hit hard by the news
of her death.

"As I believe Macek was saying, I know that Caruso is
currently transporting an odd-looking creature that claims to be
an alien lifeform into your mother's custody. I just spoke with
her, in fact. While she doesn't seem entirely happy with the
agreement Joe has made, she's withholding judgment until the
DNA results are in. She's promised to share those results with
me, as I will be sharing results from the samples your friends
were asked to provide a few minutes ago."

Given the guards Macek left outside their rooms, Claire had
a feeling that the others hadn't been *asked* for DNA, so much as
they'd been ordered to provide the sample or else. But they'd
have been giving the same samples to her mother's scientists
had they continued on to Boston and now that Kai and Kolya
were on such congenial terms, did it really matter?

"Kai may have some results even before that," Kolya continued. "They've had custody of someone named Reese for about
six hours now. She tells me he was once part of her gaggle of
assistants, as I believe you once called them." He stopped and
took several deep breaths before continuing. His voice was
strained, with the Oxford in his accent now less prominent than
his native Russian. "Janelle … are you certain she's dead? You
told me you'd only seen her once, and as I mentioned, she looks
quite different now."

"I'm certain," Claire said. "Beck was with me. He knew her for a very long time and had spoken with her just the day before. I'm sorry, Kolya. I know that you..."

He cleared his throat. "As I was about to say, *Drexel* offered me a DNA sample the last time I saw her. If everything she claimed is true, these other Watchers will have the same genetic oddities she said I would find. Either way, we won't have results until this afternoon at the earliest. And to be honest, Claire, I'm not all that concerned at this moment about purported aliens and their stories concerning the end of the world. My money is on all of this being yet another hoax by the Flock and I'll deal with it in due time. Right now, I am far more worried about the situation at Nepenthes. Shepherd's people are holding nine of our scientists, *along with their families*, at Ehden. One of those scientists is Davy. Another is Idi Ademola."

She winced, thinking not just of Idi's friendly smile as he showed them his specially engineered bamboo crop, but also of his daughter Amara, standing in front of the café at Ehden with the little lemur dog in her arms. After meeting Shepherd, Claire had believed that he was eccentric. Still, he didn't strike her as a killer and certainly not the type to threaten children or a woman as old as Davy. But apparently, the man was no better than Durav.

"What does Shepherd want?"

"His primary demand is for KTI to release the Flock members being held at the Nepenthes lab, something Davy is very reluctant to do. As am I. Not only did the Flock destroy years of her work, they killed *fourteen* of our people." He gave Wyatt a sour look. "That's Dr. Davina Monroe if you need her full name for your article."

"I'm familiar with Dr. Monroe," Wyatt said. "But her work falls more into Claire's beat than my own. And as I told Macek, I'm not here as a reporter, except in regard to my ongoing investigation of the Lone Star militia. That's something I'd think you'd be interested in as well, since I believe several of their members committed terrorist acts not just here, but on Mars as well. As far as Shepherd and the Flock, however, I simply passed on information from my source."

"A source you refuse to tell us anything else about," Macek said.

Wyatt spread his hands. "I can only tell you what he agreed to reveal. He spent time with the Flock when it was under Shepherd's leadership and has maintained correspondence through certain backchannels since Shepherd's arrival on Mars. And yes, I know you keep a close watch on messages going in and out of your colonies, but ... hey. There's always someone savvy enough to get around any roadblock you can toss up. I've got people who've helped me get through those barriers, as well. Anyway, my source informed me that Shepherd has had a change of heart about the negotiations. His information has been reliable up to this point, but I obviously haven't spoken to Shepherd or had any other form of confirmation, so it may or may not be true."

"Oh, it's true enough. I just finished speaking with Tobias." Kolya leaned back in his chair. "I suppose you're going to claim it's simply a coincidence that he's now telling me he'll only talk to Claire. Your ... *colleague*. And only in person."

Claire felt the tension leave Wyatt's body, and the slightly crooked grin he was giving Kolya now was much more like the one she was used to seeing.

"Not a coincidence at all. Claire and I are more than *colleagues*, something that is fairly common knowledge. This source contacted me because he believed I'd be able to locate her. When I figured out that she was headed to the same location where Macek's team was attacked earlier in the week, I shared that information with Macek. He reciprocated by helping me find Claire. As for why Shepherd is only willing to talk in person? You'd have to ask *him*."

Claire was almost certain Wyatt was lying on that last part.

He knew why. In fact, based on what he'd said in the car, he'd played some role in setting it up.

"I tried. Getting information out of that man is like milking a duck." Kolya was quiet for a moment, then heaved a dramatic sigh. "All he would say is that Claire is the only person he trusts not to kill him, and he can't be certain he's talking to her and not some imposter unless they meet face-to-face. The only concession he was willing to make was that he will release the four children they are holding at Ehden, which will give each side a roughly equal number of hostages. So, Claire ... are you willing to take on this task for which you are wholly unqualified?"

She didn't think the snark was warranted. Kolya probably didn't have hostage negotiation experience either. But...

"Sure. Anything I can do to help."

"Excellent. We depart in twenty-four hours. That should give Paul time to make the necessary arrangements and you time to pack a bag and make it to Tranquility. If you're not here by then, I'll go alone. I doubt Shepherd will be as obstinate in person."

"Just one condition. I need to bring two people with me. Wyatt and John Beckett."

Wyatt and Macek both gave her confused looks.

"Why Beckett?" Macek asked. "I'm supposed to deliver him to Jonas Labs."

"Why *either* of them?" Kolya amended. "We're not taking the *Ares Prime*, Claire. This isn't a pleasure excursion, and space is limited. There's no reason for Garcia or—"

"*Yes*," Wyatt said, cutting him off. "I don't know about Beckett, but there absolutely *is* a reason for me to go with Claire. The last time she traveled under your protection, she damn near died."

The pressure on her hand increased to the point of being painful. She could practically hear Wyatt begging her not to interject. He knew the accident hadn't been Kolya's fault, and he *definitely* knew that her pride was taking a major hit at his suggestion that she needed a big, brave man—or two—along for protection.

But the chest-pounding act was apparently the right track to take with Kolya. He scowled at Wyatt for a few seconds, then barked out a single laugh. "Looks like we're going to need a bigger ship. As for Beckett, my one stipulation is that *you* are the one to clear it with Kai."

"Understood," she said.

"*In person.* I'll message her to expect you shortly."

"*Understood,*" she repeated. The man was like a bulldog with a chew toy. Once he locked onto an idea, he didn't let go.

"Twenty-four hours," he repeated. "And Macek? Bring Stasia with you. I have *questions.*"

SEVENTEEN

"I'M *REALLY* SORRY ABOUT THAT," Wyatt began as they stepped into the elevator.

"It's fine. I get it." Claire pushed the button for the dining terrace. She'd messaged Beck to meet them there while they waited for Macek to confer with Paul about their travel arrangements.

"So..." Wyatt said. "I like the way you artfully dodged Macek's question back there, but I'm still curious. Why push for Beck to come with us?"

Claire glanced pointedly at the walls and then at the ceiling of the elevator, which were almost certainly recording. "Mostly a gut feeling. I think we're going to need him. But let's wait and discuss it over breakfast. And coffee, because sleep obviously isn't happening. In addition to goodbyes and shopping for travel clothes, I need to go see Kai about Beck and send Bernard my resignation. What are you going to do about work?"

"I'll tell Erica that I'm following the militia story to Mars. If she doesn't approve it, I'll ask for a leave of absence. And if she doesn't approve that, guess I'll be job hunting when I get back." He shrugged as he said it, but they both knew that the odds of Wyatt's editor refusing both of those requests were pretty much nil. "You could do the same, you know, rather than jump straight to resigning."

"What science-related story could I even claim to be chasing down?"

"I don't know. The attack on the Nepenthes lab, maybe."

She shook her head. "It's easier this way. Bernard won't have to listen to Avery's non-stop whining about all of the *pref-*

erential treatment he claims that I get. Trust me, he'll be relieved."

What Claire didn't add was that *she'd* be relieved, too. She didn't know if it was the pressure she'd been under for the past six months or the increasingly toxic work environment, or some combination of the two, but she felt done with the *Post*.

"Give Avery a day or two and he'll find something else to be pissed about. But ... what about *Simple Science*? That was your idea. You're the face of it. Are you really going to let Bernard hand it off to someone else?"

"I don't know. If I decide I want to keep it, I'm sure I can make the *Post* an offer they'll be willing to accept."

Beck wasn't on the dining terrace yet, so they parked on a bench within view of the elevators. Wyatt started writing the message to his editor. Claire considered drafting her letter of resignation, but then she saw the file that Alice had sent the night before and remembered her odd comment. *Maybe your alien friend isn't quite as alien as we thought.*

The file was another entry from the Eberin Das journal. She skimmed it quickly and was about to call Alice when she saw Beck heading toward them.

"Glad to see the hall monitors granted you a pass," she said.

"They had to check with Macek first. And it's a limited pass. Straight here and back. One of them also noted with a hint of glee that I would be forcibly detained should I attempt to leave the premises. So, yeah. They're taking their commitment to protect the property of Jonas Labs quite seriously."

"We should find a restaurant and order pretty quick. I may not have much time," Wyatt said. "Not sure how long Macek will take with his questioning."

"I've been through it," Claire said. "Twice. He's pretty thorough."

They took a moment to survey their options from the restaurants currently open. The terrace was surprisingly busy given the early hour, although the crowd seemed much more subdued than the one that Claire had waded through when she was here with Paul. Half of the diners looked like they'd just stumbled out of the casinos and were seeking food to blunt the edge of their impending hangovers. The other half looked like they'd just stumbled out of bed.

As much as she'd have preferred a quiet location, they needed a noisy backdrop. She pointed to a place near the middle of the terrace that was shaped like an old-timey jukebox. "What about that one? Mid-twentieth century décor should make you feel right at home, Beck. Who knows? They might even play some Elvis songs."

He sighed, clearly not in the mood for her teasing. "Never was much of a fan, to be honest. I've always been more of a jazz guy."

The music was indeed loud when they entered, although Claire couldn't identify the artist. And the bustle and clang of a diner would provide a bit of insurance above and beyond the privacy app that Alice had installed on her phone.

"What's wrong?" Wyatt asked, catching her expression as she slid into the red-leather upholstered booth.

"Nothing. But remind me to call Alice before we leave. Private communications will be more of a challenge once we're on the ship."

"On ... the ship?" Beck repeated.

"Yes. This time tomorrow, Wyatt and I will be en route to Mars. I'm hoping you will be, too." Seeing that he was about to object, Claire added, "Hear me out, okay? There's an armed standoff at Nepenthes between the scientists and the Flock members living at Ehden—not entirely surprising given that some Flock members bombed their lab. Tobias Shepherd initially agreed to talk with Kolya remotely, but he had a change of heart. Now he's only willing to talk to me and he insists that it must be in person."

"Why the sudden reversal?"

"I'm not entirely certain on that point myself," Claire said.

"That's Wyatt's part of the story. But let's order first, just in case he has to leave."

They quickly entered their selections on the menu pad. All three had decided on caffeine instead of sleep, so they ordered a large pot of coffee. Then Claire launched the privacy app and slid her phone toward the center of the table.

"Okay," Wyatt said. "As I told Claire when you two were at the cabin, I spent several hours yesterday talking to a new source who contacted me claiming that he had information about the attack on Jonas Labs, although that turned out to be only the tip of the iceberg. I'd hoped to get your feedback on him, but with everything else going on..."

Beck nodded. "Your source is Housen, right?"

"Yeah. How did you figure that out?"

"When I mentioned that they would likely find bodies buried on Triad property, Macek already knew. I assumed he'd gotten that information from you, and you could only have gotten it from a member of the Watch. And Durav's penchant for killing innocent people hit Housen in a very personal fashion a few decades back."

"Just to be certain," Claire said, "Housen is the one who was working with Reese when they planted the bombs at Jonas Labs, right?"

"That's him," Wyatt said. "Before that, he was at this Conclave thing with Beck."

Claire nodded. "I saw him arrive. He and Reese were two of the only faces I remembered from our surveillance."

"Drex also told me the other day that Housen was assigned to monitor the Flock for a few years before she took the assignment," Beck said. "She said he's been on sabbatical since then, but it makes sense that he might have kept in touch with Shepherd."

"Fairly close touch. He's one of the people who helped Shepherd edit his memoir. And that whole thing about the factions within the Flock and Drexel chasing Shepherd out? It was only partially true. There *was* a battle going on, but Drexel was more or less on the same side as Shepherd. Housen said Durav paid a bunch of people to infiltrate the Flock and stir up trouble, beginning about a year ago. I can actually confirm that part of the story. In the footage that I got from Devin, the Flock member whose body Claire found in New Haven, I spotted several familiar faces. Not just guns for hire, but a number of families who had been associated with secessionist militias—Lone Star, obviously, plus a few from Southern Sons and the Boise Bois. Maybe other groups, too, but those are the ones I'm most familiar with. Anyway, Housen said that an explosive took out a Flock bus that Shepherd and about thirty other members were supposed to travel on. That was six, maybe seven months back. They'd changed vehicles at the last minute due to battery problems—a common issue with the older buses they use—so the only person killed was one of their mechanics. Drexel had been pushing Shepherd to adopt more aggressive tactics, especially against the other faction, but he resisted. After that close call, though, he bowed out and quietly urged his supporters—aside from the handful who followed him to Mars—to back Drexel instead."

"Her name was just Drex," Beck said. "El is a suffix meaning *for*. And the Ufretan word for an extended kin group—sort of like a clan—is *korban*. So her chosen name translates loosely to *Drex for my people*. Her planet is one of about a half dozen that recently defected to the Hodjeri Union, so I think the name was intended as a message to the Watch. Or maybe thumbing her nose at the Alliance as a whole."

Wyatt nodded. "Housen mentioned something about a war, but he didn't go into detail. He also told me that while he didn't have *proof* that this other faction was being funded by Durav—"

"They were," Claire said. "Stasia confirmed it. She was working for Durav, too, but her conscience balked at actually killing people."

"Her conscience didn't balk nearly hard enough."

Wyatt's point was completely valid, but Claire had to fight the urge to say something in Stasia's defense. Fortunately, their food arrived at that point, sparing her the moral dilemma. She'd have plenty of time to sort all of that out on the way to Mars.

"We should probably get to whatever Housen told you about the beacon," Claire said.

Beck, who had just stabbed a bite of his waffle, returned his fork to the plate.

"I'm not sure that I understood all of it," Wyatt said. "But I gather the device is how the Triad summons the Alliance ships to pick all of you up and annihilate the rest of us?"

"Not exactly. They send drone ships. Turns out this is a one-way trip for the Watch, something that came as a surprise to all of us. Well, to all but Sandjeel and Durav." Beck gave Wyatt a brief overview of the consciousness transfer that members of the Watch went through prior to their mission and explained Sandjeel's status as a voluntary terminal. "Everything that happened tonight was because Durav discovered that the beacon in the Triad's chambers was a fake. Arbet said that after Sandjeel changed his mind about backing Drex's plan, Durav smashed the case intending to force either her or Sandjeel to provide the DNA sample, only to find he'd been duped. She wasn't sure why Durav believed Uden was responsible, but he connected a bunch of imaginary dots and assumed Uden must have passed the beacon on to Shepherd, who in turn must have left it for Claire at the house in New Haven."

"That fits," Wyatt said. "Housen told me he and Reese were about to leave to carry out their assignment at Jonas Labs when they heard that Durav totally lost his shit over something. But, as for connecting dots, that first set wasn't imaginary. Shepherd told Housen that Uden—AKA Professor Everett—left the device for him in the attic of the house he inherited, along with instructions on where to find the backup device. Housen said Shepherd never showed him the primary beacon, but he knew that Shepherd was telling at least part of the truth because he knew the location of the backup. Shepherd even said he'd sent a couple of Flock members there—some old mining camp near Kingman, Arizona—hoping they could find the device, but they never made it back."

"I'm not surprised," Beck said. "It's probably one of the best guarded roadside tourist traps in the country."

"Well, they didn't stop Housen. He retrieved the device last week. It's now somewhere at the bottom of the Pacific Ocean. He and Drex had tried repeatedly to talk Shepherd into doing something similar with the one Uden left him. Housen even went beyond what Drex had done and told Shepherd *everything* … about being a member of the Watch, what he knew about the Triad, and about the Alliance. He thought he'd convinced him to turn over the beacon, but next thing he knows, Shepherd's gone. He eventually finds out the guy is on his way to Mars, with about a hundred Flock members tagging along a few weeks behind him."

"So, Shepherd took the beacon with him?"

"Yes," Wyatt said around a bite of toast.

It was the same conclusion that Claire had reached while they were on the call with Kolya, but one thing still didn't make sense to her. "It was probably smart to keep it away from the Triad. But why didn't he follow Housen's advice and just get rid of the damn thing?"

Wyatt shrugged. "You've both read Shepherd's memoir. So, you now know the guy wasn't an entirely reliable narrator, given that he left out what I've just told you. But Housen says one thing is definitely true. Shepherd still holds out hope that there's some mothership coming to save the true believers. His long term goal was to get the entire Flock to Mars as colonists. He told Housen that Uden gave him instructions so that he'd know how and when to send the signal. And yeah, Housen tried to explain that he wouldn't be able to use the beacon, that it required specific DNA signatures, but Shepherd didn't seem to buy it."

"Okay so far," Beck said. "But how did all of that lead to the three of us on a ship to Mars?"

"Well, the guy was already more than a little paranoid—"

"Not entirely without reason," Claire interjected. "I mean, given everything we've learned."

"True," Wyatt continued. "But he's now freaking out big time because his people were blamed for attacking the Nepenthes lab. The Flock members at Ehden didn't do it— Housen said Drex contracted that out to some people Stasia knew, the same people who provided her with the bomb they used at Icarus. And while Shepherd doesn't like holding the hostages, they're also holding *his* people. That's the only reason he agreed to talk to Kolya. He doesn't trust him, he doesn't trust Dr. Monroe. Like Kolya said, the only person he seems to trust is you, Claire, because he credits you with saving his life on the *Ares Prime*. What Kolya didn't know, however, is that Housen put that bug in Shepherd's ear, saying they needed a neutral third party, and suggesting you might be someone Kolya would accept."

"Only…what Kolya said a few minutes ago was dead on," Claire said. "I'm not qualified."

Wyatt grinned. "I'm not going to fall into the trap of agreeing with you on that point. But qualified, unqualified, it doesn't matter. Resolving this standoff is just the cover for our main goal—getting you close enough to Shepherd to persuade him to give you the beacon. Or at least to locate it so that we can take the thing by force."

Claire turned to Beck. "Which is why we also need you there."

Beck shook his head. "That doesn't make sense. I've never even met Shepherd."

"I know. But the only way I can imagine Shepherd handing over that beacon is if we can convince him that the Alliance isn't on his side. He needs to understand that they're not even remotely the good guys. They never cared about protecting Earth, they don't even protect their own people. And that goes double after the section that Alice just translated."

They both gave her a confused look, so she pulled her phone back from the middle of the table and forwarded the file.

"Read it later. Just trust me for now, okay? The fact that your people aren't all that different from Earthers? It's more than convergent evolution."

"You don't really need me, though. You could let him talk to Stasia. Okay, okay," he said. "You don't trust her. I get it. But why not take Housen instead? He's had that view of the Alliance for some time now. And, from the sound of it, Shepherd trusts him to some extent. At least, enough to take his advice about asking you to mediate this standoff."

"I'm actually not sure where Housen is now," Wyatt admitted. "I tried to contact him when Macek and I were hiking up the hill earlier, but the number he gave me is out of service."

"And even if we could find him," Claire said, "Housen already tried and failed. Maybe because of what you said—he gave up on the Alliance years ago. You, on the other hand, just learned the truth. You believed they sent you here to do good. But after reading the Eberin Das journal you realized you'd been lied to. You're the one who lived through that betrayal of trust. You're the one who translated the journal—or at least most of it. I can relate all of that to Shepherd secondhand, but I don't think I can sell it."

Beck gave her a little nod of admission. "That's a valid point. But maybe you don't have to sell it. Like Wyatt said, if you locate the beacon, someone can take it by force. I just feel like I'm needed *here*, especially if there are problems keeping Sandjeel and the rest of us secret. I hate to leave all of that on Joe and Arbet."

"There's another possibility," Wyatt said, a bit hesitantly. "We may be able to convince Shepherd that the beacon is a dangerous thing to have in his possession. Because I'm guessing

Durav will eventually put the pieces together and when he does, he's going to go looking for that beacon."

Claire watched Beck's face as he realized the same thing she had during the conference with Kolya. They'd both seen the bloodied half-circles Durav left on Drex's fingers. Now they knew what she'd told him.

"Durav already knows, Wyatt. And he has a DNA sample from Sandjeel. The only question now is whether we can get to Shepherd before he does."

EIGHTEEN

KAI JONAS OPENED the door of her home office, sighed, and waved an impeccably manicured hand for her daughter to enter.

"You've redecorated," Claire said, taking in the slate blue wallpaper run through with delicate threads of gray. "It looks nice."

"That was nearly a decade ago."

Fair enough. The last time Claire had been inside this room was the night before her high school graduation, when she told Kai that she had rented an apartment in Santa Clara for the summer so that she could settle in a bit before classes started in the fall. She'd put it off until absolutely everything was arranged and had moved out the following week.

She'd also delayed this conversation until the last minute. When the chopper landed, she'd had lunch with Ro, Jemma, and Joe so that she could explain what was happening and say goodbye. After that, she'd showered and changed in her old room, digging through her closet for anything that still fit so she could add it to the bag with the rest of her meager belongings. Now, with just over half an hour until their AeroLyft to the Nova Scotia Spaceport was scheduled to arrive, she hadn't been able to delay any longer.

"I know why you're here." Kai took the chair behind her desk, nodding Claire toward the supplicant's seat on the other side. "Anton is a stubborn, manipulative fool."

Anton. She'd never heard her mother call him anything other than Kolya. An interesting development, but Claire let it slide.

"Well," she said, "I guess that's *one* thing we agree on."

Kai gave her a tight smile and got straight to business. "So … what is this favor he's forcing you to request?"

"I'm accompanying him to Mars to help mediate the hostage situation at Nepenthes. Shepherd refuses to talk to anyone else, and—"

"I *know* all of that. Kolya messaged me about Shepherd's request before he even asked you and I told him that I'm as baffled as he is. I certainly wouldn't have imagined you'd be on such cozy terms with Tobias Shepherd after everything the man has done. And my god, Claire, surely you can't believe you're qualified for this? There are *lives* on the line."

The words stung, despite the fact that Claire had been telling others the exact same thing all morning. And Kai was only talking about a few dozen lives involved in the hostage situation, not the fate of the entire planet. Maybe two planets, since she doubted that the Alliance would overlook the fact that their wayward seed had again taken root on Mars.

"No. I absolutely do *not* think I'm qualified. That's why I've asked Beck and Wyatt to come with me. And since Beck just signed something making himself your property, Kolya insisted that I ask your permission."

"Why me?" Kai opened one of the desk drawers, popped something into her mouth, and swallowed it dry. "Joe is the one who signed the agreement. And I don't know why Kolya is making such a big production out of this when I already told him that KTI could have the Ljubic woman."

The part about Stasia was true. When the Jonas Labs chopper arrived at Beekman Place around ten a.m., Stasia hadn't been allowed to join them. Macek whipped out something signed by Kai that said the company was loaning her to KTI. Stasia seemed resigned, but Arbet had fumed about it the entire flight to Boston. The only thing that had calmed her down to some extent was Beck noting that he'd be able to keep an eye on her at least until they reached Mars.

But Claire knew exactly why Kolya was forcing her to ask

Kai in person. It was the same reason he'd arranged for both of them to be at the Ares Consortium dinner. He'd been under the mistaken impression for the past six months that they would reach some sort of détente if he could just get them into a room together.

"Although I believe he's sending us another one of the supposed clones in exchange," Kai continued. "It's probably a moot point, anyway. I suspect our legal team will reject the agreement in its entirety."

"Only if you *tell* them to. We both know you've waged legal battles that were even shakier when it suited your purposes. And there's obviously no established law on whether a company can own someone from another planet."

"There is, however, case law prohibiting genetic experimentation. And while there are some exceptionally odd markers in their DNA, I'm still not entirely convinced that our new guests —yes, even the hairy one—are, in fact, aliens. Neither is Kolya. Davina Monroe isn't the only synthetic biologist with … malleable ethical boundaries."

"But Joe said he told you about the Eberin Das journal. I collected that sample and carried it back from Mars myself. There's no way anyone could have planted it inside that chamber. And Shepherd's memoir—"

"Yes, yes. Joe showed me all of the *evidence*." She made little finger quotes as she spoke the word. "I haven't had time to read everything, but kudos on convincing your brother. I'd have thought that he'd hold out for actual, scientific proof, but he seems ready to destroy everything I've built—everything *we've* built—based on little more than speculation." She shook her head, clearly ready to be done with the conversation. "I don't want Beckett here. I honestly do not *care* where he goes. Feel free to leave him on Mars. Or push him out of an airlock. But answer me this before you go—did you know about the bombs?"

Claire stared at her, furiously blinking back the tears that were threatening to surface. *"No,"* she said, when she finally found her voice. "How could you even think…"

"Well, I had to ask." Kai looked down at her desk, straightening a stack of envelopes that was already perfectly even.

"Apparently so. Because you clearly don't know me at all if you could believe for one second…" She stopped and took a deep breath to regain her composure. "Leaving aside the biodome and the buildings that my father thought of as his legacy, you actually think that I wouldn't have warned someone? That I wouldn't have called Joe? Or Wilson? Or hell … even *you*, if I couldn't get up with anyone else. I would have done my very best to stop it. Beck tried, too, and nearly got himself killed in the process."

"He didn't try hard enough."

The words were a close echo of what Wyatt had said about Stasia earlier. They had seemed somewhat unfair to her then, but in Beck's case, it hadn't been about protecting family members or the mission of the Watch. Anything he'd done was in an effort to save the entire planet. But before she could defend him, her mother spoke again.

"I suppose you've heard that Reese didn't make it?"

Claire nodded. They'd gotten the news shortly after the chopper touched down on the tennis court that now served Kai and Joe as a helipad. Beck was taking it pretty hard. She didn't get the sense that they'd been close friends, but he clearly felt responsible.

"I can't believe he worked right under my nose for nearly five years. And now, on top of everything else, we have to figure out how to dispose of an alien body."

Alien body. Judging from her expression, Kai hadn't meant to let that word slip, but she also hadn't put it in air quotes or retracted it, so Claire thought her mother was a lot closer to believing than she was willing to admit.

"I'm sure you'll think of something," Claire said. "Now if you'll excuse me, I have a lot to do before we leave."

"Of course."

When she was almost to the door, Kai spoke again. "Oh, and Claire? You're wrong about your father. Yes, he was extraordinarily proud of the biodome, proud of Jonas Labs, and his other architectural projects. But he considered you and Joe to be his legacy. Please be careful."

"You, too," she responded automatically as she pulled the door shut behind her.

Joe frowned when he spotted her coming down the stairs. "What's wrong? Did she say no? Because, you know, she doesn't really have absolute say on the matter. I can—"

"No. She's letting him go. I just … at the end there, I think she actually said something *nice.*"

"Well, she knows I'm pissed at her. Maybe she decided to mend a bridge or two so that she'll have at least one child on something approaching speaking terms. Did you get everything you needed?" He nodded toward the bag over her shoulder.

"Yeah. Everything that fits. Wyatt's going to add the pair of running shoes I left at his place in DC to his suitcase. I can probably grab anything else I need at Tranquility Base."

Joe took her by the arms and turned her to face him directly. "Are you sure about this, ClaireBear?"

"No. But I don't see where I really have a choice."

"It's just … I can't imagine that this Alliance will hold off indefinitely, even if you keep Durav away from the button. I mean, from reading that journal, it sounds like they use this testing period or whatever it is with the Watchers as a balm for their conscience, waiting until planets cross their line in the sand. But eventually, they'll decide they've waited long enough and pull the plug."

"Then my goal is to buy us as much time as possible. After that, we go public. Beck says Earth can't fight them, but maybe he's wrong. I can't imagine not even trying." She glanced toward the window. Two of the Jonas Labs security team had taken Beck to his apartment to retrieve his cat and grab a few extra things for the trip. "Do you know if he's back yet?"

"Yeah. He got back while you were showering. Said he'd meet us at the helipad. You do know he doesn't really want to leave, right? I think there may be something going on between him and the woman … Arbet?"

She nodded. "That's part of it. But he's also worried about leaving all of this on you."

"Pfft." Joe said. "It's not like I have anything else to do. I mean, you'll be home by the time I have a lab to return to. And even if that wasn't the case, I'm not sure what work I could be doing. My goal was to give people *more* time, not to sign a death warrant for the planet."

"Oh, come on." She pulled him into a hug. "You'll think of something."

He laughed. "I wasn't asking you to throw me a pity party. Beck said he thinks Sandjeel has been alive for at least *fifteen millennia*. So there's an unbelievable learning opportunity right here in the neighborhood. All I meant is that I have time on my hands. Time to think. To learn. And I can do it without feeling like every day I take off is at the expense of someone's longevity."

Claire smiled. It was the first time she'd heard Joe embrace living in the moment since … well, since they were kids. Maybe there was a tiny silver lining to the impending end of the world.

FROM THE JOURNAL
OF EBERIN DAS

Translation by Alice Dobroski
33.09.506

WHY CONTINUE THIS DIARY? It seems unwise in some sense to leave a record of my actions—actions that the Alliance will surely consider crimes. And if we fail, something that feels inevitable most days, who will ever read it?

But Navi wants me to keep writing. She has as much at risk —more, actually—than I do and she believes the journal is important. Which is why I now pick up my tale with what was almost certainly the most consequential act of my life.

Earlier this month, I gave Navi a sample of Ufretan DNA, something I should not even have brought with me to this planet. This was a grave violation of my oath, breaking my bond to both the Guardians and the Alliance. They do not know this, of course. As much as I would have liked to travel to Emperor Mountain and hand the Triad my resignation in person, I need them to remain unaware of what I am doing for as long as possible. Officially, I have just begun a cycle of sabbatical, and it is my hope that by the end of that time, I will have enough power behind our newly formed organization that we can present a compelling case to the Triad. At the moment, my only allies are Navi and a handful of her friends and family. But it's a start.

When I gave Navi the sample and asked her to analyze it, I knew there was no guarantee that she would help me. I've worked with her for five cycles and consider her a friend. But, as noted, she has a family. Even if she believed me, she might refuse, since helping me could put both their security and her job at risk.

I could, of course, have run the sample myself. We have access to the same lab, and while her clearance is higher than mine, it would only have been a minor breach of protocol. But I doubted that she would believe my results. She would inevitably ask to run the tests again, so that she could be certain. Better for her to do it from the start.

Two days later, she suggested that I meet her for lunch in a small park near the lab to take advantage of a rare stretch of pleasant weather. I arrived first, nerves on edge as I waited at one of the small tables near the lake.

I had played out this scene in my head over and over since giving her the sample. In most iterations, Navi handed it back to me and laughed, amused that I had gone to such trouble for a practical joke. In others, she was angry that I could think her so naïve, so gullible as to believe something this obviously false. I was prepared for either scenario, ready with lines that I hoped would convince her.

She appeared neither amused nor angry when she arrived. There was, however, still a hint of skepticism in her expression as she slid the envelope across the table toward me.

"You were right. That is not Martian DNA. There are many similarities, as you can see from the report, but..." She shook her head. "Where did you get that sample?"

I pulled the tiny circlet of tightly woven hair from the envelope and slipped it back onto the chain I wear around my neck, relieved to see that she'd managed to perform the test without damaging it too much.

"From my great-granddaughter."

Now she did laugh, but only for a moment. Navi has always

been adept at reading people and when she saw that I wasn't joining in, she sobered quickly and turned her attention to her lunch.

My own food remained untouched as I skimmed through her report. The first section, detailing the differences between the sample and Martian DNA are by far the most important for convincing Navi that what I'm about to tell her is true, but I concentrated on the section showing the similarities.

I know from my training that the inhabitants of the various Alliance worlds all have slight differences in their DNA, different gene expressions depending on the climate and other environmental factors. Some of their differences are immediately apparent, while others show up in tests like these.

Navi's analysis confirmed what I suspected. Martian DNA is more dissimilar than the variations between inhabitants of Alliance member worlds, but ... not by much.

When I finished reading the report, I told Navi everything. Or rather, I *began* that process. Telling everything couldn't really be done in a single conversation. I showed her the evidence that I have collected over the past few years. Eventually, I gave her this journal. Not without trepidation, I will admit. These pages show that I killed three of her people, and I feared that might be the breaking point for her. To be honest, I think something in our friendship *did* break with that confession. I hope it will mend over time, but the important thing is that it did not break our partnership. Navi is the one with the contacts, the one who can pull in people with power. People who may be able to present this evidence to the Martian government and hopefully convince them to step back from their current plans to expand to other star systems.

Earlier this week, Navi asked to borrow the sample again so that another scientist—a man one rung above her on the hierarchical ladder of our agency—could run the same tests that she had. He would want to see the evidence himself, she told me, much as I'd known that she would want to do. She returned the sample the next day, reporting that the new series of tests closely mirrored her own.

I don't know what she saw in my expression as I once again placed the braided ring on my chain, but she reached forward to place her hand over mine.

"Maybe your people don't know, Eberin. Maybe this evidence is what sways them toward mercy?"

I nod and tell her there's no harm in trying. And I *will* try. I will try anything. Because I truly want to believe that she is right.

In my heart of hearts, however, I know better.

The Alliance has known all along that Mars is one of the planets we seeded in our early colonization efforts, back when we were at this same level of development. When we possessed the same curiosity, the same desire to see what awaited us out in the vast universe.

They *know*.

And they are purposefully culling our *own* family tree.

ON ALIEN SKIES

ICARUS CODE BOOK IV

AUTHOR'S NOTE

Thanks so much for reading *Dark Little Worlds*. Astute readers may note that this series was *supposed* to be a trilogy, which would have made this the final book. Blame (or thank) Anak. His world took on a life of its own, and I follow where the story and the characters lead. The final book in the series, *On Alien Skies*, will be out later this year, and I hope you'll join Claire and company as we return to the (formerly) Red Planet.

The previous book, *First Watch of Night*, was dedicated to my furry office companion, Griffin, who was in the middle of a serious health crisis. I'm happy to report that he is still with us and more energetic than ever.

A huge thanks, as always, to my family and friends.

Some of the people listed below were involved in the current project. Others helped along the way. I owe them all a debt of gratitude: Peter Walniuk, Teri Suzuki, Oleg Lysyj, Steve Buck, Chris Fried, Theresa Kay, Cale Madewell, Karen Stansbury, Ian Walniuk, Mary Freeman, Lilly Sparks, Meg A. Watt, Aletia Meyers, Alexa Huggins, Alexis Young, Allie B. Holycross, Amelia Elisa Diaz, Angela Careful, Angela Fossett, Ann Davis, Antigone Trowbridge, Becca Levite, Bianca Najjar, Billy Thomas, Brandi Reyna, Chantelle Michelle Kieser, Chaz Martin, Chelsea Hawk, Cheyenne Chambers, Chris Fried, Chris Schraff Morton, Christina Kmetz, Claudia Gonzaga-Jauregui, Cody Jones, Dan Wilson, Dawn Lovelly, Devi Reynolds, Donna Harrison Green, Dori Gray, Emiliy Marino, Erin Flynn, Fred Douglis, Hailey Mulconrey Theile, Heather Jones, Hope Bates, Jen Gonzales, Jen Wesner, Jennifer Kile, Jenny Griffin, Jenny Lawrence, Jenny

MacRunnel, Jessica Wolfsohn, John Scafidi, Karen Benson, Katie Lynn Stripling, Kristin Ashenfelter, Kristin Rydstedt, Kyla Michelle Lacey Waits, Laura-Dawn Francesca MacGregor-Portlock, Lindsay Nichole Leckner, Margarida Azevedo Veloz, Mark Chappell, Meg Griffin, Meredith Winters Patten, Mikka McClain, Nguyen Quynh Trang, Nooce Miller, Pham Hai Yen, Roseann Calabritto, Sarada Spivey, Sarah Ann Diaz, Sarah Kate Fisher, Shari Hearn, Shell Bryce, Sigrun Murr, Stefanie Diegel, Stephanie Kmetz, Stephanie Johns-Bragg, Summer Nettleman, Susan Helliesen, Tina Kennedy, Tracy Denison Johnson, Trisha Davis Perry, Valerie Arlene Alcaraz, and the person (or, almost certainly, *persons*) I've forgotten.

THE DELPHI EFFECT

BOOK ONE OF THE DELPHI TRILOGY

It's never wise to talk to strangers…and that goes double when they're dead. Unfortunately, seventeen-year-old Anna Morgan has no choice. Resting on a park bench, touching the turnstile at the Metro station—she never knows where she'll encounter a ghost. These mental hitchhikers are the reason Anna has been tossed from one foster home and psychiatric institution to the next for most of her life.

When a chance touch leads her to pick up the insistent spirit of a girl who was brutally murdered, Anna is pulled headlong into a deadly conspiracy that extends to the highest levels of government. Facing the forces behind her new hitcher's death will challenge the barriers, both good and bad, that Anna has erected over the years and shed light on her power's origins. And when the covert organization seeking to recruit her crosses the line by kidnapping her friend, it will discover just how far Anna is willing to go to bring it down.

MORE FROM RYSA WALKER

IMPROBABLE

Improbable

Slipstream

Split Infinities

The Icarus Code

The Cold Light of Stars

First Watch of Night

Dark Little Worlds

On Alien Skies

The CHRONOS Files

Timebound

Time's Edge

Time's Divide

CHRONOS Origins

Now, Then, and Everywhen

Red, White, and the Blues

Bell, Book, and Key

The Delphi Trilogy

The Delphi Effect

The Delphi Resistance

The Delphi Revolution

Enter Haddonwood (with Caleb Amsel)

As the Crow Flies

When the Cat's Away

Where Wolves Fear to Prey

Novellas

Time's Echo (A CHRONOS Novella)

Time's Mirror (A CHRONOS Novella)

Simon Says (A CHRONOS Novella)

The Abandoned (A Delphi Novella)

Graphic Novels

Time Trial (The CHRONOS Files)

Short Stories

"The Gambit" in *The Time Travel Chronicles*

"Whack Job" in *Alt. History 102*

"2092" in *Dark Beyond the Stars*

"Splinter" in *CLONES: The Anthology*

"The Circle That Whines" in *Tails of Dystopia*

"Full Circle" in *OCEANS: The Anthology*

Time's Vault: A CHRONOS Anthology

AS C. RYSA WALKER

Thistlewood Star Mysteries

Baskerville for the Bear (novella)

A Murder in Helvetica Bold

Palatino for the Painter

A Seance in Franklin Gothic

Courier to the Stars

Comic Sans for the Ex

Coastal Playhouse Mysteries

The Phantom of the Opal (novella)

Curtains for Romeo

Arsenic and Olé

Offed Off-Broadway

Exes! Stage Right

———

ABOUT THE AUTHOR

RYSA WALKER is the award-winning author of many books, including the bestselling CHRONOS Files. *Timebound*, the first book in that series, was a Grand Prize winner in the Amazon Breakthrough Novel Awards. *The Delphi Effect* was an Amazon Editors' Pick and a finalist in the ITW Thriller Awards. Rysa's books have sold nearly a million copies worldwide and have been translated into fourteen languages.

In addition to speculative fiction, Rysa writes mysteries as C. Rysa Walker. She currently resides in North Carolina.

Check out rysa.com for the latest news or to order signed copies.